THE BOOK OF WATER

THE AZIMAR ARCHIVES BOOK TWO

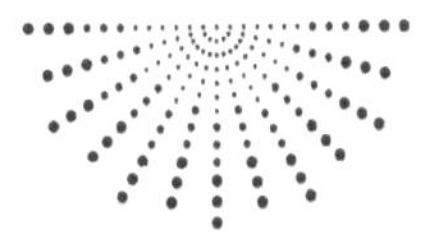

JACKLYN HENNION

DRAGON EYE
BOOKS

To Neilee - For believing in me and inspiring me all those years ago.
And, of course, to my husband. I couldn't do this without you.

PRONUNCIATION GUIDE

Alastor: Al-uhs-ter
Areanath: AIR-ee-uh-nath (*nath* sounds like *bath*)
Azimar: AS-ee-mar
Dars: DARZ
Doldural: dol-DURE-all (*dure* sounds like *lure*)
Eilonwy: eye-LON-way
Hasani: ha-SAN-ee
Mothlenor: MOTH-len-or
Nevara: nuh-VAR-uh
Nevina: nuh-VEEN-uh
Nunor: NEW-nor
Silvana: sil-VAWN-uh (*vawn* sounds like *yawn*)
Tathiel: TATH-ee-el (*tath* sounds like *bath*)
Tiryn: TEER-in
Vyris: VEER-is

1

HARLAN

Harlan was balancing the inn's books, trying desperately to suppress the giddiness he felt at the sight of the month's numbers. Business had been good over the last several months, easily better than it had ever been in previous years. It was all Silvana's work, he was sure.

That woman has turned this place around.

For years, Harlan's inn in Larten had been moderately sized. Even in slower periods there had only been just enough spare space to let his wife practice her midwifery. But his wife was long dead, and the Great Ones had seen fit to bless him with Silvana's presence instead. And Harlan's inn had grown under her care.

It had taken time, but Silvana had learned to cook, clean, and even to do her own midwifery. Harlan had often spotted her studying medicinal books well into the night while her son and Harlan's boy slept. Her skills had surpassed even his wife's; women from Emery and Hythe and all over the southern coast would travel to their little inn in Larten to have the best midwife in the Free Cities deliver their babies.

After the third year, she had taken to pestering Harlan about expanding the inn. She needed more room for her practice, but insisted that she wanted to stay close to the inn, not wanting to leave Alastor and Jaimes during the day. Rather than move, the inn should be improved on. "Perhaps we could even hire a proper cook and ship in spirits from Cardyn," she had pleaded.

Harlan took little convincing. Silvana had a certain charm about her that made it difficult to turn her down. She wanted for nothing, even if she wanted to expand his little inn to limits he thought impossible to maintain.

But she had surprised him yet again. The renovations had been completed a few months ago, and they were already seeing vast returns on the investment. Harlan shook his head in disbelief, looking down at the numbers in the ledger. *Already better than last month, and we've got another week before it's over.* He chuckled, adding one last notation. *At this rate, Silvana could have herself a whole 'nother inn to look after in a few years.*

The front door opened, the chiming of the bell fixed above the door startling Harlan out of his musings. He looked up from the ledger to see a tall man stepping in from the rain outside. Night had fallen and the dinner hour was only just over, and it was not strange for a few stragglers to come in at such an hour looking for a room. This man kept his head low, hood pulled up to cover his face, but Harlan could make out a shaggy beard and long, unkempt hair hanging limp with rain.

"Good evenin'. You lookin' for a room for the night? We've still a couple left. And some hot food to warm you, if you've the coin for it."

"I won't be staying the night. Just looking for a bit to eat. And perhaps a bit to drink, if you don't mind."

The man's accent was a crisp northern one like Silvana's. Harlan brushed the observation off. Northerners weren't terribly uncommon even this far south. "That'll be no problem." Harlan eyed the scabbard poking out from beneath the man's cloak. "I do have to ask that you leave any weapons behind. I can keep them here and return them when you leave. Or move them to a room, if you change your mind about stayin' the night." The man seemed reluctant to part with the weapon, his hand straying to hover over the sword's hilt. Harlan shrugged. "We've children here. Drinks and weapons don' mix."

The man removed his sword, dropping it on the desk in front of Harlan. And, to Harlan's surprise, he pulled first one, then two daggers out of his belt, and a third out of his boot, tossing each one down in front of Harlan.

"Are, eh, are you a knight or somethin'?" Harlan asked, watching as the pile of steel on his countertop grew.

"Or something, yes," the man answered, shifting slightly where he stood. He didn't seem uncomfortable with the question, only … Harlan considered for a second as the stranger stared at him from beneath the hem of his cloak's hood. *Disinterested,* Harlan decided.

Harlan nodded his thanks, taking the weapons and tucking them behind a couple of wooden crates at the rear of the desk. He came around the counter, leading the man through an adjacent door and into the dining area. Harlan turned towards the man, eyeing him with some concern. "As your host, it'd be rude of me not t'ask if you'd like me to dry your cloak."

The man shrugged out of the cloak, passing it to Harlan. He was about the same age as Harlan himself, but his face and neck were covered in small scars, and his hair was long and dirty. He muttered a thanks and quickly turned away from Harlan.

The dining room was empty, but the strange guest chose to sit in the far corner of the room, his back to the wall. He kept his head low, hiding his face behind his long hair. Harlan hung the man's cloak over the warm coals across the room before returning his attention to him. "What can I get for ya to eat? We've some good chicken, a bit of lamb, and an excellent fish soup."

"The soup is fine. With some bread. And a pint of dark ale, please."

Harlan was out of the dining room for only a few moments, returning with the food and the drink. The man set to eating quickly, muttering another thanks before wolfing down the soup as if he hadn't eaten in days. *Might be true, too. By the looks of him, poor fellow hasn't had a bath in a long while, neither.* Harlan turned his back on the man, keeping him just inside his peripheral vision. *At least he's polite.*

Harlan set about cleaning up the room, using the excuse to stay in the room with the man. They got their fair number of travelers, but most were fishermen straying inland for a few days of drinking and whoring. Not many were northerners, and those that were usually appeared better off than this man did. He almost pitied him. But he shook his head. Silvana pitied the folk that came through here, but Harlan took them up for a time, took their money, and then sent them off. *We both start pitying every dirty soul that comes through those doors, we'll soon be running a soup kitchen, not a profitable inn!*

There was a loud clamor from the next room, then a naked child ran through the dining area, slick with water, his black hair matted against his head. Harlan shook his head as the boy hid under a table, giggling with delight. "Silvana!" Harlan called. "I think we've a little runaway in here!" At the mention of Silvana's name, the man at the table stiffened, suddenly uninterested in his food. Harlan watched the man closely, uneasy at the stranger's reaction.

"Sorry, Harlan." Silvana entered the dining room, another naked toddler on one hip, and her damp red hair pulled over the opposite shoulder. "I was trying to give them a bath before bed, and that little worm wriggled away." She knelt down next to the table, peeking underneath at the boy. "Come on now, or I'll have to give you another bath. It's nearly time for a story!"

The little boy giggled again, crawling out from under the table and running back through the room. "You can't catch me," he called out in a singsong voice.

Harlan sighed, watching the boy run off. Out of the corner of his eye, he saw the stranger watching Alastor as well. The man's eyes followed Alastor as he took a quick run about one of the tables before disappearing into the next room. As Alastor disappeared from the room, the man's eyes quickly darted back to Silvana.

"Don't worry, Harlan, he'll wear himself out momentarily," Silvana was saying. "Jaimes, give your father a kiss good-night." She carried the sandy-haired boy over to Harlan, and the boy obediently leaned to plant a wet kiss on Harlan's cheek.

"Goodnight, Poppa."

"Goodnight, Jaimes." Harlan ruffled his damp hair, then gave him a kiss on the forehead. To Silvana, he added, "Try to keep them upstairs for a bit, we've a guest down here." He nodded in the direction of the man, who was bent over his soup again.

Silvana nodded. She walked back in the direction she'd come, pausing just inside the dining room. "Sorry to disturb you, sir. Enjoy your meal, and I wish you a good night." And she was gone in a gentle swish of skirts, disappearing through the doorway and around a corner.

Harlan gave one last side glance at the man then continued his cleaning routine.

"Was that your wife?"

Harlan was surprised he'd said anything. He paused for a moment, sure he had misheard. But the man was staring up at him expectantly. "No, not my wife. She just works for me."

There was another moment of silence.

"And the boys? They both hers?"

Harlan frowned, not quite sure why the question bothered him. "No, just one of them." His response was a little more curt than he would have liked. *Perhaps he ain't so polite after all.* The man was staring up at him again. "The sandy-haired one's mine. The dark-haired one's hers." He explained.

"Alastor," the man muttered under his breath. He might have thought he'd said it quietly enough for Harlan not to hear.

But Harlan heard it, and he stared angrily at the man for the briefest of moments, trying to decide if this wet and dirty stranger had come through before. They got a lot of odd folk in the inn, but Harlan was good with faces, and he did not recognize the one sipping quietly at the beer Harlan had brought him.

Had Harlan used Alastor's name when Silvana was in the room? He thought back to the short interaction, sure he hadn't. Harlan approached the man, arms crossed over his chest, recalling the daggers the man had handed over before entering the dining hall. Had the man kept a weapon? Would he be a danger to Silvana and the boys? "And how is it that you know the boy's name? Do you know him, or you just been keepin' an eye on him?"

"Yes. To both, in a sense." The man sounded sad, almost listless. His answer surprised Harlan, who stared down on him impatiently. "I know Silvana. From long ago. It was a different life."

Harlan's anger suddenly released. He found himself falling into the chair opposite the stranger, steadying himself with both hands on the table. "You her husband then, come to take her away?" Harlan had been hoping this day would never come. He cared for Silvana, more than a man should care for a married woman. As much as Silvana hoped that her husband was still alive, and that he would find her, Harlan had wished for the opposite just as much.

"No. Hasani is dead, I'm sure of it. I've looked for him, asked about him. I found nothing." The man sighed, dipping the last of his bread into the dregs of his soup. "Silvana was not hard to find. I just came to see her, to make sure she was alright. And to see the boy."

Harlan leaned back in the chair, crossing his arms over his chest once more. "You the brother, then? She's told me about you, too. How you stole them out of the castle to save her husband from some daft deployment meant to kill him." Harlan squinted at the man before him, trying to find a hint of the brother Silvana had described. She said he had been well kept, with bright red hair and a clean face. She'd said that he was large and muscular and trained in combat. This man was big enough, and looked strong enough, but he was also dirty and depressed. So dirty, in fact, that Harlan had a hard time telling the color of his hair. Far from the man Silvana had told him about. "If you are that brother, then show me your arms."

The man stared across at him. "She told you about the Dragon Door?" He sounded surprised.

"Ya, the magic door that could only be opened by blood sacrifice. She told me 'bout it." The words rushed out of his mouth irritably. Harlan neglected to admit that he'd thought the whole bit about escaping through the door had been a bunch of shit, meant to confuse or trick Silvana. But if this man had the proof of it, he'd never doubt Silvana again.

The man hesitated before begrudgingly rolling up the sleeve to his left arm and holding it out for Harlan to inspect. Sure enough, and to Harlan's great surprise, there were four large, perfectly round scars lined up along his arm. Harlan took the man by the wrist and turned his arm over. On the back of his arm were four more scars, perfectly aligned with the ones on the inside of his arm. Harlan released the man's wrist and leaned back in the chair again. "I'll admit that I figured Silvana for a fool. Glad to see I was wrong." Harlan paused, scrutinizing the man as he quickly rolled his sleeve back down to hide the scars. "Well met, Ajax."

The man flinched at the sound of his name. "I'm not Ajax anymore."

Harlan snorted, shaking his head at the man. "Then who the hell are ya?"

The man paused, thinking. "I guess you can call me Roland."

2

TATHIEL

I t was easy to lose her once they were in the woods. She was so concentrated on watching where she placed her feet that she didn't hear him as he slipped away from her.

Finally, she looked up, realizing he was no longer in sight. "Tathiel, wait for me!" She stepped awkwardly over an exposed root, and the sight of it almost made him snort. She came to a hesitant stop and Tathiel stopped with her, hidden in the brush not five feet from her.

"Tathiel?" Her head tilted as she listened for him. He held his breath. She might be gullible, but she was still smart, and had better hearing than he did.

"Dammit, Tathiel!" she hissed, turning to check behind her. "Where did you go?"

He chose that moment to step out of the brush, stopping a hand's breadth from her shoulder. "Eilonwy, you're a very poor hunter. You've scared all the deer away with your whining and stomping around." He shook his head to mask the sneer that stretched his lips as she jumped at his words. She hadn't heard him approach. She might not have better hearing than him after all.

Eilonwy balled her hands into fists at her side defensively.

9

"And you are the best hunter our family has." She punched him in the shoulder, though not as hard as he knew she could. "Which is precisely why I asked you to teach me." Her cheeks flushed in anger. "I want to learn how to hunt, not how to be left behind in the dirt while you run off on your own."

"Your ears turn red when you're angry, did you know that?"

Eilonwy huffed, instinctively reaching up to cover the tips of her pointed ears. Looking down, she saw the boots her brother had chosen to wear. They were smaller, lighter, and were much quieter than the ones she wore. "What are you wearing?" she asked angrily.

"Hunting boots, of course," Tathiel replied innocently.

Eilonwy groaned, exasperated. "Proper hunting boots, not these monsters you forced me to wear. No wonder I'm slower and noisier than you with these big ugly things." She crossed her arms again. "You tricked me, Tathiel. That's not very nice of you."

"I didn't trick you. I taught you a very important lesson about hunting." He paused, affecting a pedantic air. "A good pair of hunting boots can make all the difference between going around unnoticed or stomping around and scaring off all the prey."

"You could have just told me that!"

Tathiel laughed. "Yes, but then I would have missed you struggling around in those ugly things!" He dodged another punch and ran off into the woods. He could hear her following behind, but he was much faster than her. She called after him, angry. He laughed again, still running. She called again, this time throwing a curse at him. He shook his head, calling over his shoulder, "Ladies shouldn't use such words, Eilonwy." He heard her hiss in anger and change direction to follow the sound of his voice. She was closer than he'd thought, even with the terrible shoes he had told her to wear. *Perhaps she would make a good hunter, after all,* Tathiel thought. He continued running.

After a moment, he stopped. He couldn't hear her following behind him anymore. He waited, listening. *Perhaps she's trying to sneak up on me.*

"Tathiel?" Eilonwy called out again.

She wasn't far behind, but she had stopped pursuing him. He waited, anticipating some trick.

"Tathiel!" Eilonwy sounded panicked.

Tathiel's heart skipped a beat and he quickly ran back through the trees to her, leaping over logs and ducking under boughs to reach her. "Eilonwy, are you alright?" He found her kneeling at the base of a great tree, staring at something on the ground. He came around to her side, looking down among the grass and upraised roots.

A large blue stone lay partially hidden amid the tall grass and fallen leaves. Its surface was iridescent, shimmering even in the poor amount of sunlight that filtered through the dense trees. Tathiel knelt beside his sister for a closer look. "What is it?"

"I think … I think it's a dragon egg." She reached out a hand to touch it.

Tathiel did the same. "A dragon egg …" he repeated, awed.

Their hands touched the surface of the stone at the same time. Tathiel felt a strange warmth in his fingertips, then a sudden influx of energy. He jerked his hand away, staring at the stone in shock.

"We should leave it. Don't touch it." He looked over at Eilonwy, who was staring down at her hand.

"It was alive." Their eyes met. "You felt it, too, didn't you?" Eilonwy looked down at the egg again, and Tathiel's gaze followed hers. "It *knows* us. We can't leave it."

He knew his sister was right. He had sensed it; something in the egg had been alive, and had recognized his touch. He wasn't sure how it could be possible, but it was true. He reached out a hand, hesitant to touch it again. But when his fingertips met the smooth surface of the egg, nothing happened. It felt cold to the touch, but nothing more. He picked it up gingerly, tucking it into the crook of one arm and straightening up. "Come on, let's just go home."

Eilonwy nodded, straightening and matching her pace with his as he turned back towards their Homewood.

3

HARLAN

It was nearly midday, but the inn seemed quieter than usual. *Perhaps it's just Silvana's absence that makes it seem that way,* Harlan thought. Coming down the stairs from the guest rooms, he heard Tomas's voice drifting up from the dining area.

"I'm sorry, but we don' serve your kind here." Tomas sounded genuinely apologetic, and it was enough to slow Harlan's steps. His daft brother-in-law was never one to be sorry for anything.

Curious, Harlan stepped into the dining room. It was empty, save for two men sitting at a table in the far corner, Tomas standing beside them. One look at the man sitting with his back pressed against the wall was all it took. Harlan sighed and walked towards them.

"I hate to admit it, but it's just too dangerous to be seen helpin' folk … of your nature," Tomas finished lamely.

"Tomas," Harlan interjected, "I'll take it from here, brother." He laid a hand on Tomas's shoulder. "Go see to the boys, if ya don't mind. They should be 'round back, getting firewood. Might be they could use a hand."

"Sure, Harlan." Tomas nodded, eyeing their guests warily, then turned and hurried out of the door.

Harlan watched him go, then turned back to the men sitting at the table in front of him. The elf he didn't recognize, but the other man … "Roland, it's been a while."

Roland nodded in greeting. "Harlan."

Harlan gestured towards the elf. "Who's yer friend here, Roland? You know it's bad luck to be seen with elven folk nowadays, don't ya?"

But it was the elf that answered, his voice smooth as honey. "My deepest apologies. Roland said this would be a quiet little place for us to discuss some … important matters." The elf bowed his head to Harlan. "My name is Tiryn. It's a pleasure to meet you, Harlan."

Harlan huffed. "It'd be a pleasure to me if you didn't ruin my business by choosing to discuss your 'important matters' here." He sighed. "It ain't nothing personal, understand, it's just—"

Roland cut him off. "We understand, Harlan. We won't be long. I just came to check in on Alastor, make sure he's fine. We'll be leaving soon."

"Alastor, but not Silvana?" Harlan frowned down at Roland. "Silvana's not here at the moment, anyhow. She's gone away to—"

"Hythe, yes, I know."

Harlan squinted at him, crossing his arms over his chest. "Ya, Hythe. They had a bad run of sickness roll in with the traders earlier in the year. Silvana went there to help out."

Roland nodded. "Yes, I know. Why do you think I chose to come back now?"

Harlan shook his head, exasperated. "Why don' you try coming back when she is here, ya damned fool, and try patching things up with her?" He instantly regretted his words. If Silvana knew her brother was alive she might want to go with him, leaving Jaimes and Harlan behind. And that was something Harlan feared more than anything.

But Roland just shook his head. "She doesn't want me in her life anymore, I'm afraid. Not after what happened to Hasani."

Harlan didn't bother to correct him. For a time, all Silvana talked about was her brother coming to find her. And how she had tried to push him away, had blamed him for her husband's death. *But she knew that she was wrong, and she misses you, Ajax.* But Harlan didn't say anything. Instead, he sighed again. "Well, while you're conducting your business, can I get ya anythin' to drink, at least?"

"An ale would be appreciated, Harlan. We'll try not to take up too much of your time."

Harlan turned a quiet eye towards the elf, who looked up at him with a faint smile.

"I don't suppose you have Vyrisian wine?"

Harlan snorted. "We haven't had Vyrisian wine in almost ten years. Not since the imports were shut down and my last cask went dry."

The elf nodded, as if he expected the answer. "Whatever you recommend, then."

Harlan looked the elf over again. He was neat, but then weren't they all? He was also polite, and he seemed to be the friendly sort, all other things being equal. Harlan could give him something from the back corner of the winery and then write him a huge bill. He'd have no right to protest. Elves were rarely served in other cities, and those that were had grown used to paying exorbitant prices for basic fare. But the idea of deceiving someone, even an elf, irked Harlan. *And if Silvana found out, she'd give me an earful.*

So Harlan turned away from the pair of them with a gentle sigh, content to bring a pint of ale and a glass of his favorite red.

4

ROLAND

R oland watched Harlan walk away before turning back to the matter at hand. "Are you sure you're ready to commit to this, Tiryn? I don't want you to feel forced into helping me."

"We've known each other for a while. Do you really think I would walk away now?" Tiryn folded his hands carefully into his lap, glancing nervously about the nearly empty room. "There's a dwarfen stronghold east of here. Doldural. I've been working to gain an audience with their king, and I might be able to turn a few of them to our cause."

"Do you think they'll help? Dwarfs working with elves?"

"I'm working with you, aren't I?" It could have been a joke, but Tiryn's voice was level and serious. "Mothlenor threatens all of the old races, not just elves. He's made it harder than ever for someone like me to travel outside our own realm. His demons delve deeper into our woodlands every year, killing any elf they happen across. And we're not the only ones. The dwarfs are seeing the same kind of conflict. We're in this together, whether we want to be or not." Tiryn frowned, his delicate nose wrinkling in the process. "And it'll be easier for all of us if we can get along."

16

Roland nodded. "Good. I'm glad you see it as I do." He crossed his arms over his chest. "Talk to the dwarfs, then. See if you can rally some to join us. In the meantime, I have some leads of my own to investigate."

Tiryn's brows raised slightly. "Your blue winged beast? Do you think this one will work out?"

Roland shrugged a shoulder. "Can't say for sure until I go."

"Where are you headed this time?"

Roland sighed. "Back east, a few days of riding to the south of Cusch. I heard some merchants in Hythe whispering about some poor sap who lost a fine crop of either wheat or amaranth to what he swears was dragon fire."

Tiryn frowned. "Most dragons don't breathe fire."

"You and I both know that, but some drunken idiot out to get a few free drinks in exchange for a tall tale probably doesn't." Roland sighed again, stretching his arms over his head and leaning back in his chair. "Still, it wouldn't do to pass it up, just because of a little bit of skepticism on my part."

"Then I hope this is the one that puts an end to your searching, Roland."

"I'm sorry to drag you through so much, Tiryn," Roland said, giving his friend a soft frown. "I wish I'd had the sense to take Areanath's little book of clues for myself all those years ago. We might not be in this mess now, chasing down every mention of beasts and dragons and running all over Azimar."

Tiryn shrugged, an uncharacteristically graceless motion for an elf, but one that he had no doubt picked up from Roland. "I'm not sure I would have done any differently, given what you were going through at the time." When Roland made no reply, Tiryn asked, "Who does have the book? Your sister?"

Roland opened his mouth to answer, but the door to the

dining room burst open, interrupting him. Two boys walked through, each carrying an armful of firewood. They crossed the dining room, joking and laughing, stopping at the fireplace on the far side of the room. Roland nodded in the direction of the dark-haired one. "He does."

Tiryn followed his gaze, looking the boy over before turning back to Roland. "That boy? How old is he, ten?"

"He'll be nine on his next birthday. About two months from now."

Tiryn glanced over his shoulder again. "Who is he?"

The boys had dropped off their cargo and were walking back in the direction they had come. Roland got a good look at the boy then and was amazed at how much he resembled Hasani. His hair was the same, and even his eyes were the same midnight blue. The boys didn't seem to notice his staring; they kept walking until they disappeared back through the door they had come through and into the next room.

Roland dropped his gaze to the floor, his heart suddenly heavy with guilt. "He's my nephew."

5

THE TWINS

Eilonwy trod carefully over the fallen leaves, her soft steps leaving no hint of her passing. She ducked under fallen branches, carefully checking that she was still on the right path. Her prey wasn't that much farther ahead than she was; she would find it soon. She continued slowly, winding her way through trees as old as time itself, the air heavy with secrets so ancient even her ancestors had forgotten them. *If the trees could speak ...* Eilonwy thought wistfully. She shook the idea out of her head, focusing on the task at hand. Tathiel had been training her for this moment, and she was ready.

She heard the quietest rustle off to her left. Her head spun in that direction as she tried to discern what might have made the sound. A sly little smile played on her lips. *I've got you now.* She carefully stepped in that direction, eyes darting about her, looking for any sign of her prey. After a moment, she spotted him. A young buck, grazing on some weeds under one of the great trees. Eilonwy paused, pulling out her bow and the single arrow Tathiel had given her for this exercise. She hesitated, tucking a loose strand of hair behind her ear, suddenly nervous. She was a better shot than she was a tracker. She had found the buck, she could easily take him down now. She aimed, drawing back on the bow, ready to loose.

There was a loud rustling to her right, and Tathiel was at her elbow. "Eilonwy, it's time."

The noise spooked the buck, who ran off into the woods.

Eilonwy groaned, dropping the bow and placing the arrow back into the quiver on her back. "Tathiel, I had him. And you scared him off." She glared at her twin, angry that he had interrupted her. And angry with herself for not hearing his approach sooner. But Tathiel's face was flushed, worry lines etched across his forehead. She laid a hand on his shoulder, trying to read the distress on his face. "What happened, what's wrong?"

"It's time."

It took a moment for Eilonwy to understand what he meant, but her heart skipped a beat when it hit her. *After all this time ...* "Are you sure?" Eilonwy was giddy with excitement.

Tathiel nodded. "Yes, I'm sure of it."

He wasn't nearly as excited as she was, instead looking full of dread. Eilonwy ignored the concerns he hadn't even voiced yet. She had heard them many times before, and didn't want to ruin the excitement she felt. She grabbed his hand, dragging him off back towards their home. "Come on, we don't want to miss it."

He followed behind her reluctantly, "Eilonwy, what if—"

"No time to worry about what might happen. We have to get there, quickly!" Dropping his hand, she ran off for home, Tathiel a few steps behind.

It took some time, but they reached their destination at last: a remote section of woods where the trees grew the largest, shading the ground beneath them even at the height of day. Eilonwy ran to a nearby tree, placing one palm delicately on its rough bark. Breathless, she whispered, "Friend,

grant me the protection of your walls, and I will be grateful."
She stepped back, anxiously waiting.

The tree responded, its bark slowly twisting and writhing
around to form a small hole. The hole grew larger, forming
into an entrance. But it was happening too slowly for
Eilonwy, who bristled with anticipation. "Come on, come
on." She writhed her hands impatiently.

"Eilonwy, be respectful," Tathiel chastised. "Our home is
very old now, and it takes a little longer for it to recognize
requests for entrance."

"Ugh," Eilonwy groaned, tucking another loose strand of
hair behind one long pointed ear. "You sound like Mother."
But she stood still, waiting a little more patiently for the
great tree to finish. As soon as the entrance was wide
enough, Eilonwy dashed inside, disappearing into the tree's
depths.

Tathiel shook his head. *She never remembers the second
part.* Placing his palm delicately on the tree in much
the same way Eilonwy had, Tathiel whispered, "Thank you
for your kindness. In gratitude ..." He leaned in, resting his
brow on the rough bark of the tree for a moment before
straightening. "My thanks." He slipped through the doorway
as the tree writhed and contorted back into its regular form.

Tathiel took two steps forward into the darkness of the
interior of the tree before meeting a slight resistance, like
walking through a curtain of misty water. But he continued,
not faltering in his step, as the protective spell surrounding
their home swept over him. On the other side of the barrier,
their home was brightly lit with countless orbs of light
floating around. The interior of the tree had been shaped
long ago into hallways, rooms and bedchambers, ornate and
beautiful. The magic used could still be felt, warm and

comforting. He heard a single voice singing from one of the rooms nearby. Eilonwy was standing a few steps away, waiting impatiently for him, one hand on her hip. She'd already deposited her bow and quiver into a neighboring room.

"Well, come on now. Or are you getting too old to move properly as well?"

Tathiel bit his lip. "Eilonwy …" He sighed. "What if the thing is wild?"

Eilonwy rolled her eyes. "It recognized us, remember? It won't be wild." She grabbed his hand again, as she was wont to do when in a rush. "Now let's go, before we miss it."

They hurried down the hallway towards the stairs, a long, curved set that continued up the interior of the tree for several hundred feet. They had almost reached the foot of the staircase when the singing Tathiel had heard stopped.

"Eilonwy! Tathiel!"

They turned and stepped into the room the voice had called from. "Yes, Mother?" Tathiel and Eilonwy responded simultaneously.

Their mother stood alone in the center of the room. She turned towards them, looking them over. "You two should stay in for the rest of the night. Our Hometree is very distressed. I've never seen her this upset before. Something strange is happening."

Tathiel gave Eilonwy a knowing look, but she ignored him.

"Go up and change. I'd like you both back down here within the hour. It's time I taught you how to properly care for our Hometree. Aldur's father has already taught him, and he is much younger than you two."

"But, Mother—" Eilonwy began.

"When the Great Ones granted me the birth of two chil-dren, I thought myself twice blessed," their mother inter-jected. "Now I am beginning to think that I have been twice cursed." She shook her head, but there was a sly twinkle in her eye. She chuckled, a small smirk on her face. "Now go on, and hurry, I'll need your help tonight calming her down."

Eilonwy sighed audibly before rushing up the stairs, Tathiel once more just a few steps behind her. Eilonwy skidded to a halt in the doorway of her bedroom. The furnishings were sparse, all made from the same wood of their Hometree, each piece blending in and growing from the wooden walls as if it were still a part of the great tree that housed them. But it was the blue egg sitting directly on the floor of the room that fascinated Eilonwy and Tathiel. For the moment, it seemed especially boring, simply resting in the center of the open floor. Breathless, Eilonwy turned to her brother. "Did you bring it out here?"

Tathiel shook his head fiercely. "No, I just walked by and saw it in here. And then it … it moved."

Eilonwy turned back to the egg, her shoulders tense and her eyes fixed on the ovoid blue orb. They stared at the egg in silence for a moment. She seemed ready to give up when it suddenly jerked, spinning quickly before lying still once more. With a squeal of delight, Eilonwy ran to the egg, falling to her knees in front of it, watching as it rocked and spun about again. Tathiel hesitantly followed her, choosing to sit a little further away.

"Look, Tathiel, there are cracks on the egg—it's going to hatch!" She looked over her shoulder at him, excitement making her eyes bright and her cheeks flushed, but he just shook his head at her and motioned for her to move away from the thing twitching on the ground before her.

"Come on, back up a bit. We don't know what will happen when it hatches."

Eilonwy rolled her eyes at him again. "What could happen? It's just a baby, Tathiel."

"A baby *dragon*," Tathiel insisted. "It could still be very dangerous. It could be wild."

"It *won't* be wild," Eilonwy insisted. The egg cracked audibly, and she leaned in closer. "Oh, Tathiel, I think I saw an eye!" Eilonwy squealed. "It's breaking the egg!"

Despite his own warnings, Tathiel inched closer, peering over his sister's shoulder. *It's not every day you get to watch a dragon hatch.* The iridescent blue of the egg had chipped away in several places, and Tathiel was sure he saw the flash of light blue scales. He leaned forward as the crackling grew louder.

With a loud snap, the egg blew apart and shards flew in all directions. Eilonwy shrieked, her hands rising to cover her face. Tathiel instinctively wrapped an arm around his sister, pulling her down and shielding her with his body.

The dust settled quickly, but it was a quiet burbling sound that pulled Tathiel's head up. There, in the rubble of its small egg, sat a little blue dragon. Its eyes were large and watery, its scales patched with bright blues and dark turquoise hues, and it looked much too small and frail to be very dangerous. Eilonwy gasped and fawned over the hatchling. The dragon's head cocked at the sound, and when it opened its mouth, the softest little burbling noise was all that would come out. "Oh, Tathiel, look, it's trying to roar."

"Maybe it's hungry. Just back away," Tathiel said lamely. But no sooner had the words left his mouth than the little dragon rushed at him, darting around Eilonwy's outstretched hand, and crawled up into Tathiel's lap. His instinct was to scream, to fling the creature off of him, to get Eilonwy and run back down the stairs, but he was frozen in place, staring into the watery blue eyes of the little dragon. His gaze locked with the creature's and it held him there.

"Look, it likes you, Tathiel."

He was vaguely aware of his sister's voice sounding in his ears, but there was something else, something more there with it. That quiet little burbling was growing louder in his head, mixed with all kinds of strange sensations and feelings that weren't entirely his own. "Eilonwy—"

"Oh—"

Tathiel felt Eilonwy stiffen next to him. She was just as transfixed by the creature as he was.

What is happening? It was just a thought, a simple question, but Tathiel heard it echo within him.

Tathiel? Eilonwy's voice, but she wasn't speaking.

Eilonwy?

The burbling came to a crescendo, and Tathiel felt an overwhelming sense of pride wash over him.

And then the feeling was gone and Tathiel was alone with his own thoughts again. The dragon crawled from his lap to Eilonwy's chest, nuzzling itself into the crook of her arm.

Tathiel shook his head, trying to make sense of what had happened. "That noise, she was laughing."

"She?" Eilonwy looked down at the creature in delight.

"Yeah, she." Tathiel was sure that the presence that had held him so tightly had been female. "She's happy to see us." Tathiel reached out to stroke the dragon's head, unafraid. The dragon chirped loudly in response.

The sound of hurried footsteps outside the room caused Tathiel and Eilonwy both to turn. Their mother rushed in, anxious. "I heard a shout, what's going on?" She skidded to a halt at the sight of the dragon curled up in Eilonwy's arms, nuzzling Tathiel's palm.

The sound of their mother's terrified scream echoed throughout their Hometree.

6

TIRYN

T iryn sat patiently in the carved seat he had been directed to. It was stone, as was the long table in front of him, along with much of everything else he had seen thus far in Doldural. But it was comfortable enough, and surprisingly warm. Still, he had been waiting for what felt like nearly an hour. It might have only been ten minutes. This far underground, even his impeccable elven awareness of time was confused and all but useless.

A stocky dwarf stood by the only door leading to or from the room Tiryn waited in. He was broad shouldered, even by dwarf standards, and stood with both palms draped gently on the haft of the great double-headed axe that rested against the ground in front of him. His clothing was fairly plain, and his wiry hair and beard were carefully trimmed and brushed into a thick braid that ended just short of his belt line.

It had surprised Tiryn how neat and orderly the inhabitants of the dwarfen keep were. He had imagined Doldural to be a greasy, raucous, and gaudy hall filled with glittering jewels and ale. But it was quiet, clean, and tastefully decorated in a way that Tiryn could appreciate, even if it was still a tad gaudy for his simple tastes. And the dwarfs living within, the few he had seen, anyway, were much the same.

"What are you looking at?"

Tiryn blinked, surprised the dwarf in front of him had spoken. "I didn't mean to stare. I was just admiring your axe."

The dwarf made a humored snort.

"No, really. It's quite fascinating. I've never seen one like it." Tiryn held out a hand, palm up. "May I?"

The dwarf sneered at him, his beady eyes narrowing.

Tiryn almost laughed. "I'm here in an act of diplomacy. I don't intend to threaten that so far into your hall." Tiryn dipped his head towards the dwarf. "And I would never dream of damaging a dwarf's weapon."

The dwarf seemed to consider for a moment, then lifted the axe to grip in both hands and brought it to Tiryn. He held it out for him to take, and Tiryn carefully lifted the weapon from the dwarf's grasp and turned it over in his hands, inspecting it.

"Remarkable." Tiryn ran a hand down the grain of the handle. The axe was far too small for him to use comfortably. It looked almost like a child's plaything in his hands. But the blades were sharp, with carefully etched designs crossing each face.

A large green jewel, about the size of Tiryn's thumb, was set into the lip of the axe on one side. "Is that an emerald?" Tiryn tapped at the gem lightly with one finger.

"Careful."

The gem flashed a brilliant green for an instant, and a spark of energy flitted from the stone to Tiryn's fingertip. "Ah. You've stored magic in it." Tiryn touched the gem again thoughtfully. "I'm not terribly familiar with dwarfen magic, but I think I could figure out—"

"It helps to keep the edges sharp." The dwarf's voice was gruff and deep. He sounded a bit annoyed, though Tiryn supposed all dwarts might naturally sound agitated.

"Oh." Tiryn wished the stone had been for something less mundane. "I have something similar on my favorite blades. Though mine are all in the hilt, not on the blades themselves."

"Axe handles break." He held his hands out to take the weapon back. "Better to put in on the head itself."

"Of course." Tiryn gingerly dropped the axe back into its owner's hands.

The dwarf made a low sound of what might have been agreement, and retreated to stand by the door once more. Tiryn thought to ask him who had crafted the weapon, and who had filled the jewel with arcane energy—dwarfs were not known to be very skilled in the arcane—but the latch on the door lifted and Tiryn's questions died as the dwarfen king entered the room.

He was taller than most dwarfs, standing a good half a head over the two dwarfs that followed him in. Of the four of them, five counting Tiryn himself, he was the most richly dressed, but the thick banded rings and their large stones and the gemmed circlet on his head conveyed only a sense of respect and power, not of greed and opulence. At his entrance, the waiting dwarf straightened, tipping his head slightly at his king's back.

Tiryn hastily stood, bowing low. "King Darlyth. Thank you for agreeing to see me."

Darlyth waved a hand. "Get up. I don't let the other dwarfs kiss the dirt I walk on, and I won't let an elf do it either."

Tiryn straightened, waiting for the three newcomers to be seated before taking his seat once more. "I trust that you've already been informed of the reason for my visit?"

Darlyth nodded. "Yes, yes. Grinor was sure to leave no detail out of your earlier meeting with him." Darlyth gestured towards one of the dwarfs that had accompanied him inside, an older dwarf that Tiryn recognized as one of the king's advisers. "Nunor! Come join us," Darlyth shouted, peering over his shoulder at the younger dwarf that had waited with Tiryn. "Can't have you sulking in the corner— my brother would curse me from his grave." Darlyth turned back to Tiryn, not waiting for the younger dwarf to answer. "Has my nephew treated you kindly?"

Tiryn caught Nunor's eye as the dwarf circled behind the king to sit between Tiryn and the still unknown dwarf. Tiryn felt the corner of his mouth beginning to curl into a smile, but he tried to keep his voice impassive as he answered, "Only just kind enough, King Darlyth."

The king roared in laughter, the sound deep enough to vibrate through the stone table beneath Tiryn's fingertips. "Good, good." Darlyth let out a few lingering chuckles, then nodded at Tiryn. "And are you comfortable? We don't have many elven visitors anymore."

Now Tiryn did smile, dipping his head slightly to Darlyth. "If you are comfortable, I am comfortable." In truth, the chair Tiryn sat in was far too low, and he had to pull the seat back from the table to keep from grazing his knees against the underside. But it was rarely wise for a guest to complain, especially to a dwarf, and never to a dwarfen king.

Darlyth laughed again. "Spoken like a true elf." He clapped his hands together, the sound resonating throughout the room. "Now. On to more difficult matters." He peered around the table before settling his gaze on Tiryn once more. "The amulets."

Tiryn nodded slightly. "The amulets."

"The Amulet of Earth has been missing for over twelve years now," Grinor said, his voice thin and warbled. "Ours is not the only one. The Vyrisian king has reported that their Amulet of Fire has also vanished. I'm not sure which of the elven cities on this side of the Knife the Amulet of Water was hidden in, Thessala perhaps—"

"Thessala is gone," Tiryn said. There was a bitter note to

his voice. "But I can confirm that the Amulet of Water also disappeared around the same time as the others."

"Around the same time King Areanath was killed, you mean?" Darlyth asked.

"Yes, that would be general consensus," Tiryn said.

"Thessala is truly gone?" Grinor asked, face drawn. "There had been rumors, but …"

Tiryn nodded. "Thessala fell in the first year of Mothlenor's rule. Many of us were able to flee, but …" Tiryn frowned. "Not quite all of us."

"I'm sorry to hear it," Grinor said.

The fourth dwarf, silent until now, pounded a closed fist against the stone table. "The humans have broken their treaties. Now is not the time to hide behind broken promises. It is time for war!"

"Enough, Darman," Darlyth said tiredly. To Tiryn he added, "You'll have to forgive my son. He doesn't have the mind for diplomacy."

"My cousin is right, Darlyth." Nunor spoke up, leaning to gaze down the table at the king. "The treaties were broken the moment the amulets were stolen. Now the choice must be made: do we fight, or do we wait to die by Mothlenor's hand, as Thessala did?"

Darmon pounded the table again. "I say we fight!"

"I say we do neither," Tiryn said firmly, eyes settling on the restless Darmon. "I've come with what I hope is a third solution, one that we can all be at peace with."

Darmon opened his mouth to protest, but King Darlyth spoke up again, raising a hand to quiet his son. "What is that third option, friend?"

Tiryn fell against the back of his chair, folding his hands into his lap. "We find the amulets before Mothlenor does, and keep him from summoning the Great Soul."

Darmon laughed, startling Nunor beside him and causing both the king and Grinor to glare at him. "The Great Soul is a myth! Can't you see, Father? This elf wants to send us on a fool's quest, chasing after a monster that does not exist!"

"It is not a myth!" Grinor shouted feebly. "The Great Soul is a terrible creature, his power split into the amulets to keep him from destroying the whole world. If Mothlenor were to get all four of the amulets, it would mean our deaths. There is no fighting the Great Soul."

"It is only a children's story, you old fool!" Darmon cried.

Grinor scoffed, waving his robed arms at the younger dwarf. "Ancient texts going back nearly five thousand years speak of the creature they called the Great Soul. It is very real!"

"Lies! Lies, and your old mind going to dust, Grinor!"

"Enough!" Darlyth shouted. His voice rang through the small room, and Tiryn was sure it carried through the thick stone walls and into the rooms beyond. Darlyth turned to Tiryn, face pinched in irritation. "Do you know where the Amulet of Earth is?"

Tiryn hesitated for only a brief second. "No, I do not."

"Do you know where any of the amulets are?"

"No, I do not. But we have clues to their locations." Tiryn's stomach twisted uncomfortably. *Or we will soon, at least.*

Darlyth sighed, leaning to rest his forearms on the table and lacing his fingers together. "Then I can't do much to help you, I'm afraid."

Grinor and Darmon both instantly protested, their words tumbling over each other so that Tiryn couldn't make out what either was saying.

Darlyth raised his hand for silence again, glaring between the two angry dwarfs. "If it were only a matter of retrieving the amulets from their known locations, I would be happy to send some of my dwarfs along with you. But—"

"We should not be considering any aid to anyone who is not a dwarf. The treaties have been broken, Father! We must do what is best for us, and leave the elves and the men to care for themselves. Areanath—"

Darlyth slammed his fist down on the table hard enough to make it shudder. "Enough, Darmon!" He seemed to struggle with himself for a moment, taking a long breath and glaring down the table at his son. "Not another word from you on this. You've said your piece."

Darmon's eye flashed angrily, but he nodded.

Darlyth fell back into his chair, turning his attention back to the rest of the table. "Areanath did break the treaties made between the men and both the dwarfs and the elves." His eyes flicked to his son, then back to the rest of the table. "If we are to follow the treaty to the letter, that is." He once again leaned to rest his forearms against the table, running his fingers through his thick beard. "But if we are to consider the spirit in which the treaties were written, then Areanath acted as he did in our best interest, if our friend here is to be believed. And that would mean that he died wanting peace between our peoples, not war." He turned to Tiryn. "Would you say my thinking is correct?"

Tiryn nodded. "It's my belief that Areanath was trying to protect us by stealing away the amulets. It is Mothlenor that craves war, and he would have destroyed anyone in his path to collecting all four amulets."

"He would already have a second one now, if Areanath had not acted as he had," Grinor said softly. "The water amulet, from Thessala."

Tiryn nodded again. "Correct."

"So, then," Darlyth continued with a sigh, "it is Mothlenor that is our true enemy. It is Mothlenor that we must defend ourselves against." Darlyth paused for a moment, eyes on the center of the table, gaze unfocused. "And that is why I cannot just give you some of my people to help you on this quest." His eyes met Tiryn's again, and he tapped the table with one thick finger. "I need them here, to protect us from Moth-lenor. Not out in the wild, searching for lost treasure."

"I understand," Tiryn said softly. His chest felt suddenly tight as he considered the possibility that he and Roland would be taking on their quest alone.

"Darlyth …" Grinor murmured.

Darlyth raised his hand again to quiet the elderly dwarf. "However, if a dwarf here in Doldural hears of your quest, and takes it upon himself to follow you, I will not fault him. It is all that I can do, I'm afraid." Darlyth searched around the table, finally settling on his nephew. "Nunor. You have been quiet in all of this. What do you think?"

Tiryn looked to the silent Nunor, who sat with one hand stroking his beard much as Darlyth had, and the other resting on the handle of his axe, which lay across his legs. He seemed to consider the king's question for a moment, all eyes on him. "I think I will go with the elf, Uncle. I am not fond of the idea of taking a war to Mothlenor, and I have never been one to wait patiently either."

Darlyth nodded, a warm smile stretching across his face. "Excellent. I can't think of a dwarf better suited to the task. Now then …" Darlyth stood, and the others around the table did the same, Tiryn included. "I think this meeting is finished. I thank you, friend, for bringing us the information you have. I hope Nunor will be an indispensable asset."

"I'm sure he will be, King Darlyth. And I thank you for your assistance." Tiryn dipped his head politely to Darlyth.

"When you have finished discussing your arrangements with my nephew, Grinor will see you out." Darlyth extended an arm, and Tiryn took it, mildly surprised by the firm grip the small dwarf held him with. "You and yours will always be welcome in Doldural, so long as the treaty between our two races is kept."

"And you and yours are welcome wherever you might find an elf, so long as the treaty between us is sound."

Darlyth made a sound somewhere between a snort and a laugh, then turned and left the room, Darmon and Grinor just behind him.

Only Nunor remained behind. He stood beside Tiryn, both palms draped over the butt end of his axe again. "So, you have my name."

Tiryn held out an arm, and the two shook. "Tiryn."

"Well then, Tiryn. Tell me everything you know about our quest."

7

MOTHLENOR

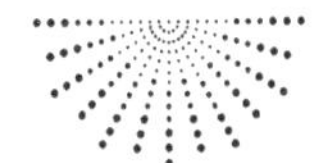

Mothlenor's apprentice padded carefully around the room, eyes fixed on the book in her hands. Anna walked gracefully, seeming to know out of instinct where each haphazard pile lay in his cluttered study. But she'd had years to learn his habits, and he hers, and she could navigate with ease what most others would stare at in dismay. Her feet were bare, the only sound of her movements the quiet swish of her dress skirts as they brushed against her legs with each step. His own work, an open book filled with meticulous notes penned in his careful hand, lay forgotten on the desk before him as he watched her, transfixed.

"Anna." He said her name without thinking and silently cursed himself for giving her reason to pause.

But she didn't. One eyebrow raised, and she made a noncommittal sound of acknowledgment without even looking up.

Mothlenor hesitated, the rich scent of jasmine wafting towards him as she swept past his work area. "Nothing," he said quietly. "Please continue."

Anna stopped, her eyes flicking up to meet his. "Did you need something of me?"

35

Mothlenor watched her for a heartbeat, wishing she would return to her quiet walk around his study. "No." He straightened, tugging the sleeves of his robe to cover his wrists. "I only wondered how your research was going."

Anna sighed, shutting the book carefully, marking her place with a thin finger. "Not well, I'm afraid. Nothing so far that we haven't already read in other books over the years." She folded her arms delicately over her midsection, turning to face him fully. "I can put in another request for more books and papers from the Azimar Archives, if you'd like. Or we can ask Archivist Vale to return—"

"Archivist Vale is a dried-up old fool, Anna." His voice was firm, but he tried to keep it kind. "I'll not ask him to return Etritia ever again. Demon-lore and curse expert, what a bunch of lies."

"You hardly even gave him a chance to speak," Anna protested. Mothlenor was sure he could see the hint of a smile in the corner of her mouth.

Mothlenor snorted, picking up his quill and glancing over his last line of text again. "I didn't need to. I knew from the moment he said curses were unbreakable that he was hardly the expert he claimed to be."

"And how can you be sure?"

Mothlenor paused, quill hanging above a blank space on the page. A fat drop of ink rolled to the tip of the quill, threatening to fall, and Mothlenor watched it for a moment. With a smooth motion, he dropped the quill back into the inkwell and once more straightened to address Anna. "I just know there's another answer. I know it in here." He tapped one temple, then stabbed the same finger at his chest. "And in here."

"But what if you're wrong?"

"I am not wrong."

Anna sighed, sitting on the edge of Mothlenor's desk and leaning to meet his gaze. "But what if we are going about this the wrong way? Instead of searching for clues to how your brother's curse worked and trying to find a way to break it, perhaps we should aim for a more direct approach? What if we searched for the amulets themselves, and—"

"I'm already working on that as well, Anna. You underestimate me." The scent of jasmine drifted closer, cloying and sweet.

"You've sent Ferrand north to find another Dragon's Eye."

"Commander Ferrand," Mothlenor corrected automatically. "Another Dragon's Eye, and another egg, yes."

"He goes up there every few months. He's always returned empty-handed."

Mothlenor frowned. His head was beginning to ache, and thoughts of Ferrand's continued disappointments were not helping. "I'm aware. Perhaps this time will be different."

"Perhaps. Perhaps not. We won't know until he returns. And that won't be for another week, maybe even two."

"What are you suggesting, Anna?" He felt his annoyance at her growing, though she was normally immune to his often unsteady temper.

"I am suggesting," she began, a thin smile curving her lips, "that you are going about this the wrong way. You are not a hunter. You are a sorcerer. You should be finding ways to find the amulets with magic, not with trinkets some mercenary has brought you from beyond the mountains."

Mothlenor gazed at her for a moment. Her eyes were alight, their normally soft hazel brightened and excited. Her smile, though not large, was sincere. And the scent of jasmine clung heavy around her, pleasant and relaxing. He had considered her idea in the past, and had dismissed it without giving it a second thought. It wouldn't have worked then, but now ... *With her, it might.*

He took Anna's hand, running a thumb over the back of her knuckles. Her skin was soft, but he could still see the faint ring of small scars circling her wrist. They were old now, white and almost invisible. She seemed to stiffen at his touch, but perhaps he was only imagining her apprehension. "Stay with me a while longer tonight."

Anna straightened, her smile suddenly gone, and nodded once. "Of course, my lord."

8

ALASTOR

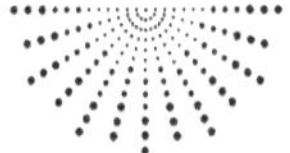

Alastor stepped into his mother's room, his brother Jaimes a half step behind him. Together, they crept silently up to the edge of the bed where his mother lay under a pile of thick covers. The heavy scent of illness filled the small space and burned the back of his throat.

"Mother?" Alastor called softly. For a moment, nothing happened. *Perhaps she is already gone.*

But then his mother's chest rose and fell, and she turned her head slightly. "Alastor?" Her voice was weak, weaker than it had been yesterday, and weaker still than the day before. One thin hand stretched out from under the bedcovers and reached for him. Alastor sat on the edge of the bed and took her hand before it could stray too far from the warmth, gripping it as gently as he could. Her hand seemed more bone than flesh, and he was shocked by the cold of it. "Where is Jaimes?"

"Right here," Jaimes said, stepping to stand just behind Alastor's shoulder.

"My boys." Silvana sighed, craning her neck to look between the two of them. There was sweat dotted across her brow, and it caught the soft light filtering in from the half-

39

shuttered window on the far wall. "You're bigger than I remember. I've been stuck in bed for too long."

Alastor smiled. She'd said the same thing the day before. "It's alright. You'll be better soon enough," he lied.

"I'm not sure I can remember the last time I was ill for this long." She thought for a moment, her eyes half shutting. "Maybe when I caught that terrible chill when we were little. Do you remember that, Ajax?" Silvana craned her neck again to look up at Jaimes. Her eyes were far too bright, and her cheeks a deep red.

"Y-yes," Jaimes stammered, his voice cracking.

Alastor bit his lip, knowing what was to come.

Silvana tried to laugh, but it came out a croaking wheeze. "Great Ones preserve the two of you. You never left my side then, and you haven't now."

"Of course not," Alastor said quietly.

His mother's eyes locked on to his, and her face broke into a wide smile. Despite the sickness that had ruined both her mind and her body, her smile was still radiant, and Alastor found himself smiling to match her. "Hasani. I wondered if you might finally find me again. I've missed you so much." Her grip on his hand tightened slightly. "And look, Ajax is here. We can be a family again."

Alastor could only nod, trying to keep his mother's smile from fading. Beside him, he sensed Jaimes shifting uncomfortably, but he remained silent. They had agreed to say nothing, and to let his mother have her delusions.

"Hasani, you should see Alastor. He's grown into such a good boy."

Alastor's chest tightened, but he nodded again. Her wide smile seemed to shimmer for a moment, and Alastor realized his eyes were filling with unshed tears.

"You'd be so proud of him. And his brother, too, I think." She shook her head, seeming to guess at a question Alastor hadn't asked. "Not blood brothers, but you couldn't tell from the way they treat each other." She hesitated for a moment, her smile faltering slightly. "I have never loved anyone but you, Hasani."

There was a low mumble and an unsteady shuffle from the hall. Alastor turned, catching sight of Harlan's back as the man shambled away from the sickroom. The knot in Alastor's stomach twisted. *He's been drinking. And he heard what she said.* But it couldn't be helped. Silvana was no longer in her right mind. Surely Harlan would realize that.

He turned back to his mother. She was still smiling up at him, her too-bright eyes fixed on him. He patted her hand gently. "I know."

"I-I should go check on Harlan," Jaimes whispered. He moved to pass Alastor, but Silvana's hand caught his sleeve, moving so suddenly that Alastor hardly caught it.

"Wait, Ajax." Silvana tugged Jaimes back a step, pulling him closer to her. "Don't leave me."

Jaimes's gaze shifted to Alastor. His eyes were wide and frightened, and his breathing hitched slightly as he drew in a sharp breath.

Alastor frowned at his brother, momentarily frustrated with the ease in which Jaimes could find himself in a panic. He leaned forward, carefully freeing Jaimes's sleeve from his mother's grip and holding her hand in his once more. "He'll only be gone a moment."

Jaimes straightened, lips pursed together, and Alastor shot him an apologetic smile as he hurried passed.

"No, don't let him leave, Hasani!" his mother cried. "Please, make him listen! Tell him to take it back, to return what we stole. It's the only way we can be happy again!" Silvana sat up in bed, staring around Alastor at the departing Jaimes. "Come back, Ajax!"

Alastor carefully coaxed her back against the pillows. "Hush, Ajax already knows."

His mother's weak struggles eased, and she let Alastor

pull the covers back over her. "He knows?" The words sounded childish, full of concern and fear.

Alastor brushed Silvana's hair back from her sweating face. "He knows. That's where he's going now. To take back what we stole." Her face was flushed, her cheeks an even deeper shade of red after that little effort she had expended. "He'll be back soon. So we can be a family again."

The bedside table, normally cluttered with books and assorted potted plants, was now empty, save for a small bowl of cool water and a few dampened cloths. Alastor took one of these and folded it with a few quick motions. "You should try to rest." He draped the damp cloth over her forehead, watching as an errant drop of moisture rolled down her temple to be lost in her hair. "I'm sure Ajax will be back when you wake up again."

"I've missed you both so much," Silvana murmured. Her eyes closed, her body relaxing as she drifted to sleep.

Alastor watched her for a moment, counting the seconds between each shallow breath. Three seconds, then a breath out. Another three, then a breath in, long and wheezing. Three seconds, and a slow exhale.

Three seconds.

Five seconds.

At eight seconds, Alastor squeezed Silvana's hand. "Mother?"

She inhaled sharply, her eyes flitting for a moment, then opening and settling on him. "Alastor? You just missed your father."

Alastor smiled, silently willing the lump in his throat away. "I'm sure he's still around. I'll find him."

Her breathing seemed normal again, and her eyes were already closing once more. "You're such a good boy. Your brother too." She exhaled in a long sigh.

Alastor knelt to kiss her cheek. "Rest. You'll be fine in a few days."

Her eyes were already shut, and her breathing continued in a slow rhythm. Alastor stayed with her for a few moments, watching her chest rise and fall with each shallow and rattling breath. Finally, he stood and left the room, closing the door most of the way behind him.

Jaimes was waiting for him at the end of the hall, leaning against the wall and staring at his feet. "I'm sorry, Alastor. I just don't know what to do when she gets like that."

"I know." Alastor leaned against the wall next to Jaimes, nudging his brother's shoulder with his own. "It's alright. Things will be fine soon enough."

"Sure..."

There was a heavy silence in the hallway. Alastor was sure his brother was considering the same questions he was. Would his mother be fine in a few days? A few weeks? Or would she never be fine? Would whatever illness she had eventually kill her?

There was a string of mumbled curses and the sound of glass clinking together in the adjacent room, and Alastor and Jaimes both looked up at the closed door to the dining area.

"How is he?" Alastor asked.

"I haven't checked."

Alastor sighed, stepping away from the wall and motioned for Jaimes to follow him. "Come on, then. Let's go see."

Harlan was drunk, that much was evident as soon as the door was opened. There were empty ale bottles arranged in an untidy semicircle on the table around him, and a mostly empty crate of full ones sitting on the ground beside his chair. There was a pungent sour scent in the air, and a spot of dark liquid on the stone floor nearby. Alastor's first thought was that Harlan had drunk enough to piss himself, but there were shards of dark glass littering the ground as well. A broken bottle, and a broken man. *Great Ones preserve us.*

Alastor shook his head, stepping around the spilled

alcohol to start collecting empty bottles. "Don't you think you've had enough, Harlan?"

"I know when I've had enough," Harlan grumbled, taking another swig from the bottle in his hand. "You heard her in there. She's never loved another man but him."

"That isn't how she meant it," Alastor pleaded. He deposited the first armful of bottles into an empty crate nearby. "She meant that she had never—"

"I know how she meant it, Alastor," Harlan hissed. He finished the bottle he held, then offered it up for Alastor to take. "And it's true. Your mother and I were never together." His bloodshot eyes seemed to bore into Alastor's. "But I love her, same as I love Jaimes's mother. And to hear her say that …" He rubbed both hands over his face then ran them through his dirty hair. "Well, it just ruins a man."

"Harlan …"

"Ah, forget it." Harlan reached for another bottle and struggled to his feet. "Get to bed, both of ya." He stumbled off, heading for the door that led out to the small garden Silvana kept. "Just leave me alone."

Harlan's drinking grew worse as the days passed. The inn all but closed, with the few regulars they had for drinks and company in the evenings abandoning the little inn. Alastor and Jaimes spent their days alternating between each parent, occasionally finding solace in a quiet corner, far off from the scent of disease and from the sounds of drunken stumbles and curses.

At the funeral, Alastor and Jaimes stood silently on either side of their mother's open grave as the Elder Vyrik, brought in from Hythe, gave the ceremonial death speech. Alastor hardly heard the words and could only stare numbly ahead at the assembled crowd, eyes unfocused.

When it was finished, Elder Vyrik gave Alastor and Jaimes each a small shovel, little more than a gardening trowel, and the two of them knelt in the earth to begin the burial.

The soil was hard, having been dug up several days earlier and allowed to bake in the sun before the hole was needed. Alastor could feel small stones in the earth cutting at his hands as he worked, and small blisters formed where he gripped the handle of the shovel. But he kept working, dumping small amounts of dirt over his mother's body.

When the work was about halfway done, a commotion in the gathered crowd caused Alastor to look up. Sweat and tears stung his eyes; he wiped at them with the back of one dirty to hand to see the crowd parted and Harlan taking drunken swings at a man Alastor didn't recognize. A gasp came from the gathered mourners as Harlan made a poor throw, which the stranger caught and used to pull Harlan off balance, sending Harlan to sprawl across the packed earth. The stranger looked up, realizing he had the attention of everyone around him. He looked over at Alastor and Jaimes, hesitating for a moment before turning and rushing away.

Elder Vyrik hurried to Harlan's side, helping him to his feet and admonishing him for causing such chaos during a time of grief. Harlan cursed him, shoving the Elder away and stumbling off towards the inn.

Alastor looked across the half-filled hole to Jaimes, who was staring wide eyed after his father. "Jaimes?"

Jaimes turned to Alastor reluctantly. Sweat clung to his face and neck, and his hair was matted to his forehead. Jaimes only shrugged, casting one last glance in the direction Harlan had gone before continuing his work again.

Alastor picked up another scoop of dirt, dropping it into the hole.

Then another.

And another.

Until the hole was finally filled.

9

ROLAND

Roland waited patiently, crouching behind a large tree. He had been there for nearly an hour, wondering if anything would even come from this meeting. There had been so many leads and so many disappointments, but this was the best tip he had received thus far. Roland was hopeful that it would finally lead him to the beast with deep-sea wings. After a few moments, Roland saw movement between the trees and three elves stepped into the clearing in front of him. Their faces were covered, but Roland could tell by the fluid way they moved that they were indeed elves. Highborn, too, judging from their loose and shapeless clothing and the long silver hair that was visible beneath their hoods. Roland stood carefully, making his presence known, and stepped into the clearing with his arms raised in peace.

One of the elves instantly turned towards him. "Begone, human, you have no business in these sacred woods." Her voice was a midnight storm, both soothing and terrifying.

Roland winced, but took another step towards them. The other two elves tensed at his approach. "Actually, I do have business here. I've come to speak with the elf Aniri, regarding her children." He took another step closer before stopping in his tracks. "I've been Marked, if that eases your concerns any." He tried his best to show no sign of fear, but his heart was pounding. *If this goes wrong in the slightest way, I'll be dead before I can blink.*

At the mention of a Mark, however, the female turned to one of her male companions, giving him a slight nod. The male strode towards Roland, who offered out his right arm for inspection. The elf took the arm in hand, pushing the sleeve of Roland's tunic up to the elbow. The inside of Roland's arm appeared to be bare, until the elf grasped it firmly with both hands. Roland felt a tingling sensation throughout his arm, and within seconds, a faint silver mark appeared on the inside of his wrist. Roland, not understanding the elven language, could not read it, but the elf squinted up at Roland in surprise.

"It's a nice Mark, human." The elf's voice was rich and light, not unlike Roland had expected.

"Thank you, I guess. A friend gave it to me."

"Uthil?" the female elf called. The elf obediently released Roland's arm, turning to give his companions a slow nod.

The three elves before him removed their hoods; all three were very similar in appearance, with silver hair and sharp, angled features. *Highborn, just as I had suspected,* Roland thought. He had never met a highborn elf before, but Tiryn had described their appearance well enough, as well as their more defined facial features, and their longer, pointier ears.

"I am Aniri. I apologize for my rudeness, but I was expecting …" Her voice trailed.

"An elf?" Roland suggested, and Aniri nodded. "I'm sorry for my deception, but I was worried you wouldn't come if I had divulged that I'm human."

"I suspect that you were right to worry." Aniri sighed. "Still, you have the Mark. You must have done something great for one of my kinsmen to bestow that gift onto you, especially in these trying times."

It was Tiryn's idea, actually. But Roland kept his thoughts to himself. Tiryn had applied the Mark without hesitation, describing it as a hidden rune, one that meant "friend" or "ally", and would be seen as a sign of his good faith.

Aniri beckoned him closer. "Come. You wanted to speak of my children? Then I shall lead you to them."

Roland followed closely in her footsteps. "Your letter said that your children began acting strange suddenly. In what way, exactly?"

Aniri tilted her head, contemplating. "I didn't realize it at first. They are still very young, and I thought it was the normal progression into their adulthood. Eilonwy had always been excitable, but suddenly she would go through phases where she was too much to handle, and she would often forget herself and her responsibilities." Aniri paused, sighing. "Tathiel handled it differently. He had always been a bit of a trickster, especially with his sister. But then, one day, he was suddenly constantly worried about nothing at all, and he fell into a depression." She looked over her shoulder at Roland. "They've both returned to their usual selves, if you were concerned. They pose no harm to you, human."

Roland had been concerned. A manic sister and her anxious brother? Aniri continued speaking, and Roland put aside any additional worries of her children to follow her words.

"One day, they rushed inside, like they did most days, and ran straight for their rooms. It was silent for a time, until I heard Eilonwy scream. I rushed to them, only to see *it* when I got there."

"The blue winged beast." Roland nodded. They walked side by side now through the woods. The trees were large, larger than any Roland had ever seen before, but he kept his eyes focused ahead, not wanting to seem distracted to his host.

"A *dragon*." Aniri shuddered, reeling from the memory.

Roland nodded. Aniri looked at him, puzzled. "You already know that. How?"

"There were rumors … They eventually led me to you." Roland tried to keep his answer vague. He didn't want to admit to her that it was a dwarf that had first said the word "dragon". Dwarfs should never know the private matters of an elf, even if those private matters were flying all about the woods with her children in tow.

"And it does not shock you?"

"Oh, it shocks me. Wild dragons haven't been seen in centuries." Roland skirted around a large tree root poking from the ground. He vaguely wondered if they were walking through Aniri's Homewood. Tiryn had told him once that highborn elves still lived within ancient trees while most other elves had decided to live in dwellings that more closely resembled human houses and towns.

"The dragon isn't wild. She and my children *belong* together." She said the words with some difficulty, as if she didn't quite believe them.

"She?" Roland's interest was suddenly piqued. Off in the distance, he could hear peals of feminine laughter.

"She, yes." Aniri lifted the skirt of her dress a few inches as she stepped over a broken branch that lay in their path, and Roland saw that she was barefoot. "She told us someone in need would be coming, but I must admit I had hoped she would be wrong."

Roland paused, one hand resting on the rough bark of a large tree. "She told you I would be coming?"

Aniri smiled. "Sometimes she seems to know things that she simply should not. If you can connect with her, perhaps you can see for yourself."

"Connect with her?"

"You'll understand, perhaps." Aniri raised her head, eyes scanning the skies above. She pointed. "Look, here she comes."

Roland scanned the skies where Aniri had pointed, but the trees grew too tall, blocking his view. But he heard something … like a strong wind blowing through trees. The sound grew louder, until a large shadow covered them all in darkness. Roland barely had time to panic before the shadow was gone, heading further into the woods.

Roland turned to Aniri. "Was that her?"

Aniri nodded, smiling faintly at his shocked expression. She turned to the two elves that had accompanied them through the woods. "Thank you, Uthil and Aldur, but you can go. I will be fine from here." She bowed to them, and they bowed in return before turning back and disappearing among the trees. Aniri beckoned Roland further into the woods. "Come, I'll introduce you to my children."

They walked in silence for a few moments, Aniri leading Roland deeper into the woods. Roland heard more laughter, louder and closer this time. Soon, they stepped into a large clearing where another elf was standing. She was smaller and younger than Aniri, but looked almost just like her. The young elf was gazing up into the sky, her hands clasped together and a smile lighting up her face. As soon as she caught sight of Aniri, however, the grin grew larger, and she ran into Aniri's arms, hugging her around the neck. "Mother, you came this time! They'll be returning soon, watch!" She turned to stand next to Aniri, one arm wrapped around her mother's waist, and pointed up into the sky.

Roland followed their gaze, but again could see nothing. The sound of wind rushing through the trees came again, and Roland knew what to expect. The shadow loomed over them, closer to the ground this time, and Roland heard more laughter coming from above his head. The shadow was gone in an instant, but a large … *something* was falling from the sky. To his horror, Roland realized it was a person. He started to run further into the clearing, to perhaps break the person's fall with his own body, but a small hand gripped his wrist with surprising strength, keeping him back.

Roland looked over to see the young elf, Eilonwy, looking up at him. "Just watch."

So Roland turned back, watching the body tumble through the air. His heart was beating fast, and he was sure he was watching someone plummet to their death. But suddenly, the dragon had returned, and neatly caught the person on her back. Roland's tension immediately released, as did Eilonwy's grip on his wrist. Roland looked over to Aniri, to see that she had been just as panicked as he was, with her own wrist held tightly by Eilonwy.

"She's coming around once more to land." Eilonwy's voice was full of excitement. "Step away from the center."

Aniri and Roland did as they were told, and Eilonwy leaned in to whisper to Roland. "Well met, traveler. Melonya has been expecting you."

"Melonya?" Roland looked down at Eilonwy and was surprised to see a pair of wise old eyes that did not belong to the young elf staring back at him. It was the same look Nevina had when …

Roland blinked hard, pushing the memories from his mind. Eilonwy smiled up at him, her eyes once more twinkling with youthful energy. "Melonya is the name she chose for herself."

There was another strong gale, but rather than pass over them for a third time, the dragon turned downward, headed straight for the clearing. At the last moment, she pulled up, correcting her landing by buffeting the ground with her great wings. She landed with a great thump, and her rider slid off her back and onto the ground.

Eilonwy ran to the rider, a taller, male version of both Eilonwy and Aniri. "Good job on the recovery. You looked like some sort of big ugly bird while falling."

Her brother smiled down at her. "I'll try to make it look a little less ugly next time."

Roland heard their banter, but only vaguely. He was more focused on the great dragon before him. She was huge, with large blue eyes staring right at him. Her body was easily three, no four times as wide as his, with muscular shoulders and forelegs squared against her broad chest. Her neck was long and lithe, her tail the same, and her wings were an almost translucent blue, with veins visible throughout the thin webbing. And all over her were blue scales of varying size and shade.

The blue-winged beast.

There was a loud buzzing noise, and an uncomfortable pressure in Roland's ears. He winced at the pain just as a musical voice sounded in his ear. *"Welcome, Ajax."*

Her voice was soothing, and with the words came a wide range of emotions: excitement, wistfulness, a twinge of sadness. And also a full spectrum of colorful explosions in his mind's eye with each syllable she spoke. He could not only hear her words, but see and feel them. He stood for a moment, trying to recover from his connection with her. Finally, finding his voice, he corrected her numbly, saying aloud, "My name is Roland."

I haven't used that name in years, he thought quietly to himself. But the dragon had heard that, too, he realized. There was a rumbling of bells, laughter, and the over-whelming sense of amusement.

She started again. *"Well met, Roland."*

Roland realized they were no longer alone in their conversation. Eilonwy and Tathiel had slipped into his mind as well, following Melonya's example. Their minds were dull compared to the dragon's, without the waves of emotion and the display of colorful lights he got when Melonya spoke. But Roland could sense their intentions and knew them to be honest and trustworthy.

"Well met, Roland," Tathiel repeated.

"We've been expecting you," Eilonwy added.

Roland was struck with a realization as he connected to the elves so intimately. They weren't just brother and sister, they were twins. With the same light hair, same light eyes, and nearly identical mental connections. He was silent, letting their minds wash over his. They did not intrude, only waited patiently for him to gain some sort of familiarity with them. After a moment, Roland tried to delve deeper, to understand what was happening more fully. He found the connection linking his mind to Eilonwy's, barely able to discern it from her brother's. He started to follow it, to reach out for himself, unsure if he even could. It was easier than he thought, and suddenly he was reaching out to her, rather than the other way around.

"Hello." Eilonwy's voice shifted in his mind, and Roland realized it was amusement he could sense from her.

Unsure of how to respond, Roland just continued to wander through Eilonwy's mind, engrossed in this incredible method of communication. He fell upon something, roaming through. He suddenly saw a glimpse of woods, a bow in his hand, Tathiel at his side.

But the connections instantly vanished, and he was back in his own mind, with only Melonya holding her connection with him. The twins had vanished from his mind.

Realizing what he'd done, he turned to Eilonwy. "I'm sorry, I didn't mean to—"

She smiled. "It's alright. Just a harmless memory of hunting. Now you understand how it works?"

Roland nodded. "I think so." He shook his head, trying to relieve the sudden strangeness that Melonya's presence in his mind gave him. "I've never done that before."

"It's the only way Melonya can speak to us," Tathiel explained. "It can take some getting used to."

"Roland." Aniri stepped to his side, careful to stay just out of arm's reach. "You've met my children, and the dragon." She seemed to waver, her gaze shifting slowly between the great dragon and Roland as she spoke. "Melonya has told us that you would need her help, but not to what end."

Roland had forgotten Aniri was there. "Yes, well …" he stammered, not sure how best to explain the situation. "It's something better suited for more private quarters."

Aniri shook her head. "You might be a friend to elves, but I will not welcome you into my Hometree." She crossed her arms over her chest, "We discuss this here. Or you leave." She didn't sound angry, Roland realized. Aniri sounded worried.

"Very well." Roland sighed. "The problem is …" He paused, not sure how to continue. "You see …" He paused again. He had spent so much time worrying about getting to this moment, yet he had never stopped to think of what to do once he had found the blue-winged beast. But then he remembered that feeling he'd had when Tathiel and Eilonwy had been connected to him. That sense of honesty pouring from the twins. He could still feel it even now, coming from Melonya. He took a deep breath and held it for a moment, trying to calm his nerves. Letting out a long sigh, he turned to the twins and their dragon. "I need your help finding the Amulets of Power."

The twins said nothing. It was Melonya who replied. *"I've known this day would come for some time. I've felt the imbalance in the world left by the disappearance of the amulets. Mothlenor must be stopped before he can find them and summon the Great Soul."* She paused, and Roland was again hit by a wave of emotions that were not his own. Fear, sadness, and a hint of grief rolled through him. *"We will go with you."*

Roland was grateful, and he felt a large weight lift from his chest. He had found the blue-winged beast, and had convinced Melonya and the twins to help him. It was only a matter of time before they found the first amulet, he was sure.

Aniri's shoulders slumped slightly, and she looked to her children with resignation. "I had hoped this wouldn't come to pass. That Melonya had been wrong about your place in this nonsense. But I would not be so lucky, to keep the three of you so close to me."

"Come with us, Mother," Eilonwy said, reaching for Aniri's hand.

Aniri shook her head, folding her fingers over Eilonwy's. "I must stay here. Vyris grows smaller with each passing year, and I must remain behind to keep her from falling away completely." Aniri released Eilonwy's hand, opening her arms for her children to step into her embrace. "Just promise me that you'll return to our Hometree when you can."

Roland turned and left them to each other, stepping just outside the clearing. He pulled a small leather pouch out from the inside of his vest, flipping it open with one hand to inspect the contents. Inside the pouch were spare bits of parchment and a small coalstick. *Time to tell Tiryn about this.* He paused, thinking. *Hythe. Hythe would be the best place to start.*

Tiryn hesitated outside the door. Already, there was an air of misuse about the building, and some parts of the once great inn were falling into disrepair. Tiryn sighed in resignation. *This might be harder than I thought.* He quickly pushed open the door, the sound of the little bell above making him wince as it echoed through the empty inn.

Tiryn heard movement in the next room, followed by what might have been the sound of a chair falling over. After a moment, the door swung open, and Tiryn was shocked at the sight of the man that entered. It had been only a few years, but Harlan had aged very poorly. His hair was greasy and streaked with grey hairs, and his entire body looked fatigued and weak. Harlan stumbled through the doorway, taking a swig from the large tankard in his hand. He looked Tiryn up and down, not seeming to recognize him. One look at the pointed ears, though, and Harlan was quick to shake his head. "No rooms for elves." He turned away, heading back into the next room.

"Harlan, it's me, Tiryn." Harlan waved his hand over his shoulder, dismissing him. "We met once, some time ago." Still no response. Tiryn sighed, already regretting his next words. "Roland sent me."

At the mention of Roland, Harlan paused his drunken retreat. "Roland." The name came out as a growl. He turned back to Tiryn. "And where is Roland? Too busy bein' some self-righteous runabout to come see Silvana's son for himself? Decides to send his little elf friend instead?" Harlan took another swig from the tankard. "Well, ya can tell 'im Silvana is dead, and see if he chokes on it."

"He already knows," Tiryn said sadly.

Harlan chuckled, his head tilting, as if he only just remembered something he hadn't realized he'd forgotten. "'Course he already knows. He was there, wasn' he?" Another swig from the tankard. "What do ya want?"

"I've come to take the boy to his uncle."

"Alastor ain't goin' nowhere with you. 'Specially not to tha' bloody bastard." Harlan was shouting now, swaying unsteadily on his feet.

"Silvana would have wanted him to be with family, Harlan."

"He is with family! I've been more of an uncle to him than *he* has. He stays here."

"Silvana—"

"Silvana is dead." He drained the tankard. "She wants nothing, now." Harlan's voice had dropped off to a whisper. "Fifteen years, I've loved her. Fifteen years, I've cared for her. And when the fever took her, it was him she called for. Him, an' her husband. Not me. Not once did she call for me." He stared down into the empty tankard in his hand. "I was there, but she didn' want me. She called for him, and where was he?" Harlan looked up at Tiryn, glaring. "Alastor stays with me. And we have no rooms for elves." Harlan turned and walked back into the next room, leaving Tiryn standing in the foyer. He heard crashing and thumping as Harlan wandered his way through the dining room, presumably out into the backyard.

Tiryn paused for a moment, unsure of what to do. He couldn't really leave without the boy; Roland needed him. He sighed, thinking.

"Don't worry about him, he'll be fine in the morning."

Startled, Tiryn turned towards the voice, recognizing Alastor right away, though he looked much older than he'd been before. At fifteen, he was nearly a man full grown, and every inch looked as such. His broad shoulders and muscular arms were strangely offset by his dark eyes and his thin face, and his speech lacked much of the characteristic slurring of the southerners he had grown up around.

Tiryn nodded back in the direction Harlan had gone. "Does he get drunk every night?"

Alastor nodded. "Most nights, yes. Though he doesn't exactly give himself the chance to sober up during the day, either." The boy shrugged his shoulders. "He'll go out into the garden, probably pass out, then come in tomorrow and start all over again."

Tiryn glanced back the way Harlan had gone. "How long has he been like this?"

Alastor sighed. "For a few months now." His voice dropped, and he looked down at his feet. "Ever since my mother died."

Tiryn stayed silent, unsure of what to say.

A moment passed, then Alastor piped up again. "I heard Harlan shouting. He said my mother's name. Did you know her?"

Tiryn shook his head. "No, I never knew her. I only knew of her."

"Of her midwifery? She was the best in the Free Cities before the sickness took her." There was pride in Alastor's voice, mixed with sadness. "Is that why you came? To ask her for help?"

"No, actually ..." Tiryn hesitated. *What do I tell the boy? I came to get you, because you have something we need to prevent the complete destruction of our way of life?* Another idea slowly formed. "I came to offer your mother my aid. I have a great deal of knowledge when it comes to medicine. I thought she might appreciate the continued education." Tiryn sighed, dropping his head. "If I had come sooner, I might have saved her. And for that, I'm sorry."

Roland had begged Tiryn for his help when he realized that Silvana had fallen ill. But by then, it was too late. Her illness was too advanced, and Tiryn was too far away. Roland himself had hardly made it to Larten in time for her burial. Tiryn had made a similar apology to his friend then, too.

There was another pause.

Alastor looked up at Tiryn. "Do you ... need a room for the night?"

Tiryn's head tilted. "Harlan said that there were no rooms."

"Harlan said there were no rooms *for elves*. I don't see an elf, I see someone who could have been a good friend to my mother, if fate had not intervened. And we have plenty of rooms for friends here." Alastor smiled. "My name is Alastor." He held out a hand.

Tiryn took the offered hand, returning the smile. "Tiryn."

Tiryn was led through the inn to the guest quarters, and from there up a flight of stairs and into a cozy room with a large window. Night was falling quickly, and there were a handful of stars peering through the cloudy sky. Far off in the distance, Tiryn could see the ocean.

"Would you like a fire made?" Alastor asked politely, using a tinderbox to light a small candelabra with the practiced ease of someone who is used to playing the host.

"No, thank you," Tiryn said.

Alastor gave him a surprised look, one eyebrow arched

high. "You sure? It can get quite chilly in the evenings, even this far inland."

Tiryn gave the young man a polite nod. "Elves grow to be quite adaptable to weather extremes. And I quite like the chill."

Alastor's lips twitched into a quick grin, and he set the brightly lit candelabra onto a bedside table. "Alright, then." He cast a glance around the room, motioning back towards the hall with a jerk of his chin. "If you don't like this room, there are plenty of other rooms. The inn is actually empty at the moment. Harlan fired all the staff, and we don't get many quests anymore." Alastor stepped into the middle of the room and turned to face Tiryn. "So you can stay in whichever room you want to, I suppose."

Tiryn smiled, setting his bag down just inside the door. "This room will be fine, Alastor."

"This one is my favorite, actually. I like to come in here sometimes and gaze out across the water, and imagine what it must be like out on the sea." Alastor gazed longingly out the window. "Have you ever been on a ship?"

Tiryn nodded. "A few times, yes. It's harder to get passage now. No captain will take on an elven passenger unless there's significant financial gain." Tiryn looked down at Alastor, smiling. "But it is a very … adventurous life."

"You'll have to tell me about it sometime, then." Alastor grinned excitedly. "But not tonight. It's getting late, and I'm sure you'd like some rest. I still have a few things to do before I can tuck in for the night." He walked back towards the door, turning and giving a small bow just inside the doorway. "Goodnight, and I hope to see you well rested in the morning." He hesitated for a moment, fingering a knot in the wood of the door frame. "And I'm sorry about Harlan. He wasn't always like this."

Tiryn returned the bow, saying nothing, and Alastor left, shutting the door behind him.

Tiryn stayed awake for quite a while longer. He paced the length of the room, pondering how best to convince Harlan to let Alastor leave with him. Perhaps he should explain to the old innkeeper why they needed Alastor's help. Or perhaps he could go straight to the boy, come clean about why he was there. Convince Alastor to come with him, or at least to part with the book. Roland seemed convinced that Alastor was necessary, but perhaps that was just his past guilt clouding his judgment. It was the book that was truly needed, not the boy. Tiryn pulled a small piece of parchment from the inside of his jerkin. It was worn in spots from being folded and unfolded so many times. Tiryn opened it once more, peering down at the smeared and faded words. They were nearly illegible now, but Tiryn knew what they said.

Meet me in Hythe.
Bring the boy.
I've found the blue beast.

Tiryn sighed, folding the parchment and tucking it away again. No details, no reason why Roland couldn't collect Alastor himself. Just three little sentences, hastily scrawled before being sent off. He sighed again, shaking his head, and collapsed into the bed, hoping sleep might come easily. But he tossed and turned for a while longer, considering the options at his disposal.

Finally, after some time, he drifted to sleep.

A shout awoke him. At first, Tiryn was sure he had imagined it. But then he heard wailing and more shouting, followed by hurried footsteps. Tiryn leapt from the bed, rushing to the door and throwing it open. Alastor was already halfway up the stairs, headed straight for him.

"It's Harlan. Please, you have to help." There were tears in his eyes.

Tiryn rushed down the stairs, following Alastor. They ran

through the house, the first hints of daybreak casting every-thing in an eerie blue-grey light. Alastor led him outside into what Tiryn presumed was the garden. There, lying on the ground, was Harlan. Tiryn recognized his son, Jaimes, clutching Harlan close to his chest, weeping. Tiryn didn't need a closer look to know that it was too late to help.

But he stepped closer anyway, kneeling down to inspect the body. He smelled stronger of alcohol than he had the night before. *He must have kept drinking after dismissing me.* But there was something else … something sweeter. It was a scent Tiryn recognized immediately. He stood up and began searching through the garden. *An odd thing to keep in a common garden,* Tiryn thought. *Silvana must have grown it for her practice.*

"What are you doing?" Jaimes's eyes followed him, anger and resentment visible behind the tears.

Tiryn continued searching. "I think I might know what happened. There's a plant …" Tiryn spotted it. "Here we are." The plant had been heavily damaged, with several stalks snapped and twisted as if someone inexperienced had been foraging from it regularly. *Or someone drunk.* Tiryn carefully broke off a twisted sprig, taking a small whiff from the long, thin leaves. It was the same scent he had picked up from Harlan's body. He brought it over the Alastor and Jaimes.

"This is called sweet tansy. The flowers can be used as a kind of anesthetic, when used with a few other things. And the leaves can be eaten as a sleep aid. That's why your mother grew it here." He nodded to Alastor.

"I know what sweet tansy is. Why does it matter?" Jaimes's voice was thick, and he glared again at Tiryn.

"It seems Harlan has been abusing the leaves for quite some time. After a while, and in combination with his drink-ing, the leaves became … toxic." Tiryn's voice trailed off.

Jaimes looked up at him. "Can you save him?"

Tiryn bit his lip. "It's too late. There is no saving him

now." Harlan had already been dead for a few hours—surely the boys realized that as much as he did.

Jaimes wailed again, and Alastor put an arm around his shoulders. "He didn't suffer, Jaimes. He must have been in a lot of pain to use that plant so much. He's better now."

But Jaimes was inconsolable.

After some time, Alastor left to find someone who could take the body away. Tiryn went back upstairs to hide from the men Alastor brought. *I'm sure I would be blamed for this if they knew I was here.* Through the open window, he could make out the sound of Alastor's voice, explaining to the men how Harlan died, and he was smart enough to imply that the inn was empty of guests. Harlan's body was removed, and the boys followed a few short hours later to oversee the burial.

Tiryn watched them depart from the window of his room. Their heads were down as they walked shoulder to shoulder up a nearby hill. Perhaps half a dozen people attended the burial and, after the ceremony, the two young men knelt in the earth to bury Harlan's body.

Their second burial in less than a season. Tiryn sighed, turning away from the window. *The world has not been kind to them.*

The boys returned to the inn alone when it was all said and done. Tiryn had rummaged through the inn's larder for provisions and had prepared a small meal for them when they returned. But neither one would eat.

Tiryn was the first to break the long silence. "I'm sorry, Jaimes. I met Harlan once. He was a good man."

Jaimes said nothing. He stared at the untouched food in front of him.

"If you want, I can make something else for you." Tiryn tried to sound pleasant.

Jaimes turned his head to look at Tiryn. "And just who are you, exactly?"

Tiryn was surprised by the sudden hostility, but it was Alastor who answered.

"Jaimes, we've already discussed this. Tiryn came here to teach my mother. You heard him, he said he knew Harlan. He's a friend, and we don't have many of those left." Alastor took a slow bite of his food. "You should eat, Jaimes."

Jaimes shook his head. "What are we going to do, Alastor? We can't manage this place on our own."

"We can get by, until Uncle Tomas returns." Alastor took another bite. "He can help us."

"We haven't heard from Uncle Tomas in over a year. What if his ship was wrecked? What if he's dead, too? It's just you and me, Alastor."

Tiryn saw his opportunity. "You could come with me."

"With you? We don't even know you." Jaimes glared at him.

Tiryn nodded. "Fair enough. What if I told you I could help you find your uncle? Where was he, last you heard from him?"

"Hythe," Alastor replied. "He'd already passed Emery, and wrote to apologize for not stopping in to see us—they didn't stop long enough for him to ride over." He paused. "Larten, obviously, is too far inland for ships to port here directly. And Hythe is too far east to really stay here for any length of time before they're due back aboard their ship. It was just a bit unlucky, I suppose, that he wasn't able to come and visit us."

"His captain's plan was for them to sail around the entire Azimar coastline, fishing and trading as they went, then sail first to Emery again, then Hythe, before turning back and going all the way around again. He's been with this crew for a couple of years now, and they've made this same trip several times before." Jaimes sighed, pushing his uneaten food around with a fork. "They should have made it back to

Hythe again by now. He was going to take a year off and come home for a while."

Tiryn nodded his head. "Alright. I can take you to Hythe. I'm meeting a friend there anyway. We can ask about your uncle, and if we still can't find him, I'll let you stay with me until we find out what happened to him." Tiryn paused. "Does that sound fair?"

Jaimes looked apprehensively over at Alastor, but it was Alastor who made the decision. "Alright, that sounds fair." He nodded slowly, contemplating. "We'll go with you to Hythe. Any leads on Uncle Tomas's whereabouts, we follow. And if we find him, we'll leave you, with our deepest gratitude."

"And if we don't find him?" Jaimes asked.

Alastor paused, poking at a bit of fish on his plate. "We'll just have to figure it all out then, if it comes to that." He turned first to Jaimes, then to Tiryn. "Deal?" He struck his hand out over the table, palm down.

Without hesitation, Tiryn placed his hand atop Alastor's. "Deal."

They both turned to Jaimes, who sighed before reluctantly placing his hand on top of Tiryn's. "Alright, let's see how this goes. You've got a deal."

The boys quickly retracted their hands, returning to their meals with renewed vigor. But Tiryn watched each one from the corner of his eye, contemplating how best to get Alastor to stay with him. *I hope you have some sort of trick up your sleeve, Roland. One little glimpse of their uncle Tomas, and they're both gone, the book with them.*

ROLAND

R oland was dreaming, he was sure of it. But it felt real enough. He could feel the weight of her in his arms, the way her embrace tightened around him. He could even catch the scent of roses that always seemed to hang about her.

They were in his old room, back in Etritia. There was a fire, the heat of it tantalizing. That winter had been cold and cruel. As had every winter since.

She was wearing a white dress, her veil undone and hanging loosely from one hand, and her eyes were a bright blue in the firelight.

"Nevina." His voice came out in a croak. "I've missed you."

"I have always been here, Ajax."

He ran a hand over her pale hair. "Here in my dreams, you mean?"

Her lips quirked into a small smile. "Something of the sort, yes."

"It feels so real. Like it's more than just another dream." Roland's grip around her loosened and she stepped out of his arms. Memories came to him, slow and clouded. Nevina shuffled through the stack of papers on his desk, searching for a sketch she seemed to know she would find. "This has happened before?" Roland asked. "Us meeting like this?"

Nevina nodded, her gaze focused on the task before her. Her fingers found the page she wanted, and she pulled it from the others. "I've always enjoyed looking at this." Her nose wrinkled as she looked up at him with another smile. "Even if the eyes are wrong."

"I … I don't do much drawing anymore," Roland said.

Nevina nodded again. "I know. It's a shame. You're really very good."

Roland reached for her, and she set the sketch aside to settle in his arms once more. "Why are you here? And where is here? My memories?"

Nevina shrugged his arms into a more comfortable position around her waist, wrapping her arms around his in return. "I only wanted to see how you were doing after finding the blue beast at last."

Roland sighed. "I'm fine. I don't know what to expect now, but at least I'm on the right path."

"There is so much more to be done."

"I'm trying, but I don't know where to go from here."

Nevina's form began to fade, growing weightless in his arms. "You'll find out soon enough."

"Nevina," Roland pleaded, trying to tighten his arms around her. "Please don't leave yet."

Beside them, the fire flared, filling the room with hot flames and smoke. Roland shrank back, bringing his arms up to shield his face from the flames. And as his arms released her, Nevina's thin frame dissolved entirely.

From the heavy smoke around him came her soft reply, nearly lost in the crackling of the fire. "Find the boy. Find the book. Finish what has been started."

"Nevina!" Roland searched for her, coughing as the thick smoke filled his lungs. But she was gone.

The fire flared again, pushing Roland back. He stumbled, falling into the flames, falling into darkness.

Roland sat up, breathing heavily. There was sweat on his brow, and the air still stank of smoke. But the smoke was from the small campfire a few feet away, and on the other side two thin figures were lying next to each other in the dark.

Roland threw off the blanket covering him, his flesh warm and slick with perspiration. He covered his eyes, burying his face in his palms, and drew several breaths to help slow the rapid beating of his heart.

"Are you alright?"

Roland jumped at the sound of the great dragon's voice. His eyes flicked around him, but she was nowhere to be seen. *"Where are you?"*

"Close." He sensed a flicker of worry from her, and she repeated the question. *"Are you alright?"*

"I'm fine." Roland wiped at the sweat on his face. *"It was just a dream."*

"I know. I saw it."

"You saw it? How?"

Melonya seemed to consider the question for a moment, and Roland's connection with her fell quiet for a moment. Her voice came back to him in a slow monotone. *"I can feel emotions easily. If you are afraid, a part of me, the part that is connected to you, is also afraid. When you feel loved, a part of me also feels loved."* Melonya paused for a moment again, and Roland sensed her searching for the right words to use. *"Sometimes, when the emotions are strong enough, they bleed into my other senses. If you are very afraid, I can not only feel that fear, but I can taste the bile building in your throat, or see the thing that causes your heart to panic."*

"And when I dreamed, you could see the dream," Roland added.

"Yes."

"*And I was afraid?*"

"*Afraid, confused. Bitter, even.*"

Roland felt Melonya sigh; the effect oddly rippled through his mind.

"*There was something else, too. Pain, maybe. But not physical pain.*" She huffed slightly, exasperated with herself. "*I'm not sure, but it seemed like your heart was in pain.*"

"Heartache."

"*Is that what it is?*"

Roland nodded in the dark, then remembered that Melonya couldn't see him. "Yes."

"*For the woman in your dream? Nevina?*"

"Yes." Roland dropped his head between his knees, releasing his breath in a long sigh.

"*Who was she, Roland?*"

"She was ..." Roland hesitated, unsure of the answer. "*How can I explain who she was? She was Nevina.*" And with the thought of her, an image of her formed in his mind. Nevina, veil covering her eyes, laughing as her face tilted up to his. And with the image came a tide of emotions that Roland had not expected. For a long moment he could only sit in the quiet dark of the camp, head bowed and eyes shut tight against the image his mind had conjured of the woman he loved.

In the silence that followed, Melonya's voice was a welcome disruption. "*I see.*"

Roland didn't answer.

The silence continued, broken again by Melonya's deep voice echoing through his mind. "*Get some sleep, Roland. If you can. I can keep watch from here.*"

Roland obediently fell back into the dirt, tucking one arm under his head. Across the fire, one of the twins rolled in their sleep, and Roland's eyes shot in their direction at the sound.

"*Sleep, Roland.*"

He lay awake instead, gaze fixed on the stars above him, listening to the crackling sounds of the fire until the eastern sky lightened into grey morning.

1 2

TIRYN

Tiryn and the two young men now in his care spent much of the following morning packing. Jaimes, to be more precise, spent most of the morning packing, while the others waited. Tiryn always carried very little, but was sure to collect some extra provisions for the road, unsure of what would happen once they reached Hythe. Alastor had only packed a small bag filled with a handful of clothes and a few additional provisions.

"Is that all you plan to bring?" Tiryn asked Alastor. "It might be some time before you can come back to this place."

Alastor shrugged, closing the pack and setting it carefully on the ground between his feet. "I don't have any material things that I'm terribly attached to. I have a little toy that Harlan made for me when I was young, but that's about it."

A thought came to Tiryn. "Is there something your mother left behind that could be useful? Books, perhaps?"

There was a loud thump on the table behind him. "She left all of these behind. Do you think some could be useful to us?"

Tiryn turned towards Jaimes's voice, but couldn't see the boy behind the stack of tomes he had dropped onto the table.

Tiryn felt a sudden wave of anxiety as he eyed the books. "Are you planning on taking all of these with us?"

"No, not all of them. Just the important ones. Trouble is, I can't figure out which ones are the most important." Jaimes began sorting through the stack. "I'd like to take this copy of *Medicine of the Harvest*, but *Herbs and Fungi and their Medicinal Properties* seems more useful. And then there's *The Mystery of Medicine* …" He stepped out from behind the books, turning to Tiryn, a large book in each hand. "What do you think? You said you know medicine, right?"

Tiryn read a handful of the titles. They were all about medicine, most of them regarding midwifery and herbology. "Have you read any of these books, Jaimes?"

Jaimes frowned, his face scrunched up in contemplation. "Do you think I should only bring ones I haven't already read?"

In the end, Jaimes brought half a dozen different titles. Tiryn had helped him pick them out and had tucked them away as carefully as he could, at Jaimes's insistence. The rest were to be locked back into a trunk tucked away in a corner bedroom. Tiryn helped Jaimes carry the books back up the stairs and eyed the room with some reverence. There were some womanly things in the open closet, such as dresses and aprons, but there was also a large shelf full of books next to the tidy bed in the corner. These books, Tiryn noticed, were mostly for children. Storybooks, simple history books, and the like. *This had been her room*, Tiryn thought. *Silvana's.* Indeed, Jaimes treated everything with extreme care, handling the great wooden trunk at the foot of the bed as if it might crumble beneath his hands. He neatly stacked the books he had removed back into the trunk, locking the lid with a tiny key kept on a chain. This he pulled over his head, letting the key drop onto his chest beneath his shirt.

Alastor had gone back and retrieved a few more useful

things, including, Tiryn hoped, the little black book Roland desperately needed. Tiryn had scoured the rest of the inn, looking for the book, but had not found it. His only conclusion was that Alastor had it on him, or that Silvana had destroyed it. When Jaimes and Tiryn met him back in the dining room, Jaimes offered the key to Alastor, holding it out without a word. But Alastor shook his head. "Better for you to keep it. I'll just lose the little thing." Jaimes shrugged, tucking the key back into his shirt. Finally, with their belongings tucked under Tiryn's arm or tossed over their shoulders, they left the inn. Jaimes locked the door behind him, this time with a much larger key, which he also dropped around his neck.

"You think anyone's going to bother it while we're gone?" Alastor asked, turning to Jaimes.

Jaimes shrugged, an empty look to his eyes. "By tomorrow, everyone in town will know what happened to Father, and they'll all know that we've left. But I think they'll leave it. Because they all know there's nothing of much use to them in there. Any food worth taking we have with us, and my father made sure to use up anything worth drinking." Jaimes's voice was bitter, and Tiryn caught the worried glance Alastor cast his brother's way. "I think it'll be mostly unharmed when we return."

Tiryn bit his tongue, not wanting to admit to the boys that they might be gone much longer than either of them anticipated. *Better to let it just happen.* They turned their backs on the inn, headed southeast.

The walk from Larten to Hythe was pleasant, though long. The gentle sea breeze blowing in from the south cooled them as the sun hung high and hot in the sky above. The boys asked Tiryn many questions. Jaimes wanted to know about medicine, and what Tiryn knew about it. Tiryn was amused by his questions, and was glad to answer them. *He might make a good herbalist one day,* Tiryn thought while listening to Jaimes explain to Alastor the difference between nightshade and hemlock.

Alastor, on the other hand, wanted to know about Tiryn's various adventures. So Tiryn told him about sailing on the ocean, and about the trip he had taken through the dwarfen lands a few years before. He left out Roland and the hunt for the amulets, unsure of the proper time to mention it. Both boys listened to him in complete awe the entire way, right up to the center of town. Neither Alastor nor Jaimes gave any indication they noticed the open stares or the looks of disgust Tiryn received on their way through the small harbor town, but Tiryn grew worried as they neared the squat building that served as Hythe's inn.

He turned to the boys just outside the entrance. "Perhaps you two should stay out here while I go inside and see if I can find us a place to stay tonight."

Alastor nodded, pulling Jaimes aside to stand by the door. "We'll wait here."

Tiryn opened the door to the inn, once more flinching as a little bell sounded his entrance to an inn he was surely not welcome in. There were a handful of men sitting in the lounge just inside the entrance, talking and laughing loudly. Tiryn stepped up to the bar, waiting to catch the attention of the innkeeper behind the counter. It only took a moment for a hushed silence to fall over the inn, and Tiryn felt all eyes on him.

The innkeeper looked up at the sudden quiet, catching sight of Tiryn almost immediately. "We don't serve your kind here," the innkeeper all but shouted. Murmured approvals rumbled through the assembled guests at Tiryn's back. The man behind the counter went back to his work, waiting for Tiryn to leave.

Tiryn's mouth was dry. "I'd just like some food. And a room for the night, if you've got it." He swallowed hard, tying to dislodge the lump that had formed in his throat. "I have plenty of money, and I won't cause any trouble." He pulled a purse from his belt and dropped it onto the table with a loud thump. Sometimes the promise of gold was enough to sway even the staunchest of innkeeps, and Tiryn hoped that would be the case this time as well.

The bell rang again as the door opened for the second time. The innkeep leaned in towards Tiryn, his sour breath wafting over the distance between them. "I said we don't serve your kind here. Now get out, before I put you out."

"Tiryn?"

Tiryn winced at Jaimes's worried voice. He turned to see Alastor and Jaimes standing meekly just inside the doorway. "I asked you to wait outside." He ushered them back out, hoping the two boys could leave without being noticed.

"I'm sorry, Tiryn," Alastor said quickly. "Jaimes said he heard shouting—"

"I did not! You said you heard shouting—"

"Them ain't your boys, now is they?" It was one of the patrons, a burly man who was clearly more than a few drinks in. He stood up, knocking his chair back. "Them boys is human, and you ain't." He took a lumbering step towards Tiryn. "Who'd you steal them from?"

"Steal?" Tiryn's voice came out in a startled squeak. He stepped in front of the boys, protecting them, but the innkeeper snaked a thin arm out over the counter and grabbed hold of Jaimes's wrist.

"Did he kidnap you?" The innkeep's foul breath blew into Jaimes's face, and the boy wrinkled his nose. "Where are your parents?"

"Dead, more'n likely." Two more men stood, and they rounded on Tiryn. "I heard your kind are good at killing innocents."

"I didn't kill their parents." Tiryn backed Alastor against the wall, putting as much distance as possible between him and the drunks. If it came to blows, Tiryn was sure he would have no difficulty with the inn's patrons. But to bring down a roomful of men in front of the children?

"Let go of me!" Jaimes tried twisting his way free, but the innkeeper held him tighter.

"Please, let go of the boy!" Tiryn reached for Jaimes, but one of the patrons stepped in his way. The bell chimed again, but Tiryn barely heard it.

"We're just doing our duty to the king and freeing these boys from their captor."

"I did not kidnap them!" Tiryn yelled, trying to reach around the man for Jaimes.

"Let go, let go, let go!" Jaimes pounded on the innkeeper's arm, trying to free himself, but his fist did nothing to loosen the man's grip.

"I would do as the boy says, if I were you."

Everyone turned to the newcomer standing in the doorway of the inn. He was short, shorter even than Alastor and Jaimes. His face was covered in a thick black beard, and his voice was gruff and deep.

"Nunor." Tiryn sighed, thankful to see the stout dwarf again.

One patron grumbled loudly, spitting on the ground in disgust. "A dwarf!"

"Do that again," the dwarf threatened, "and I'll rub your face in that spittle." His voice was startling calm. He turned to the innkeeper. "Now let that boy go. Before I cut you all down to my size."

"This is really none of your concern, dwarf. Leave, we don't serve your kind here," the innkeeper replied dryly. The patrons protested loudly, while Tiryn pleaded and Jaimes struggled with the innkeeper.

"Kill them both, the monsters!"

"Let me go, let me go!"

The bell chimed again, but it was ignored.

"I bet a rope would look nice around that ugly little neck of yours, dwarf."

"Please, release the boy, and we'll leave quietly."

"Jaimes! Get out of my way, Tiryn!"

"Release the boy, or I'll cut that hand off." The new voice was a booming basso, and all present turned to it, momentarily silenced.

"Roland!" Tiryn felt his shoulders relax at the sight of his friend. Behind him stood two young elves Tiryn did not recognize, highborn siblings, by the look of them, their long white hair and angled features perfectly mirroring each other.

"You know this elf?" The innkeeper eyed Roland distrustfully, ignoring the threatening hand Roland held on his sword.

"I do. Now let the boy go."

"What's it to you? You know the boys as well?" a patron asked, eyeing Roland and Tiryn distrustfully.

"They're my nephews. And I won't have them harmed."

"Your nephews, you say?" the innkeeper asked. "Then what are their names?"

Roland's reply came out in a dry rasp. "The dark-haired one's name is Alastor, and the other is named Jaimes. As I said, they are my nephews, and I will not have them harmed." Roland gripped the hilt of his sword tight enough to make his knuckles turn white.

Jaimes looked up at the innkeeper, crying out, "He's telling the truth! Let me go!"

The innkeeper eyed Roland's sword before releasing Jaimes's arm with a huff.

"Tiryn, take the children outside. I have some business to discuss with our friends here." Roland's eyes never left the innkeeper's face as he stepped aside to let them pass.

Tiryn nodded, guiding the boys and the two young elves Roland had brought with him back out the door. "You heard him, let's go." The door had barely shut behind them when they heard a loud shout and a crash from within.

The elven sister turned to Jaimes. She looked only a little older than he was, though Tiryn knew she was closer to two hundred years than ten. If she had been human, Tiryn guessed she might have been sixteen or seventeen. "Roland isn't really your uncle, is he?" She was almost laughing, her lips turned up into the smallest of smiles. Her brother stood behind her, staring silently at the door to the inn.

Jaimes shook his head. "No, I've never seen him before."

There was another crash inside, louder than the first. Tiryn and the dwarf both instinctively stepped closer to the four children, protecting them.

"Good to see you again, Nunor. I take it you got my last message to Doldural?"

"Darlyth delivered your news to me himself. I was on my way to Hythe before the courier had caught his breath."

"I'm surprised you made it here so quickly." Tiryn turned to the dwarf. "But I'm also thankful."

The dwarf nodded, eyes fixated on the door to the inn. More shouting could be heard within. "There's a saying in Doldural: that a dwarf can sense when an elf is in trouble. It helps our legs move just a bit faster, so we don't miss the show." He looked up at Tiryn, a twinkle in his eye.

Tiryn smiled. "And if that elf is a friend?"

The inn had grown oddly quiet.

"Not sure that makes much of a difference to our speed." The dwarf chuckled deeply. "But I'm glad I was here to see you squirm a bit, Tiryn. It does the old heart good to see an elf uncomfortable."

Tiryn said nothing, letting the smirk tugging at the corners of his mouth share his thoughts with his small companion.

Roland kicked open the door from the inn and stepped out into the plaza. A large bag was slung over his shoulder, and there was a small splattering of blood across the front of his tunic.

"How did your business go?" Tiryn asked hesitantly.

"Well enough for us. Not so well for the innkeeper." Roland shrugged the bag into a more comfortable position.

"You didn't kill him or anything, did you?" Tiryn asked.

"No, no, of course not." Roland shook his head. "I did break his arm and take some provisions from his larder, but he's still very much alive." Roland sighed, patting Jaimes on the head as he passed him. "I also impressed upon him the importance of not grabbing little children and trying to pull them away from their guardians."

Alastor frowned up at Roland, crossing his arms over his chest. "He's not a child!" His frown deepened. "And neither am I!" he added hastily.

Roland paused, looking Alastor over. "You're right. You're nearly full grown now, aren't you?" He reached into an exposed pocket of the bag he was carrying and pulled out two simple daggers. "Which is why I snagged these for you." He held them out to the boys, hilt first. Alastor took them both, passing one to Jaimes while keeping his eyes on Roland. "If it happens again," Roland said, his face blank, "stab them."

Jaimes's eyes widened at Roland's words, but he held the dagger firmly in one hand.

Roland readjusted the pack on his shoulder. "Now come on, all of you. Let's rid ourselves of this place. I know of a quiet little nook down by the harbor we can all enjoy."

The twins followed after Roland, and the boys went behind them. Tiryn hesitated, glancing back at the inn. He cursed, shaking his head. "Great Ones preserve us."

Nunor snorted at him and followed after Roland as well.

ROLAND

Roland's quiet little nook was little more than a patch of sandy beach not far from the harbor proper. He dropped the pack of stolen provisions down into the sand and sank down beside it. "I don't know about you, but the twins and I haven't eaten in some time. Do you mind if we rest a while?" It wasn't to Tiryn he had aimed the question, or even to Nunor, but instead he looked to Jaimes and Alastor for permission.

Jaimes nodded timidly before sitting in the sand next to Tiryn, distancing himself from Roland. He clutched a heavy bag close to his chest, and Roland could sense his unease.

But Alastor stood his ground, arms crossed defiantly over his chest. "Who are you? How is it that you could tell that innkeeper our names?"

Roland saw Tiryn stiffen at the question, but Roland had already considered the simplest answer to that very question.

"I know Harlan. I've visited the inn a few times over the years, and got to know a bit about the two of you through him." Roland shrugged, reaching into the bag and pulling out two wrapped packages, handing one to each of the two younger elves. "I wouldn't say Harlan is overly fond of me, but he treats me well when I stop there, and he's very quick to talk about his two boys and how proud he is of the both of you." He turned to Jaimes, unfurling a third package and revealing strips of salted beef. "I must say I'm surprised Harlan let both of you come along for this little adventure."

"Harlan is dead." Tiryn spoke softly, placing a hand on Jaimes's shoulder. Jaimes shrugged the hand off, clutching his bag closer.

Roland frowned. *Harlan, dead?* It would certainly explain why both of the boys were here. "When? How?"

"The night before last. Tiryn says it was sweet tansy and drinking that did it," Alastor answered sadly, dropping into the sand across from Roland.

"That sounds more like heartache to me." Roland paused before continuing. "He cared about your mother very much, Alastor." He sighed. "I'm sorry for your losses."

There was a moment of silence, broken first by Alastor. "We have to find our uncle."

"Your uncle?" Roland's heart skipped a beat. Had Silvana told them about him?

"Uncle Tomas." Jaimes spoke up for the first time. "He's a sailor. He should have come through here recently." His voice was shaky, but confident. "If we can find him, we can go back home. The three of us can run the inn together, I'm sure of it."

Roland drew an unsteady breath, letting it out slowly. "Alright. That sounds like a plan to me. Run on down to the docks, see if anyone has seen this uncle of yours. We'll follow behind shortly to help out." Jaimes and Alastor jumped to their feet, already running down the beach to the docks. "Make sure you stick together!"

As soon as the boys were out of earshot, Tiryn turned to Roland. "I'm so sorry, Roland, I wasn't sure what to do. Harlan died, and I wasn't sure how to get them to come with me, so I told the boys I would help them find their uncle—"

Roland raised a hand to quiet Tiryn, turning to the dwarf. "Nunor, is it? You heard of our quest from Tiryn?"

Nunor ran a thick hand through his long black beard. "Aye, you lot are off to find the four Amulets of Power, before Mothlenor gets his hands on them and uses them to 'purify the lands'." He spat into the sand in disgust. "He also told me about this blue beast you've been searching for. A dragon? Am I to assume one of these young elves is the dragon's owner?" He jerked his head back at Tathiel and Eilonwy.

Eilonwy huffed. "You don't *own* a dragon."

Tathiel smirked at Eilonwy's remark. "What my sister means to say is that we are both the dragon's riders. She belongs to both of us, just as we both belong to her."

Tiryn's eyebrows raised appreciatively. "And where is she now?"

"Hiding. Out in the sea." Roland reached into an inside pocket of his vest, pulling out a small, iridescent orb. "The important thing right now is that the only ones who don't yet know of our quest are the two young men who just ran off to find Jaimes's uncle. One of them, the dark-haired one, has the key to finding the amulets. I want to gain their trust before telling Alastor about his family's quest." He gripped the orb tightly in his palm, looking at each of the four clustered in the sand around him. "They're young, they're frightened, and they are alone. They need someone to trust, just as much as we need their help."

"What do you plan on doing?" Tiryn looked down at the orb in Roland's hand.

"I'm going to find their uncle."

"With that little rock?" Nunor snorted.

"It's a Dragon's Eye. It can be used to locate others." Tathiel shook his head. "But it only works if you've already met the person you're looking for. Can you find their uncle?"

"They said his name was Tomas. The same Tomas,

perhaps, that denied us service that day at Harlan's inn?" Tiryn asked Roland pointedly.

"My thoughts exactly. I can give it a try, at least." Roland held the orb close to his face, peering into the depths of the stone. The colors buried in the stone's surface suddenly came alive, shifting and swirling and changing. Once again, Roland was momentarily entranced by the display, though he had seen it more times than he could reliably count over the years.

Roland waited for several seconds, growing agitated as they stretched on. It had never taken this long for the eye to find whoever Roland searched for. *Except Hasani,* he thought. *It was never able to find Hasani.*

The colors buried in the stone's depths brightened, causing Roland to squint to keep from being momentarily blinded. But he continued to look into the stone, waiting. The colors shifted faster, almost in a frenzy. Just as he was about to give up, to say that perhaps it wasn't the same man, the stone turned a soft blue. Roland saw strange colorful plants flowing in the breeze. Everything looked so strange. There was so much blue … *He's underwater?*

But then Roland spied a hint of bright white hiding among the seaweed. *Bones,* he realized with a shudder. He was seeing Tomas's bones. He caught another glimpse of white, not far away. Then another, and another. Roland realized with horror that he was looking at an underwater graveyard. And with that realization, the stone went black.

Roland blinked rapidly, trying to erase the images burning themselves into his mind. He was lightheaded and faintly nauseous.

"Are you alright?" a faint and feminine voice asked.

"Fine. Just side effects from staring into the eye for so long." Roland pressed his eyes tightly shut, willing the vertigo to fade.

"What did you see? Did you find Tomas?" Tiryn asked.

"Tomas is dead. Lost at sea with the rest of his crew, it looks like. The stone showed me a watery graveyard, and his remains were there." Roland slipped the stone back into his vest and dropped his head between his knees. "At least this way, we don't have to worry about the boys finding Tomas and running back home with him."

"That's a rather selfish way to look at it, Roland," Tiryn grumbled. "They've lost their whole family now."

"Alastor hasn't lost me," Roland corrected, looking up at his friend. His voice sounded bitter even to his own ears, and Tiryn's thin mouth turned down as a delicate frown crossed his features.

Tiryn could be as annoyed with him as he wanted; it didn't change the fact that he was the only relative Alastor had left. *There will be time to set things right later. But for now ...* Roland stood, picking up the pack from the sand and slinging it over his shoulder. "Come on, let's go help those boys find their uncle."

<hr>

Alastor and Jaimes were not difficult to track down. They were the only children wandering about the harbor. Most others were sailors, either loading supplies and gear for the next voyage out, or hauling fish and trade goods out of their vessels after coming to port. After spotting the two boys, Roland called to them, and they rushed back, red faced and already sweating in the sun. "Any luck yet?"

"Not really." Alastor squinted up at him, one hand shading his face from the sun.

"We just keep getting ignored. Or worse, they yell at us to get out of the way," Jaimes grumbled.

"Are you trying to talk to the men loading and unloading the ships?" Jaimes and Alastor both nodded. Roland shook his head. "Those aren't the men you talk to if you want answers. Follow me, I'll show you."

As Roland led them down the pier, he noticed that most of the ships moored there were fishing ships, smaller vessels with a single mast and what looked like miles and miles of casting nets. Even as they watched, one of these further along the pier cast off from the harbor with clean nets and, Roland presumed, empty barrels tucked away in the small hold. Within minutes, another took its place, and the crew immediately disembarked, rolling barrels full of fish down the gangway to be sold elsewhere. The pier was busy, as it could be during the height of summer, when the fishing was best, Roland assumed. But perhaps it was busy like this all year round, he had no idea.

He ignored the fishermen, weaving in and out of the crowd. Jaimes started to protest, but Roland cut him off. "These men don't sail around, as your uncle does." Roland had to force himself to not use the word "did." "They only sail straight out, perhaps as far north or south so that they just lose sight of Hythe proper. But they never stray far, and they are never gone for very long. They won't know much about the habits of your uncle's vessel."

"So what do we do, then?" Alastor asked, looking up at Roland.

Roland gestured with one hand up ahead of them. "We talk to the traders." Jaimes and Alastor followed the gesture and saw the vessel Roland was pointing at.

The ship was large, much larger than any of the fishing boats they had already passed. Its size made the ones surrounding it look like little more than toys. They were still a way down the pier, but Roland could already see the marked differences between the two types. This one was much longer and wider than the others they had already passed, and was taller as well. While the others had one, perhaps two masts, this had three. The largest mast stood so tall, Roland's stomach rolled at the thought of standing at the top. The whole ship had a sleek, decadent look to it, and the two boys gazed up at it in open-mouthed awe.

"That's the one we want?" Jaimes asked, looking back to Roland.

"It's a good place to start." He placed a hand on Jaimes's shoulder as they walked closer, guiding him around a large man with a mass of netting slung over one shoulder. "Watch your step, or you'll be trampled." He walked both boys closer to the massive merchant ship, looking over his shoulder only once to make sure Tiryn and the others were following. Tiryn had pulled the hood of his cloak over his head, presumably to hide his elven features, but the twins walked with their heads uncovered and their eyes wide with silent wonder. Behind them trailed the dwarf, one hand stroking his beard as he gazed around him.

At the foot of the large gangplank that led up to the deck of the merchant ship stood a strange-looking man. His head was bald, and his face was clean-shaven, giving him the appearance of a large infant. His thick neck and fingers were glittering with jewels, and he wore a heavy purple robe, belted above his round stomach, and matching slippers. In one hand he held a long roll of parchment, in the other a large and colorful quill. As Roland and the two boys approached, the large man stopped another man descending the gangplank with an armful of furs and exchanged words with him. Roland stopped before him as the large man motioned the sailor away with a wave of the quill.

"Excuse me, sir," Roland started. "Could you—"

"Just a moment," the man answered brusquely. He was making a note on his parchment, the quill waving furiously. With a final jab at the parchment, he looked up at Roland and the two boys on either side of him. "What do you want?" His voice hardly matched his appearance. While he was large and richly colorful in his purple robe, his voice was a high-pitched, whining monotone.

"Could you tell me where we might find the captain? These young men have some questions they'd like to ask him about their missing uncle." Roland pushed Jaimes and Alastor a step forward to meet the man.

The man ignored them, fixing his beady eyes on Roland. He sighed heavily, and his jowls shook with the heaving of his chest. "The captain is busy." He huffed. "As you can see—" he stopped another sailor descending the gangplank and quickly inspected the cage of hens the sailor carried over his shoulder before waving him on with the quill, "—we've only just docked and are beginning to unload our wares."

He made a quick note on his parchment before continuing. "I'm the quartermaster, and questions you think the captain might be able to answer, I can answer on his behalf."

"Our uncle is missing. We hoped someone might know where his ship last docked," Alastor piped up.

"What's the name?" the quartermaster was looking down at his notes, scribbling furiously as another sailor came down the gangplank with another cage, this one full of roosters.

"Tomas," Jaimes answered timidly.

The quartermaster finally looked down at the boys, sighing heavily again. His breath was sickeningly sweet, like the smell of rotting fruit. Roland also caught the scent of what might have been perfume. "Not your uncle's name, the name of the ship."

"Oh." Jaimes looked at Alastor, who shrugged. "I don't know."

The quartermaster rolled his eyes. He bent down to look Jaimes in the face. "Do you at least know the name of his captain?" He smirked cruelly.

"Mathius," Alastor replied, scowling at the quartermaster.

The man glanced sidelong at Alastor before straightening up. "Mathius, you say?"

"Th-that's right," Jaimes stammered. "His captain's name is Mathius."

The quartermaster sighed, looking back up to Roland. "Mathius and his … tub … are just down there." He motioned over his left shoulder with the feather of the quill. His eyes widened as he noticed the presence of Tiryn and Nunor. "Now I won't be answering any more questions, understand." His voice had risen slightly in pitch. "I'm a very busy man, and it doesn't do to be seen with such … persons … as yourselves." He waved furiously with the quill. "Now go on. Go," he shouted.

Jaimes jumped and gasped, backing into Tiryn in his fright. Roland gestured to Tiryn, telling the elf with only a nod to take the boys on down the dock.

As Tiryn passed, with a hand on each on each of the boys' shoulders, he bowed slightly to the quartermaster. "Thank you for your help." Eilonwy and Tathiel walked behind, each glaring at the quartermaster. The man only sniffed and looked away from them.

Nunor paused as he stepped passed, snorted loudly, then spat at the man's shoes. The gleaming spittle landed just next to one of the quartermaster's purple slippers. The man glanced down, then glared at Nunor, his eyes gleaming angrily.

"Damn," Nunor grunted. "I missed." He continued, following behind Tiryn and the twins.

Roland nodded pleasantly at the man, trying to stifle a snort, before bringing up the rear of their group.

They followed the direction the quartermaster had indicated, passing a few more fishing vessels before reaching what must have been the ship they were looking for. It was significantly smaller than the first merchant ship, but still larger than the fishing boats. The ship was still triple masted but wasn't quite as wide as the other merchant ship. Where the first ship had sharp edges and seemed elegant, this one had rounder features, and the whole thing looked worn and well loved.

This time, it looked like the crew members were loading things onto the ship, rather than unloading. From the looks of the barrels and crates, it was salted and dried foods, as well as water or ales. There was another man, this one trimmer and shirtless, standing at the foot of the gangplank, also taking notes. He carried a heavy ledger, and his quill flourished only modestly as he noted what went aboard.

Roland led Jaimes and Alastor up to the man. "Are you the quartermaster?" he asked.

"Quartermaster, captain. It's all the same on this ship." He continued making notes in his ledger, but glanced up at Roland with a quick smirk.

"So you're Mathius?" asked Jaimes.

"That's me." Mathius made a quick jot in his ledger as another man walked past him, then he shut the book and looked down at Jaimes and Alastor. "How can I help you gentlemen? Come to try the sailing life? You're the right age for it, I suppose." His smile was pleasant, much unlike the first man they had spoken to.

"N-no," Jaimes stuttered. "We're looking for my uncle Tomas."

"Ah." Mathius frowned. "I know him, but I'm sad to say that he's no longer sailing with me."

The boys exchanged a troubled look.

"He didn't die, did he?" asked Alastor, and Roland suddenly panicked at the thought of what the captain might say. If he told them that Tomas was dead, the boys would just turn around and head home.

"No, he's not dead. Tomas and a bunch of my crew sailed off." Mathius's frown deepened. "They stole my ship and my cargo, and left me and a few of my better sailors stranded. They didn't kill us, so I guess that's something."

"Oh," Jaimes said sadly.

"Do you know where we might find him?" Alastor asked.

Mathius snorted. "If you happen to know where the Isle of Onia is, sure."

"The Isle of Onia?" Jaimes asked. "What is that?"

"It's an island that's supposed to be off the southern coast. Sailors have been telling stories about it for centuries. The Isle of Onia is said to hold fantastic beasts and seams of gold and iron in the hills, just waiting to be mined," Mathius said with heavy sarcasm. He opened his book once more and jotted out a quick line as another sailor climbed the gangway up to the ship's deck.

"So it's a myth?" Roland asked.

Mathius gave him another smirk. "Didn't stop Tomas and his friends from deciding to mutiny."

"Is there any way to know where they might have gone searching?" Alastor asked.

Mathius considered it for a moment, looking Jaimes and Alastor up and down. "There's a small port, up along the coast. It's along our route, though we don't normally stop there. It's pretty seedy, if you ask me. But if Tomas was heading south, he would have stopped there for supplies before hitting open water. It's the last place along the coast for some time, and there weren't enough provisions left on the *Seahawk* to brave the ocean." Mathius scratched at his bearded chin, the tip of his short quill coming dangerously close to marking his face with a smear of ink. "I'd be willing to take you for a price. And if your father here agrees."

"He's not our father," Alastor said quickly.

Mathius raised an eyebrow. "As long as he agrees, and you can pay, I'm not sure that I care how he's related to you."

Jaimes and Alastor both turned to Roland. "What do you think? Do you think it would be worth looking into?" asked Alastor.

"I told you I would help you find your uncle." Roland shrugged a shoulder. "It sounds like a good plan to me." *And the chance to search for the amulets is good enough reason for the rest of us ...*

Mathius nodded. "So it's settled, then?"

"Sounds like it. How much for us to sail with you?" Roland asked.

"Five gold each, with the understanding that you might need to help out around deck on occasion. I can't let fit and healthy men like the three of you just sit around, my crew might get the wrong idea, you understand." Mathius said, winking at Alastor and Jaimes, who smiled excitedly at each other.

"I understand. It will be good for the boys, anyway," Roland answered, pulling out a pouch and counting out fifteen gold pieces for Mathius.

"What about us?" Tiryn asked, stepping from behind Roland.

Mathius's eyes widened, but out of surprise, not fear. "Elves? And a dwarf?" he added, spotting Nunor. "I've never had a dwarf sail with me before." Mathius looked back at Roland, smiling widely. "You keep interesting company, mister ..."

"Roland."

Mathius nodded slightly. "Mister Roland. Interesting company indeed."

"We want to go, too," Eilonwy said.

Mathius's smile faded. "Ah, well, you see—"

"You won't take us?" Tathiel asked.

"Most wouldn't, no," answered Mathius. "I will, but it will cost more."

The twins frowned at that, and Nunor grumbled, but Tiryn nodded. "I understand, and I thank you."

"The money isn't for me, it's for the crew. Everyone on this side of the world is highly critical of the other races right now. I'm sure the same is true up north."

"It is," Tiryn answered, his voice a little hard. "How much will it cost?"

"Twenty for you, sir, and fifteen each for the young ones," Mathius answered.

"And for the dwarf?" Roland asked.

"Another twenty."

Nunor growled. "Twenty? I cost the same as an elf? It should be twenty-five, thirty even!"

Mathius smiled. "I'm sorry if I've offended you, master dwarf. As I said, I've never had a dwarf sail with me before, so I'm not sure of the normal pricing. But I would be happy to raise the cost, if that would please you."

"It wouldn't," Roland said. "Consider the difference a discount due to your size, Nunor. You're easier to pack than the rest of us." He counted out more coins from his pouch, dumped all but a few back in, and handed the pouch over to Mathius. "Seventy gold coins, for my friends."

Tiryn protested. "I have gold, Roland."

"I imagine that some of the crew thinks that my gold is better quality than yours," Roland answered, glancing up to the deck of the ship. There were a handful of men standing there, watching the interaction.

Mathius sighed, noticing Roland's glance. "You might be correct, sir." He turned to Tiryn, Nunor, and the twins. "You would do well to keep to yourselves, below the deck. At least during the day. I'll make sure no harm comes to you, but you'll be harassed less if you're out of sight. If we reach our destination without incident, I'll refund half of your seventy gold."

"I understand. And thank you again," Tiryn said, dipping his head in a bow.

Mathius pocketed the coins, waving them ahead of him. "Welcome aboard the *Kingfisher*, then," he said. "I'll show you below decks and let you get settled in while I have a word with my crew, then we'll be ready to depart."

Mathius led them up onto the deck, and Roland once again took up the tail end, one hand gripping the hilt of his sword tightly.

"Captain …" One of the crew members stepped in front of Mathius, blocking their path. He was tall and well built, with light blond hair and leathery tanned skin. "You really shouldn't—"

"I don't want to hear it, Reed." Mathius said, glaring at the blond. "This is my ship, not the king's, and they have good money for an easy journey." He waved Reed off. "Now step aside, so I can get them to their cabin."

Within minutes they were all down below deck, after suffering nothing more inconvenient that a couple of glares as they passed by Mathius's crew. Mathius left them to return to the deck for a few moments, giving them the chance to survey their quarters.

The room they would be staying in was a good size, but still rather cramped for all seven of them, even if most of their company was made up of children and a small dwarf. There were four folding bunks chained to the interior wall of the room, and it took only a few seconds for everyone to agree that the elf twins and Jaimes and Alastor should be the ones to use them. Eilonwy was quick to pick a bunk for herself, and sat atop it, watching the others organize their few belongings around the room. She pulled off her traveling cloak and tucked her long pale hair behind her ears.

"You shouldn't do that, Eilonwy," Tathiel warned, tossing their shared bag onto the bunk beneath hers.

"Do what?" Eilonwy asked insolently, smirking slightly at her brother.

"Tuck your hair behind your ears. It makes them stick out more."

"You want me to hide my ears? They all already know that we're elves, what's the point in trying to hide it?"

"He just wants you to be safe," Tiryn said, handing a stack

of large books to Jaimes, who carried them reverently to the lower bunk next to Tathiel's.

"He just wants me to be afraid. Why should I be?" Eilonwy asked, crossing her legs and glaring at her brother.

"You shouldn't be afraid of them," said Roland, sitting down on the cabin floor and leaning his head against the wall opposite the bunks. "You have no reason to be afraid. But you should be careful."

"What do you mean?" Eilonwy asked, turning to look at Roland.

Roland shrugged, realizing everyone had paused to look at him. "You are stuck in an enclosed space with several people who automatically dislike you through no fault of your own. You can try to make them your friends, and I hope that we can do that. But if that will not work, we can at least try not to make them our enemies." Roland sighed, leaning his head back again. "Sometimes that means hiding who you really are, for the sake of your own survival. It's not fair, but it is what it is."

Eilonwy looked uncomfortable, smoothing her hair back in front of her ears, trying to hide the tips. "I suppose that makes sense."

There were a few seconds of silence, broken when Nunor grunted in amusement. "Fuck all of that."

"Nunor!" Tiryn frowned. "There are children. If you're going to curse … well, do it in Dwarvish."

"But then the children will know Dwarvish curses," Eilonwy said slyly, winking at Alastor, who had climbed into the bunk beside hers. He smiled back at her, amused.

"All I'm trying to say is that you don't have to hide who you are, so long as you have a big stick to beat everyone with when they try to come at you," Nunor said, crossing an arm over his chest and looking the four on the beds over slowly. He stroked his beard, his face scrunched together in concentration. "Though I suppose you're all a bit too slight to be carrying big sticks around, but I'm sure we can think of something."

"Great Ones preserve us," Roland muttered, unable to hide his smile.

"Why do they dislike you?" Jaimes asked Tiryn, one of the books already propped open in his lap.

"They think an elf killed King Areanath," Tiryn replied, glancing over at Roland.

"They also think a dwarf killed Areanath," Nunor grunted.

"I thought someone in the Coven killed King Areanath," said Alastor, and Roland stiffened at the mention of the Coven.

"So, who is right then?" Jaimes asked, looking from Tiryn to Nunor.

"They're all wrong," Roland replied, not opening his eyes.

"Then who did kill King Areanath?" Alastor asked.

"My father said that the king was attacked by demons, and that means someone used magic to kill him," Jaimes said.

Roland opened his mouth to reply, but at the sound of footsteps on the stairs leading up to the deck, he stopped himself. He stood up, spotting Mathius coming down the stairs and heading for them. "Perhaps that's a question better left for a different day."

Mathius stepped into the cabin room and passed a pile of thick blankets over to Roland. "It can get a bit chilly down here, so I thought you might want these. We're ready to shove off, but the wind isn't in the right direction for us to leave port, so a bunch of my crew will be coming through here to get down to the oars at both the fore and aft ends of the ship. You shouldn't be bothered, but I wanted to warn you."

"How long will it take to get to the port we want?" Jaimes asked.

"Four days. Maybe early on the fifth day. Not too long, I promise," Mathius replied with a smile.

"Thank you, Mathius. You've been very helpful." Roland said.

"It's my duty as captain," Mathius said, shrugging. "I'll return later, but for now you should just stay down here, out of the way, if you don't mind." Roland only nodded in reply, and Mathius turned and nodded to everyone as a group before turning and leaving to go back up the stairs.

There was a moment of silence following Mathius's departure then Tathiel turned to Jaimes. "What will you do if you can't find your uncle?"

"I'm not sure, honestly," Jaimes replied sadly.

"What about you?" Eilonwy asked, turning to Alastor. "You're not really brothers, right? Where is your family?"

"My mother is dead," Alastor answered. "She got really sick last winter." He frowned, thinking. "I'm pretty sure my father is dead, too. I never got to meet him, but my mother told me he would have found us if he was still alive. He saved our lives, apparently." Alastor shrugged. "And … I have an uncle, I think." Tiryn glanced again at Roland, but Roland ignored the pointed look. Alastor continued, "But I think he's dead too, or he would have come and found me."

"You can come with us," Eilonwy said, jumping down from her bunk to land silently on the cabin floor.

"And where are you going?" asked Jaimes.

Eilonwy smiled, putting her fists on her hips and puffing her chest out in pride. "We are going to save the world."

MOTHLENOR

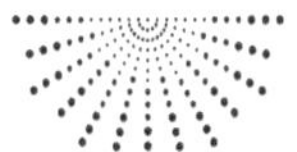

The two waiting guards pulled open the doors to the hall as Mothlenor approached them, and he continued his hurried pace into the room and up the dais to the throne. The man waiting for him turned abruptly at his entrance, his one good eye fixing on him as a wolf might glare at a rival male. The rest of his face, burned mess of scars that it was, was unreadable. And the sight of it made the steady burn of anger in Mothlenor's heart suddenly flare.

"My king, I'm glad you were able to come. We have some news."

Mothlenor settled himself into the stiff and overstuffed throne, steepling his fingers together and resting his chin against them to stare down at his commander. "I certainly hope that you do. I was in the middle of some important work." He'd been rereading an old passage about dragon lore, hoping another pass through it might give him some insight into finding another egg, but Ferrand didn't need to know how fruitless his evening had actually been so far.

"Should we wait for your adviser, my lord?" Ferrand's question was polite enough, but the way his eyes gleamed at the mention of Anna was not.

"I have her working on another task for me. She'll be informed of anything useful to come out of this meeting."

Ferrand crossed his arms behind his back, a smirk pinned firmly in place on the unburnt half of his face. He made his way down the length of the hall at a crisp pace. "No matter, though she will be missed." He came to rest at the foot of the dais, tilting his head slightly to look up at Mothlenor. "I received a message from one of my men down south. It seems he's been spotted boarding a ship."

Mothlenor's eyebrows raised, and he straightened in his throne. "He? You mean Ajax?"

Ferrand smiled. "That's correct, my lord." His smile faded. "Though my little rat couldn't be positive. The man he saw had long hair and a beard, but the spy was fairly sure it was Ajax."

After all these years … "Fairly sure I can deal with. Was he taken into custody?"

"No," Ferrand replied bitterly. "He was with friends, it seems. Some elves and a dwarf. Plus a couple of children, one of whom looked remarkably like your former adviser."

"Intriguing." Mothlenor paused for a moment, thinking. Non-human species were supposed to be banned from receiving passage on ships. Clearly someone was trying to make themselves the exception to the rule. "What ship was it? And where was it going?"

"It's a merchant ship, sailing the southern and eastern coastline. It will be back in the Southern Cities in about six months' time."

Mothlenor sighed. "I'll have to see what I can do in the meantime. Is it too late to get a man on board that ship?"

"My man would have found a way on if he was able. But I won't know for sure until I hear from him again."

Mothlenor nodded, rubbing absently at his temple. He could feel a headache coming on. "And what of the other tasks I gave you, were you successful?"

"No, my lord," Ferrand began, dipping his head apologetically. "I was unable to locate another Dragon's Eye, or an egg. But with more time—"

"I can't be sure how much time we have left," Mothlenor hissed. "If your spy did see Ajax, and he was indeed with Hasani's son, then they are surely working together on whatever fool's errand my brother gave his adviser before his death." Mothlenor groaned, pressing harder at his temple, where the pain in his head was beginning to deepen. He narrowed his eyes, glaring down on Ferrand. "I wish you had killed Ajax when you had the chance, you idiot."

Ferrand crossed his arms defensively. "I thought I had. But I was injured. Badly, you might recall." He gestured at the ruined half of his face, his good eye narrowed in anger.

Mothlenor snorted. He'd heard the excuse many times before, every time there was a possible sighting of the wanted former captain of the guard. "Yes, yes, you ran home to get patched up, then sent twenty of your strongest men to bring his body back, and he was gone." Mothlenor sneered down at Ferrand. "Why did you send so many men if you were sure that you had killed him? You can never seem to give a satisfactory answer to that question, Ferrand."

Ferrand pursed his lips, silent.

"I will think of something," Mothlenor said bitingly. "I always have, and I always will. You just let me know if your man was able to get aboard that ship as soon as you find out."

Ferrand nodded. "Yes, my—"

"Just go, Ferrand. It would seem I have some work to do."

15

WITCH

She was frantically tossing belongings into bags and trunks when her son came in. She turned at the sound of the front door swinging shut to see him standing in the middle of the room like he was standing in the midst of a storm. And, in a way, he was. There were papers strewn about on every available surface, and half-empty bottles of who besides herself knew what littered the floor. The look on his face told her that he knew exactly what was going on.

"Good, you're home." She sounded breathless to her own ears. Great Ones, was she starting to get old? She'd packed up and slipped town dozens of times, and it had never made her out of breath before. "We're leaving this place."

"Why?" The tone of his voice made it clear that he was really asking her, "Why, what did you do this time?" But she ignored the implication.

"There's a nasty rumor going around that Farmer Henrey's goats have gone dry because I put a curse on them when he refused to pay me for his hip ointment last month." She scooped up an armful of dried herbs that she had painstakingly sorted out just the morning before and

100

dumped the whole lot of them into a trunk on top of some spare clothes.

"Did you?"

She turned back towards him, hurt. "No." *How could he think such a thing?* "I don't even know how I would do such a curse, and Farmer Henrey didn't pay me last month because I owed him after he helped me put a new wheel on the wagon the month before." She plucked an armful of bottles from the kitchen floor and tucked them gently between the folds of her old dresses. "His goats have stopped giving milk because they're fucking old." She bit her lip, hating herself a little for cursing. She shut the lid to her trunk with a little effort, then motioned for her son to lift it from the table for her. "Come on, we have to leave."

"I'm not going."

She laughed, brushing her yellow hair from her face. They always had this argument. She had hoped this time he might be more understanding, considering how much worse things had gotten this close to the capital. They could really be in trouble if they lagged too long, and someone decided to send for one of the numerous King's Guard that always seemed to linger around the town's outskirts. She lifted another empty trunk onto the table, next to the full one, and began stacking books and papers into it, rushing around their tiny home to gather them up. "This isn't really a good time to get sentimental, darling. There will always be another town."

"I'm not going," he repeated. "I mean it this time. I'm staying right here."

She turned and took a long look at her son. There was a serious expression to his brown eyes that troubled her. His eyes had always troubled her; they were the only part of him that wasn't a clear reflection of herself. No, his eyes he had gotten from his father, she could only guess. Looking into those dark eyes, a thought hit her like a stone.

He was no longer a little boy that needed his mother, no matter where she dragged him off to. He was nearly a fully grown man. He could survive without her. Curse that, he would probably thrive without her. She wanted to cry. But there wasn't the time for it. "Why?"

"Lana is pregnant. I've asked her to marry me." He smiled, picking up a stack of papers that she had missed and passing them to her. "Her father offered to come let me work on his farm. I could live with them, and we could start a family. And when the time comes, that farm would be mine."

"You really mean it then?" She had always known that a day like this would come, but she had hoped it wouldn't for many more years.

"I mean it." Her son picked up the last few bottles from the floor around them and helped her arrange them in the last trunk. "I can't keep living the way you do. Always helping people, then always running away."

She felt a tear stain her cheek and she wiped it away, angry at herself for crying. "You could bring Lana with you. And wherever we end up, we could stay there. For always, I promise."

Her son laughed. "You always say that. 'For always, I promise.' But it never works out, does it?" He pulled her in close, hugging her to his chest. She realized with a strange sense of awe that at some point he had grown to be taller than her. *When did that happen?*

"I want this place to work out." He stared at her, his brown eyes clear and bright. For the first time in many years, she looked away, unwilling to hold his gaze for long.

In the end, she rode off in their little wagon on her own. It seemed almost empty, though her son had never packed much. Most of their belongings had always been hers, and had been mostly for keeping up with her herbal practice. Still, it seemed emptier … and lonelier as she guided their old mare down the back path and away from the home they had known for the last year. Or had it been two years? She could never remember how long they stayed at each place.

She promised to write to him when she was settled wherever she saw fit, and he promised to write her back, and to come and visit after the baby was born.

But she knew it would never come to pass.

16

ROLAND

The sound of crying woke him. Roland was disoriented for only a second before remembering the events of the days before. He had found the twins Tathiel and Eilonwy, they had gone to Hythe to meet not only Tiryn and Alastor, but the boy Jaimes as well. Nunor had found them, led to Hythe by a missive sent by Tiryn to the dwarfen king in Doldural. They had found a ship that would take them around the southern coast on a fool's errand to find Jaimes's uncle. And now Jaimes was sobbing quietly in his bunk.

Roland wasn't good with children, but the sound of one crying was still upsetting to him. He could surely do *something* to help him.

He had barely shifted his weight when an arm shot through the dark to stop him. Tiryn's face was barely visible in the dimness of the cabin, but Roland could just make out the elf's frown and firm head shake. Roland opened his mouth to protest, but a woman's soothing words stopped him.

His heart skipped a beat until he recognized the voice. For a moment, he had been sure he had heard Silvana in the darkness around them.

But it was Eilonwy's voice drifting across the cabin, her thin figure just a shadow as she slipped from her bunk and sat next to Jaimes on his. She spoke softly, her words unrecognizable, but the boy quieted instantly.

Roland released his breath with a sigh, turning to look at Tiryn.

The elf smiled thinly. "You're not the mothering type, Roland."

Roland snorted, looking around the cabin. Tathiel was surely awake, if his sister had woken, but he lay unmoving in his bunk. Alastor was still snoring gently. There was no sign of their brazen dwarf friend.

"Nunor went up to the deck about ten minutes ago," Tiryn said, noting his roving gaze.

Roland nodded and stood, patting Tiryn on the shoulder. "Get some sleep."

He left through the open cabin door, finding a lantern hanging at the foot of the stairs to the deck. Roland followed the light and the scent of salt to the ship's deck. Nunor was close by, leaning against the railing and looking out across the sea. Roland noticed with a smile that the dwarf had found a small metal crate to stand on, the added height making him tall enough to lean against the railing and look out across the water. The sky to the east was starting to brighten with the coming dawn, and Nunor's eyes were half shut against the light.

"You couldn't sleep?" Roland asked.

Nunor turned his head at Roland's words. "I slept fine. I just knew morning was coming, and I wanted to see the sun before I was confined down there for the day." He turned away from Roland. "And you?"

Roland stopped to stand next to the dwarf, leaning against the railing as Nunor did. "One of the boys had a night terror."

Nunor nodded in understanding. "Tiryn caring for him?"

"Eilonwy, actually."

Nunor nodded again.

They stood in silence. Roland stared at the wake created in the water as the ship sailed, nearly mesmerized. The water stretched on forever on this side of the ship, a seemingly endless blue. Roland had been sailing a few times, and the same feeling of incredible insignificance always caught him while he watched the ocean stretch out around him. He briefly wondered what kinds of creatures lived in these waters, and made a mental note to ask Melonya later.

"When do you plan on telling the boy that we need his little book?"

Roland shook his head. Tiryn had asked him the same question the night before. "I want to gain his trust first."

Nunor grunted. "We don't need his trust. We need his book."

"*I* need his trust." Roland looked sideways at Nunor. "He's my nephew, but he doesn't know it. He thinks his uncle abandoned his mother, after letting his father die. I doubt he wants anything to do with the man he thinks I am, but I want him to trust the man I want to be." Roland frowned, turning to lean his back against the railing. "It's the only way I can think of to keep him here with me. With us."

Nunor grunted again, running his stubby fingers through his short beard. "You humans are good at making things more complicated than they really ought to be."

Roland couldn't help but laugh. "I guess so."

Nunor sighed, looking past Roland. "Looks like the rest of the crew is waking up." A single member of Mathius's crew was climbing the last few steps from below deck. He eyed Nunor darkly as he walked by, but said nothing. "I guess it's time for me to go." Nunor stepped down from the metal crate. He crossed his arms over his chest and gave Roland a squinting look over. "I suppose I can understand why you want him to stay with you, but you seem to be forgetting that the longer you keep your identity away from him, the more he'll resent you when he does find out." Nunor shrugged. "Or so I would think. I can't be sure. You're a strange bunch."

Roland nodded, thinking. "I'll keep that in mind. Thank you, friend."

Nunor chuckled. "You're too quick to call a stranger a friend, as well." He shook his head, walking away.

Roland smiled, watching Nunor descend the steps that led to their cabin.

"He's right. You should talk to the boy soon."

Roland jumped at the voice, stumbling hard against the railing. The lone crewman looked over at him, glaring suspiciously. Roland shrugged apologetically. "Haven't got my sea legs yet, it seems."

The man turned away, shaking his head and continuing to check the knots on the riggings.

Roland turned to prop his elbows against the railing, looking out across the sea once more. *"Melonya?"* he thought, hoping she would be able to hear it.

"Who else?"

She sounded almost amused. Roland smirked at the idea, then realized she may very well have enjoyed startling him. *"I guess I just wasn't expecting you to be listening in to my conversations. Are you close?"*

"Close enough to hear your talk with the dwarf without even needing to be connected to you. But if it's unsettling, I can leave you alone. I just thought you might like to hear my opinion on the matter."

"No, I'd like to hear your thoughts." Roland shifted his weight, reaching up to run a hand through his dirty beard. He wanted to bathe, but it'd probably have to wait until after they reached the next port.

"Are you going to listen, or daydream about baths?"

Roland smirked again, closing his eyes to concentrate on her words. *"I'll listen."*

"*Good.*" Melonya sighed, her exasperation rolling over him like a gentle wave. "*I can understand your desire to keep the boy close. He is, after all, your kin. But Eilonwy seems to think the boy has a stubborn streak in him, and that might suggest that he will run off if you displease him. You need to give him a reason to stay. A reason other than familial bonds. And don't neglect the other boy. The two are brothers in every way but blood, and if one decides to leave, they will both go.*"

"*I know all of that, Melonya.*" Roland rubbed the back of his neck, sighing in frustration. "*I'm just not sure what to do.*"

"*They already like Tiryn. If he is the one to ask them to stay, they might be more inclined to do so.*"

"*Great.*" Roland snorted, a bitter pang of jealousy making him frown. Alastor was his nephew, yet Alastor already preferred Tiryn over him?

"*Don't be a child, Roland. They like Tiryn because he is differ-ent, and because he was there when Harlan died. He cared for them and offered to help them when they felt alone. You can do that, too.*"

Roland nodded, forgetting that Melonya couldn't see him. "*I suppose you're right.*"

"*Of course I am.*" Melonya sounded amused again. Roland could feel her emotions almost as if they were his own. "*Another thing. It wouldn't hurt if you could offer them something they might not otherwise get if they just went home. And come clean about who you are sooner, rather than later.*"

"*I did have one more question, Melonya.*"

Melonya laughed, the sound of it echoing through his mind like a gentle chorus of bells. "*I've yet to run into anything extraordinary down here, Roland.*" He smiled, realizing she had known exactly where his thoughts had wandered. "*There are a lot of fish. Some sharks, and a few whales. Normal sea creatures, big and small. Most seem to ignore me. The dolphins are friendly, though a bit stupid for my taste in company. There's nothing that one wouldn't normally expect to find.*"

"*Thank you, Melonya.*" Roland smiled again, refocusing his

gaze on the water before him. He took a moment to consider her words, realizing that the deck around him had grown busier as more members of the crew woke up to begin their duties. The sun had fully risen, and the heat of it warmed him. It was pleasant, being on a ship. If only he could ignore the occasional glance that was thrown his way by the crew members.

"Tiryn said I might find you up here."

For the second time that morning, Roland was startled into an involuntary jump. He turned, finding Alastor a few feet away and watching him. "Ah, Alastor. I didn't realize you were there."

"Sorry, didn't mean to surprise you." He crossed his arms over his chest, shaking his dark hair out of his eyes.

"It's nothing, I was just thinking about a few things." Roland motioned for Alastor to join him, shoving Nunor's crate aside with one foot. Alastor propped his elbows on the railing in much the same way Roland did. "Did you sleep well? And how is Jaimes?"

Alastor grimaced, looking up at him. "He woke you too, did he? He's pretty embarrassed about that, I wouldn't mention anything to him." Alastor sighed. "I slept fine. I feel bad about it, actually."

"Why?"

Alastor paused, clearly unsure if he should answer. "Jaimes is upset about his dad. He's prone to fits of panic and night terrors, and I should have guessed they might come back. I should have woken up. Done something to help him." Alastor's eyes squinted against the morning sun as he stared over the railing of the *Kingfisher*. "He's my best friend, and Harlan was basically my father."

Roland nodded, turning to face Alastor. "I understand. But you shouldn't let it bother you. We can all be here for both of you, if you want us to be."

Alastor frowned, gazing vacantly across the water. "I

guess you and Tiryn did know Harlan. And Tiryn said he was even familiar with my mother, though he didn't know her personally. It might be nice to have someone to talk to about them. At least until we find Uncle Tomas."

Roland hesitated, choosing his words carefully. "And if you don't find him? What will you do then?"

Alastor folded his arms over his chest again, leaning even deeper over the railing. "Tiryn asked us the same thing. I'm not really sure what we would do. Go home? We can't run the inn on our own, I don't think." He shrugged, looking up at Roland. "What do you think?"

Roland fought the immediate desire to tell the boy that he should stay with them, and instead considered the question for a moment. "I suppose it depends on what you would like to do. You could go home, sure. Harlan had a pretty profitable inn, though Tiryn tells me that he ran it into the ground in the last several months. But the foundation of a successful business is still there. It might take some time, and a lot of ingenuity, but you and Jaimes are smart enough to figure out how to get it going again." Roland smiled, shaking his head. "But it would be a very boring life. I would perhaps sell it, or give ownership to someone I trusted, and travel instead. I would try to see the world. I would want to learn new things. As much as I could. The world is so big, and Larten is only one small part of it." Roland laughed, catching Alastor's surprised look as the boy straightened to look at him. "That's me, though. And I am not you. You have to decide what you would like to do."

Alastor thought for a moment, head turned to look across the water again. "I'd like to find my uncle."

"You mean Tomas?"

"No, *my* uncle."

Roland swallowed away the sudden knot that formed in his throat and willed the erratic beating of his heart to slow. "You said you thought your uncle was dead."

Alastor shrugged a shoulder. "I'm not sure. But I'd like to know what happened to him. I'd like to know why he never came to see my mother. She asked for him a lot, when she was sick …" Alastor's voice trailed, and he chewed on his lower lip for a moment, lost in thought.

"Perhaps he thought it was best to stay away," Roland said carefully. "Maybe he thought that she didn't want him in her life."

"Maybe." Alastor turned to look at Roland, squinting in the brightening sunlight. "Will you and Tiryn be traveling together for a while? For this *quest* thing that Eilonwy mentioned last night?"

Roland nodded. "Yes, it seems so."

"How long will it take you?"

Roland rubbed at his beard, thinking. "Years, perhaps. I have no way of knowing."

"And where will you go? All around the world?"

"Probably." Roland narrowed his eyes at Alastor, though he felt a smile tugging at his lips. "Why do you ask?"

"I'm curious. You said you would want to see the world, if you were me." Alastor looked Roland over. "And what could you teach me, if I traveled with you?"

Roland's smile deepened. "Do you know how to fight?"

"Some," Alastor said with a smirk. "There were other boys in Larten besides Jaimes and me."

"Do you know how to fight with a sword?"

Alastor's eyes glinted. "You can teach me that?"

"In another life, it was my job to teach boys like you and Jaimes how to use a sword."

"And what about Tiryn? What could he teach us?" Alastor was excited, leaning in to hang on to Roland's every word.

"Well, he's good with herbal medicine. He's patched me up a few times."

Alastor shrugged lightly. "Jaimes would enjoy that."

"But not you."

"No, not really." Alastor shook his head, smiling sheepishly.

Roland glanced around them. The deck was busy, and soon they would surely be underfoot. But for now, their little corner of the deck was still private. Roland hesitated, looking Alastor over. The boy was tall, even for his age, but still several inches shorter than Roland. He looked almost just as his father had when they were still young. He dropped his voice down low, waving Alastor in closer. "Tiryn can also do magic."

Alastor's eyes narrowed, his easy grin shifting into a sneer. "You're joking."

Roland laughed. "I've seen it, I swear. He doesn't like to talk about it, but he can. And he might be able to teach you, if you have the aptitude for it. You won't learn any of that in Larten, I can promise that much."

"You're probably right." Alastor leaned his back against the railing, arms folding over his chest once more. His smile faded, and he looked over to Roland again. "Will you tell me about this quest sometime? You stopped Eilonwy before she could say anything about it, but the idea of traveling the world is appealing."

Roland considered for a moment, then nodded slowly. "Not today, and probably not tomorrow. But I will sometime soon. Let's see what we can find out about your uncle Tomas first." Roland sighed, waving Alastor towards the stairs. "Now let's get back downstairs. I'm sure Tiryn is wondering where we are, and we're going to be in the way soon enough."

Alastor obediently turned towards the stairs and started walking away. Roland was only a step behind him, but the sound of Melonya's voice made him pause.

"Tell him the truth soon, Roland."

17
TIRYN

Tiryn watched and listened as Eilonwy soothed the grieving Jaimes. It didn't take long for the boy to calm himself, sitting carefully on the edge of his bunk, Eilonwy close to him, one of his books open across her lap. Jaimes's eyes were rimmed in red, his cheeks flushed with embarrassment, but he answered questions from Eilonwy when prompted. Eilonwy smiled, pointing at the text and making some crude remark, and Jaimes laughed, giving her a soft smile in return. Tiryn closed his eyes, tuning their words out. He heard movement outside their little room as sailors woke and headed for the deck of the ship.

Heavy footsteps clunked down the stairs, coming to a stop in the open doorway beside Tiryn. "How's the boy doing?" Nunor murmured.

Tiryn opened his eyes once more, surveying the room. Alastor and Tathiel were both awake. Tathiel was quietly watching his sister's interactions with Jaimes, while Alastor tousled his unruly hair with one hand and tugged a boot on with the other. Jaimes and Eilonwy still sat together, heads bowed over the book in Eilonwy's lap. "Better. Though I'm sure it will take time to find peace with his father's death."

Nunor made a sound like a low snort. "I'm sure the attention of a pretty girl will help him."

Tiryn eyed the way Jaimes's smile seemed to grow deeper as Eilonwy shifted her weight slightly to sit closer to him. "Perhaps you're right."

Nunor snorted again, his back already on Tiryn as he walked deeper into the cabin.

Alastor was shuffling tiredly in his direction, his mouth stretched in an impressive yawn.

"Good morning, Alastor." Tiryn gave him a small nod from his spot on the cabin's floor.

"Morning, Tiryn. Where's Roland?"

"The deck, I believe. Go have a look, but don't stay too long. It sounds like it's getting busy out there."

Alastor nodded, smoothing his hair flatter as he went. He left the cabin, bound for the stairs to the deck, and Tiryn listened to his retreating footsteps.

There was a muffled thump from the hallway, and Tiryn tilted his head at the sound of a sharp and startled shriek and the thuds of heavy objects hitting the wooden floor of the hold. Tathiel and Eilonwy both looked up at the sounds, but Jaimes and Nunor seemed unfazed.

"I'm so sorry!" came Alastor's soft apology. "Please, let me help you with those."

"Oh, it's my fault, really," an unfamiliar voice replied. The voice was pitched high and sounded slightly nasal but friendly. "I wasn't paying any attention at all."

Tathiel gave Tiryn a quizzical look, but Tiryn waved him off, standing to investigate. Eilonwy glanced between her brother and Tiryn, then quickly turned her attention back to Jaimes as he made some quiet comment about the book she held.

Tiryn stepped out of the cabin, spotting the source of the commotion right away. Alastor was scrambling to gather up several heavy books from the floor, stacking them carefully back into the waiting arms of a thin and rather frail-looking man. The stranger was peculiarly dressed, wearing an over-sized robe with trailing sleeves, pale-colored trousers tucked into short boots, and a belt cluttered with heavy pouches hanging loosely around his waist. His dark tunic was buttoned almost to his neck, and hung down to just above the knee, making him look like a small child in his father's clothes.

Alastor stacked a book onto the man's already towering pile, then peered around the impressive collection to address the man. "That's all of them. Can I help you carry them somewhere?"

"No, no. That's quite alright, young man," the stranger said. His voice was strained, and his knuckles were white as he struggled to maintain his hold on the heavy stack. "I've grown used to such a delightful burden, it's really nothing at all."

Tiryn knelt to pick up a stray book that had landed further down the hall than the rest of its companions. "You missed one, Alastor."

Alastor turned. "Oh, Tiryn. This is … uh …"

"Lord Brynne, at your service!" The man held out a hand, aiming it about a foot to Tiryn's left, then quickly retracted it as his tower of books leaned precariously and nearly toppled again. "But Brynne is fine," he added, straightening the stack of books before they could find themselves on the floor again.

Tiryn added the final book to the pile, then took the top half and lifted them from Brynne's arms. The man's face was suddenly visible; dark and beady eyes surrounded by squint lines sat above a small nose with a line of dried ink smeared across it and a pouty, feminine mouth. He was younger than Tiryn had anticipated, not quite into the full years of his adulthood, though his slim build and thin voice suggested a frail man in his later days. "It's a pleasure to meet you, Brynne." Tiryn dipped his head politely to Brynne, then turned to give Alastor a quick nod and a smile. "Go on, Alastor, I can help our friend with his belongings."

Alastor returned the smile, then rushed up the stairs to the deck above.

"Oh, just the man, or elf, I suppose, that I was looking for!" Brynne exclaimed. "I'd heard Mathius had taken on elven passengers and I was hoping I might have the chance to meet one of you!"

"You were?"

"Oh yes, of course." Brynne's small eyes were bright, and a warm smile lit his face. "Who wouldn't want to meet an elf? Such polite company, and such engaging conversations." He began walking, his now manageable stack of books leaning heavily against his thin chest, and Tiryn followed beside him as they made their way slowly down the narrow hall of the first level of the hold.

"I have to admit that it's been some time since anyone has shown such pleasure in meeting me, Brynne," Tiryn said. They passed the open door to the cabin Tiryn and his companions shared, and Tiryn chanced a quick glance inside. Everyone was as they had been a moment before with the exception of Tathiel, who stood close to his sister and Jaimes with his arms crossed defensively over his chest and his eyes fixed on the door. Their gazes met, and Tiryn offered him a reassuring nod as he and Lord Brynne continued. "The last several years have sown only disgust and hatred at my approach."

"I can't say that I'm surprised. Though I can promise you that you'd hear such excitement more frequently if you surrounded yourself with scholarly peoples like myself."

"Scholarly?" Tiryn asked politely. He had guessed as much on seeing Brynne's ink-stained face and his towering stack of reading, but if there was one thing Tiryn had learned from his time around humans, it was that they enjoyed talking about themselves and their interests at great length.

"I am a researcher, Tiryn," Brynne said. They rounded a corner, coming to a row of open-entry cabins roughly the size of a larder. Each one held a slim bed against one wall, and a number of them had a trunk or similar lying at the foot of it, with only enough spare room to turn around in. A few of the cabins were occupied by sailors, and each looked up with a glare at Tiryn and Brynne as they passed. But Brynne continued walking and talking, either not noticing or not caring about the stares from the crew. "I'm on the *Kingfisher* as part of a sort of scholarly expedition. I requested several books from the local libraries of the Free Cities, and Mathius picked them up yesterday in Hythe. But some thickheaded sailor," Brynne said with a huff, oblivious to the surrounding company, "decided to tuck them away down in the lower hold below, with the wines and furs and chickens." Brynne shuddered, making a small sound of disgust. "I explained to Mathius just days before that these books are too delicate to be left in the damp like everything else, but I suppose the message was lost in translation somewhere in the journey from captain to deckhand."

Tiryn looked down at the books he carried. The front cover of the topmost book was blank, with no embossed title or description. The spine of each book was similarly blank, their external appearance giving no clue as to what could be read within. "What are you researching, Brynne?"

Brynne paused, turning to Tiryn and giving him another wide smile. "I shouldn't say. Not until it's done." He tapped the side of his nose twice with one ink-stained finger and winked, and Tiryn realized how the smear of black might have ended up on Brynne's face.

"I thought Mathius asked you and your companions to remain in your cabin during the day, elf," a low voice called from the next cabin, and a tall blond man emerged from the doorway to stand before Tiryn and Brynne. He was broad shouldered, nearly taking up the whole width of the narrow hall, and he stood perhaps a hand's breadth taller than Tiryn himself, making him simply tower over the slight Brynne.

Tiryn started to explain, but Brynne surprised him by stepping forward and jabbing one pale finger into the man's tanned chest.

"Now listen here, Reed," Brynne said, his voice taking on a stern edge. "Tiryn was helping me out at my request. It simply won't do to insult a man, or an elf, for just trying to be helpful."

Reed's lips thinned for a moment, his nostrils flaring slightly. He gave Brynne a stiff half bow, followed by a curt nod in Tiryn's direction. "Forgive me, Brynne. It is only for his protection that the captain has asked him to remain in his cabin."

Brynne gave an exasperated squeak, glaring up at the sailor. "Well, you can tell Mathius—"

"It's alright, Lord Brynne," Tiryn said, his eyes fixed on Reed's glassy stare. "I'm sure Reed means no disrespect, and I would be happy to return to my quarters, if only there was someone to assist you."

Reed matched his stare, and Tiryn wondered if the small glint to his dark eyes was an angry hint of malice or one of disgust. "Evert," Reed called over his shoulder, turning his head slightly. Another sailor, this one bald and nearly twice as wide as Reed, slipped from a tiny cabin just behind Reed, turning sideways to fit his large frame through the doorway. "Please help the good Lord Brynne with his books. I'm needed on deck." Then, with a hard glare and a small wave of one hand, Reed added. "After you, *Tiryn.*"

Tiryn silently passed the books he held to the sailor Reed had called Evert, and the whole stack seemed to fit neatly within the palm of one enormous paw. He turned on his heel, dipping his head to Brynne in farewell. "I'm sure you'll have no trouble finding me later, should you wish to continue our conversation, Lord Brynne."

"Certainly, Tiryn." Brynne nodded enthusiastically, his face split into a wide grin. "I'd be delighted to meet your companions, as well."

Tiryn made his way back, feeling Reed's hot stare on his back with every step. They turned the corner, Reed nearly on his heels, and continued in silence until Tiryn reached the open door of his cabin, where Jaimes's soft voice carried out into the hall. At that moment, Reed brushed past him, hurrying to take the stairs to the deck two at a time and disappearing in the warm sunlight above.

Tiryn felt the tension in his shoulders slowly ease, and he stared after the sailor for a moment before shaking himself and stepping into the large guest quarters. As he shut the door behind him, the open space around him suddenly felt just as cramped and confining as the crew cabins just down the hall.

"Well?" Tathiel was standing where he had been moments before, though his arms now hung loosely at his sides. Behind him, Eilonwy gave Tiryn and her brother only the barest glance before directing her attention to Jaimes once more. Nunor sat apart from the others, inspecting the edge of his axe, but Tiryn was sure he would be listening to whatever might be said.

Tiryn crossed the room to stand beside Tathiel, watching as Jaimes flipped idly through a few pages of the same heavy book. He thought of Brynne's excitement at seeing him, and of Reed's matching mistrust and that odd glint in his eyes. "I think we might have a new friend. And perhaps a new enemy as well."

1 8

ANNA

The house was dark and smelled of sweat and urine. They all did, in this corner of the city. As well as most of the other corners, as well. The common people of Etritia were too poor to afford the candles and lamp oil that the castle burned through without a care and were often forced to keep their homes dark in the evenings.

Anna didn't mind the dark, not here anyway. But the smell was another thing. Not that any of them could be blamed. Most of the bathhouses had closed down, or been converted into brothels, and the ones that were still operating were also expensive. Those few that were lucky enough to have washrooms in their homes were usually not lucky enough to afford basic amenities such as soaps and a good source of clean water.

It wasn't just the smell of the living that filled the streets of Etritia. The dead had their own stink of decay as they hung from the rickety gallows in the center of the main square. Ferrand, ever hungry for violence, found amusement in hanging Etritians for even the smallest of crimes, and they were left until the combination of their weight and the passing of time finally broke the nooses that held them.

It was no wonder the population of Etritia had fallen drastically since the beginning of Mothlenor's reign. Those who weren't killed outright by the Commander of the King's Guard were beaten, harassed, and raped by the men that should be their protectors. And those that survived had disease and starvation to worry about.

And that was why Anna was really down in this forgotten part of Etritia in the first place, wasn't it?

Anna had brought her own candle to the makeshift clinic, and in the soft light that it cast, she dabbed carefully at a nasty cut on a young girl's arm. The cut was thankfully not a deep one, and the wound was already knitting itself back together nicely. The skin around it was red and inflamed, but the edges were cleanly cut, as if from a short blade.

"How did you say this happened?"

The girl, only a few years younger than Anna, hesitated before answering. "I fell, Lady Anna. Down some stairs in one of the alleys."

"Hm." Anna didn't pry. Lots of girls "fell", and it wasn't her place to force the truth from them. Only to bandage them up. "And when did it happen?"

"Just last week. I tried to come see you when you were here last, but ..."

"But I didn't come, yes," Anna finished. "I'm sorry, Deidre." Anna scooped a generous amount of white cream from a pot in her lap and lathered it around the cut. "I wish you had come to the castle. Cookie would have let you in the kitchen door. She would have made sure I could look at it."

"I thought about it ..." Deidre said slowly. "But it's not safe for us to go up there. Even to the kitchens."

Anna couldn't argue with the girl on that point. It *was* dangerous to stray too close to the castle, especially for a young woman like Deidre.

"I wasn't up for the walk, anyway." Deidre gave a small chuckle. "I banged myself up pretty good on those stairs."

Anna frowned. "Are you hurt anywhere else?"

"There are other cuts." Deidre's face reddened in the candlelight. "In other areas."

"Ah." That was as close to the truth as Anna was going to get. "Do they look like this?" She pointed at the wound on Deidre's arm. "Red and angry looking? Shallow?"

Deidre nodded. "Will I be alright?" Her voice was flat, as if she didn't care how the question was answered.

To accept the thought of death at such a young age ...

"You'll be fine, Deidre. Just a bit of infection." Anna pressed the lid back onto the jar of ointment and held it out for the girl to take. "Put some of this around each of the cuts. It'll fight off the infection and help them heal." Deidre's eyes were wide as she listened to Anna's instructions. "Do that twice a day, every day, for a week. Keep the cuts clean. Make sure you change the wrappings every night before bed." Anna made a mental note to send more bandages out to all her clinics around the city. They were likely low again. "Can you wrap the other cuts?"

"Yes, I think so." Deidre's voice was almost breathless. "I remember how, after you showed everyone last year."

"Good." Anna patted Deidre's hand, closing the girl's fingers around the little pot. "If you have any left after the week is up, save it, just in case." Anna thought for a moment, then reached into a pocket of her robes and pulled out a short squat vial of cloudy liquid. At the sight of it, Deidre's tense shoulders relaxed, and she let out a small sigh. "And take this with you." Anna pressed the vial into the girl's hands. "Just in case."

Deidre's hand wrapped around the fragile vial. "Thank you, Lady Anna."

"Don't forget, it needs to be—"

"Warmed up, yes, I remember." Deidre nodded solemnly.

"And if you don't need it, give it to someone who does. They don't last long." Anna pointed at the tiny vial as Deidre slipped it into the top of her blouse. "That one is still fresh, and will last for another three months. Don't forget. Use it yourself, if you need it, or give it to someone who can use it. It's no good if it's old, so don't hoard it."

"I remember, Lady Anna. I promise to do as you say."

"Good." She bent to kiss Deidre on the forehead, checking for fever. Her head was warm, but not alarmingly so. The girl smelled of the city, of urine and sweat, but Anna kissed her anyway. "You're going to be fine. We're all going to be alright, in the end."

"If you say so, Lady Anna." Deidre nodded, getting to her feet.

"Don't forget to take a parcel on the way out. There's soap and a few silver pieces in each one. And an apple tart, fresh from the kitchens." Anna gave the girl a smile as Deidre's eyes lit up.

"Thank you, Lady Anna." Deidre gave a clumsy curtsy, then rushed for the door, snagging a parcel from the large basket sitting just inside the doorway. The basket was nearly empty, only a few more packages lying in the bottom.

Anna sighed, leaning back in the chair she had been sitting in for the better part of the day. "Is that the last one, Cookie?" Anna turned towards a second small candle glow, not ten feet away. She knew Cookie was there, though she couldn't see the old woman in the dark.

"That's the last of them." Cookie's frail voice warbled as she spoke. "Seems we had more than usual today."

"I missed last week, remember?"

"Ah, right, right. I remember."

Anna wondering if the old cook actually did remember. Her memory was failing more and more these days. "Are you ready to pack up, then?"

"Yes, yes." Cookie got to her feet with a groan, and Anna did the same. It felt good to stretch her legs. "Best be getting back soon, before the sun goes down completely."

Anna looked out of the open doorway as Cookie shuffled around the table that stood between them. The sky outside was already darkening into a reddish purple. She hoped Deidre could make it back home before it got too dark. The streets weren't safe after nightfall.

"You all fresh out of that tonic?"

Anna didn't have to ask Cookie which tonic she meant. "Yes, I just gave the last vial to Deidre."

"You'll be needing more ingredients for a fresh batch, I suppose, then?"

Cookie tried to lift the basket and drape it over one arm, but Anna stopped her, taking the basket and carrying it herself. She dropped a few odds and ends from her robe pockets into the bottom of the basket with the remaining care packages. After such a long day, there was only a single tub of ointment and two small bundles of bandaging left. "That's right. Do you think I can get more so late in the season?" Anna blew out both candles with a quick breath, then followed Cookie out of the old house that had served as their clinic for over two years now. She locked the door behind them with an old key, more out of habit than out of necessity. No one in this part of the city would rob the clinic.

"Ishta can get some for you, she's got a stash hidden around somewhere." Cookie looped an arm through Anna's free one, and they started down the cobbled path back to the castle. "She should have time to stop here herself soon enough. I'll have her meet you tomorrow morning. Perhaps the two of you can make one of your little exchanges."

Anna made a mental note to track Ishta down herself, in case Cookie forgot. Last time Anna had waited for over an hour for a supply exchange that Ishta had never been told to prepare for. "Would she give me some of her own?"

Cookie scoffed. "You? Of course she would." They walked slowly, Cookie careful with every step. "With all you do for us, I wouldn't be surprised if she handed over most of hers to you. We need you, Anna. Etritia needs you and your little tonics."

Anna let Cookie lean against her, supporting some of her weight as they walked. "I wish it wasn't needed. I wish things were different."

Cookie patted Anna's hand. Her skin was thin and wrinkled, but her hands were still sure. "But they aren't. That's the truth of it. We're just grateful for everything you do."

Anna was silent. She had never meant to take on Etritia's poor and injured. But there was no going back now.

"I consider myself lucky," Cookie said. "I've never needed one of those little vials. But I can't turn a blind eye while the city suffers. And I've my daughters to consider." Cookie's grip on Anna's arm tightened as she nearly stumbled over an upraised stone in the path. "We might all live in the castle, but that doesn't mean we're safe."

"No," Anna said, her voice hard. "It doesn't."

When morning came, Anna took a basket full of needlework and went out to the gardens. They were in terrible disarray, a fact Cookie was sure to complain about at length at every opportunity. Apparently, the former king had been fond of the garden, especially of the numerous rose bushes that were dotted throughout the greenery. But the shrubs and bushes had been left untrimmed, letting them grow into wild shapes and sizes, and the roses were left to either wilt and die or grow wild and thorny with unchecked abandon.

They were ugly and disorganized, but they were close to both the kitchens and the main market square, and they made for a good spot to plan a chance encounter. The heavy scent of rose and greenery helped to cover the stench of rot that drifted from the main courtyard, where Anna knew half a dozen men and women still hung just out of eyesight. To Anna, the untamed gardens were perfect.

So she sat, heavy basket at her feet, a scrap of old linen in her lap, and a needle and thread in her hand. Anna stared at the white cloth draped across her knees for a moment, waiting and listening. The waiting was always the hardest part. It was always in those quiet moments that she truly feared something would go wrong. That Mothlenor, or worse, Ferrand, would find her out here on her own.

A door behind her opened and closed softly, and Anna's shoulders tensed.

"Lady Anna, a pleasure to see you," a woman's voice called.

Anna didn't even turn, but brought the needle tip to the coarse fabric, tilting her head to watch the newcomer as she stepped into view. "Ishta." Anna dipped her head, then focused on the fabric on her hands again. The needle hadn't yet pierced the material.

"Do you mind if I join you for a moment?"

"Not at all." Anna shifted over a few inches on the bench she sat on, giving Ishta enough room to sit beside her.

Ishta placed her basket of washing on the ground, the edge of it brushing against Anna's ankle lightly, then sat beside her, hands folded carefully in her lap. "How goes the needlework?"

Anna's lips curled, though she tried to hide the smile. "It's going as well as usual."

That got a small snort from Ishta. "You'd think, after all this time, you might have actually learned how to do the damn work, Anna."

Anna let the fabric fall and tucked the needle back into its little leather purse. "Cookie tried teaching me, but I just don't have the head for it." Anna finally looked up, not to Ishta, but to the small path that led from the gardens to the main square.

Ishta's gaze followed hers. "There's no one out there. I checked before coming."

"And the kitchens?"

"Empty." Ishta sighed. "Mother has everyone out running errands around the castle."

Anna turned, her eyes scanning the castle walls for any visible windows.

"Anna." Ishta placed a hand over the one Anna had resting on the bench. "No one can see us from the windows. The hedges have grown too tall." Her fingers slipped around Anna's and gave her hand a gentle squeeze. Only then did Anna meet Ishta's eyes. "We checked everything, no one can see us down here."

"I know, it's just—"

"Anna." Ishta lifted Anna's hand to her lips, giving her palm a gentle kiss. Anna's body relaxed, and she let out a deep breath. "You're safe here. With me." Ishta leaned forward, her free hand reaching for Anna.

Anna closed the distance without a thought, her hands pulling Ishta closer as their lips met. They held each other close for a few moments, Anna grateful to find comfort in Ishta's touch.

When their lips broke apart, Anna rested her forehead against Ishta's, her eyes shut tight.

"You're crying," Ishta said.

"I know."

"You always cry when we meet like this."

"I know."

Ishta snorted again. "Is the kissing that bad, then?"

Anna let out a small laugh, lifting her head to look into Ishta's eyes. "No, no, of course not." She ran a hand over the side of Ishta's face, trying to memorize the angle of her jaw with just the touch of her hand.

Ishta smiled, her hand playing with a loose lock of Anna's hair that had fallen over her shoulder. "Good."

"How are you?" Anna asked, wiping away the last of her tears.

"Fine. Finding resources for the clinics keeps me busy. You?"

"I'm fine," Anna lied. She didn't want to tell Anna about Mothlenor's latest plan. It would just hurt them both too much. "Ferrand is away on another one of his trips, so it's been quiet."

"Ah, I wondered where that murderous bastard went," Ishta said bitterly, her whole body instantly seizing up. "Do you know when he'll be back?"

Anna shook her head. "No, sorry. He's never gone for the same length of time."

Ishta grimaced, pulling away from Anna slightly. "I wish someone would just kill him and be done with it."

"He's too—"

"Dangerous, yes, I know." Ishta frowned. "Doesn't mean I can't still hope he dies spectacularly."

"If he keeps failing the king, I'm sure he will."

Ishta let out a sigh, her arms briefly tightening around Anna. "We should go."

"Already?" But Anna knew she was right. They only ever had a few moments to make their exchange before one or other of them was needed.

Ishta stood, Anna following her example. Anna took the basket closest to her, draping her linen over the top and tucking the needle case down the side. It was lighter than the basket she had brought out to the gardens, but still heavier than expected.

Beside her, Ishta's eyebrows raised. "I guess I've got more washing to do than I thought."

"The clinics are running low on dressings. I fashioned some new ones from some old dresses. I also wanted to send a tub of white nettle cream around to each one. It seems Dirk is back from whichever rock he crawled under. I've seen an increase in the number of girls coming in with dagger cuts."

Ishta grimaced again. "Will one tub per clinic be enough?"

"No, but it's a start. I'll bring a few more during my next round."

"And when will that be?"

Anna sighed. "Whenever I can slip away from Mothlenor's tower for more than a few hours. You can manage fine without me for a time, right?"

Ishta nodded then leaned to give Anna a quick kiss. Anna held her close, savoring the comfort.

"Before you go, Ishta, I wanted to talk to you about Cookie."

Ishta nodded. "Her memory is going. We've all noticed."

"I want you to take her place."

"Me? You think I could handle it?"

Anna nodded. "I do. You're Cookie's daughter, after all. You can do it."

Ishta shrugged. "Alright. I can ask Illa to pick up the slack on the supply chain. We can make do."

Anna leaned in for the kiss this time. "Go. I'll see you when it's time to make another trip around the city."

Ishta nodded, then turned and took her basket of fresh dressings and white nettle cream down the path to the main square.

When Anna shut the door to her rooms behind her, she threw back the layers of fabric that covered the items Ishta had brought her. Nestled in the bottom of the basket were two potted plants, as well as half a dozen leather satchels and what looked like a large leather pouch.

Anna let out a low sound of awe, setting the basket carefully on the bed and lifting the plants out of the basket. "Ishta, you shouldn't have." They were only trimmings, but they were healthy and beautiful trimmings. And they would give her everything she needed to keep the women of Etritia supplied with her little tonic for years to come, if she cared for them properly.

She hurried to a window set in the far wall, propping the

plants up and into the sunlight that streamed through the shutters. It wasn't ideal, but it would do for now, until she could arrange something more fitting.

The rest of the supplies were more along the lines of what she normally received from Ishta. Dried herbs and flowers, including the sweet tansy that now sat in the window, as well as a sealed jar that seemed to be filled with animal tallow. But the leather pouch was new.

Anna unrolled it across the bed, staring at the interior. It was filled with small pockets, the first half dozen of which already had empty vials tucked inside. Anna counted the vials' sleeves. There were thirty, in two rows of fifteen. Precisely the number of vials each batch of tonic produced. She knew it wasn't coincidence.

Anna slowly rolled the pouch back up, inspecting the soft leather as she did. There, about halfway down the length, was a small gap between one pair of pockets and the next. And stamped into the leather in that gap was a small, stylized letter A.

Anna rolled the pouch up the rest of the way, then held it to her chest. It was a little large, and would be even larger when the pockets were all full, but it could easily be hidden beneath a cloak or a robe. No more slipping a few vials in the pockets of her robe and hoping it would be enough for that day's visit. Now she could bring them all.

And Ishta had made it herself.

Anna held the pouch tighter and wept.

19

TIRYN

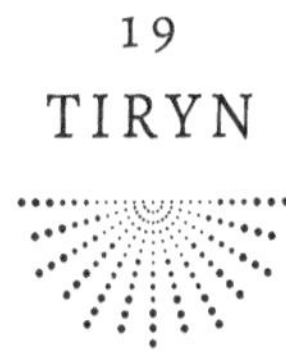

Tiryn paced the length of the small cabin, glancing up the stairs to the deck with each pass by the door. It was sunny outside, he could see that much, but his limited view gave him no sign of the ship's surroundings. He turned, pacing back toward the bunks on the far wall. "We should be reaching the port soon. I'm surprised no one has said anything yet."

"I'm sure everything is fine, Tiryn. The boys are working hard with Roland. Someone will come down soon enough." Tathiel sat cross-legged on his bunk, idly polishing a small dagger and watching Tiryn pace. His sister lay on the cabin floor in front of him, legs propped up to rest next to him. Tiryn noticed with some amusement that she was flipping absently through one of Jaimes's books on medicine. The book was on herbal remedies, judging by the figures Eilonwy casually glanced over before turning the page.

Tiryn turned again, heading for the door once more. Tathiel was right. Tiryn could hear the sporadic sound of sticks knocking together, and knew that Roland was teaching the boys swordplay. Yesterday they had come down for dinner sweating and bruised. Jaimes had apologized

131

profusely over a particularly nasty bruise on Alastor's arm, but the other boy had laughed it off as part of their training. And Roland had asked Tiryn if he would be able to teach the boys magic. Tiryn turned once more, shaking his head. How could he teach anyone magic if he was stuck down in the belly of the ship, forgotten?

"Will you quit that pacing? You're making my axe-hand itch," Nunor grumbled, glancing up from his plate of food long enough to give Tiryn a dirty glare.

"Sorry, Nunor." Tiryn stopped where he stood, sliding down the wall to sit on the cabin floor. They would be arriving at the port Mathius had told them about at any moment, and Tiryn desperately wanted to leave the ship for a few hours. Their little room was starting to feel like a prison, and he wasn't sure he could handle it for much longer. Tiryn sighed, realizing that his fingers were drumming absently on his leg, and stilled them.

He turned to the twins. "Do you two know how to use a sword?"

Eilonwy answered, turning a page in the book as she did. "We know how to use swords, bows, and even staffs. We're also somewhat skilled in the arcane, though it's not our strongest skill."

"It's not *my* strongest skill, you mean. You're much better than I am, Eilonwy," Tathiel mumbled.

Eilonwy smiled, nudging her brother with one foot. "We can't both be great at everything. Besides, I might be better, but I'm still not very gifted."

"Can you cook?" Nunor suddenly asked. "I'm already getting tired of fish. Maybe they'll let you down into the galley to make something."

"Isn't that a little presumptuous, assuming that she's the better cook between us?" Tathiel asked, setting aside the dagger he had been working on and picking up another from the bed.

Nunor shrugged. "It's the dwarf women who always cook."

"Actually, Tathiel makes an excellent venison dish. And now, thanks to this book—" Eilonwy snapped the book shut loudly, turning her head to look at Nunor, "—I can make a poison that kills your fingers and toes and makes them fall off."

Nunor shrugged again. "So we send Tathiel."

Eilonwy and Tathiel laughed. Tiryn could only shake his head, but he was glad to know that their odd circle of allies was getting along nicely, despite their differences in race.

The sound of rushed footsteps coming down the stairs brought Tiryn to his feet, but it was only Alastor who came running into the cabin. He was sweating and red faced, but seemed energetic. "Roland asked me to come down and let you know that we should be anchoring soon. The port's just come into view. Roland wants you to go ashore with him."

Tiryn looked Alastor over, noticing the bruise on his arm was already healing to a nasty shade of green. "Are you and Jaimes going as well?"

"I think that was the plan, yes." Alastor nodded excitedly, brushing the sweat-dampened hair from his eyes.

Tiryn turned to face the rest of the room. "Nunor—"

Eilonwy interrupted. "Don't worry, Tiryn. Tathiel and I will babysit the dwarf." She smirked, sitting up and turning to look at Nunor. "I'm sure he'll behave himself while you're gone."

"I can make no promises on that, Tiryn," Nunor said, accenting his words with a small belch. "Dwarfs do fine in enclosed spaces for long periods of time, but only when there is ample beer and work to keep us occupied."

"I'm sure the twins can find something for you to do." Tiryn motioned for Alastor to lead him out. "We'll be back soon, I hope."

Alastor smiled at Tiryn. "I almost hope Uncle Tomas isn't there—I'm not sure I want this trip to finish so soon."

Tiryn forced a smile in return. "We'll see what we find, Alastor. But I'm glad to have you and Jaimes with us."

<hr>

The questionable port Mathius brought them to had only a small dock, hidden in a little inlet on the coastline. Mathius insisted on dropping anchor in the sea proper and letting Tiryn and the others row a small raft to shore. He claimed it was because the *Kingfisher* was too large a ship to make port in such a small harbor, but Tiryn was sure Mathius just wanted to stay as far away as possible from the dubious and secluded spot. Tiryn could hardly blame him for being so cautious after Mathius had already lost one ship. As he and Roland rowed, Tiryn wasn't sure he wanted to walk into whatever misadventure might be waiting for them beyond the thick strip of woods that lined the shore. But he wanted to be there in case Roland needed him, and that was enough to keep rowing them further from the safety of the *Kingfisher*.

The waters along the coast were a perfectly clear blue, and Tiryn could see the silt and pebbles that made up the seafloor eddy in their wake. Tiny fish darted around his oar as they paddled, and Tiryn realized it might have almost been peaceful if not for their unknown destination.

It took only a minute to pull the raft up onto the shore and tuck the oars away, and then the four of them were walking through dense underbrush on what could have been a walking path. Tiryn instinctively took up the rear, keeping Alastor and Jaimes between him and Roland. The woods were humid, and Jaimes's shirt dampened with sweat as they struggled their way through the weeds and grasses. Roland kept them on the footpath, and they finally managed to break through to a large clearing. The makings of a fairly decent camp were evident, including a small open-air tent with a table and a set of barrels and crates to serve as chairs. In the center of the clearing was a stone ring with evidence of a recent fire within. There was no one in sight, though signs of life were evident at every turn. He could smell freshly cut wood and the faint hint of some sort of animal, but there were no marks on the surrounding trees and no sounds of living creatures.

Roland fell onto a nearby bench, roughly made from might have been the wreckage of a ship, and tugged his shirt from his trousers to wipe the sweat from his face. Alastor and Jaimes both collapsed into the sand, pulling off their shirts and tossing them aside. Roland squinted up at Tiryn and shook his head. "Fucking elves."

Tiryn looked down at himself. His shirt was unstained with sweat. He was uncomfortable, but clearly not as uncomfortable as the other three. He could only shrug at Roland's irritated glare. "Sorry."

A rustling in the grasses around them brought Tiryn's gaze up. Roland's head snapped up too, but Jaimes and Alastor lay groaning in the sand, unaware that they were no longer alone. Six men and a boy roughly the same age as Alastor and Jaimes stepped into the clearing. They each carried a sword, and stared down at the four of them in apprehension. Only then did Alastor and Jaimes sit up, their eyes wide and startled, but with a look from Roland, they remained seated in the sand.

One of the men stepped further into the clearing, and Roland barked out a laugh at the sight of him. "Is this how you treat your guests, Myka?"

The man tilted his head, looking Roland over. "Roland? Is that you? You need a good trim, old man." He wrinkled his nose, grinning. "And a bath." His eyes were bright and intelligent, and he kept his sword up as he stepped closer to the four of them.

"Do you know these people, Roland?" Tiryn asked.

"I know him, in a way," Roland answered, eyeing Myka as he stepped closer.

"In a way?" Myka raised an eyebrow, tilting his head once again. "My sister found this man bleeding and alone in the woods. She dragged his bloodied ass back home, and we patched him up. He slept under our roof, ate our food, then stole our horse and left without so much as a thank you."

Roland lifted a placating hand. "I did say thank you. Many times. And I had your horse sent back to you, as soon as I got to the next town and could buy my own." Roland furrowed his brows, glaring up at Myka. "And I left you some money. And a note." Roland scoffed. "You can't really be angry about all of that?"

"Of course not, you old bastard." Myka smiled, dropping his sword back into its scabbard. The others around them instantly did the same. He stepped closer to Roland, pulling him off the bench and into a hug. "I'm just surprised to see you again."

Tiryn relaxed, and he released the arcane power he had been silently directing towards his palms.

Roland beat a hand affectionately on Myka's back, then released him. "I could say the same. What are you doing all the way down here? And how is Myra? And your wife?"

Myka laughed, his eyes twinkling. "Cora is fine, as is Myra. They're both still up north."

"I bet they aren't too happy about being left behind," Roland said, smirking.

"They are not," Myka replied with a sigh.

"Roland," Tiryn said pointedly. "I'm glad you've found an old friend, but we came here for a reason."

Myka's eyebrows rose again. "I would hope you wandered

here with some sort of purpose. And I'll be happy to help, if I can."

"We're looking for someone," Tiryn said, offering a hand to Jaimes to help him stand. "He should have come through here a few months ago."

"Why would he come here?" Myka frowned, waving them over to the tent, where someone had already set out half a dozen mismatched mugs of water. "There's nothing really here but the few of us who made the move south."

"It's our uncle Tomas we're looking for." Alastor spoke up, his shirt tossed over one shoulder. "He and a bunch of his fellow crew members stole their captain's ship and were headed south in search of the Isle of Onia."

Myka crossed his arms over his chest, a mug of water grasped loosely in one hand. "The Isle of Onia? Why stop here? That's supposed to be out in the southern waters."

"The best we can figure is that they wanted to stop for supplies before leaving the coastline." Roland fell into a chair at the rough-hewn table, and Alastor and Jaimes followed his lead without hesitation. Tiryn remained standing, feigning interest in his water as an excuse to let his gaze wander once more over their surroundings. The camp was as tidy and clean as could be expected for something that was clearly not meant to be permanent. Most of the furnishings appeared handmade and were mismatched, and the smell of animals was stronger than it had been a few moments before. The rest of Myka's men had returned to milling about the semi-permanent camp, but it was clear they were doing nothing productive, and the way their heads tilted and turned every few seconds told Tiryn they were paying just as close attention to their guests as he was to them.

"I see." Myka frowned, turning a chair around and sitting with his arms wrapped around the back of it. "We wouldn't have been able to help them, I'm afraid. We've only just begun settling here ourselves."

"Why?" Roland asked. "You have a nice home up north. Why did you leave it?"

Myka sighed, his shoulders slumping at the question. "There was a territory dispute. I lost."

"I'm sorry." Roland's expression was pained, only adding to Tiryn's confusion.

Myka shook his head. "It's only fair. There are no hard feelings. It was an old family that made the claim, we've known them for a long time. Times are tough, with your current king and his army. At least the women and children will be safe while we build a new home here."

"I don't understand," Tiryn said. "Your homes were stolen from you?"

"Myka and his family are wyres, Tiryn," Roland answered.

Tiryn felt his eyebrows lift. "Really?" He looked Myka over again, but he seemed … normal. As human as Roland was. But there was still the stink of animals about the place, though none had yet to make an appearance.

Roland continued as if he hadn't heard Tiryn. "I'm assuming one of the wyre families to the far north was discovered and run out?"

Myka nodded, then met Tiryn's stare with his own. "Wyres make a practice out of claiming land to settle on, rather than purchasing like humans do. If another family disputes a land claim, then the family alphas fight to resolve it. When that first family was run out by Mothlenor's army, it caused a ripple of disputes and upheavals. A lot of families have lost homes that they've lived in for a couple of centuries. It's been a very difficult time."

Tiryn nodded slowly. "I imagine it will only get worse over time."

"The only way to break that chain is to claim and settle new land." Myka smiled, looking across to Roland. "Which is why we're here."

Tiryn looked around the clearing again. "So all of this is you trying to build a new town?"

"This is just an outpost of sorts. The real work is being done a bit further inland."

"And the dock on the shoreline? You built that?" Roland asked.

"For trading, yes." Myka's mouth twitched into a wry smile. "When we're ready."

"I don't understand what this has to do with our uncle Tomas, though," Alastor said, pulling his tunic back over his head and sweeping his black hair back from his face. "If they never came here, then where did he and his crew go?"

Myka sighed, drumming the fingers of one hand against the rough wood of the table. "They were here, though. For a night, at least. Luka can tell you more about it." Myka turned, waving over the youngest of the wyres. Luka seemed to have been waiting for such an invitation, and moved with an almost preternatural speed at Myka's beckon, at his side in a second and taking the last seat at the table.

"This is Luka?" Roland asked with a soft chuckle. He extended a hand to the young man, and with a nod from Myka, Luka accepted it. "The last time I saw you, you were still a screaming babe."

"Aunt Myra's told me stories about you," Luka said with a smirk. "The swordsman that stole her heart and then stole her horse."

Roland laughed, shaking his head. "Myra still has a way with words, I see."

"Luka, tell these people about the sailors that came to our outpost a few months ago," Myka said, draining his mug and turning to the boy expectantly.

"It was closer to six or seven months ago, actually," Luka began. "It was a fairly normal afternoon, until we heard several people stumbling through the woods from the beach. We aren't ready to accept traders or visitors, and they sounded drunk and rowdy. So I made the decision to pull everyone out of the outpost and watch them from the surrounding woods until we had a better idea of who had arrived."

"Like you did with us?" Tiryn asked.

Luka turned a pair of warm amber eyes towards Tiryn and smirked. "Exactly as we did with you."

"Luka …" Myka warned. "Play nice, these are friends."

"Like you ever play nice," Roland said with a snort.

Luka's smirk became a genuine smile at the comment, and Tiryn noted a strong resemblance between Luka and Myka. "You made the decision to watch them?"

"I wasn't present when this occurred," Myka answered, accepting another mug from a third wyre with a murmur of thanks. "Luka is my son, which makes him the family's beta." Myka motioned for Luka to continue his story.

"There were several people. Eleven, to be exact. More than we could handle if it came to a fight." Luka crossed his arms over his chest, leaning the crate he sat on back until it stood on only one edge. "So I decided to let them be and see if they left. Until my father returned, at least, and we would have a better chance of dealing with them if things got ugly." He sighed. "They ended up staying the night. We had a few members of the family keeping watch on them throughout the night. They were pretty loud, but mostly harmless. They kept arguing over a map. Something about making port somewhere along the coast, but they couldn't decide where. There was a bit of a row." Luka chuckled suddenly. "But everyone was so drunk, it was more amusing than dangerous. They must have come to some sort of agreement, because they left early the next morning and returned to their ship." The young wyre shrugged. "We never saw them again."

"The question is, did they go to the next port or did they set sail in search of the Isle of Onia?" Tiryn asked.

Myka clicked his tongue a few times, fingering a knot in the table. "The nearest port of any reputable size is another few days or so further along the coast. It's possible they went there. Unless they turned back the way they came."

Roland shook his head. "I doubt it. Their ship was stolen. They were likely intent on staying as far ahead of the King's Guard and the Mercantile Guild as possible."

"Then it sounds like you're headed for the Isle of Onia." Myka drained the rest of his water and thumped the empty mug down.

Roland laughed. "Where do you go to find a mythical island?"

"I think we'll need a bird's-eye view, Roland," Tiryn said pointedly.

Roland grunted, giving Tiryn a side glance, but he said nothing.

"There you have it, I suppose." Myke shrugged, getting to his feet. "Whatever that means."

Tiryn's brow furrowed, and he looked Myka over once more. "Can I ask you one more question before we leave?"

Myka nodded enthusiastically. "Sure, sure. Anything."

"What kind of wyres are you?" Luka's eyes widened in shock at the question, and Roland and Myka simultaneously barked in laughter. Tiryn frowned again, surprised at their responses. "There are types of wyres, aren't there?"

Myka nodded, his laughter dwindling to a few chuckles. "There are different types, yes. But it's not a polite question to ask."

Tiryn felt his cheeks warm. "I'm sorry. I didn't know."

"I made the same mistake many years ago, Tiryn," Roland said, still laughing. "It's nice to hear someone usually so polite do the same."

The warming sensation crept up to Tiryn's ear tips, and he stammered out another apology before Myka waved his words away dismissively. "It's not very often anymore that the different races are able to interact so freely together. I take no insult, and only add that it's an honor for an outsider to see a wyre in his animal form. We do not give that information away freely." Myka stood, beckoning for Luka to do the same. "But for now, you have your answers, and I'm sure that you have a captain waiting for you." Myka smirked, then reached for Roland's hand. "It was good to see you again, Roland. Myra will be very happy to hear that you're doing well."

"I can only hope that we run into each other again soon, Myka. I can never repay you for the kindness your family showed me." Roland took the wyre's hand then pulled him into another embrace.

<hr>

They returned to the ship, Tiryn leading the way back to their raft and letting Roland follow behind Alastor and Roland. The waters were as calm and clear as they had been on the way to shore, and Tiryn was reluctant to return to the confines of their cabin after feeling the sun on his face and sand and earth under his feet. At least the salty sea air would stay with him, and there was always nightfall to look forward to, when he would be allowed to walk the deck under the stars.

Mathius was waiting on the deck of the ship, his arms crossed as he stood at the railing. "Well?" he asked. He didn't even wait for the four of them to scramble out of the raft. Jaimes and Alastor hurried past, heading straight for the stairs to the cabins below. "Did you find him?"

Roland shook his head, giving Tiryn a careful look as they worked together to secure the raft to the aft side of the ship. "Just a small settlement of displaced Etritians. They remember Tomas and his friends coming through, but they had nothing to offer them." He fastened the final knot with a hard tug. "They moved on, bound for the Isle of Onia."

"Shit," Mathius grumbled. "How can we possibly find them?"

"Perhaps it's time to give it up, Mathius," a tall man called from across the deck. "If Tomas was not at this settlement, and if he is not at the next port, then perhaps our friends should part from our company and search for him elsewhere."

"Dammit, Reed." Mathius turned towards the sailor, giving him a glare. "This whole adventure might be for the sake of finding that boy's uncle, but you know it's my ship I really want. And if I can find those damned thieves and get the *Seahawk* back, then it'll be worth the trouble of chasing them all around the coast of Azimar."

"But they aren't on the coast." Reed's voice was scathing, and he eyed Mathius with a stony glare. "They're out in the Southern Sea, headed Great Ones only know where. You asked the question well enough yourself, Mathius. How can we possibly find them?"

"I think we might be in luck there, Mathius," Tiryn said. "We happen to know a pair of elves that could help us find the *Seahawk*."

2 0

MATHIUS

"You can't still think this is a good idea, Mathius?" Reed asked, hot on his heels as he climbed the stairs from the lower hold up to the cabins.

"I do." Mathius counted the freshest lines in his ledger, careful not to smear the drying ink. *The hold should be fairly empty after bringing all of this to port. All the more room to stock up on supplies before heading after the* Seahawk.

"If I didn't know better, I would think you've gone mad."

"Then I'm glad you know better." Mathius crossed in front of the open door to the cabin the elves and Roland shared. It was quiet inside, but he could see Tiryn pacing the floor. "I plan on taking all the precautions I can, and I've only given them three days."

"Only three days?" Reed rushed around him, stopping in front of him on the lowest stair up to the deck. "Three days sailing out into open and uncharted waters with nothing but the word of a pair of elf children to say that we are headed in the right direction."

Mathius sighed, scratching at his beard. "Yes, Reed. Three days. We'll sail on a curved trajectory. If nothing comes of

144

our detour, we can make it back to the coastline and the next port with little impact to our schedule. We can make up the time."

"It's not the lost time I'm concerned with."

"Then what is it you're concerned with?" Mathius snapped.

Reed hesitated, but his gaze shot over Mathius's shoulder. When Mathius turned, it was to see Tiryn pacing, his chin cradled in one hand.

"Oh, Great Ones take it, Reed." Mathius stormed around the sailor and climbed the stairs to the deck, barking out an order at a pair of passing crewmen. "I wish you would stop with that nonsense."

"I'm not the one dealing in nonsense."

Mathius sighed, closing his eyes and rolling his shoulders. They ached terribly, though he had done little to work them up. *Perhaps it's just the stress of this journey getting to me. It'll be over soon enough, and if I can get my ship back ...*

He took a deep breath and held it for a moment. Reed stared at him expectantly, arms crossed. Mathius let the air out slowly through his nose, matching Reed's narrowed gaze. "Three days."

Reed huffed, turning away from Mathius.

"Head down to the market and get double the usual, will you?" Mathius called after him.

Reed waved a hand over his shoulder, already heading for the port.

"No, get triple the usual. And take Evert with you!"

Reed tapped a large sailor on the shoulder and motioned for him to follow.

"And get my damned money from that thieving port master!"

Reed waved a hand over his shoulder again, the motion sharper than the first.

"Increasing the port tax again, fucking unbelievable …" Mathius muttered.

"Everything alright, Captain?"

Mathius jumped, nearly dropping his ledger. "Master Brynne." Mathius turned to see the small man standing terribly close, one large book tucked into the crook of his arm. "I didn't hear you come up the stairs."

Brynne tapped the side of his nose with one thin finger. "It's from years of walking around the Azimar Archives, my dear captain. You learn how to be silent when one misstep could send a herd of rampaging librarians after you."

The image of a dozen men looking remarkably like Brynne crossed Mathius's mind, and he smiled at the thought. "I see. How can I help you, Master Brynne?"

"I was going to ask you the same, actually." Brynne straightened to his full height, bringing him another inch or two closer to Mathius's own height. "I have quite the record with settling little spats back home. I would be happy to try my ministrations with you and Mister Reed."

Mathius laughed, but quickly stopped when he saw that Brynne's expression did not change. "No, no, Master Brynne. Reed will cool down of his own accord. We might not always see things the same way, but he's faithful. We'll both go about our own duties and pretend this little disagreement never happened." Mathius guided Brynne away from the stairwell as a small group of sailors emerged from the hold below with assorted goods slung over their shoulders. "It's not the first time we've had our differences, and it likely won't be the last. But I know Reed will always be there to nag and heckle me."

"You have a lot of faith in him, Mathius," Brynne said. "It's nice to see that you can still trust your crewmen, after what happened to your first ship."

Mathius snorted, making a small check next to a line of text in his ledger as another sailor crossed the deck to the dock. "You heard about that, did you?"

"It wasn't exactly hard to hear about. Some of the other merchants in Emery were practically singing about the theft of the *Seahawk*."

"Of course they were," Mathius muttered. *That fucking pest Artran. It wasn't enough that I had to tell the Mercantile Guild, but for him to go and spread it around like wildfire ...*

"I hear we're going to go searching for your ship out in the Southern Sea?"

Mathius nodded. "If you'd rather not come with us, I can understand. We can wait for you to collect your belongings and escort you to an inn if you need it. Another vessel will here within a week or two that can take you the rest of the way to Cusch."

Brynne scoffed. "And miss out on such an adventure as sailing for the mythical Isle of Onia? Nonsense."

"It could be dangerous."

Brynne shrugged. "With the company of three fine elves and a sturdy dwarf, I have nothing to fear from a little danger."

Mathius sighed. He wasn't sure he wanted the small fellow on his ship for what could end up being a risky expedition. But he couldn't very well turn him away, either. *The money he gave me for his journey would go a long way to replacing the* Seahawk *if it can't be found or salvaged.* Mathius nodded, extending a hand to Brynne. "Very well then, Master Brynne."

Brynne shook his hand, his grip surprisingly firm for such a feeble-looking scholar. "Good. Now please excuse me. I can smell some delicious pastries down at the end of the harbor, and they are calling my name."

The small man descended the gangplank to the dock, his huge book still held firmly against his chest. Brynne wove his way through a handful of sailors and fishermen with an ease that Mathius could only assume he had picked up working in the Archives. He lost sight of Brynne in the milling crowd of fishermen rushing across the dock on the far end. He sighed, scratching at his beard and taking up his usual position at the foot of the gangplank. "This will be an adventure, alright."

21

ROLAND

Roland stepped carefully down the steep ramp, a small cask of some sloshing liquid under each arm, grateful to be back on solid ground for a short time. Mathius waved him over, inspecting the casks and making a quick note.

"Those can be taken down to that red-faced fellow down there." Mathius jerked a thumb over his shoulder to indicate a plump man in his later days with a large nose and thinning hair. "And when you've finished, go ahead and take some time to enjoy the town. We can finish up on our own."

"Are you certain? I don't mind helping."

Mathius smiled. "It's not you I'm worried about, it's the boys." Mathius's eyes shifted to a spot behind Roland and his smile seemed to deepen for a moment. "I'm not quite sure they're cut out to be sailors just yet."

Roland turned and spotted the pair of young men struggling down the ramp with a cage of chickens held between them.

"Let them get some fresh air. Maybe buy them a drink, get some hair growing on their chests." Mathius snorted as Jaimes's grip slipped, and one corner of the cage hit the wooden deck with a metallic crash and loud squawking. "Be back within an hour, I think, and we can get back out on the open water soon enough."

Within a few minutes, the casks had been delivered to their new owners, the chickens had been sent off to be sold, and Roland walked between Alastor and Jaimes through the village surrounding the small dock the *Kingfisher* waited in.

It was a dirty town, so small that Roland couldn't remember the name of it, or if his map even had a name for the smudge of dirt so many called home. There was a scattering of houses on one side with a building that doubled as both an inn and a tavern. The attached stable was large enough for perhaps three horses, but Roland saw nothing to indicate that anything was stabled. There were a couple of vendors lining the street, and Roland bought a dozen small cakes from a fat baker for a single gold piece. He passed one to each of the boys, and they chewed through them slowly as they meandered down the town's single dirt road.

"It's kind of a sad little place, isn't it?" Alastor asked through a mouthful of pastry.

"I didn't realize places could be so small," Jaimes said.

Roland scuffed at a small patch of green peeking through a crack in the hard-packed earth of the street. "Places can be as big or as small as they want to be." He looked up and around, squinting against the afternoon sun. "I've seen smaller. Villages that were just a few tired houses grouped together. I guess you can't really call that a village, though." He worked at the persistent weed with the toe of one shoe, working the roots loose from the soil.

"What about bigger?" Jaimes asked. "What's the biggest place you've ever been to, Roland?"

"Etritia, probably," Roland answered, not realizing his mistake until Alastor let out a small gasp.

"You've been to Etritia? My mother was from there."

Roland shrugged, cursing himself. "I've seen it, yes."

"She used to tell us stories about the place. Is it as nice as she said it was?"

Roland thought for a moment, his gaze still on the ground in front of him. "It was, once." He finally worked the roots of the stunted weed free, and kicked it to land a few feet away. "Not anymore."

"Oh," Alastor murmured.

There was a hesitant pause; Roland looked up again to survey the street—and caught sight of a familiar figure weaving through the few pedestrians still on the road.

"We can still go, Alastor. Once we find Uncle Tomas. We can go to Etritia ourselves, right, Roland?"

Roland hardly heard Jaimes's question. "Sure, if you want." He was still tracking the tall blond as he disappeared behind a worn-out shed. He held what looked like a letter in one hand, tapping it lightly against one leg as he walked. "You two stay here for a moment, will you?" He passed the wrapped package containing the remainder of the sweets to Alastor. "Don't eat those. And don't run off."

Alastor only shrugged, and Roland tousled his hair gently before stepping around the pair of them and started after the man he'd spotted.

He followed Reed down to the town's inn, which seemed to be the only lively spot around. Roland slid into the dimly lit building only a moment after Reed and quietly sat in a dark corner where he might be overlooked. He spotted Reed easily enough, the sailor's shock of light hair making him hard to miss at the far end of the bar. The room was mostly empty, but the few patrons were loud enough to prevent Roland from eavesdropping on Reed's conversation with the man behind the counter. Roland could only watch as Reed passed the letter over to the innkeeper and dropped a few coins onto the counter.

Roland's view of the exchange was suddenly blocked by a slim-waisted figure standing over him.

"Anything you'd like?"

Roland looked up at the woman blocking his view. "Sorry?"

She smirked at him, something like greed shining in her eyes. "Do you see anything you'd like?"

"No." Roland looked her over, shaking his head. "I didn't come for that."

The woman frowned at him. "You want a drink at least?"

"No."

She stepped aside, pointing at the nearby door. "Then get out. We don't allow squatters."

Roland glanced at the bar, sighing when he saw Reed's seat now empty. "I was just on my way."

He felt the woman's eyes on him as he left the tavern, but his attention was more focused on where Reed had disappeared to. He'd only been distracted for a few seconds, and yet Reed had managed to slip away without him noticing. *Great Ones damn that woman*, Roland thought sourly.

Roland began the short walk back to Alastor and Jaimes, watching for any sign of the blond sailor along the way. He reached the boys without spotting him and took the wrapped package of sweet breads back from Alastor without a word.

"You just missed Reed," Alastor said.

"I did?" Roland scanned the road back to the docks. He spotted Reed down the road, his light-colored head weaving between the other men bustling around the dock.

"He said the *Kingfisher* would be leaving soon, and that we should get back if we don't want to leave our friends alone for too long."

"He's probably right," Roland said. He watched as Reed rose to the deck of the *Kingfisher*, pausing briefly to glance back in Roland's direction. "Come on, we should get going."

Roland guided the two boys back to the waiting ship, motioning for them to go on without him up the ramp. Mathius was making notations in his ledger, and Roland waited patiently for him to finish before addressing him. "I need a word, Mathius."

The captain looked up at him, an eyebrow raised. "Did you get those boys a drink?"

"Do you trust the men on your ship?"

Mathius scoffed. "I trust that they'll do as I ask, so long as I pay them." He narrowed his gaze, glancing quickly up at the busy deck of the *Kingfisher*. "Why? Should I not?"

Roland crossed his arms over his chest, sighing. "I'm not sure." He glanced around them to ensure the dock was fairly empty, then leaned closer to Mathius. "Do you think any of them would turn you in? For carrying elves?"

"Not if they want to get their money." Mathius laughed. "I think perhaps you're being a bit paranoid."

"Perhaps. But ..."

"But what?"

"I saw something. Reed, carrying a letter to the inn. I thought maybe he was sending a complaint to the King's Guard."

Mathius frowned, letting out an exasperated sigh. "It could have been any kind of letter, being sent to anyone."

"Perhaps."

Mathius raised a hand to quiet Roland. "And out of all those men up there, Reed is the one I trust the most. He has his problems. Most do. But he's been loyal to me, and if I ask him to look the other way for a few weeks, then he'll look the other way."

"Are you sure?" Roland asked. *If Mathius is wrong, if Tiryn and the others are captured ...*

"I'm sure, Roland." He patted Roland on the shoulder, snapping his ledger shut and waving up to the deck of the *Kingfisher*. "Now come on, let's get out of here. This place always makes me a bit depressed."

22

MATHIUS

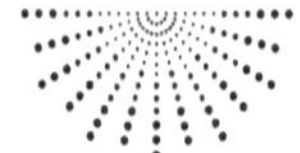

Mathius watched Roland follow the two young boys back to their cabin, his shoulders tense as he walked. Roland had hardly disappeared down the steps to the hold when a gruff voice spoke up behind him.

"Captain. A word, if you don't mind."

Mathius turned, letting out a frustrated sigh at the sight of his second standing just behind him. "Reed. Just the man I was looking for."

"I came across the two boys out in the town. Alone." Reed's face was drawn into a scowl, his tanned arms crossed angrily over his broad chest.

Mathius brushed past the man, knowing he would follow, and took to double-checking the last batch of merchandise that had been brought up from the dock. "I know, Reed. I sent them off the ship to enjoy themselves. They're hard-working boys, but they were getting in the way."

"And their guardian?" Reed asked pointedly.

Mathius snorted. "I'd hardly call Roland their guardian." He knelt to inspect a roll of deer pelts on their way north. "Clean, minimal tool marks. Good quality, as usual," he muttered to himself.

Reed waited for him to straighten, then stepped in front of him as he turned to continue his inspection. "They shouldn't have been left alone. And perhaps Roland shouldn't be left to wander the ship unsupervised."

Mathius huffed. "Reed, I don't have time to indulge your moral quandaries at the moment. What exactly are you wanting?"

"I want them kept under a watchful eye, Mathius. All of them." Mathius snorted, opening his mouth to protest, but Reed cut him off with an upraised hand. "It would be for the good of everyone on this ship."

"Treating our guests as so much unruly cattle?"

"We could keep them out of trouble. And keep ourselves out of trouble, as well."

"Your meaning?"

"Great Ones damn you, Mathius," Reed growled, stepping closer. "You know as well as I do that it's illegal to carry non-human passengers. They should not be here! If someone—" Reed bit the rest of his words, glancing quickly around them before continuing in a lower voice. "If someone were to send notice to Etritia … If there were King's Guards waiting for us at one of the next ports …"

Mathius laughed softly. "Funny that you should bring up those concerns."

Reed frowned, brows pinching together. "Why?"

"Because Roland just brought the same worries to me not five minutes ago."

Reed was silent for a moment, eyes flat and blank. "Roland thinks I would be the one to betray them."

"You have made it easy for him to distrust you, Reed." Mathius stepped around the other man, making the final comments in his ledger. They would be ready to depart soon, and as soon as Roland and his company found Tomas and the *Seahawk* this mess could be behind them.

"Just as he has made it easy for me to distrust him," Reed

snarled. "He travels with elves and a dwarf. He has no concern for the law—"

Mathius rounded on Reed. "And when it comes to that particular law, I have no concern for it either." Reed fell back a step, eyes wide and mouth agape. "No one will be treating anyone else on this ship with anything less than civility."

"Civility and legality are not the same thing, Mathius."

Mathius snorted. "Life would be a lot simpler if they were."

Reed sighed, arching his back and staring at the bright sky through slitted lids. Mathius heard small snaps and cracks where the sailor's spine popped and the joints stretched. "Let's be reasonable with each other for a moment."

Mathius shifted his feet further apart, squaring his shoulders. "Alright. Let's."

Reed raised a finger. "Only one of the non-humans on the deck at a time. For an hour."

Mathius nodded. "I suppose that's fine."

"And not during any periods when they might get underfoot, or when we're close to any ports or any other ships. If only to make sure they aren't spotted, and the Guild doesn't revoke your membership."

Mathius gritted his teeth. "Fine."

Reed sighed again. "And I think we both know that the rest of the crew would be a lot more comfortable if they were watched by someone while they were up on the deck."

Mathius shook his head. "I will not have my men following them around. They have as much right to their privacy as we do, and I won't take that from them."

"What if we asked Roland and the two boys to be their keepers instead? Tell the elves that it's for their own protection. They're less likely to be bothered if one of the others is with them." Reed shrugged. "It wouldn't be a lie."

"I don't like it."

Reed gave him a pained smile. "You don't have to like it to agree that it's the best way to make sure everyone gets what they want. The men want to pretend we don't have illegals on our ship. The boys and Roland want to find Tomas." Reed waved his hand at Mathius. "You want to find your ship. And the elves want whatever the elves want."

Mathius scowled. "They just want to be treated like guests, and not animals. They want to see the sun, Reed."

Reed nodded. "Then they can see the sun, and help us find the *Seahawk*. If they follow the rules."

Mathius sighed. "Fine. I still don't like it, but fine." He snapped his ledger shut, letting the sharp snap convey what he couldn't find the words to say. "Now get us out of here, Reed."

Reed squared his shoulders, lifting his chin. "Yes, Captain."

"Just get a move on it," Mathius barked. Then, before Reed could leave, he added, "And thank you for trusting me, Reed."

Reed's body relaxed, and he gave Mathius a curt nod before turning on his heel and shouting orders to the sailors milling about the deck.

"Problem, Captain?"

Mathius once again turned to find someone standing just behind his shoulder. Brynne was climbing the ramp up to the deck, head cocked and his usual cheery smile lighting his face. His heavy book was still tucked under one arm, and he held a wrapped package in his opposite hand.

"Nothing serious, Master Brynne," Mathius said, forcing a smile.

"Still having your scuffle with Reed?" Brynne asked, tapping an ink-stained finger against his equally ink-stained nose.

"Nothing that requires your intervention, I assure you." Mathius widened his smile, resisting the urge to shout curses at the sky above. *Great Ones take it, I fear my head will explode before I ever lay eyes on the* Seahawk *again.*

"You know what might help?" Brynne held out the wrapped package, offering it to Mathius. "One of these sticky buns. I've found that sweets are always an excellent remedy to even the shortest of tempers. Would you care to indulge?"

"No, thank you, Master Brynne," Mathius said, giving the short scholar a stiff bow. He wondered how much of a splash such a small man might make if he were thrown overboard. "We'll be leaving port momentarily. It would be best if you returned to your quarters."

Brynne nodded enthusiastically, slipping his package of sticky buns into the inside of his vest. "Of course, Mathius. Let me know if you change your mind about the sweets."

Mathius forced another smile to match the one Brynne gave him. "I'm sure I won't."

Brynne shrugged, scuttling around Mathius to descend the steps to the hold. "More for me, then!"

Mathius let out an annoyed sigh as Brynne disappeared. He stared down at the half-lit landing of the first level of the hold. His own quarters were down there. And there was a half bottle of expensive Cardyn red, a gift to himself when he first became a captain. *Perhaps a taste of wine and a bit of shut-eye will—*

"Mathius."

"Great Ones damn it all, what now?"

Reed appeared before him, flecks of sweat and seawater staining his face. "We're ready to depart." Behind him, sailors stood with halyards gripped in dirty and calloused hands, waiting for the order to raise sails.

"Excellent," Mathius said with a sigh. *The wine will have to wait, I suppose ...*

"Shall I take the helm?" Reed's face was still stern and unpleasant, but there was a certain glint in his eyes that suggested all had been forgiven between them, even if all was not wholly forgotten.

"That …" Mathius started, thinking of the cool darkness of his quarters. He sighed, giving Reed a small smile. "That would be very much appreciated. I just need an hour of quiet, no more."

Reed gave him a quick nod, turning to shout to the men on the decks. They immediately jumped into motion, hoisting sails and gathering pooling lines and shouting amongst themselves. Reed stepped around Mathius, heading for the helm, but Mathius stopped him with a hand around his upper arm.

"Reed." Mathius narrowed his eyes at his second. "If you hear anything from the men about sending notice off to the king regarding our passengers, remind them that there is easy money to be had if they just keep their mouths shut. They don't have to like it, but I know they'll still put up with it for a good bit of coin."

"And if these kinds of passengers become routine?" Reed asked, his gaze once again hard. "Do you think they will still keep silent?"

Mathius thought for a moment, letting his grip on Reed's arm drop. "I won't take be taking non-human passengers again, I suppose."

Reed's face softened. "I can admire what you're doing, Mathius, though I doubt many of the crew would understand. But it is still illegal."

Mathius nodded. "I know, Reed. But I will not ask for your forgiveness." Reed nodded, his eyes once again showing that small glint, and he hurried to the helm. "An hour, Reed. No more. Or they might start to think that you're the captain, and not me."

Reed only waved an irritated hand at him.

Mathius snorted, then jogged down into the blissful coolness of the hold, where his half bottle of Cardyn wine waited patiently for him.

23

MELONYA

Melonya waited until nightfall to leave the cold waters of the Southern Sea. It had been a struggle at first, trying to figure out how to make the leap from water to sky. But she soon figured out that if she propelled herself hard enough, she could emerge from the surface of the water with enough momentum to ease the transition from swimming to flying. It was not easy, and it was not graceful, but it could be done.

She reached out to touch her mind to Roland's. As her conscious mind brushed against his subconscious one, the bitter tang of regret filled her mouth and weighed her body down for the briefest of moments. But the feeling faded as Roland acknowledged her presence.

"On your way already?"

"I can find the Seahawk *better from the sky than I can from the sea."* Melonya shook herself, disgusted with how the motion resembled a dog shaking water from its fur, and turned on silent wings to head south. *"Did anyone notice anything?"*

"No. We got lucky. The moon will be full in a few days. You would have been spotted easily if not for the cloudy skies."

Melonya made a sound that was as close to a laugh as she could manage. *"That isn't luck, Roland. Tathiel and Tiryn are pulling moisture from the air and sea to conceal me. It will dissipate in a short time."*

Roland was silent for a second, and Melonya took the time to enjoy the sensation of wind rushing over her scales and along the underside of the thick webbing of her wings. It felt good to be in the air again. She felt alive and complete in a way that only flight could bring her. The only thing that could improve the feeling would be having Tathiel and Eilonwy on her back. And if the salt drying between her scales was not there.

"I didn't realize they could do something so complicated," Roland finally said.

"It is not easy. It will tire them both out. Tathiel especially, I think. His arcane talents are not as strong as Tiryn's." Melonya stretched her neck, breathing in the cold air. She could smell the humans on the ship below her; they smelled of sweat and dirt and hate. Hate towards her Riders, as well as the dwarf and Tiryn. It was the most unpleasant scent in the stink that rose from the *Kingfisher,* and Melonya was glad to be leaving it behind. *"Eilonwy will stay in contact with me while her brother rests. And if the need arises, she can help Tiryn procure more clouds."*

Melonya's connection with Roland was fading, though she was not far from the ship. Roland must have sensed it. Before they broke contact, he wished her luck. *"I hope you find the* Seahawk *quickly. I know the twins will not be happy until you've returned."*

Before Melonya could reply, the link between their minds severed.

She was only alone for a moment, then Eilonwy's mind brushed against hers in greeting. Melonya caught the tether that led back to Eilonwy's consciousness and anchored it to her own.

"How is Tathiel?"

"Tired," came Eilonwy's reply. The familiar feel of her mind calmed the anxious beat of Melonya's heart. *"He'll sleep well tonight. He and Tiryn have already stopped feeding energy into the clouds. They should be dissipating."*

Melonya sensed the shift in the air as the clouds began to thin. They would not hold for very long without the magic that pulled them together. *"And you? Will you sleep tonight?"*

"No. I will stay with you. I don't like the idea of you being out there alone."

The muscles along her spine relaxed, and Melonya was ashamed of the relief that she felt at Eilonwy's words. *"Thank you. I don't cherish the thought of being apart from you and Tathiel."*

"You'll be home soon," Eilonwy said with a small laugh. *"How long can it take to find a ship out on its own in the sea?"*

Mothlenor and Anna were already waiting for him by the time Ferrand made his way into the council hall. He would have been more surprised if only Mothlenor had made it, and if Anna had been absent. But the king was sure to always keep his pretty pet close by, and Ferrand knew they had been working together in his study when Ferrand's message found Mothlenor.

The king sat in his usual place, across from the empty head of the table, and Ferrand noted the small look of distaste that pursed his lips together as he sat straight and stiff.

Anna was seated just beside him, hands folded demurely and resting on the smooth wood in front of her, her hair done in a loose braid that curled over one shoulder and over her chest. She stared ahead at some spot above Ferrand's head, avoiding his gaze. From this distance Ferrand couldn't smell the light scent of her jasmine oils, but the sight of her called the memory of them to him, and he briefly entertained the thought of wrapping the length of her dark hair around her neck until her body went limp. And then …

"I hope you've called us down here to discuss news about Ajax, Ferrand. I'm not sure I have the tolerance for anything else at the moment," Mothlenor said.

Ferrand slowed his steps, nearing his seat, and bowed. "That's precisely why I asked for your company, my lord. I've received another letter from my spy."

"Oh?" Mothlenor arched one silver-brown eyebrow, motioning for Ferrand to take his place. "And was the news good?"

Ferrand slid into the seat across from Anna, smiling at the eagerness he could hear in Mothlenor's voice. "He is certain that the man is Ajax, though he's been using the name 'Roland' instead."

"Was he able to get aboard the ship with him?"

"Yes. He's given descriptions of each of his companions, including the two boys traveling with him. Additionally, he's sent me the ship's schedule, and their estimated arrivals at several of the ports along the southern and eastern coasts." Ferrand chanced a quick glance at Anna, but her face was blank, her gaze still fixed on some distant spot.

"And you have a plan on how to proceed?" There was an unpleasant edge to Mothlenor's voice—either because he had seen Ferrand's wandering gaze, or because he was reminded of how well Ferrand's last dealing with Ajax had ended.

Ferrand scowled up at his king. *The man was all but dead. His blood stained that stretch of earth for weeks afterward. He should not have survived.*

To Mothlenor he only said, "I have a plan, yes. Ajax shouldn't be a problem for too much longer."

"And what about the children?" Anna asked suddenly, surprising Ferrand.

"You mean the two boys? What about them?" Ferrand asked, delighting in the way her eyes couldn't quite meet his.

"They're innocent." Anna looked from Mothlenor to

Ferrand and back again as if searching for confirmation from the king.

Ferrand scoffed. "I'd hardly call two young men traveling with a couple of base creatures and a known criminal innocent, Anna."

She never looked away from Mothlenor, ignoring Ferrand's protest altogether. "They're just children," she repeated. Her voice was firm, not pleading, and Ferrand hated the confidence in her words.

An hour alone with her, and I can make sure she never speaks up like that again.

Mothlenor hesitated for a moment, then nodded once, turning back to Ferrand. "Anna is right. They are innocent." Anna sighed, giving Mothlenor a soft look of gratitude, but he continued without giving her a second glance. "They should be brought in for questioning but left unharmed. If one of them is indeed the son of my brother's adviser, then perhaps he knows what Areanath tasked his father with."

Ferrand nearly choked. "My lord, I don't recommend—"

"I think I understand what you may or may not recommend, Ferrand," Mothlenor snarled. "But I have given my opinion on the matter."

Ferrand chewed his tongue for a moment, a muscle in the ruined side of his face twitching unpleasantly as he fought to control his anger. *That stupid bitch. She doesn't understand anything. She needs to learn to let the men do the thinking for her, and to keep her mouth shut and her legs open.* And with that thought, Ferrand's mind once again pulled together the fantasized image of Anna's face in the midst of sexual pleasure, Ferrand's hand fastened around her pale neck. He went hard, his shoulders relaxing and his anger at Mothlenor dissolving. "Yes, my lord."

"Is there any additional news you've come to share?" Mothlenor asked.

Had there been anything else? He couldn't remember now.

In his mind's eye, his fingers tightened around Anna's neck, deep enough to leave lasting marks. Her face darkened slightly, but the expression on her face hardly changed. *Would I kill her, if such a chance arose?*

"No, my lord."

"Then I'll call this council meeting adjourned. Dismissed."

Mothlenor had hardly finished the word before Anna was out of her chair, heading for the exit. Ferrand got to his feet half a heartbeat behind her. *Time to see if a small lesson in manners can't still be taught.*

"Ferrand," Mothlenor called. "Another moment of your time."

Ferrand hesitated, watching Anna slip from the room and out of sight. He wanted to curse and chase after her, but he turned and gave Mothlenor a short bow. "Yes, my lord?"

"How well do you trust your spy?"

Ferrand frowned, the muscle in his face twitching again. "He's one of the better ones. Very adept. And loyal."

"Good," Mothlenor said, eyes narrowing. "Because if your plan fails, he might need to step in and take care of Ajax himself."

Ferrand snorted, momentarily forgetting about Anna. "*If my plan fails, my lord, you might need to step in yourself to kill the man, because surviving might mean he's been granted some sort of arcane blessing. Send your shadows, if my plan fails. Or rain fire down around him, and end him that way.*" Ferrand smiled. "But my plan will not fail."

"Good," Mothlenor repeated. "Because my shadows could not make the trip to the coasts to destroy Ajax. They have yet to recover from their last excursion into Vyris."

"I see. Still sending them to hunt for the lost egg?"

"If I had another Dragon's Eye, it wouldn't be quite so difficult to find." There was a venomous bite to Mothlenor's words that made the muscle in Ferrand's face twitch in irritation.

Ferrand scowled. "I'll find you another Dragon's Eye. And I'll kill Ajax."

"Good."

2 5

E I L O N W Y

Eilonwy leaned against the railing of the *Kingfisher*'s deck, looking out across the water. It had been four days since Melonya left in search of the *Seahawk*, and Mathius had reluctantly angled their course back to the shoreline. But Melonya was still out there, and there had been no word from her in over a day. It had been difficult enough to not worry about their closest companion when she and Tathiel could still stay in contact with Melonya, but it was near impossible when the distance between them grew too great for even their close bond to hold together.

"Dammit all, come back to us!" Eilonwy cast her thoughts out across the sea, hoping they might find Melonya.

"She'll return. Don't worry." The reply was Tathiel's, from down in their cabin below. He sounded sure, but there was a nearly imperceptible lilt to his words that betrayed his own concerns for Melonya.

"Eilonwy?"

Eilonwy started, looking down at Jaimes, who sat on the deck at her feet. "What?"

Jaimes frowned, the creases in his brow deepening. "I asked if you were alright. You seem worried."

169

Eilonwy smiled, shrugging a shoulder. "I'm fine."

Jaimes raised an eyebrow, giving her a skeptical look. "Are you upset that you and Tathiel weren't able to find the Isle of Onia? Or the *Seahawk*?"

"A little." Eilonwy turned to press her back to the railing. "There were a lot of people counting on us. Mathius wanted so badly to reclaim his stolen ship." She tucked a strand of hair behind her ear. Jaimes was staring up at her, his eyes wide. "And you and Alastor …"

Jaimes shook his head. "There's nothing that can be done about it now." He gave her a sympathetic look. "My uncle made the choice to sail off on a stolen ship. He could be home with us, if not for that."

"You would be fine giving up the search and going back to Larten?" Eilonwy asked.

"I … I don't know." Jaimes crossed his arms over his chest, shivering slightly at the cool wind that blew across the deck. "I think I might like to stay."

Eilonwy took a seat beside him, crossing one ankle over the other and nudging Jaimes's shoulder with her own. "I think we might like it if you did."

Jaimes gave her a quick smile, but said nothing. He shivered again, and Eilonwy caught the way his jaw tightened as he tried to keep his teeth from chattering.

"Do we need to go back down below deck?"

"No," Jaimes said firmly, shaking his head. "I want to stay up here with you. This will be your only chance to leave the cabin until nightfall."

"Yes, but you're freezing." Eilonwy huffed, catching sight of Reed at the aft end of the ship in conversation with a thin deckhand. She pitched her voice louder, hoping her complaint might reach the sailor's ears. "It's ridiculous that I need an escort just to get a little fresh air. You shouldn't have to catch a chill for something so silly."

Reed turned, a scowl stretching across his face, but he made no move toward them.

"I don't mind," Jaimes said. "I like being up here with you. A little chill won't kill me."

Eilonwy sighed. "Jaimes, I don't need protecting. And this whole situation is insulting …"

"I'm not sure you understand the half of it, my lady," a bright voice called from the nearby stairs.

Jaimes and Eilonwy both turned to see Brynne ascend the last few steps to the deck. "Good morning, Master Brynne," Jaimes said. "Care to join us?"

"No, no, young sir," Brynne said, emphatically waving the hand not clutching his ever-present tome. "I just wanted to have a quick word with our captain, but Mathius seems to have vanished from the ship." He tapped the side of his nose and gave Jaimes a smirk and a knowing wink. "I suppose Reed will have to do to hear my complaints."

"What did you mean?" Eilonwy asked. "About not under-standing the half of it?"

Brynne's eyebrows raised. "My dear lady, have you really no idea of the state of the world? And of the sad place they've given elves and dwarfs in it?"

Eilonwy lifted her chin. "I have a very good idea, yes."

"Then you know that in most places elves are killed on sight? That those left alive are taken captive and sold into various … unsavory markets?"

"Unsavory markets?" Eilonwy swallowed, and a slight shiver tickled her spine.

Brynne's expression softened. "I don't think it would be polite of me to go into detail."

Eilonwy shook her head. "I would appreciate it if you didn't."

Brynne sighed, staring down the ship at Reed and the other sailors around him. Compared to the rest, Reed stood out plainly with his light hair and towering build. "I do not like the way you are being treated one bit. But when the alternative is to have your ears clipped and your power sealed away while you're passed around from one bidder to the next—"

"Stop talking like that!"

Brynne and Eilonwy both jumped, surprised by the outburst from Jaimes. Even Jaimes seemed shocked; his eyes were wide and his cheeks flushed with embarrassment. "Can't you see you're scaring her, Brynne?"

Brynne's mouth worked silently for the space of a few seconds, then he let out a short sigh and composed himself. His heels snapped together, and he gave a deep and respectful bow to both Eilonwy and Jaimes. "I'm very sorry if I have frightened you, my dear. It was only my wish to help you to understand that while things on the *Kingfisher* are far from ideal, they could also be much worse." He straightened, pulling his book to rest against one hip. "I hope you can forgive me, lady."

"You have my forgiveness, Master Brynne. And my thanks." Eilonwy returned the bow with a slight nod of her head. "It appears my understanding of the world is not entirely accurate."

"Perhaps …" Brynne started, glancing down the deck at Reed once more, "perhaps that should be something you and your brother discuss at some length with Tiryn. He's a wise fellow, and has surely seen more of Azimar than you have yet to experience. He can tell you more than I, and hopefully without causing too much stress."

"Perhaps you are right, Master Brynne."

Brynne gave one more nod, then turned on his heel and hurried towards the aft end of the *Kingfisher*, calling for Reed.

"Are you alright?" Jaimes asked, shifting to sit so he could face her. "I'm sorry, I shouldn't have scolded him like that. But you seemed uncomfortable."

Eilonwy suppressed another shiver as she thought over Brynne's words once more. "It was not pleasant to listen to him talk like that."

Jaimes frowned. "Your face got so pale. And when he talked about your ears getting clipped …" His frown deepened. "Well, you did that." He motioned towards her, and Eilonwy was surprised to realize that one hand had instinctively risen to brush against the tip of her ear.

She let her hand drop, covering the hand that Jaimes used to prop his weight up and giving it a delicate pat. "Thank you, Jaimes."

The red flush to Jaimes's cheeks returned, and he gave her a shrug before turning to press his back against the rails once more. "Of course. It was nothing." He shrugged again. "And, if it would make you feel better, I could always be the one to come up to the deck with you. Just to make sure Brynne doesn't try to give you any more lessons on life in Azimar."

Eilonwy laughed. "I think that would be very nice."

"Yeah?" His face brightened, and Eilonwy nodded. Jaimes smiled, his cheeks still stained with a bright flush. "And what does Brynne know, anyway?"

Jaimes tried to hide his excitement. It was amusing to think he had taken any kind of interest in her. But it would be a fleeting one, surely, and when their journey on the *Kingfisher* ended, there would be nothing to keep them together, and nothing to keep his interest from fading.

The wind shifted, and with it came the whispered conversations of the men at the aft end of the deck. Eilonwy thought she heard her name, but she brushed the observation aside. No doubt Brynne and Reed were discussing her presence on the deck.

"I mean, I know he's smart and all that, but he doesn't exactly get out of the Archives much, does he?" Jaimes was saying. "He carries that big book around all the time—"

"*Eilonwy.*"

"—but I've never actually seen him reading it."

Eilonwy's head snapped up.

"What good is a book if you never open it?"

"Eilonwy, Tathiel! I found it!"

Eilonwy got to her feet, leaning over the railing. She let out a laugh, loud and breathless, and slapped the worn top of the balustrade with open palms. "We did it, Jaimes!"

Jaimes got to his feet, looking out over the water. "Did what?"

Eilonwy turned, cupping her hands around her mouth. "Reed!" Behind her, there was a muffled shout and the hurried sound of footfalls on the stairs from belowdecks. "Reed!" she called again, and this time the sailor turned, a fresh scowl on his face.

Tathiel slid to a stop beside her, leaning out to stare across the water. He was already in conversation with Melonya, and Eilonwy pushed their excited talk aside as Reed stormed his way across the deck towards them.

"Great Ones take it, what do you want?"

Eilonwy smirked at him, planting one fist firmly on her hip. "We found the *Seahawk*."

NUNOR

For the first time since Nunor had stepped down into the cabin of the *Kingfisher*, he was on her deck in the brightness of full day. The sun was hot, and beads of sweat trickled down his face and into his beard. He hated the heat, and had chosen to ignore Mathius's invitation to leave their cramped and dark cabin for the freshness of sea air and some sunlight. Dwarfs did not do well in heat, and sunlight was overrated. Nunor was used to small spaces and darkness, and the air blowing across the deck was just as salty in the dark of night as it was in the heat of day.

But here he was, standing on a metal crate Roland had procured for him, with a human child on one side and an elf easily three times his age on the other. They were all up here, including the two elf twins, all lined up against the starboard baluster and looking across the thin stretch of water that separated them from the shoreline of a small island.

Beside him, Mathius cursed, turning to look at Roland. "That's the *Seahawk* alright." He groaned, looking back at the ship moored in shallow waters. "That's the ship that my old crew stole from me."

The island the stolen ship was now harbored in was unremarkable in appearance. The sands were clean and white, and Nunor could hear birds cawing and chirping from the numerous trees that covered the isle in dense green foliage. The grey point of some small clifftop could be seen poking its way through the canopy, and Nunor briefly wondered if the island might hide some collection of minerals or gemstones. Not that he was much of a miner. His skill had always been behind a forge, not behind a pickaxe.

"Roland," Nunor called, pointing to a section of coast behind the dilapidated ship. From this close to the shore the tidy row of rafts pulled up on the sandy beach was obvious. "I count four rafts. They probably went further inland. It's likely they'll still be over there somewhere." Behind Roland, Alastor and Jaimes exchanged an anxious glance, but Roland grimaced sickly. They knew Tomas was dead. The only ones who didn't know were the two boys looking for him. And Mathius, Nunor supposed. If Tomas and his crew were on that island, it was only their bodies they would find. Perhaps not that much.

"I'm going over to her," Mathius said. "She looks to be in distress."

Nunor almost laughed. Distressed was an understatement. The *Seahawk* was pitched dangerously on her port side and her mainmast was nearly split but still standing. Her prow was washed up on the shore, and it would be a miracle if her sails were at all intact. It was clear that a storm had beaten the ship mercilessly, and she had floundered with no crew to protect her.

"I want to help," Jaimes's soft voice piped.

Roland turned to him, eyes widened in surprise. "Are you sure? We might find your uncle here."

Jaimes smiled softly, his brown eyes unable to meet Roland's. "Yes, but I'm beginning to think that the sight won't be something I'd like to see."

"I understand," Roland replied, placing a hesitant hand on

the boy's shoulder. "We'll find out what happened to your uncle and his crew."

"I'll take the boy's place, Roland," Nunor said, crossing his arms over his chest to stop the agitated twitching of his fingers. "A bit of walking on some solid ground would do me good."

"That's fine, Nunor. I'm sure we could use your company." Roland turned back to Mathius. "We'll meet you on the beach in a couple of hours. Will you take the twins with you?"

"Sure, I suppose," Mathius replied, eyes narrowed. "Why?"

Roland sighed. "I'm not sure I want to leave them alone on the ship, to be honest, Mathius." He waited for Mathius's reluctant nod, then continued. "Alright then, let's go. Alastor, you can come with us, if you want."

They split into their two groups, each one taking an identical raft and waiting patiently as the remaining crew of the *Kingfisher* lowered them into the water. During the descent, Mathius shouted orders up at his first mate, a large blond man with a name Nunor couldn't quite recall. As soon as Mathius's raft hit the water, he took two oars and rowed swiftly for the downed *Seahawk*. Jaimes and Tathiel each took up an oar and did their best to match the captain's hurried pace, and they soon passed Nunor and the others. Roland and Tiryn set out at a more moderate pace, declining Alastor's offer to help. Nunor already knew that he would be no help—his arms were much too short to handle the oars properly—so he sat quietly in the middle of the raft, watching the water slip past.

"Alastor, listen for a moment." Nunor craned his neck to address the boy seated behind him. "You should stay close to the rest of us. Don't wander off, no matter what. We don't know what happened to your uncle or his crew, but you can bet your bony ass that they haven't been sitting around a campfire singing songs for the last six months."

Alastor huffed, much to Nunor's disappointment. "I can take care of myself, Nunor. Roland has been training me in combat."

"Aye," Nunor said. "And Roland says that you're doing quite well. I bet you could take on someone your size and beat them nicely." He paused, trying to turn further and look the boy in the eye. "But I doubt that it's a fifteen-year-old boy we'd be facing over there. It might not be human. It might not be anything that can be fought. Maybe they all ate a bunch of poisonous berries and took a nice long nap in the dirt." Alastor frowned at that, thinking. "We don't know. So just stick close, and be careful."

Alastor nodded slowly. "Alright, Nunor. I'll be careful."

They continued their row to the shore, giving Mathius and the others a quick wave as they passed the *Seahawk*. Jaimes and Eilonwy were the only ones to return the wave; Tathiel was in the process of boosting Mathius up to the bottom rung of a weathered and broken rope ladder that led to the tilted deck of the ship. Nunor watched with amazement as Mathius grabbed the lower rung of the ladder and pulled himself hand over hand up the tattered thing until his foot found the bottom rung. The man was much stronger and more motivated than Nunor had given him credit for, and Nunor found himself respecting the young sea captain a great deal more. Tathiel took a small leap and grabbed the bottom rung of the ladder himself, an impressive stunt for a human, but nothing outside of the ordinary for an elf. Between Tathiel's outstretched hand, and Eilonwy's help from the raft, Jaimes was able to quickly get himself onto the ladder and climbed right behind Tathiel. Finally, with a leap similar to her brother's, Eilonwy took to the ladder, and within moments all four had disappeared over the railing and onto the deck.

Roland and Tiryn pulled their raft onto the shore only a few moments later, setting it to rest beside the four rafts that

Nunor had noted earlier. There were half-empty crates of amber bottles in the bottom of each raft, and a basket of something that might at one point have been food, but had since rotted and molded beyond recognition. Nunor was tempted to stab the damned thing just to see what kind of putrid maggoty mess leaked out, but decided against it at the ill look on Alastor's face. They put the sea to their backs and headed inland, forcing their way through dense underbrush and over sandy soil.

The humid heat from the thick woods brought sweat beading across Nunor's forehead in no time at all. He felt it running down his cheeks to settle into his beard, and the haft of his axe slipped dangerously in his hands until he was forced to fasten it away on his belt. Without a weapon or even a carving knife in his hands, he felt suddenly restless. Swatting insects kept his hands busy enough, until a fat mosquito landed on Alastor's shoulder and Nunor slapped the boy across the back hard enough to send him to his knees.

"Sorry, lad," Nunor muttered, surprised when his words came out dry and breathless. Alastor shook his head, brushing dirt from his trousers and giving Nunor a disgruntled look. The boy's face was red and the front of his shirt was stained with sweat. He looked like he might fall over at any moment, but he fell into step behind Tiryn without a word.

The forest on either side slowly thinned, letting blessedly cool air sweep between the trees. Over the noise of buzzing flies and chirping birds, the sound of splashing water could be heard further ahead.

"There must be some sort of lake or small waterfall further in. Maybe Tomas stopped there," Nunor said, panting. "Can we stop there? Just for a moment?"

Roland looked down at Nunor, smirking slightly. Even he looked hot and exhausted. "Are you getting tired, Nunor?"

Nunor tried to grunt angrily, but it came out as only a wheeze. "It's your damned legs! They're too long. I have to almost run to keep up." He leaned over, resting his hands on his knees. "And all this damned fresh air! It's going to kill me!" Nunor straightened with a proper growl, jogging to keep up with Roland and Tiryn. "I haven't stepped outside Doldural for any good length of time in over ten years, and now I'm running, uphill, in a damned forest. And it's so damned hot."

Ahead of him, Roland laughed, not pausing in his march. "If you can make it back to the beach, we'll break open some of those bottles you found and have a nice drink, Nunor. How about that?"

"You're fucking right we will." Nunor huffed. Beside him, Alastor laughed, stopping suddenly when he caught Nunor staring at him. Nunor shook his head. "No, go on, keep laughing at the poor bastard. What a damned mess, with his freaky long legs and his fully functional lungs." Alastor laughed again, and it made Nunor smile. "What a damned mess," he repeated, continuing to follow Roland and Tiryn deeper inland.

The sound of flowing water became stronger as they neared the source, and Tiryn suggested that they circle around to see if they could find a better way to access the lake than to just wade right into it. They circled off to the east, keeping the sound of flowing water in earshot. They finally found the source, hidden behind a thick stand of trees. Nunor had been right when he said that there might be a lake or a small waterfall. There were both. The lake was fairly small, almost a pond, with a nice strip of dirt and gravel about fifteen feet wide that led right to the edge of the water. Tiryn had managed to guide them from this side, and Nunor couldn't be sure if it was pure luck or if the elf had known that the eastern side of the lake might be more accessible. Across the water, the lake's source was plain to see. A small waterfall cascaded down into the lake, coming from what Nunor could only assume would eventually lead to the cap of the hill they had seen from the *Kingfisher*.

"This is it," Roland said. "This has to be where they ended up at some point." He crossed to the center of the dirt stretch and began kicking and scraping dirt and leaves aside. "Look here." He pointed down at his feet, turning to look at the others. "The remains of a fire. There are some stacked stones and the bones of small rodents or birds. And fish."

Nunor looked around them, catching sight of something stuck in the ground nearby. He walked towards it and pulled it from the ground. "An ale bottle here." He turned it over and gave it a shake. Nothing came out. "Empty," he grumbled. "Figures."

"There are some more over there," Tiryn said, pointing. "They're all over the place. There's broken glass everywhere." Tiryn grimaced, turning back to Roland. "How many people did Mathius say there were in the crew?"

"Eleven," Roland answered.

Tiryn looked around once more. "There seems to be far more than enough debris to suggest that they had another drunken night here." Tiryn frowned. "And then what?"

Roland glared at Tiryn, then glanced sidelong at Alastor, who had wandered down to the lake's edge. Nunor rejoined the two of them as Roland answered in a hushed whisper. "We know what happened then, Tiryn."

Tiryn shook his head, frowning. "They just died? You said his bones were underwater, right? Did they just decide to go swimming while drunk and drown?"

There was a loud splash, and all three turned to the lake, startled. Alastor stood with his back to them, pitching his arm back to toss a small rock into the water of the lake. Nunor sighed in relief, and he was surprised to hear Roland do the same beside him.

Roland turned back to Tiryn, continuing his angry whispering. "Stranger things have happened."

"Can't you just double-check?" Nunor grumbled. "Get your little magic ball back out and take another look?"

Roland rolled his eyes, but reached into the pocket of his vest. He pulled out the small orb Nunor had seen him use before, then took a quick look over his shoulder to make sure Alastor couldn't see what he was about to do.

There was another splash as Alastor tossed a rock into the lake, and Nunor glanced up at the boy to see him digging out additional rocks from the dirt around him. Nunor turned back to see Roland staring at the small orb as it swirled and shimmered in variegated colors. It settled into a deep blue in moments, speckled with white shapes. This time, Nunor could more clearly make out the muddy bottom of a seafloor. Or more appropriately, he realized, a lake floor. The mud looked strikingly similar to the dirt they stood on. The image faded from the orb's surface, and Nunor looked up to see Tiryn and Roland eying each other.

"So they did drown," Tiryn said over the sound of another splash from Alastor.

"In that lake," Nunor added, jerking his head back behind them.

Roland was shoving the orb back into his pocket, his face pinched. "We don't have any way to prove it, though. We'll just have to tell everyone the truth. We didn't find them, but we found evidence that they had been here. It's been so long, we just have to assume that they died in the forest somehow."

"That's fine with me," Nunor said, turning back to the lake's shore to collect Alastor. But the boy wasn't anywhere to be seen.

Beside him, Roland glanced around them as well. "Where's Alastor?"

27

ALASTOR

Alastor tossed a rock into the dark waters of the lake, trying to ignore the whispered conversation of the adults behind him. He knew they were just saying aloud what he had already realized. His uncle Tomas had been here with his crew. They'd had a night of drunken festivity, judging by the broken bottles strewn on the ground around them, and then they had simply disappeared. Whether they had continued into the forest and gotten lost and died of hunger, or had been attacked in their sleep by a pack of wild animals and dragged off into the night, he would probably never know. But he did know that his uncle was very probably dead. He'd known that as soon as he had seen the *Seahawk* sitting tilted in the bay, so tattered and busted that to him she seemed unfit for sailing.

He bounced the last rock he'd picked up onto his palm a few times, then tried to skip it across the water. It skipped only twice before plunking into the depths with the others.

He'd gone with Roland and the others in the hopes that he might at least find out what had happened to his uncle, but even that seemed too much for the Great Ones to give him.

"What a damned mess," Alastor muttered as he bent to select more stones from the ones around his feet. He'd liked the way Nunor had used the phrase more, but it seemed appropriate to this situation as well. And it had made the dwarf sound confident and impressive, despite the fact that he was a whole head and shoulders shorter than Alastor himself.

Alastor selected another four smooth stones, these ones flatter than the last set, and straightened to skip another one across the lake. He bounced a stone against his palm, sighted down the lake to take aim, then halted suddenly.

In the cascading shower of the waterfall on the opposite end of the lake stood a girl, bathing herself. *Not a girl*, Alastor thought. *A woman.* Somehow the difference was crucial, though Alastor couldn't be sure why. He tried to turn away from her naked form, but he didn't seem to be able to stop his staring.

She was beautiful, with long dark hair draping wet over her shoulders and barely concealing her breasts. Alastor was fascinated by the way the water ran down her neck and chest, then down her waist and into the lake, and suddenly he wished he could see the rest of her body. He'd never seen a woman fully naked before. There were girls in Larten, but they had all been young. There had been no curves to their figures and little in the way of seductive charm. The same could not be said of the woman in the lake, and Alastor found himself wanting very much to see more of her.

The woman noticed him staring, and she quirked a smile at him, turning to face him. She tossed the hair from one shoulder, exposing the breast beneath, and crooked a finger, beckoning him into the water. With hardly a thought, Alastor quickly stripped his shirt off and kicked off his boots. He strode into the lake, watching as she dipped deeper into the water and began swimming out to meet him. A few feet into the lake the floor suddenly dropped, and Alastor fell into the water with a splash. When he came back above the surface, treading water, the woman was gone. He looked around desperately, worried he had lost her, but the touch of someone's hands on his waist told him that she had found him first.

He felt a hand pulling at the lacing of his pants, and a pleasure he had never felt before rippled over him. Her other arm wrapped around his waist and began to pull him down. Alastor took a deep breath and let himself be pulled under as the tugging at his pants became more insistent. Once fully submerged, he opened his eyes, and saw the woman only inches from his face.

Up close, she was even more beautiful, with dark eyes that matched her dark hair drifting around her body. Her skin was pale, and her lips full and dark red. She smiled at him, her teeth a stark white against her lips. With one hand she stroked him, while the other hand wrapped around the back of his neck and pulled his mouth to hers.

Alastor would have groaned in pleasure if his lungs had had the air for it. He had kissed a few of those girls in Larten, but none of them had been filled with so much passion and fire. And he knew that he would never in his life have another kiss that felt as good as this one. Her lips were magic, and her hands even more so. His whole body ached for her. His mouth burned for hers. Even his lungs burned for her. She wrapped her legs around his waist, pulling him closer. He felt her guiding him, leading him into her. Any second, and he would be inside her. Any second and—

Alastor felt a heavy hand rip them apart, and was shocked to see Tiryn put himself between him and the woman. With a single shove, Tiryn pushed the woman several feet away, and Alastor heard her scream in pain as a strange rippling wave drove him and whatever monster held him further from the intoxicating woman.

Alastor and his attacker broke the surface of the water,

and Alastor gasped and spluttered, filling his lungs with air. He hadn't realized how much they had been burning. He tore at the arms that held him, desperate to swim his way back into the arms of the woman of the lake.

"Stop struggling, you fucking idiot!" Roland yelled into his ear. "Nunor, help me get him out of the water."

Alastor felt another pair of strong hands, smaller than the first, grab him by the shoulders and pull him up. Within seconds he was out of the lake and lying on his back on the dirt, panting.

There was a splash, and Alastor heard Tiryn's voice. "She's coming back, get out of the water. Quick!"

Roland fell to the dirt on Alastor's left, scrambling to his feet and reaching for the sword lying on the ground nearby. Tiryn fell to the ground at his right, brown hair dripping with water.

Roland leaned into his line of sight, glowering angrily down at him. "What the fuck do you think you were doing?"

Alastor struggled for another deep breath, then angrily spat up to Roland. "What the fuck does it look like I was doing?"

Roland's eyebrows raised, his beard and hair dribbling water onto Alastor's face. "It looks to me like you almost got yourself killed by a water nymph." Roland frowned down at him, shaking his head. "Pull your pants up, you're embarrassing yourself."

"Roland," Tiryn warned, and Alastor sat up to see a rolling wave riding toward the shoreline. As it reached the drop-off Alastor knew was hidden feet from the water's edge, the wave crested, and the naked woman surged from it, planting herself nimbly onto the shelf of the drop-off, breasts and thighs exposed, feet dangling in the water's depths. The cresting wave splashed innocently back into the lake, hardly rippling as it did.

"That's close enough," Roland said, pointing the tip of the sword at her exposed chest.

The woman smiled. "You know as well as I do that I cannot set foot on land."

Her voice was rich and sultry, and Alastor found himself drawn towards her again. He tried to stand, but Nunor pulled him back firmly. Instead he stared at her, muttering, "You are on land."

Her smile deepened as she turned her dark eyes on him. "Not my feet, little one." And with a kick, she sent water splashing from the lake's depths. She leaned forward, arms pressing her breasts together, and looked Roland over with a sensual lick of her lips. "Give him back to me. We were only getting started."

"No," Roland answered flatly.

The nymph rose to her knees, placing them a provocative distance apart, and ran a hand absently over her inner thigh. Tilting her head, she looked Roland over again. "Then why don't you join me? With a body like that, you might be able to finish me off." She smirked. "You might even kill me."

"Great Ones preserve us," Nunor muttered, pulling Alastor back again as he leaned toward her.

"No," Roland repeated.

"What a shame," she nearly moaned, her lips pouting seductively. "Then what will you do with me?"

"I have some questions for you." Roland's voice was dry and flat, but Alastor swore he was struggling to stay calm. The nymph was getting under even his skin.

"Oh?" The nymph ran her hands over her breasts and up to her neck, then bundled her dark hair and made a show of wringing the water from it. "I'll answer them." She quirked her lips again. "For a price."

Roland glowered at her. "What do you want?"

The nymph crossed her arms over her chest, pressing her breasts together, and brought the long nail of her forefinger up to trace across her lower lip. "You, of course. Even a little will do."

Roland looked to Tiryn, who gave him a hard shake of the head. "Don't, Roland."

Roland drew a breath and held it, staring at the nymph. He held out a hand to Nunor, palm up. "Your dagger, please."

Tiryn groaned, but Nunor obliged Roland, passing a dagger hilt first to Roland without taking his eyes off Alastor.

Roland rolled up the sleeve of his left arm, bringing the tip of the dagger to the inside of his elbow. Alastor saw a rash of old white scars crisscrossing Roland's forearm, as well as some curiously round markings that were oddly familiar. The nymph let out a soft moan, pulling Alastor's attention back to her, and he gave the markings no further thought as he focused on the seductive beast fondling her breasts only meters away.

"A hand, Tiryn, if you don't mind," Roland said.

Tiryn made an aggressive motion of one hand, and the red that trickled from the cut that Roland put into his arm balled itself up and floated through the air towards the nymph.

The nymph held out a finger, and one fat blood drop burst against her pale skin. She slipped the finger into her mouth, moaning again. Her eyes rolled back for a moment, and when they focused again the dark of her irises had grown to fill her eyes entirely.

"Delicious." The nymph gently prodded a second drop of blood into her mouth, letting it burst against her outstretched tongue. A shiver shook her, and her back arched delightfully. Alastor almost sat up again, but Nunor pushed him back so he could hardly move.

"Now," the nymph sighed, "your questions."

Roland's hands were shaking, but he took a deep breath and visibly steadied himself. On Alastor's other side, Tiryn moved to step closer to Roland, seemingly unaffected by the nymph's seductions, but Roland stopped him with a quick jerk of his uninjured hand. "We're looking for some men who we think might have come through these parts. There were eleven of them. Sailors. It would have been roughly six months ago. Were they here?"

The nymph smiled, her bright teeth suddenly terrifying against such dark lips. "They were." There was an odd emphasis on the last word that pricked Alastor's nerves, and the magic of her was suddenly lost to him.

Alastor leaned forward, sedately brushing Nunor's hand aside as he tried to push him back. "What happened to them?"

The nymph's eyes flicked to Alastor, and the hunger he found in them made him shrink away. She looked away, settling her sights on Roland again. "They got drunk. I waited until dark. Then I lured them into my lake and killed them."

"You killed all of them?" Tiryn asked, sounding both disgusted and awed.

The nymph never looked away from Roland. "A few of them drowned on their own, unfortunately." She pouted, hands roving back over her chest. "I was only able to ride them down to the depths *after* they had breathed their last."

"Why Alastor?" Roland asked, pointing behind him. "He's just a boy." The finger pointing at Alastor was shaking slightly again, and he wondered if Roland would need Tiryn's help after all.

The nymph laughed, and the sound of it both aroused and sickened Alastor. "A boy will someday turn into a man. Why wait?" She looked over to him again, and Alastor felt her hunger radiating out towards him, trying to reel him in like a fish. "Besides, he would have enjoyed himself. They always do." The nymph smirked. "And you all taste the same in the end, don't you?"

"Roland," Tiryn warned, and the nymph's eyes snapped back to Roland's. Tiryn stepped to Roland's side, putting a hand on his injured arm. "We have our answers, now let's get out of here."

"Right," Roland muttered, letting Tiryn pull him back in the direction they had come. But Roland's eyes never left the nymph's form. Nunor helped Alastor to his feet, silently handing him his discarded tunic and boots.

"Oh, come now, Roland," the nymph purred. She sat back on her haunches, legs spread far enough apart to see every inch of her. "Won't you stay with me?" With one hand she caressed herself, and with the other she beckoned Roland forward with one pale finger. "It's been so long since I've had anyone join me in my lake."

Alastor shivered, an intense wave of grotesque delight passing over him. Tiryn tightened his grip on Roland's arm, pulling him further along. Nunor pulled Alastor into the trees, and Tiryn tugged a slightly resisting Roland into the woods after them. They continued their slow retreat until the lake was out of sight, although the burbling of the waterfall could still be heard.

Alastor leaned his wet head against a tree, closing his eyes and taking in deep breaths to calm himself. He opened his eyes to see Roland crouched down, head hanging between his knees.

Tiryn put a light hand on Alastor's shoulder. "Are you alright?"

Alastor nodded. "I'm glad you were all there. I would probably be dead right now. I'm sorry, Roland."

Roland stood with a grunt of effort. "It's alright, Alastor. Water nymphs are very powerful creatures. I'm sure I would have fallen for the same trick, if I had been in your shoes."

"You almost did," Tiryn said, worriedly.

"I'm alright, Tiryn," Roland grumbled.

"Is your arm still bleeding?" Alastor asked.

"No, it's fine." Roland had already tugged the sleeve into place, and there was no red stain to indicate that the wound was bad enough to need much attention.

"Tiryn, how were you able to overcome her … advances?" Alastor asked, feeling himself redden. He quickly retied his pants, realizing that they were still undone, and pulled his tunic over his head.

"The power of nymphs simply just doesn't work quite as well on elves." Tiryn shrugged. "And I wasn't really interested."

"And you, Nunor?" Alastor asked, standing on one foot to replace a boot.

"Oh, I was interested," the dwarf answered, grinning. "A woman like that, all naked and wet. Very interesting, indeed." Nunor sighed. "But it's like Tiryn said. The attraction just isn't quite strong enough to get over the realization that she'll kill you and eat you as soon as the deed is done."

Alastor shivered, partly from the chill settling into him, and partly from the reminder that he had almost died.

"Come on," Roland grunted, struggling to regain his proper gait. "Let's just get as far away from here as we can."

2 8

ROLAND

Roland dropped himself onto the sandy beach, glad they had finally found their way back out of the woods and away from the water nymph's lake. He could still feel the magic of her seductive charms working its way out of him, and he shivered at the memory of her naked figure beckoning him towards her.

"Damn elementals," he muttered, trying to shake his head clear. Alastor sat close by, chin dropped to his chest and taking deep breaths. Roland reached out and thumped him on the back half-heartedly, and Alastor lifted his head long enough to grimace and nod in agreement.

"They're not all like that. Most are fine," Tiryn called over his shoulder as he rummaged through the abandoned rafts nearby. "The water nymphs are really the only ones who tend to be so …" He paused, tilting his head as he considered. "Feisty." He straightened and turned, holding four intact amber bottles of what Roland very much hoped was something strong.

"I'm just glad you and Nunor were there. I'm not sure what Alastor and I would have done if you two didn't have your wits about you." He took the bottle Tiryn offered with a hand that still shook slightly. "Thank you."

"It was my pleasure," Nunor replied in his usual grumble. "It's not every day I get to see a beauty like that, shaking all of her bits around."

"Clearly you've never been to the inn at Hythe." Roland pulled the cork from his bottle, looking apprehensively down the mouth. "If you go downstairs, there's a little stage. For a few gold pieces, you can see all kinds of beauties shaking their bits around." He took a tentative sip, surprised when the taste of honeyed mead filled his mouth. "Or so I've heard."

Nunor laughed, tugging the cork from his own bottle and chugging half of it in one pull.

Tiryn held the remaining bottle out for Alastor to take, but the boy only looked up at him, confused. "That's mead, right?" He looked to Roland, waiting for permission.

"You almost died today, Alastor. If that isn't excuse enough to drink, I'm not sure what is." Roland shrugged, taking another sip of the mead.

Alastor took the bottle gingerly from Tiryn, giving the worn label a scrutinizing look. He tugged the cork free easily enough, no doubt from years of practice in Larten's inn. He looked down the neck of the bottle, then gave Roland a shrug and took a large swig. His face soured, and he swallowed hard. Nunor bellowed, seeing the look of disgust Alastor made, and Roland couldn't help but smile.

Even Tiryn chuckled laughed lightly. "You don't have to finish it if you don't like it. I'm sure Nunor can handle the rest."

Before Alastor could say anything in answer, there was a shout from further down the beach. Roland looked up to see Mathius and the other children walking towards them. Jaimes and Eilonwy held what looked like a small fishing net between them, and Mathius and Tathiel followed behind.

Roland stood and walked down to the beach to meet them. "I was hoping you would make it back soon. We need to discuss a few things."

"Ah," Mathius said, looking Roland over. "Something bad happened, huh?"

Jaimes's eyebrows raised. "Did you find my uncle?"

Roland sighed. "Yes and no. Let's wait to talk about it until we're all comfortable." He motioned for Jaimes and Eilonwy to continue down the beach, and Tathiel fell into step behind them. "Go ahead and have Tiryn and Alastor help you with that. Tathiel, can you get a fire started? I think we'll be camping here tonight, if the captain doesn't mind anchoring the Kingfisher overnight."

Mathius shrugged. "It sounds fine to me. It'll be dark soon, and it's not wise to sail out of such shallow water without the sun to guide you." Mathius cast a glance back over his shoulder at the *Kingfisher*. "I'll return to the ship and inform the crew of what we found on the *Seahawk*."

"Fish for dinner, hm?" Roland asked, eyeing the net as the younger ones walked away. "I'm sure Nunor will be thrilled at the news."

"It's not so bad," Mathius said with a grin. "When I was young, my father used to say that his father had taught him a dozen ways to catch a fish, and—"

"And a dozen ways to cook it," Roland finished without a thought.

"Oh, so you've heard that one too, have you?" Mathius chuckled.

Roland shrugged, trying to ignore the sudden racing of his heart. "It's a common saying where I'm from."

"And where is that, exactly?"

Roland forced a smile. "A long way away, I'm afraid."

Mathius paused, waiting for Roland to elaborate, then only shrugged when he remained silent. "Your little elf twins are very good at net fishing," Mathius said, changing the topic with a nod to Eilonwy and Tathiel. "We found some old gear on the *Seahawk*, and they had dinner caught in no time at all." He shook his head. "It was fascinating to watch."

"I suspect they have a lot of talents they don't talk much about," Roland replied, shuffling his feet in the sand.

Mathius chuckled nervously. "That's not at all worrisome to hear."

Roland laughed. "They're good people, Mathius. I trust them." He looked over his shoulder, seeing Tiryn instruct Jaimes and Alastor while Nunor stood nearby, drinking away at what was probably no longer his first bottle.

Mathius sighed. "I see you found some more of the mead. There were only three cases of it left on the ship."

"You can try to take the rest away from Nunor, if you want." Roland gave Mathius another smile. "I'm not sure how pleased he'll be. It's very good quality."

"I would hope so." Mathius frowned, watching the dwarf reach for another bottle from the bottom of one of the rafts. "It's made by the master brewers of Cardyn. It was on its way to the capital when my ship was stolen from me." He shrugged. "I've already paid for the loss, go ahead and enjoy what you have."

"Thank you," Roland said, surprised by Mathius's generosity. "I'll be sure to let Nunor know he should savor it a bit more."

Mathius sighed, his gaze shifting once more to look Roland in the eyes. "Did you find my crew? The *Seahawk* was trashed. It's clear no one has been on her in months. Are they dead?"

Roland nodded. "They happened on a particularly nasty water nymph. They got drunk, and she lured them all to their deaths. I'm sorry."

"Don't be." Mathius shook his head and tugged at his beard as he seemed to do when upset. "They died like fools, running away from the realities of life, and chasing a silly dream of easy glory."

"We want to keep sailing with you for a bit longer," Roland said. "Not as crew, mind you, but as passengers."

Mathius raised one bushy eyebrow. "Where to?"

"I'm not sure yet. I'm hoping to find out tonight."

"It will cost you."

Roland smirked. "You can keep the other half of our gold."

"And if that doesn't cover it?" Mathius asked.

"I have enough to cover any extra cost," Tiryn called from behind Roland. Roland turned, startled by his sudden appearance. "We have a job to do, Mathius, and this was only the start of it."

"Very well." Mathius's eyebrow lifted higher. "I'll take you wherever you need to go." He smiled, clearly intrigued. "So long as you have the coin for it."

***

J aimes and Alastor did an excellent job of preparing the fish, with a certain amount of oversight on Tiryn's part and the occasional half-drunken word of advice from Nunor. They ate their fill, surrounded by the warmth of a campfire Tathiel built from what he could scavenge from the very edge of the woods. Jaimes, who Roland knew had already strongly suspected that his uncle Tomas was dead, took the story of their journey to and from the nymph's lake rather well in Roland's opinion. He was clearly despondent, nursing his bottle of honeyed mead in silence while the others joked and laughed together. But he was able to muster up a small smile at Eilonwy's mention of storytelling.

"I don't really have any stories for such young ears," Nunor said with a small belch. "Tiryn might get upset if I tell the good ones." The dwarf smiled over his bottle at Tiryn, who sat across the fire from him.

"Actually," Eilonwy said, interjecting before Tiryn could answer Nunor's remark. "I thought we could each tell everyone a little about ourselves. We're going to be traveling together for a while longer, right? It could be a good chance to get to know one another better."

"It's not a bad idea …" Tiryn said, catching Roland's eye. Roland only shrugged noncommittally, knowing full well where Tiryn's thoughts had gone, and still unsure if he wanted to share his identity with the young men seated across from him.

"Great. Then Tathiel and I will start," Eilonwy said, crossing her feet and tucking some loose hair behind one ear. "We live with our mother, in our Homewood to the west. We're twins, if you hadn't already gathered." Eilonwy rolled her eyes slightly, casting a quick glance at Jaimes. "Twins are very rare among elves, and we're considered to bring good luck to our Homewood because of it." Eilonwy suddenly laughed, recalling something. "In fact, for our fiftieth birthday—"

"You're fifty?" Jaimes asked, bewildered. For a moment, he no longer seemed depressed and quiet, and was scrutinizing Tathiel and Eilonwy. Roland smirked to himself, familiar with the struggle of accepting that some creatures lived much longer lives than humans.

"Well, we're over a hundred now," Eilonwy answered shyly. "We're still considered young, by elven standards."

"You forget that elves can live for hundreds of years, Jaimes. We really still have a lot of growing up to do," Tathiel added.

"I'm almost four hundred," Tiryn added cheerfully, grabbing another bottle from the collection sitting in the nearby sand.

"It's just …" Jaimes furrowed his brows, considering. "You look only a little older than Alastor and me."

"In the lifetime of an elf, we *are* only a little older than you," Tathiel said, exchanging an undecipherable look with his sister.

It was quiet, and Roland waited for Eilonwy to continue. But she gave a small shake of her head and a thin smile. "Never mind. It's not that great a story." She folded her hands and dropped them into her lap. "That's all there really is to us, I guess."

Jaimes seemed ready to protest, but Tathiel shot him a disapproving glare and he remained silent.

A brief moment of silence was broken by Nunor. "Enough of this silly whining. It's my turn now." He chugged the bottle he held in his hand, but to Roland's relief didn't reach for a fresh one. "I'm Nunor Halfhelm, son of Noren Halfhelm, and—"

Tiryn burst into laughter, much to Roland's surprise. He'd never heard Tiryn laugh so hard, and certainly not while someone was speaking. *How much has he had to drink?* Roland wondered, trying to count the bottles scattered around the campfire.

"You're a Halfhelm?" Tiryn asked.

"Yes ..." Nunor said, his eyes narrowed and staring at the elf.

"What's a halfhelm?" Alastor asked, leaning around the fire to direct the question to Roland.

"Well," Roland started, "it's a piece of armor, but I'm not sure—"

"It also happens to be the surname given to my family after my idiot great-great-great-great-great grandfather wore a rusted-out helm into battle during the Great War," Nunor said, still staring at Tiryn. "At least the foolish mudeater had the sense to leave a pregnant wife behind, or I wouldn't be here today." Nunor grabbed another bottle, ignoring Roland's shake of his head at the move, and yanked the cork from it in one hasty motion. He took a large swig, then shoved the bottle down into the sand to stand on its own. "All it took to kill him off was a well-placed blow to the head. A child could have done it."

"A child did do it," Tiryn said with a grin, shaking his head at Nunor. "An elven child, barely a hundred years old. He shot him right through a rusted hole on the top of his head."

Nunor laughed. "That's right. The poor bastard was buried with the arrow still firmly lodged in his brain. His wife was furious, but she was pretty batty too. She swore vengeance against the elven child that killed him."

"Does that mean your uncle, King Darlyth, is a Halfhelm as well?" Tiryn asked.

Nunor wiped at some spilled mead that dribbled through his beard. "He's really more of a cousin than an uncle, and he's not so close in blood as to have the same cursed name as I do."

Tiryn lifted his bottle, and Nunor leaned dangerously close to the fire to clink his own to Tiryn's. "Lucky for him then," Tiryn said.

Nunor laughed, hiccuping as he did.

"Who killed Halfhelm, Tiryn?" Alastor asked, wide eyed.

"His name was Aishe," Tiryn said, sipping from his bottle again. "But enough of these old war stories, Nunor. You're frightening the children."

Nunor snorted. "Fine, fine. Tell us who you are then, elf."

Tiryn smiled, looking across to Nunor. "I'm Tiryn, son of Aishe."

There was a pause. Roland looked back and forth between Tiryn and Nunor, not sure which one would move first. His breath held in his throat, and he wondered if they might still be able to seriously hurt each other if they were both drunk.

But Nunor barked out a laugh, startling Roland and the younger ones into a jump. Tiryn's smile only widened, and Nunor's laugh grew louder and harder. The dwarf lifted his bottle again in salute. "Well met, Tiryn, son of Aishe." Tiryn copied the motion, and they both drank. Nunor let out a large belch before continuing. "You've nothing to fear from me. My great-great-what-have-you grandmother made that vow of vengeance, and she's long dead now. Everyone knows that any idiot mudeater that goes into battle with a rusted-out helm will only come home dead or a coward."

"Thank you, Nunor. We are well met indeed." Tiryn saluted Nunor once more, taking another swig from his own bottle.

"What about you, Roland?" Alastor asked, looking across the fire towards him.

Roland's heart skipped a beat, and he felt his body chill suddenly, despite the warmth of the campfire. "Ahh, well …" He floundered for a moment, Alastor watching him expectantly.

"It's getting pretty late," Tiryn interjected, the cheer in his voice gone. "I'm not sure we have time to continue this—"

"It's alright, Tiryn." Roland put a hand on his friend's arm, hoping that the touch might quell his own anxiety. His heart felt like it was pumping ice, and it was much harder to take full breaths. Alastor's staring eyes weren't helping, so Roland looked down at his hands twisting around each other in his lap. "I'm originally from Etritia. I used to work in the castle. A long time ago." Roland felt a lump form in his throat, and he forced his hands to remain still, placing one on each of his knees. "I had a sister, and she was married to my childhood friend. I fell in love with a beautiful woman. I was the commander of the King's Guard." In his peripheral vision, he saw Alastor stiffen. "I had everything." He slowly let out a deep breath. "And then I lost everything." He laughed, despite his fear of what might happen in the following moments. "I even lost my name." He looked up, meeting Alastor's eyes and watching the boy slowly stand to glower down on him. "My name isn't actually Roland."

"What are you saying?" Alastor's voice was shaking.

"My name is Ajax," Roland said carefully. "And I'm your uncle, Alastor."

Alastor laughed, a short and shocked sound. He shook his head, looking up the sky and rapidly blinking. "I'd ask you to prove it, but I've already seen the proof. Those scars on your arm. They're from when you helped my mother and father escape the castle. Mother told me about that."

"Yes," Roland said. It was all he could say; his throat was too closed up to let any other words out.

"And you just left her?"

"Yes." Roland swallowed hard, struggling to his feet. "Sh- she told me to. It was what she wanted."

"You never came to visit? Never checked in to see how she was doing? How I was doing?"

"I did—I came all the time!" Roland was pleading now, he could hear it in his voice, but he didn't give a damn. This was his nephew, his sister's little boy. Hasani's son. And he would plead until his dying day if it meant that Alastor would understand and maybe stay. "And I checked in on both of you." He scrambled into his pockets, pulling out the Dragon's Eye and holding it out for the boy to take. Alastor did, glancing over it before reverting his glare back to Roland. "I used that to check in on you, to make sure you were safe and happy."

"He did, Alastor," Tiryn said soberly. "It's how we met Harlan. He knew who Roland was. And we knew when your mother fell ill, and we both tried desperately to get to her before her time ran out." Alastor glared down on Tiryn, but the elf was unmoved. "I'm sorry, Alastor."

"It doesn't change the fact that you were never there for me," Alastor spat.

Roland held his hands up, surrendering. "I didn't think you or your mother wanted me."

Alastor shook his head. Then he stretched out his hand

over the fire, prepared to drop the Dragon's Eye into the flames.

"No, don't!" Roland yelled, watching the firelight dance on the surface of the stone.

Alastor hesitated. "Why shouldn't I?"

"Because I need it to find your father," Roland said quickly.

Alastor paused, then retracted his hand and dropped the Eye into Tiryn's lap. "My father is dead."

Roland sighed. "I thought he was too, but now I'm not sure." He gestured towards the Dragon's Eye with a wave. "I looked for him in that for years, and I could never see him. I thought he was gone. But when I looked for Tomas, and I saw his bones—"

"You knew Uncle Tomas was dead?" Alastor hissed. "You knew he was dead, and you still dragged us along with you?"

Roland closed his eyes. How could he have been so stupid? "I'm sorry, Alastor. I just wanted you to stay …" He was pleading again, and he didn't care. Roland opened his eyes to see Alastor shaking his head at him, mouth open in stunned silence.

Alastor blinked, finding his voice long enough to say, "What kind of monster are you?"

And then he turned and hurried away into the dark.

Jaimes stood and walked after him, casting one fearful and angry look back at Roland.

Roland wanted to follow them, but he couldn't put his legs into motion. He was sure his heart had stopped, and it took him a second to realize that he had stopped breathing. He exhaled in one shaking sigh.

He could vaguely see Eilonwy and Tathiel going after the boys in the dark, but his vision was blurring.

Tiryn wrapped a warm arm around his shoulders, squeezing him gently. "It'll be alright, Roland."

"What if it isn't?"

ALASTOR

Alastor buried his feet into the cool sand, surrounded by unfamiliar shapes hidden in the darkness. It had been stupid of him to run from the campfire while it was so dark, but he just couldn't stand the sight of Roland. If he turned, he could still see the amber glow of the fire from where he sat, and that would surely be enough to guide him back when he had calmed enough to face the others. He wrapped his arms around his legs, resting his head against his upraised knees.

He'd told Roland that he wanted to find his uncle, and part of him was glad to know that the man he had heard so much about growing up was still alive. But how could Roland have kept himself so distant for all these years? Alastor could remember his mother crying some nights because she missed her family so much. His father was dead, but his mother had known that her brother was still out there somewhere. And Roland had chosen to stay away.

Worse, Roland had chosen to maintain some sort of one-sided relationship with his family. He had known Alastor, had watched him from afar. He had even known when Alastor's mother fell ill. But he had never reached out to let anyone know that he was still alive and doing well, and wanted to reconnect. Roland had decided to wait on the fringes of their lives, and had swooped in only when Alastor was left alone in the world.

Alastor sighed, beating his forehead against his knees. And Roland had known that Uncle Tomas was dead, and had tricked Alastor and Jaimes into joining their party in search of him. Had Tiryn known as well? Nunor? Had everyone known but him and Jaimes? They had been lied to, pulled into a voyage that they were unprepared for, all so that Roland could try to befriend him.

"Are you alright?" Eilonwy's voice startled him, and he jerked up to see her standing in front of him. A small orb of blue-green light bobbed around her head, illuminating her face and most of her body.

"I'm fine," Alastor grumbled, letting his knees drop to the sand and crossing his ankles between them. "Just angry." He shrugged. "I feel betrayed."

Eilonwy nodded, but said nothing.

Alastor wanted to continue, but the irregular bobbing of the light around her head distracted him. "What is that?"

Eilonwy smiled, her nose wrinkling as she did. "I think you might call it a witch light. But the elves taught the witches how to cast it, so it might be more appropriate to call it an elf light." She lifted a hand, and the light bobbed against her fingertips. "Do you like it?"

Alastor nodded. "Could you teach me how to make one?"

She tilted her head, considering it. "Perhaps. Though Tiryn would be a much better teacher." She sat in the sand across from him. "I can ask him again to teach you, if you want."

Alastor groaned. He did very much want to learn magic. And he wanted to continue learning how to use a sword. But he wasn't sure that he wanted Tiryn or Roland to be his teachers. "Did you know about Uncle Tomas?"

Eilonwy took a slow breath, then nodded. "I did. Roland found out right after you and Jaimes said that you wanted to look for him. After he sent you down to the docks in Hythe to ask about him."

He remembered that afternoon. It seemed like forever ago, but how long had it been? A few weeks? "Why did no one tell us?"

Eilonwy bit her lower lip, thinking. "I'm not sure, but I think Roland wanted you to trust him before he asked you about something. Something to do with our quest. He wants you to come with us."

"Will you tell me about this quest?"

She shook her head vigorously, the witch light around her head bouncing around her ears as she did. "It's not my place to say anything about it. Roland wanted to be the one to explain everything to you."

Alastor rolled his eyes, brushing his hair away from his eyes. "I don't understand the secrecy. I don't understand why Roland felt he had to lie to me. I just …" He tugged at the ends of his lengthening hair, searching for the right words. "I don't understand."

Eilonwy's soft eyes stared into his own. She looked only a little older than him, thin and young and full of the kind of energy Alastor had only ever seen in people his own age. Except for those eyes. Her eyes looked like they had seen the world, and had grown wiser for seeing it all, and the sight of them in someone who otherwise looked as young as himself was unnerving. "Would you like to?"

He blinked at her. "What?"

Her nose wrinkled again as she smiled, and suddenly she was just a young elf again, her eyes sparkling with excitement. "Come on, I want to show you something." With hardly any effort, she was standing in front of him, hand extended to help him to his feet. Once he was up, she tugged him further down the beach, closer to the shoreline. Her witch light bobbed along, alternating between shoulder and knee height, presumably giving her enough light to guide them. The pale blue-green light hardly helped Alastor see more than a few feet in front of him, but Eilonwy pulled him along unerringly, her hand pleasantly warm in his grasp.

"Where are we going?" His steps slipped in the shifting sand of the beach, but Eilonwy continued without slowing down.

"You'll see in a moment."

"Wait." He tried to tug his hand out of her grip, but she held him tightly. So he planted his feet as firmly as he could in the sand and pulled her back. "The last woman that led me away from the others tried to drown me." *And have sex with me,* he added to himself. "Where are you taking me?"

Eilonwy paused long enough to cast an annoyed look over her shoulder at him. "Not to drown you, if that's what you're worried about. Or do anything else with you, for that matter." She smirked at him before turning away. "Now come on, there's someone I want you to meet."

Alastor reluctantly let himself be pulled along, silently cursing whoever had shared the story of the water nymph with Eilonwy. She guided him around a rocky outcrop, pulling him to the left as they continued towards the beach. They waded through ankle-deep water, skirting around the fallen *Seahawk* and further from the campsite. "This is ridiculous, Eilonwy. Where is this person? Out in the ocean?"

"Yes, actually. She'll meet us up ahead." She sounded almost breathless, and Alastor had to assume it was from excitement, because she didn't seem to be tiring as they waded deeper and deeper into the water.

Someone out in the ocean? Another nymph, perhaps?

Alastor tried once more to slip away from Eilonwy's grasp, but she turned to give him a sly smile, her witch light bobbing at chin height and casting a delicate glow across her sharp features. "Don't you trust me?"

"I haven't exactly had the best day so far," Alastor said. "Are you sure you know where you're going?"

Eilonwy laughed, the sound relaxing and comforting. "You're safe with me, Alastor, I promise."

She tugged him further along, and Alastor let himself be led further out into the sea with slightly less reluctance.

Eventually, she stopped. The water was halfway up his calves; the gently rolling waves that hit them came to his knees. With a gentle wave of her free hand, Eilonwy sent out half a dozen additional witch lights, and they formed a semi-circle in front of them, hovering at chest height. Alastor looked around him, seeing no one in sight. The *Seahawk* blocked his view of the shore, putting the camp out of sight. He realized he also couldn't see the *Kingfisher*, where Mathius and his crew were likely getting ready to bed down for the night. It was just the two of them, standing alone in the ocean, surrounded by magic lights.

Except he didn't feel alone.

There was a nagging sensation in his mind, alerting his senses to the fact that there was *something* else out in the darkness. The sensation grew stronger, and the sound of heavy splashing drew his attention off to their left. A looming shadow lumbered into the soft light of Eilonwy's witch lights, and Alastor's heart skipped a few beats as it came into view.

"Hello, Alastor."

"Great Ones preserve us," Alastor managed, struggling for a moment to remember how to speak. "A dragon." He had read about them in old history books, and there had been a few drawings. The creature before him was easily recognizable, though smaller and less spiny than he would have thought.

"Yes," the great dragon said, her large dark eyes closing and reopening slowly. *"My name is Melonya."*

Alastor realized with a start that the dragon was not

speaking aloud to him, but that he could hear her words in his mind. It felt like her words were reverberating through him, becoming a part of him. A smug sense of satisfaction wrapped around him, and Alastor realized that her feelings were washing over him like the waves washing over his legs.

"This is incredible." Alastor was faintly aware of Eilonwy giggling behind him, but he didn't care. He reached out a hand, stretching it towards the dragon, then hesitated. "Can I pet you?"

"I'm not a dog." Alastor was hit with a deep sense of displeasure, then a second wave of glum resignation. *"But if touching me will help you to come to terms with my existence, then I'll allow it."*

"Amazing." Alastor brushed a hand down the side of the dragon's neck, feeling the hard scales under his palm and fingertips. Her body was cool to the touch, and the scales wet and rather slimy. "This is amazing," he repeated. Melonya let him stroke her neck for a moment, then broke the silence with a soft rumble of annoyance; Alastor backed away apologetically.

"I understand that you're having a difficult time. I thought I might be able to help."

Alastor remembered what had caused Eilonwy to drag him away from his angry seclusion, and he frowned up at Melonya. "I'm not sure how." He shrugged. "What Roland did was incredibly selfish and stupid. He hurt my mother. I'm not sure I could ever understand him. Or forgive him for it."

"I think you might be wrong, but let's give it a try."

Alastor stiffened. "What are you going to do?"

Melonya huffed, warm air buffeting Alastor's face. *"I'm only going to act as a conduit, so that you can see and feel what Roland cannot explain to you in words."* She blinked slowly at him, bringing her large head in close to his. *"Just close your eyes, and see if you can feel the connection between you and I."*

Alastor did as he was told, closing his eyes with a skeptical glance at Eilonwy. He was surprised to realize that he could feel his connection to the dragon almost immediately. The link between them was strong, anchoring itself in his mind like an old memory. "I can feel it," he muttered, jaw slackened in surprise. "It feels … powerful."

"Only because we are so close together, physically. It would fade with distance. And grow stronger with time and affection."

"Amazing."

"Can you visualize it? Imagine a rope, tying the two of us together."

In his mind's eye, Alastor saw himself standing beside a softly glowing post with a rope fastened around it. The rope was pulled taught, its length stretching out into the great unknown before him.

"The other end of the rope leads back to me. Follow it."

In Alastor's mind, a second post appeared in the distance, larger than the first, with many more ropes connected to it. Without hesitation, he followed the mental connection between him and Melonya, reaching what seemed to be some sort of nexus. "Is this … your mind?" he asked, staring around him. He could see where other connections started at this nexus point, but their opposing ends were hidden from him.

"Only a small part, little one. My mind is far too complex for you to go exploring through. You might get lost."

A third post lit up in the distance, this one similar to Alastor's own.

"That is Roland. I cannot allow you to wander all the way back to his mind, but I will let you touch his connection with me, and see what you might find lurking on the very surface of his mind."

Alastor hesitated, not sure if he wanted to know what Roland was thinking and feeling. "What do you think is there?"

"I don't need to guess. I know what is there. And I know it will help you understand him better."

"Is he fine with you doing this?"

Another wave of annoyance washed over Alastor. *"I'm sure he will appreciate the gesture, though he did not think to ask me for the help."*

Alastor's hand stretched out almost of its own accord, reaching for the connection between Roland and Melonya. The rope he envisioned in his mind's eye was thicker and stronger looking than his own. Was it because Roland had known the dragon longer, and their connection was stronger for it? Alastor brushed his palm delicately along the corded surface of the connection Melonya had shown him, still uncertain if he wanted to know what he would find tangled within.

Melonya's feelings of annoyance and impatience vanished in the instant his fingertips brushed against the thickly braided rope. In its place, a deep sense of anguish and hurt settled deep into Alastor's heart, and flighty feelings of panic and fear strummed through his body, leaving him rooted where he stood. He reflexively tightened his grip on the mental connection Melonya had opened to him, searching for stability in the sudden turmoil of emotions and sounds that cascaded over him. He could hear his mother's voice, telling him that he was dead to her. He heard another woman's voice, this one pitched a little deeper, warning him of tremendous heartbreak. He saw a man that could only be his father, with dark hair just like his, darting up from where he crouched beside him and running towards a dark forest, and he felt the pain of knowing he might never see his brother again.

He felt the compressive weight of years of tormented thoughts of self-doubt and self-hatred pushing him down to his knees. He was worthless. He let his brother die. He couldn't save the woman he loved. He couldn't save his sister. And now his nephew, the last of his family, wanted nothing to do with him.

He could never redeem himself.

He was useless.

He was a failure.

He was a monster.

He was—

He was on his knees, the gentle waves of the ocean buffeting against his chest. Someone had their hands on his shoulders, calling his name.

Alastor released his held breath in a ragged gasp, then immediately sucked in another mouthful of air. His heart was beating so hard in his chest that he could feel it throughout his body, and his head was pounding in a matching rhythm.

"Alastor, are you alright?" Eilonwy sounded panicked, and she tried to pull him back to his feet, but his legs were too weak to hold his weight. Another set of arms grabbed him from around the middle and held him steady.

"Easy there. We've got you." Tathiel's soothing voice was oddly calming. "You're alright now. Just take some deep breaths."

Alastor did as he was told, trying to focus his blurring vision on the witch lights bobbing frantically around. He noticed numbly that some of them were greener than Eilonwy's had been. *Tathiel's, probably,* he thought.

"I'm sorry, Alastor. I should have realized that Roland's current state might not be the best for that sort of thing," Melonya said, her shame rolling over him in dark waves.

"It's alright," Alastor managed. He straightened, gently pushing Tathiel and Eilonwy away from him. "I'm okay now. It was just ..." He drew in another ragged breath. "I felt like I was him."

"We know." Tathiel looked Alastor over, wide eyed. "There was a lot of overflow from you. We felt everything, too." Tathiel's gaze was caught by something over Alastor's shoulder. "Some of us more than others."

Alastor turned to see Jaimes standing a few feet away, motionless. Even in the dim light cast by the witch lights around him, Alastor could see that he was crying. He couldn't blame him; tears were blurring and stinging his own eyes. "Jaimes …"

"He thinks he's a monster," Jaimes muttered, his eyes unfocused and staring.

"Yeah," Alastor replied numbly.

"He's only alive right now because he wanted to be here for you." Jaimes's eyes snapped to Alastor's, then flitted away again.

"Yeah." With a shudder, Alastor recalled the bitter self-hatred and the thoughts of suicide that had felt so *real* only a moment ago. But they had been very real. They just hadn't been his.

Jaimes seemed to collect himself, drawing a slow breath and giving his head a firm shake. "I don't want to leave him now. I think he needs us. I think he needs you."

Alastor nodded, considering it. "I think you're right."

ROLAND

Roland paced the sand close to the fire, arms crossed over his chest and one hand rubbing absentmindedly over his chin. "I should have told him sooner," he muttered under his breath. From the corner of his eye, he saw Tiryn watching him as he paced. *Tiryn was right,* Roland thought. *I was being selfish and thoughtless, and look what it's gotten me.* He turned, rubbing his hand over his face again. *Alastor called me a monster. Is that what I've become? Am I failure? First I lost Nevina, then my chosen brother. Silvana said I was dead to her. Now my nephew thinks I'm a monster.* Another turn. *This could have been avoided if I had taken the book from Silvana. Alastor would be safe at the inn, still thinking I was dead or missing.*

"Why didn't I just take the book from her before I left?" he asked himself. He paused, turning to Tiryn. "I know you can hear me over there." The elf looked up from where he sat, looking annoyingly unperturbed. "What do you think of all of this?"

Tiryn tilted his head, considering for a moment. "I think I picked up my anxious pacing from you." He grimaced, looking Roland over. "It's a bad habit to fall into."

Roland scoffed and continued walking, turning after a

few feet and starting again. "They've been gone for over an hour."

"They'll be back. Tathiel and Eilonwy are with them, they'll be safe."

"You should have let me go after them."

"So you could make an even bigger ass of yourself?" Tiryn smirked, shaking his head. "No."

Roland could only glare at Tiryn and continue his pacing. But Tiryn was right. Tiryn was always right. *The damned elf.* He took a deep breath, letting it out slowly. "Alright, Tiryn. In the future, will you tell me if I'm being a selfish idiot? I'll try to listen to your advice more often. You seem to be much better at dealing with other people than I am."

"Roland …" Tiryn started, his voice sincere. "You're my friend. I trust and care about you. I will always tell you when you're being a selfish ass."

Roland looked the elf over. Tiryn never cursed. "You're still drunk."

Tiryn shrugged. "A little. At least I'm still awake." He jerked his chin to the opposite side of the fire, where Nunor had passed out some time ago. The dwarf had finished off a whole case of mead on his own, had drunkenly tried to play a lute he pulled out from Great Ones only knew where after the boys had run off, then had simply fallen over and started snoring.

Roland sighed, pausing long enough to catch Tiryn's eye. "Thank you for staying with me. You're a good friend." Tiryn only shrugged again, and Roland continued his pacing in silence.

The quiet only lasted for a moment more before being broken. "Roland." Tiryn stood in one smooth motion, coming to stand next to him. "They're on their way back. I can see lights down by the shore."

Roland looked out across the stretch of sandy beach. The night was so dark and complete, he could hardly see more than a few feet beyond the circle of light cast by the fire. But Tiryn's eyesight was much better than his. "Are all four of them there?"

Tiryn nodded. "They'll probably still be very upset."

"I know." Roland sighed.

"And honestly, they have every right to be."

"I know," he said a little more forcefully.

"You did lie to them, and—"

"Tiryn," Roland growled. Tiryn turned to look at him. "I know what I did. I know it was wrong. I just hope I can convince them to stay."

They waited, standing side by side, as the others came into Roland's view. Tathiel and Eilonwy were both walking at a leisurely pace, with Jaimes between them. Alastor followed more slowly behind, head down. When they reached the fire, the twins ignored Roland and Tiryn completely, apparently content to pretend that the last hour or so had never happened. Jaimes gave both of them a small smile as he passed, but Roland couldn't be sure if it was meant to be affectionate or a smirk.

Alastor alone remained standing, his hands twisting together anxiously. "After giving it some thought," he said slowly, "Jaimes and I have decided that we want to continue on this journey with you. We want to help you with whatever it is that you're trying to do."

Roland's shoulders relaxed, and his breath let out in a quiet whoosh of air.

"Are you sure?" Tiryn said.

Roland turned to look at his friend. From so close, he could see the bright sheen to Tiryn's eyes, but the elf seemed more sober than not at this point. "You can't be serious," Roland mumbled.

"What I meant was ... that—" Tiryn waved a hand around them, his brows raised. "That did not go well."

"Dammit, Tiryn."

"No, he's right," Alastor said, nodding slowly. "It did not go well." He paused, seeming to weigh his words. "But I had some time to think about your past decisions. And I had some help understanding them."

Roland's head cocked, and he glanced over to Eilonwy, who sat silently in the sand, twirling a small stick through the fire. At her side, Tathiel swirled a finger through the sand, creating intricate whirls. "Help from who?"

Alastor smiled, a genuine one that lit up his dark eyes. "We met Melonya." His eyes widened, and he looked down at his open palms in wonder. "We met a dragon. I got to *pet* a dragon! It was incredible."

Roland laughed, remembering his own wonder at meeting her. "She let you *pet* her?"

"You weren't supposed to tell them that, Alastor," Tathiel said teasingly. Eilonwy smirked at his words, glancing up at them.

Alastor shrugged, tossing his hands up. "I got to meet a dragon. I'm sailing on a real ship. I'm traveling with elves and a dwarf. I'm learning how to use a sword, and I might be able to learn how to use magic." He paused, looking up at Roland with a small smile. "And I was finally able to meet the uncle my mother always told me stories about."

"Alastor …" Roland started, but Alastor raised a hand to quiet him.

"You made a lot of mistakes over the last several years. But I can understand your reasoning for a lot of those decisions." Alastor smiled, holding out a hand for Roland to take. "I'd like to make sure I'm here to keep you from making any more ridiculous mistakes in the future. So, will you let Jaimes and I stay with you?"

"Of course," Roland said, nodding emphatically. "Of course you two can stay with us." He grabbed Alastor by the hand, pulling him into an embrace. The boy was tall and thin, like his father had been. Holding his nephew close reminded him of hugging Hasani all those years ago, and the thought was both painful and comforting. After a respectful moment, Roland released Alastor, blinking his eyes rapidly to stave off the sudden threat of tears again.

Tiryn clapped his hands together once, the sharp sound rolling through the air like thunder. "Well, now that all of that is done with, let's get down to our real business."

"I'll drink to that," Nunor mumbled in a drunken slur from the stretch of sand he had collapsed in before rolling over and continuing his soft snoring.

"I think we could all do with a nice chat, yes," Roland said, sitting himself once more in front of the fire. Alastor resumed his place across from him, next to Jaimes, who patted him affectionately on the back.

"Alastor," Roland began, "what did your mother tell you about the night we left the castle?"

Alastor glanced at Jaimes, who said nothing. "She told Jaimes and I about the Dragon Door, and how you were able to get her and my father out of the dungeons by making a blood sacrifice to open it." Alastor pointed at Roland's arm. "She said that you somehow healed almost immediately, but that it left you with four round scars on your left arm."

Roland nodded, his hand instinctively touching a spot just above his navel. "Those weren't the only scars I earned that night, but that's correct."

Jaimes squinted, concentrating. "She mentioned once that they had to leave before the king sent Alastor's father off to kill the Coven." He shook his head. "But they were killed anyway, weren't they?"

Roland nodded again, pained at the mention of the Coven. "They were, shortly after we made it out of the castle, I think. Anything else?"

Alastor and Jaimes looked at each other, and Jaimes broke the eye contact by looking down at his lap. Alastor answered the question, not quite meeting Roland's gaze. "When my mother was ill, she talked a lot about how the king had come to kill her, because they had stolen from him. We tried to ask her about what she and my father had stolen from him, but it just made her more upset."

"She didn't steal anything. *I* stole the Dragon's Eye from him, as well as a dragon's egg." Roland sighed. "Mothlenor wanted to use magic to force the egg to hatch, so he could control the dragon within and use it to purify the lands of all non-human creatures. I stole it to prevent that."

"And it hatched into Melonya?" Alastor asked.

Roland frowned. "No, Melonya's egg was found by Tathiel and Eilonwy in their Homewood. The dragon egg I stole was gold, and your father had it on him when he fled into the elven woods west of the Knife." Roland paused, tossing a nearby twig into the fire and watching it curl. "I can only hope that it was lost in there somewhere, and that Mothlenor hasn't found it yet."

"I don't really understand what this has to do with what you're all doing," Jaimes said, crossing his arms over his chest. "You might have lied about trying to find my uncle, but you're sailing with Mathius for a reason, right?"

Roland sighed again. "I'll get to that in a moment. I'd just hoped Silvana had told you a little more of the story. But I can do that, I suppose." Roland picked up another twig from the sand nearby and tossed it onto the fire, watching as it curled and burned away.

"It all started when Areanath's adviser, my sister's husband, was given a small book for safekeeping. That book, which was passed from Hasani to Silvana and, hopefully, down to you, holds all that we need to know to keep Mothlenor from destroying Azimar as we know it."

Alastor hesitated. His brows knitted together, and Roland wondered if he was struggling to understand what had just been said. After a moment, he reached into a pocket sewn to the inside of his tunic and pulled out the little leather book

Roland had first seen over fifteen years ago. He held it out for Roland to take. Roland took it from him gingerly, letting it rest against his chest for a moment. There was a sudden lightness to his heart that felt almost surreal. "Finally," he whispered, "we can truly begin Areanath's quest."

Nunor whistled, startling everyone around the fire. "It's a good thing you took your shirt off before running off to fuck that nymph, boy. The fate of the world could have washed away if you hadn't."

3 1

MELONYA

Melonya lay in the cooling sand of the beach, grateful to spend a few hours on dry land. Nunor and Tiryn had taken her appearance at their campfire very well. Tiryn had been respectful, even by elven standards, and the dwarf had been as crass and delightful as Melonya had hoped he would be. But now they had all retreated to separate corners of their small camp, and Melonya quietly watched them.

Well, nearly quietly.

"You sound like a big house cat, Melonya," Jaimes said. He stood just behind the joint of her left wing, where bone and sinew met hard muscle.

The loud hum emanating from her chest paused as Melonya turned to look at him, baring her teeth. *"I do not."*

He turned to Eilonwy, who stood on Melonya's other side with a fistful of sand in each hand. "Does she always make that noise?"

Melonya shifted her long neck in time to catch Eilonwy's cheeky grin. "Only when she's happy." Eilonwy slapped the damp sand against Melonya's back and massaged it across her scales. "And I think she is very happy." She reached one hand under Melonya's lower jaw to scratch at her chin.

"Aren't you, my darling?" Eilonwy's voice took on a motherly tone and her eyes glinted mischievously.

"Stop that." But even as Melonya protested, the rumbling purr grew louder. It was hard to admit it, but Eilonwy's fingertips had happened upon a rather delightful spot.

Eilonwy chuckled, both hands now rubbing along her lower jawline and down to her neck. "You sure you want me to stop?"

Melonya jerked her head away and thrashed the tip of her tail, sending sand spraying in Eilonwy's direction. *"I'm not a cat."*

Eilonwy and Jaimes both laughed, the former wiping sand from her clothing as she did. "Come on now, I'm only playing. Do you want us to get the brine from your scales or not?"

Melonya settled down in the sand once more, turning her long neck so she could keep them both in sight. *"Yes,"* she said glumly. *"I'd prefer a proper bath, but this will have to do until we can return home."*

"Will you go back to Vyris then, after you've found the amulet Roland was talking about?" Jaimes asked. While he might have tried to make his question sound innocent enough, Melonya sensed a deeper blend of emotions that she could not altogether understand.

Eilonwy shrugged, her attention too focused on a spot between Melonya's haunches to notice Jaimes staring at her. "Probably. It's not safe for us here in Azimar. As Brynne was helpful enough to point out."

"Do you think we could come visit you?"

Eilonwy looked up. The smile she gave Jaimes was warm and kind. "I'd like that very much." She turned her attention back to Melonya's side and slapped another handful of sand against her blue scales. "My only regret is that we never found the Isle of Onia."

Jaimes frowned, stepping back to inspect his handiwork

in the light of the campfire. "What makes you say this isn't it?"

"Well, the Isle of Onia is supposed to be the source of all arcane energy, right?" Eilonwy paused, lifting her head as if to survey their surroundings. But she only shook her head. "There's nothing here. No more energy than any other stretch of beach might have."

Melonya snorted. *"That's not quite right."*

"What do you mean?" Eilonwy asked.

Melonya rolled onto her side, and Jaimes circled around to stand beside Eilonwy as she began scrubbing sand against Melonya's underbelly. *"This might not be the source of arcane energy now, but I think it once was a source. And a good one, too. You can still feel it. Like …"* Melonya struggled for words that might make sense. She felt the energy flowing through the island as easily as she felt the coarse grit that rubbed away the salty crust from her scales. But the sensation was different. And it somehow reminded her of something she could not quite recall. *"It's like the last few drops of moisture in the bottom of a glass. You can see it. If you tried, you could even get to it. But it will not quench your thirst. It can only remind you of what was once there."* Melonya stretched her hind legs, the long claws digging into the sand. *"Besides, how else would so many elementals have come into existence on such a small island?"*

"There are more elementals here?" Jaimes asked, his eyes widening. "You mean like that nymph that tried to kill Alastor?"

"There's only the one nymph. Likely because there is only the one lake, and nymphs are very territorial." Melonya yawned, exhaling in a hot breath of air that hit Eilonwy and Jaimes in the face. *"But there are others. A couple of golems up in the hills. Some jinn and faeries scattered around. I wouldn't be surprised if a fire spirit were hiding in the embers of the campfire, gnawing away on the burnt wood and ashes."*

"Are we safe?" Jaimes exchanged a look with Eilonwy, who seemed undisturbed by Melonya's revelation.

"We are safe." Melonya blinked slowly, surprised by the fatigue that was settling over her. She looked around their little camp once more, making careful note of the various activities each member of their party was involved in. Nunor was still nursing a bottle of honeyed mead, but it sat in the sand at his feet as he carved away at a broken branch that looked comically large in his small hands. Tiryn and Tathiel were both lying in the sand to rest, though Melonya was sure neither was sleeping. Tathiel made a habit of keeping a close eye on his sister, and Tiryn seemed to be a similar sort when it came to Roland and the two young boys. And Roland and Alastor sat close together, their heads dipped in murmured conversation. *"There are enough of us to warn of anything that may approach, and there is nothing out there interested enough to venture out of the woods."*

"Numbers didn't help my uncle and the men with him," Jaimes said.

"Your uncle didn't have a dragon and three elves with him," Eilonwy said softly. "Things might have ended differently if there had been someone like Tiryn there."

Melonya yawned again, giving her tail a quick flick. *"Eilonwy is right. Roland himself said he and Alastor might not have survived the nymph if not for him."*

Jaimes only shrugged, brushing sand from Melonya's stomach.

"You should get some rest, Melonya. It must have been exhausting, searching for the *Seahawk*. When was the last time you slept?"

"I'll be fine," Melonya said with an irritated grunt. But her eyelids were already growing too heavy to keep open, and she wanted nothing more than to curl up in the warm sand and sleep.

"Don't be silly. Let someone else keep an eye on things tonight."

Melonya took little convincing. She couldn't honestly remember the last time she had slept. It was difficult to sleep in the depths of the ocean, and she almost never had the opportunity to leave the cold waters long enough to get a good rest. *"Try not to wander off and cause any trouble, will you?"*

Eilonwy laughed. "Of course."

Melonya closed her eyes and settled herself down deeper into the sand, twisting once more to lie on her stomach. She could hear Jaimes and Eilonwy murmuring, and their weight was comforting when they sat in the sand and leaned against her side.

And as she faded into sleep, Melonya opened her mind to the arcane creatures of the island. The golems were disinterested, but the others accepted her without hesitation. They offered themselves to her curiosity, and Melonya did the same for them.

Melonya dreamed, and as she dreamed she shared with them all that she had come to learn about the world outside the little isle. They shared with her as well, and her dreams were filled with visions of great dragons soaring the skies above. Melonya fell into a deeper slumber, and the sound of Jaimes's and Eilonwy's voices faded as she tried to count the winged beasts that filled the skies in her mind's eye. There were dragons of every shade imaginable, and Melonya's heart leapt when she spotted a large and heavily spined one with blue scales flying close to a ruby-colored dragon roughly half its size.

Never had Melonya felt such peace as she did in that dream the few inhabitants of the island gave her. Her chest let out a rumbling purr, loud and lusty.

nd out in the wide world, the energy of the Isle of Onia carried the emotions that poured from Melonya out to another sleeping creature. And while the other did not dream of flying through the clouds, the deep hum that reverberated sympathetically with Melonya was enough to disturb even a centuries-long sleep.

The creature stirred, surprised by the strangely familiar power that teased at old and forgotten memories.

"Onia, is that you?" the creature asked. *"It has been too long."*

32

FERRAND

"Please, sir," the man whispered through cracked and bleeding lips, "it won't happen again."

Ferrand weighed the whip experimentally in his hand and gave the vermin locked in the pillory a frown. "I can't let you go unpunished. If I let one misdeed go without consequence, others will follow. Precedence is precedence, after all."

The man sobbed. "Please. I've been here for three days. Has my penance not been fulfilled?"

"It will be," Ferrand said. A muscle in the burned half of his faced twitched unpleasantly. "After ten lashes."

The vermin sobbed again, but no tears fell. He likely didn't have enough fluid left in him to muster any up. But the sight of his dried and wrinkled face scrunching up in such a way filled Ferrand with disgust. "Fucking pathetic."

Ferrand took his stance at the rear of the pillory. The man's back curved and hunched against the shackles he was fastened in. Ferrand let the length of corded leather skate across the stained wood planks and measured the distance between himself and his target with a tilt of his head and a careful narrowing of his only remaining eye.

The first lash landed low, hitting the man across his bony

haunches. The sound of the whip closely followed by a piercing scream echoed across the market. The few people still milling about in the heat of the day, all men by the look of them, quickly turned tail and hurried away.

"One," Ferrand called.

The second lash landed high, cutting across the back of the man's neck. Fortunately for him, it had also been a weak landing, and the ensuing cut was thin and likely shallow.

"Two."

The third strike landed squarely where it should, and by the fifth the man had let his weight fall with each blow, his legs too weak to keep him on his feet. If it pained him to have the bottom of the pillory digging into his throat every time he collapsed to his knees, he made no complaint. Or perhaps his sobs and screams of pain were complaint enough for both the agony of the pillory and the agony of the whip.

"Six."

The man let out a particularly loud scream, and Ferrand was pleased to see a deep break in the skin through the numerous tears in his ragged tunic.

"Commander Ferrand," a man's voice called from behind Ferrand.

Ferrand turned to see a King's Guard standing a few feet away, breathless and sweating. The man was familiar, but Ferrand could not put a name to his face. "Can't you see I'm busy?" Ferrand turned back to his task, snapping the whip over the pest's flesh once more. "Seven."

"My apologies, Commander."

"Shut up, you imbecile. Or you'll be next." The eighth lash landed with hardly a whimper, and Ferrand cursed. *This fucking idiot has ruined my concentration.*

Ferrand pulled the whip back, letting the leather fly through the air with a whistle. It struck very well, and the man let out a rasping scream and arched his back so deeply the heavy bars of the pillory strained against the back of his neck. And then he fell into a slump, blood staining his tunic enough to make the original color hard to discern.

Ferrand waited for him to struggle to his feet once more, but it quickly became clear that he would not be getting up without assistance. Ferrand let the whip strike for a tenth time, and then twice more in quick succession. The man hardly moved with each strike.

Ferrand cursed, coiling the whip on itself and turning to face the King's Guard. "What is so important that you felt the need to interrupt my work?"

"I-I'm sorry, Commander," the knight stammered. "But Madam Moira says that the twins are ready. They're waiting for you in your quarters."

Ferrand couldn't help the sneer that curled the unburnt side of his mouth. "Already?"

"Yes, Commander. You said you wanted them quickly."

Ferrand handed the whip to the King's Guard. "Best to not keep Madam Moira waiting, then." He rolled the shoulder of his whipping arm, feeling the muscles stretch. *I should have warmed up a little more before coming here. I might not have wasted so many lashes.*

"And do you have any other news for me?"

The King's Guard gave him a blank stare. "Like what, Commander?"

Ferrand groaned. How he had ended up with so many imbeciles in his employ, he would never know. "Like news from our men along the southern coast. About the ship we're looking for?"

"N-nothing, Commander. We have no new reports on the whereabouts of the *Kingfisher.* But our men are in place and ready to act as soon as the ship docks."

Ferrand scowled, his eye narrowing. "Good." He waved a hand over his shoulder at the flogged vermin behind him. "Take care of that mess. If he's alive, drag him down to the dungeons. If he's dead, toss him into the Knife."

The King's Guard hesitated. "What did he do?"

A new King's Guard then, to pity the rabble of the streets.
Ferrand sneered again, even the ruined half of his face
twisting uncomfortably. "I can't recall."

Ferrand left the King's Guard to his duty and picked his
way through the torn cobbled square and up the steps to the
main entrance to the Etritian castle. Once inside, his pace
increased. His quarters were dreadfully far from the main
foyer, but Madam Moira would wait for him. She always did
when his coin was involved.

Another King's Guard tried to flag him down as he
crossed from the more formal section of the castle into the
residential halls. All Ferrand had the chance to see was a red
and blue checked surcoat hailing him. He didn't even give the
man the opportunity to speak.

"Not now, you idiot!" Ferrand brushed him off, his eagerness increasing with every step.

Madam Moira was waiting for him right outside his door.
She stood tall and erect for a woman in the years just beyond
her prime. Her cheeks had been dusted with rouge and her
dress had been carefully styled to reveal the barest hint of
pale breasts. If she didn't already have the pick of the girls
left in Etritia for him to choose from, Ferrand could easily
see himself taking her. And before she had become Madam
Moira, he had done just that.

"Commander Ferrand." Madam Moira greeted him with a
low bow and a flutter of her eyelashes. "I'm delighted that
you have chosen my girls to satisfy your appetite this
evening."

"They're ready?" Ferrand asked, tugging his tunic free of
his pants.

"Ready and waiting."

"Good." He tossed a bag of coins her way, and Moira
caught it deftly. "I'll return them to you when I've finished
with them."

"Of course, Commander." Moira bowed again, then turned to walk away.

Before she could get too far, Ferrand grabbed her tightly around the elbow and pulled her close. Any other woman might have been afraid of him, but Moira only gave him a delicate smirk and another flutter of her lashes. "Perhaps next time I'll have you join us."

Moira's smirk deepened. "Perhaps next time you'll bring a bigger purse."

Ferrand's hand left her arm, and he sent her away with a sharp slap on her rear. "I'll keep that in mind, Moira."

The door to his quarters opened and shut with the slightest of sounds. Through the open doorway to his bedroom, across from the sitting area, he saw Moira's twins waiting for him.

They were naked, lying in wait atop his covers. Each was fair haired and pale skinned and identical to the other in every way. And each wore a red silk scarf tied around her neck.

If Moira had thought that the single article might entice him, she had been wrong.

Ferrand crossed the open sitting area, undoing the lacing of this pants as he went. "Take those off."

The girls exchanged a glance.

"Now."

They did as they were told, pulling the scarves away and tossing them to the floor.

And that was where the single difference between them could be seen.

One twin was perfectly flawless from head to toe. The other twin had a fading bruise in the vague shape of a hand-print around her neck.

Had long had it been since Moira had last brought the twins to him? And yet they still bore his mark. No one else would dare to bruise his girls, and indeed few others in Etritia could even afford the opportunity to do so.

Ferrand kicked off his boots and pulled his shirt off. "Begin."

They were less hesitant this time, and he had hardly started pulling his trousers off before the sisters were wrapped around each other, their mouths meeting in hot earnest.

"I said begin."

The unmarked twin jumped as his command, but the other was quicker to comply. She slipped one hand down between her sister's thighs, wrapping the opposite hand through the girl's long tresses and holding her close.

Ferrand watched for only a moment before joining them. He was never one to be patient. And when he was finally through with them, both twins carried his mark around their necks.

3 3

MATHIUS

Mathius stood on the aft end of the *Kingfisher*, a small paring knife in one hand, a half-cut apple in the other. Not far away, Alastor and Jaimes were engaged in a mock fight, using two heavy wooden swords carved from a large piece of driftwood Nunor had found on the beach of the Isle of Onia. The new weapons were an excellent upgrade from the slimmer and more fragile practice swords they had been using previously, and the boys seemed to be improving their techniques nicely. Mathius sliced off another piece of his apple, watching Jaimes circle Alastor, looking for the opportunity to strike. Alastor was becoming a fairly well-rounded fighter, but surprisingly Jaimes was the better of the two when it came to offensive strategies. Though he was usually the quiet and reserved type, often seen sitting in the small amount of shade offered by the mainmast and reading one of the various books he had brought, the young man seemed to awaken in some strange way when he held a weapon in his hands. Though he did have one major flaw in his technique …

Jaimes lunged in for the attack, and Mathius grimaced as Alastor easily sidestepped the maneuver and whacked Jaimes on the hip as the boy passed. Jaimes quickly turned, already looking for the chance for a counterattack, but Roland shouted a halt command, and both boys instantly straightened.

"You keep leading with the wrong foot, Jaimes!" Roland yelled, more from frustration than from anger. Mathius almost laughed after hearing the same exclamation for perhaps the twentieth time in the last week.

"I know, I know," Jaimes answered, clearly just as annoyed. "I'm just doing what feels natural, and I don't realize until I'm already moving that it's going to get me tripped up."

"You could have had Alastor there. It was a good attack, if you had just led with the—"

"The right foot, I know," Jaimes grumbled. "I'll get it right, I promise."

Roland ran a hand over his freshly trimmed beard, which was now clearly red after he'd taken the time to scrub down properly. Though Mathius could understand why he might prefer to wear his beard longer; there was a bald scar that ran the length of the right side of his face, from cheekbone to chin. "I wish I could show you this stuff better, but Tiryn and the twins are just far too fast for me to spar with properly, and Nunor is too short."

"I could help, Roland." Mathius was surprised to hear the words coming out of his mouth, but didn't retract them. Instead, he cut another slice off his apple as Roland looked him over.

"Can you fight?" Roland asked, an eyebrow raised. There was something to his voice that suggested he already knew the answer.

"I'm pretty good, I think. Good enough to show the boys proper footing, anyway." Mathius smiled, pocketing the knife and setting his mostly finished apple onto a nearby barrel. He motioned to Alastor, and the boy tossed him the weapon he held. Jaimes passed his over to Roland in silence, and Roland took it hesitantly.

"We'll go pretty easy on each other, and I want both of you to watch how we move our feet. And Alastor, I want you to watch how I block Mathius's attacks," Roland said to the two.

"If you *can* block them, mind you," Mathius joked. It had been some time since he'd last held a sword, but even the blunted wooden stick felt familiar in his grip. He took a relaxed stance, legs shoulder-width apart and knees slightly bent, and waved for Roland to begin.

Roland fell into a similar stance, though with his right leg slightly behind the other. Mathius saw the ensuing step and lunge coming before Roland's weight had even shifted. He sidestepped, much as Alastor had, catching Roland's sword on his own and pushing it aside. Adjusting the momentum into a turn, he brought his sword up to hit Roland's shoulder. But Roland was already expecting the move, and recovered himself enough to roll forward, out of the reach of Mathius's sword. Roland sprang up to his feet easily, and Mathius let him recover his stance before moving in for his own attack. He led with his right foot, hoping Jaimes was paying attention, and went with an overhead strike. Roland blocked it, as Mathius knew he would. The boot to the chest Roland had not expected, and although Mathius didn't intend to hurt him, Roland stumbled back several feet.

"What the fuck, Mathius?" Roland grumbled, rubbing at his chest. "That's not how you're supposed to fight."

"It's how just about everyone fights, Roland. Now stop being a child. I didn't kick you that hard." He fell into his stance once more. "Let's get serious for a moment, shall we?"

Roland's weight shifted in the smallest of motions, and he was on Mathius in a second. Mathius was able to block the first attack, but was forced to dodge the second. He came back with an attack of his own, stepping closer to Roland as he did. Roland's block was a little clumsy in such close quarters, but still effective. Mathius used the block to shove Roland back a step, then forced the retreat with another advancing attack. Roland anticipated the move, and side-stepped to the left rather than let himself be pushed against the ship's railing.

They went back and forth for a few moments more, switching quickly between attacking and defending. Finally, their swords once more locked into a block after Mathius had led with another shoulder-height stab, Roland called a halt.

"I think they've seen enough for today," Roland panted.

Mathius could hardly blame him for breathing heavily. He was out of breath as well, and beads of sweat were rolling into his eyes, burning them. He stepped back, running the sleeve of his tunic over his forehead. "You're pretty good, Roland."

Roland snorted, wiping sweat from his own brow. "You're certainly the best I've had in a while."

Mathius laughed, leaning to rest against the starboard railing. "I've only ever heard that from women, but thank you."

Roland shook his head, chuckling quietly under his breath.

"That was amazing, Roland. You both moved so quickly, it was hard to catch everything." Alastor held out a hand for Roland's practice sword, and Roland passed it over and fell heavily onto a nearby crate.

"Were you able to see what I was trying to explain?" Roland turned to Jaimes, who had taken Mathius's weapon. "Do you better understand the importance of good foot-work, Jaimes?"

Jaimes nodded. "I think so. You two were incredible."

"It's from years of practice. You could be that good too, Jaimes." Roland waved them away tiredly. "Go work on your footwork again. And Alastor, watch out for opportunities to block his attacks. Dodging only works for so long. Eventually your opponent will catch up with you and land a hit."

The boys obediently stepped back to the center of the deck, taking up their sparring positions once more. Roland was watching them, but Mathius was paying more attention to Roland. "Where'd you learn to fight like that? Were you a knight or something?"

Roland glanced up at Mathius for an instant before his gaze was drawn back to Alastor and Jaimes again. "Or something, yes." He sighed, leaning forward to rest his forearms on his thighs. "What about you? You're very skilled."

"When I was young, I had this idea that I could make something of myself by joining the King's Guard. My father trained me." Mathius frowned, remembering. "I was ready to go and present myself to the captain of the King's Guard, but Areanath died." Roland's eyes met Mathius's own, but Mathius could only shrug one shoulder half-heartedly. "I suddenly lost interest in becoming a knight. I left after Mothlenor's coronation. I went south, and instead of becoming a knight I became a sailor. After eight years I became a captain myself."

"You grew up in Etritia?"

"I did." Mathius watched Roland for a reaction, but he only nodded once and went back to watching the boys. "You know, you look a lot like him."

"Who?" Roland asked stonily.

"The captain of the King's Guard. I didn't notice at first, with the shaggy hair and the long beard, but it's pretty clear now. You don't even look much older, which is surprising."

"You're wrong." Roland's eyes narrowed, and Mathius saw his jaw tighten.

Mathius laughed. "I'm not wrong, *Roland*."

The emphasis on his name drew his gaze back up. "What

do you want?" The sudden venom in his voice was startling, though Mathius knew he shouldn't have been surprised.

Mathius shook his head. "You misunderstand. I don't want anything from you." He crossed his arms over his chest. "Quite the opposite, in fact."

Roland raised a quizzical brow, but said nothing.

"It wasn't Areanath's death that changed my mind about becoming a knight. I changed my mind after it was announced that you would become a Peace Guardian. I trained to serve under *you*, Ajax, like my father did. I didn't want to fight with anyone else." Mathius looked over to Jaimes and Alastor, momentarily distracted by their sparring. Jaimes's footwork seemed better, though Alastor was still a little faster than he was. "In a way, you made me the man I am today. Indirectly, of course. But you did, all the same."

Roland grunted noncommittally. His focus was back on Alastor and Jaimes, and Mathius wondered if he was really watching them or just staring off somewhere else.

After a quiet moment, Roland sighed. "And to think Dars was worried about you getting accepted into the King's Guard."

Mathius laughed. "So you do remember me?"

Roland shook his head. "Not well. But you look a bit like your old man. Not too much, lucky you. But enough." Roland lifted his head long enough to flash him a small smile. "It was mostly that stupid line about catching fish that made me sure you're his son." Mathius laughed again, and this time even Roland let out a small chuckle. "I only ever heard him say that, and he said it so often …" Roland's voice drifted, and after a hesitant moment, he looked up at him again, his expression serious. "Have you heard from him? From Dars?"

Mathius shook his head. "Not in a long time. You?"

"Not since I left Etritia."

Mathius shrugged. "I've just learned to accept the worst. That he's gone, and that I'll never see him again."

Roland nodded slowly, staring down at his clasped hands. "Do you know where you're going?"

"Not really. We'll know when we get close."

Mathius nodded, not entirely surprised by the cryptic response. "You've already been aboard for several weeks. We'll run out of ports eventually, and we'll need to turn back. I can't take you further than that, but you're welcome to stay aboard for that long, at least."

"Thank you, Mathius," Roland muttered, not looking up.

Mathius straightened, stepping away from the railing. He was ready to walk away, but remembered another question. "Is Tiryn teaching them magic?"

Roland's gaze flicked up to Mathius, but he didn't answer.

Mathius sighed, shaking his head. "Great Ones preserve us. Just don't damage my ship, damn it." He walked back to the aft end of the ship, snagging his apple along the way. "Great Ones preserve us," he muttered again, bit off a chunk of his apple and tossed the core overboard.

3 4

JAIMES

They once more walked the dirt lane of some small coastal town, Roland walking between Jaimes and Alastor. Only this time, the lane they traveled was muddy and torn from carts and endless foot traffic. It had rained a few days past, and while the deck and sails of the *Kingfisher* had dried quickly under the hot sun, the roads and footpaths of their latest stop hadn't had the same chance. Jaimes's boots squelched and stuck slightly with every step, which only added to his general fatigue and annoyance.

His arms were sore, his legs throbbed and twitched with every step, and the muscles of his shoulders were hard and tense. The night before, he and Alastor had both collapsed into bed without so much as a goodnight to their companions, and were awoken in the morning with a gentle shove from Eilonwy and a hasty breakfast of lukewarm hash before getting to work once more.

In the mornings, they did whatever work Mathius could find for them, often involving carrying various heavy objects —ropes, crates, and other assorted equipment—up and down the length of the *Kingfisher*'s deck. In the afternoons, during the heat of the day, Tiryn trained them in the arcane arts

down in their cabin, often paired with lessons in the medicinal arts. Jaimes found these lessons fascinating, but Alastor
had the annoying habit of staring off at nothing within
minutes. It was during this time that Roland or Tiryn would
make them recite the first poem from Areanath's little book
of clues, until they could recite it word for word upon
request. And after the evening meal, Roland took them back
to the deck to practice their swordplay, often until the sky
had faded into black and the two of them could no longer see
the end of the heavy wooden weapons in their hands.

The endless routine left Jaimes exhausted most days, but
Roland's intense schedule was beginning to pay off. Jaimes
hardly ever misstepped when fighting anymore, and he and
Alastor had both been given the highly regarded compliment
of being "passable beginners" by both Roland and Mathius.
The muscles of his arms and legs were filling out more, and
what little childhood fat that had stubbornly remained had
melted away under the hot sun and Roland's training. His
sand-colored hair grew lighter even as his skin grew darker
and tanned. A handful of weeks aboard the *Kingfisher* had
done more to change him than his entire lifetime working at
his father's inn in Larten.

Roland passed a sweet roll to each of them, and Jaimes
tucked his into his mouth whole, letting the warm pastry
melt on his tongue. It was sweeter than the last batch they'd
purchased in that tiny village further down the coast, and
Jaimes savored the taste of it for a moment, licking the last
bits of honey from his fingertips with relish.

"Where do you think they get the bees?" Alastor asked
suddenly, and Jaimes peered around Roland to see that his
brother was also licking his fingers clean of anything that
remained of his sticky bun. "For the honey, I mean."

Jaimes looked to Roland for the answer, but he seemed
distracted, gazing off in the distance with a sort of dazed
expression on his face. Jaimes glanced around, noting

quickly that, while there were several people in this small town, there was very little plant life. "Maybe they ship them in? Someone cares for them, and harvests the honey?"

"You can ship bees?" Alastor frowned, his face scrunching around his sunburnt nose. "Is that safe?"

"As long as you're careful, sure. I read about it in one of Mother's books. Honey has a lot of medicinal properties." Jaimes paused for a moment, remembering. "She and I were going to see about starting our own colony," he added quietly. He shook himself, giving Alastor a small smile and a light shrug. "Maybe they just ship in the honey."

Alastor considered for a moment, sidestepping a particularly deep rut with a few inches of standing water. "The buns would have been more expensive in that case, I think."

Jaimes shrugged again, then looked Alastor over more carefully. He seemed taller than Jaimes remembered. And his shoulders were broader and more pronounced. "You need a haircut, Alastor. You should let Eilonwy do it."

Eilonwy had cut his own hair a few nights before, and though she had cursed his small and rounded ears for confusing her, it had turned out well enough. So far as Jaimes could tell, anyway.

Alastor flicked his dark hair out of his eyes with a quick shake of the head. "I kind of like it this way. I might keep it."

Jaimes snorted, stepping over another muddy puddle. Beside him, Roland stepped right into the fetid water without so much as a wince. "You'll like it until some poor shopkeeper mistakes you for a girl and offers to sell you some lovely ribbons for your lovely locks."

Alastor opened his mouth to protest, but Roland hushed him with a raised hand.

"We're being followed."

Jaimes's and Alastor's eyes met for a moment around Roland's figure. Alastor's eyes were wide, the dark irises suddenly very small in the surrounding whites. Their footsteps slowed, and Jaimes chanced another look around them.

"No," Roland barked in a low voice. "Don't look around. Don't stop moving. Act like nothing has changed."

Jaimes swallowed around the hard lump that had formed in his throat. His mouth was suddenly dry, and the sweetness of the sticky bun threatened to rise back up as bile. "How long have they been following us?" Jaimes asked quietly. His head was bowed, as if watching his steps, but his eyes glanced frantically all around them, searching for some sign that might give their pursuers away.

"Since the docks, probably. Though I wasn't sure until we stopped at the bakery." Roland carefully wrapped the remaining sticky buns in their linen wrappings and handed them over to Jaimes, who took them numbly.

"How many are there?" Alastor asked. His voice was thin, but steady, and Jaimes wondered briefly how he could be so calm.

"Four, maybe five. I can't be sure." Roland looked up, squinting at the hint of sun that peeked through the clouds overhead.

"Can we fight them?" Alastor asked, and the thought of it made Jaimes's stomach roll. Fighting some unknown men, in a strange town, with no weapons?

"We will not fight them. I will try to lead them away from you, and let you get back to the *Kingfisher*."

"What do you want us to do?" Jaimes asked, his heart beating heavily in his chest.

"Do you see the shop up ahead? The one with the painted sign out front?"

Jaimes saw it. Unlike the others on this end of the street, this shop was in an actual building, while the others were in moving carts. The paint on the sign was peeling, the letters nearly illegible, but it looked to be a tailor house; racks of colorful fabrics could be seen just inside the shop windows.

"When we get close, I want you two to fall back, and then head inside and wait for me. I'll lead them further down the street. If you hear fighting, I want you to run back to the docks. As fast as you can. Do you understand?"

"But Roland—" Alastor began.

"Do you understand?" Roland repeated.

Both boys nodded.

"Good." They were nearing the tailor house, and Jaimes saw a short man with pins pressed between his lips pinning a taller man's sleeve to the shoulder of his tunic. Roland turned to them both, and Jaimes was surprised to see that his eyes were just as wide as Alastor's and full of worry. "I'll see you later, then." He turned and continued in his sedate pace further down the road.

Jaimes and Alastor watched him for a moment, then Jaimes tugged on Alastor's elbow, pulling him closer to the entrance of the shop. "Come on, Alastor. Let's go inside."

The inside of the tailor house was cooler, almost chilly, but it was bright, with several windows and a number of hanging candles dotted around the room. Jaimes and Alastor immediately went to the nearest rack, a low wooden frame with bolts of heavy fabric arranged neatly along it, and stood where they could watch the open doorway.

"I can't believe Roland made us stay behind. We could be helping him," Alastor complained.

"How?" Jaimes asked, tucking the wrapped sweets into his vest. "We have no swords, we don't know how to fight hand to hand. We'd just be in the way, and in danger."

"Didn't you see his face, Jaimes?" Alastor said, glaring at him from over a bolt of deep red fabric. "He was scared."

"He was scared for us, Alastor." Jaimes looked up as the tailor's customer left the shop, ducking his head to avoid the low overhang. "He was worried about what would happen to us."

"Can I help you?"

Jaimes and Alastor both jumped at the voice behind them, and they both turned. Jaimes stammered out a quick "Y-yes," at the same time Alastor answered with a curt "No."

The tailor's eyes narrowed, and he looked between the two of them. He was shorter than either of them, but not by very much, and the way he stood before them suggested he wasn't at all worried about their difference in size.

"W-what we mean is that we're just looking at the moment," Jaimes stammered out. "For a gift. For a friend." Jaimes swallowed hard, feeling the tailor's eyes on him. "For my lady friend, that is."

The tailor's eyes narrowed further as he looked Jaimes over. "There are brooches and various accessories along the back wall. They might be better suited as a gift." The man seemed to consider him for a minute, staring up at Jaimes with a look of distrust and skepticism. "Tell me about your lady friend. What color are her eyes?"

Jaimes hesitated, surprised by the sudden question, and his racing mind immediately fell on Eilonwy. "G-green, her eyes are green."

"And her hair?"

"Light. Almost silver."

The tailor's head tilted slightly at his answer. "And is she your age, or …?"

"No," Jaimes answered automatically. The tailor's raised an eyebrow, and Jaimes silently cursed himself. But he gave the tailor a small smile and dropped his voice lower. "She's a bit older than I am, actually." *By over a hundred years …*

Beside him, Alastor snickered, but Jaimes quieted him with an elbow to the ribs.

All sign of suspicion was gone from the tailor's face, and he gave Jaimes a sly smile and a wink. "In that case, might I suggest a nice hair accessory? Something with a green stone, perhaps. To match her eyes." He gestured over one shoulder to the back wall. "Off to the right, you should find something that suits your needs easily enough." The tailor's gaze drifted over Jaimes's shoulder as another customer stepped noisily through the doorway. "And I shall be back along shortly, to assist you further, should you need it."

Jaimes and Alastor both sighed as the tailor swept around them and greeted the waiting customer.

"That was some quick thinking, Jaimes," Alastor said, dropping his voice down to a whisper.

Jaimes felt his blood pounding in his ears. "I-I just panicked and said the first thing I could think of." He raised a finger to his lips, listening. Other than the soft sounds of conversation between tailor and customer, and the general sounds of a busy street just outside, there was no other noise to be heard. "No sounds of fighting. Maybe Roland was able to lead them off and lose them."

"Well, come on then. Let's go look at brooches and hair accessories until he finds us." Alastor pulled Jaimes by the sleeve further into the shop, stopping when they reached the far wall.

"I don't actually want to look at—"

"You've already told a nice story, Jaimes," Alastor said, peering at the collection of combs and brooches that were arranged in the back corner. "Might as well act the rest of it out to keep him from getting suspicious again. We can make up some excuse not to buy anything when Roland gets back."

Jaimes sighed, looking over the assorted goods lining two large tables encased in glass. There were far too many pieces to choose from, in a variety of sizes and styles, and Jaimes shook his head at the large collection. "I don't even know how to pretend to buy something for a girl."

"You're not buying something for a girl. You're buying something for a woman," Alastor corrected, leaning over the glass top to inspect a piece in the back row. "A woman you love very much."

Jaimes swallowed hard, wishing Roland would hurry

back soon. "R-right." He glanced over the collection again, rubbing his sweating palms along his trousers nervously. "A woman. That I love."

"There." Alastor pointed at an item in the back of the case, tapping lightly on the thin glass. "That's the one."

"W-what?" Jaimes leaned to look at the comb Alastor indicated. It was small, with silver metal leaves protruding from the spine, and a cluster of tiny green gems in the center. At the sight of it, Jaimes imagined Eilonwy wearing it, tucking it into her hair behind her long ear, and his palms began to sweat again. "What do you want me to do?"

"You should ask about it," Alastor said with a smirk.

"Why?"

Alastor huffed, giving Jaimes an annoyed look. "Do you want to play the part or not? It'd make a nice gift. Green stones and everything. So ask about it."

Jaimes considered for a moment, chewing the inside of his cheek thoughtfully. "Alright. But let's not get carried away here."

Jaimes turned, bumping into someone standing just behind him, and fell back with a surprised grunt. "I'm sorry!" The man in front of him was wide and heavyset, standing several inches taller than Jaimes himself. The stranger steadied himself with a light hand on Jaimes's upper arm, and Jaimes instinctively shrank away, pressing himself further into the table behind him. "I, uh, I didn't see you there."

"Are you boys lost?" the man asked in a soft basso. His arms were spread out as if to block them, and Jaimes stepped nervously to one side.

"N-no." Jaimes shrank away from the man's outstretched arms, searching the shop behind him. "We're just looking for the tailor." Jaimes saw where the tailor had fallen, the toes of his soft leather shoes sticking out from behind a rack of fabric.

"Perhaps you two should come with me."

Jaimes's mouth worked wordlessly as he looked from the man blocking their path to where the tailor lay mostly hidden.

Alastor lunged at the man, knocking him partially off balance and grappling with him. "Run, Jaimes!"

Jaimes froze, watching with horror as the upper hand Alastor had briefly had turned. The man regained his balance quickly, and his face contorted in fury as he pulled one of Alastor's arms off him.

"Run, damn you!" Alastor groaned through gritted teeth, bringing his knee up to hit the man in the stomach. The blow connected, and the stranger let out a grunt of pain and redoubled his efforts to subdue Alastor.

Jaimes turned and ran, his breath coming in panicked bursts. Behind him, Alastor let out a shocked gasp, and the sound of shattering glass brought Jaimes to a skittering halt.

He looked back to see Alastor pinned to the ground, the stranger holding him in place with one thick arm to his neck. The floor was littered with broken shards of glass, glittering with the light from the many candles in the shop. Alastor was still fighting, trying to buck the heavier man off him, but Jaimes could tell it would be useless. He heard shouts and hurrying footsteps from the street outside, and he turned to the open doorway, hoping someone had heard the commotion. But the people passing in the road ignored the sounds of Alastor's struggles and rushed further down the street, where Jaimes could make out the faint sounds of fighting.

Alastor made a gagging sound, pulling Jaimes's attention back to the struggle in the back of the tailor house. Jaimes groped along the rack beside him, pulling off the largest bolt of fabric he could find. It was heavy, the thick fabric wrapped around a plank of smoothed wood about the width of Jaimes's torso. He hefted it experimentally in both hands, then stepped behind the stranger.

Glass crunched beneath Jaimes's feet, but the man looked

up too slowly. Jaimes let his breath out in one calming sigh, and swung the bolt of fabric with all his might.

The broad side of the bolt connected with the side of the man's face, and he crumpled instantly. Alastor spluttered and choked as the man's weight on his throat fell away, and Jaimes pulled his brother to his feet.

"Come on, let's get out of here."

Alastor nodded, rubbing at his neck, and gave the fallen man a hard kick to the ribs.

Jaimes left him to rush to the tailor, who was struggling to sit up, one hand pressed to a small cut on his head. Jaimes slid to his knees beside the small man, offering him a supporting arm. "Are you alright?"

"That man attacked me," the tailor said weakly. "Where did he go?"

"He's in the back. He should be out for a bit. Long enough to get someone down here to arrest him, at least." Jaimes stood, helping the man to his feet.

"Was he trying to rob me?"

Jaimes bit his lip, glancing up at the open door again. The sounds out in the street were growing louder, and Jaimes wondered if Roland would make it back to them after all. "Yeah, I think so. He made right for the tables in the back. There's broken glass everywhere."

The tailor groaned, more from frustration than pain.

"Will you be alright? Do you want me to find someone to help you?" Jaimes was sure they didn't have the time to search for help, but if the tailor was seriously injured …

"I'll be fine, just a bump on the head," the tailor said irritably. "Just go, get home. Sounds like chaos outside. You shouldn't be caught up in it."

Jaimes sighed in relief and beckoned for Alastor to follow him. "Let's go, Alastor."

"Wait." Alastor held a small object up for the tailor to inspect. "How much for this?"

The two boys ran down the muddy road back to the docks, leaping over puddles of water and skirting around carts and the few remaining pedestrians. As Jaimes ran, he held one hand pressed to his torso to keep the sweet rolls and Alastor's hasty purchase tucked inside his shirt from slipping and falling into the mud. Every few seconds he glanced over his shoulder to see if anyone was following them. There was no sign of anyone, not even of Roland, and Jaimes's panic began to return at the thought of Roland's capture. Or his death.

Their feet pounded heavily against the wooden boards of the dock as the *Kingfisher* came into view. Mathius waited at the foot of the ramp, red faced and worried.

"Hurry, hurry!" He gestured for them to head up the ramp. "Get down to your quarters and don't leave." He stopped Jaimes with a hand to his shoulder as Alastor rushed past and down the steps to the hold. "Where's Roland? We need to go."

"W-we were being followed," Jaimes rushed through panting breaths. "Roland led them off. We heard fighting." Mathius wasn't looking at him, his eyes roving over the dock below. "I don't know where—"

"There he is!" Mathius raised a hand, waving at a red-haired figure rushing down the dock. "Come on, Roland! Let's go!"

The few sailors milling about on the long dock leapt out of Roland's way as he made for the *Kingfisher* and reached the deck with only a couple of long strides up the ramp. The two men knelt, pulling the ramp up and back onto the deck with a series of quick motions. Mathius shouted at the gathered crew, then to a sailor that stood waiting at the helm, and they were off in a matter of seconds.

Roland searched the busy deck, his eyes falling on Jaimes

in an instant. He went to him, dropping his arms heavily on Jaimes's shoulders. Blood intermingled with sweat along Roland's bare forearms, and his shirt clung to his chest.

"Where's Alastor?"

"Roland, you're bleeding."

"Where's Alastor?" Roland asked more forcefully.

"H-he's downstairs. He's fine. We're both fine."

Roland let out a hard breath, pulling Jaimes into his arms. "Thank the Great Ones." The stink of sweat and blood burned Jaimes's nose, but Roland only held him for a moment before releasing him. "I passed the tailor on my way back, but I couldn't find you."

"We came back here, just like you said to," Jaimes said. His voice was thick, but he fought to keep his voice steady. "We heard the fighting, and we ran back."

Roland was still panting, and he patted Jaimes weakly on the shoulder. "Of course you did. You're smart boys."

"Have some trouble, did you?" Mathius asked, coming to stand beside them.

"Yeah, of a sort," Roland answered.

"So did we," Mathius said with a snarl. "Of a sort." He motioned for the two of them to head down the stairs ahead of him. "Come on, then."

TIRYN

Tiryn leaned heavily against the cabin wall just next to the open door, trying to keep his fingers from drumming impatiently against his crossed arms. Nunor was whittling again, long strips of wood falling to the floor as he cut out a rough shape that only he could see. The twins sat together on one of the lower bunks, facing each other with their eyes closed and their shoulders relaxed, knees barely touching. They might have been meditating but Tiryn knew otherwise. He felt a restless energy in the room, though it didn't seem to bother Nunor, and if he watched the two younger elves closely enough he could see faint facial twitches and jerks.

They were sparring, pitting their wills against each other in an intense exercise that only they could truly experience. Tathiel let out a quiet snort and Eilonwy simultaneously gave a great sigh, and Tiryn knew who had won the latest bout.

"One more time?" Eilonwy asked, head cocked playfully.

"You said that last time," Tathiel said, rolling his shoulders slowly, eyes still closed.

"One more time," Eilonwy repeated, giving her brother a rogue smile. "You won't win again."

"I think I could do one more. But not with you." Tathiel fixed his gaze on Tiryn as if he knew that he had been watching them. "What do you say, Tiryn?"

Tiryn felt his lips twitch into a small smile. It had been some time since he'd practiced his mental abilities. "Alright. Do you have your anchor ready?"

Tathiel rolled his shoulders once more before settling into a relaxed position. Closing his eyes, he nodded once. "I'm ready."

"Then begin."

Tiryn sensed the rushing of Tathiel's consciousness as it dove into his mind. Tiryn let him in, providing no resistance to the heavy blow of Tathiel attempting to invade his mind.

Tathiel hesitated, confused by the ease with which he had forced himself into Tiryn's mind. And in that moment, before Tathiel realized that he had been tricked, Tiryn launched his own offense, striking Tathiel's mind while it was distracted. There was a mental wall around his anchor, but Tiryn was able to maneuver through it with little trouble, and it was over.

The fight ended in only a few seconds.

Tathiel gasped in surprise, opening his eyes and looking at Tiryn once again. There was a single bead of sweat standing out on his forehead. "How did you do that?"

Tiryn shrugged one shoulder lightly. "I can teach you sometime, if you'd like." He thought for a moment, recalling the anchor memory that Tathiel had used to build his mental defenses on. "You should consider using a different anchor. If someone were to capture you, break your defenses…" He mused on the small image he had seen after entering Tathiel's mind. A tiny blue dragon, cuddled in his arms, watery eyes staring up at him. "They would know you have a dragon."

Tathiel and Eilonwy exchanged a glance, and Tathiel nodded slowly. "Alright."

"And what was my anchor?" Tiryn asked, knowing Tathiel would be unable to answer.

"I'm not sure I got close to seeing it."

"You didn't," Tiryn said. "I'm glad you recognize that."

"Fascinating," came a high voice from the doorway, causing everyone in the room to jump. "Simply fascinating!"

Tiryn turned to see Brynne standing just inside their cabin, a heavy book held tightly against his chest. "Master Brynne," Tiryn said, surprised. "I didn't hear you coming."

Neither, apparently, had any of the others, and the thought bothered Tiryn. Had he heard Tiryn's mention of Melonya?

Brynne winked one beady eye, tapping the side of his nose with an ink-stained finger, and said nothing.

"What can we do for you?"

Brynne hurried to stand in the center of the room, shaking that same ink-stained finger at Tiryn as he walked. "I was hoping I could ask you some questions about how the tensions between humans and elves have affected you personally." He patted the book against his chest affectionately. "For my research, you see." He turned to Nunor, who had hardly glanced at the man since his entrance. "And you too, of course, Master, uh …" Brynne waited for Nunor to offer his name, and when he didn't, Brynne finished with a quiet, "Master dwarf."

Tiryn was about to ask what sorts of questions Brynne had in mind, but several sets of hurried footsteps on the stairs leading to the deck drew his attention to the open doorway. He straightened, stepping away from the wall of the cabin, and leaned his head out of the door just in time to have a large and hairy hand shove him roughly in the chest and back into the cabin.

A total of six sailors rushed into the cabin, the last one kicking the door shut as he entered. They had weapons drawn, pointed at the group of them, and each wore a matching scowl across their face.

Tiryn glanced behind him to see that Tathiel and Eilonwy had both jumped to their feet, and Tathiel held a dagger in one hand. Eilonwy was shoving Brynne behind her, shielding the small man from any harm. Nunor was also getting to his feet, holding the small carving knife tightly in one hand and glaring at the intruders. Nunor's axe, Tiryn remembered with a frown, was tucked under one of the lower beds with the rest of their weapons, out of sight and out of reach.

Tiryn turned to face the intruders, noting that while they were dressed to look like sailors, he didn't recognize any of them. *A disguise, then, to get on the ship ...* "Can I help you gentlemen?" he asked, looking at each of the men in turn. Two of the fingers on his left hand twitched, the motion barely more than a muscle reflex, but Tiryn hoped that Tathiel had seen it. If the young elf had noticed ... *Well, he's been in my mind now, after all.*

"Surrender yourselves to us, and we'll see that the captain of this vessel receives only the lightest of punishments for agreeing to carry base creatures," the man in front said. One of the men behind him grinned; there were gaps in his smile where a few of his yellowed teeth had fallen or been knocked out. "Refuse, and we'll kill all of you and arrest the captain. He'll be tried for his crimes and hung." The man's eyes flicked to Eilonwy, Brynne cowering behind her. "The elf girl we might keep alive. Though she'll wish we hadn't."

Tiryn took a slow breath, willing his heart to stop beating so quickly. "I'm sorry, but we'll have to refuse."

The man's eyes narrowed and he attacked.

Tiryn slid inside the man's defenses, sidestepping the short sword aimed for his chest, and delivered a quick punch to the man's ribs. He felt bones snap beneath his knuckles, and another sharp blow to the back of the head brought the man down in an instant. Tiryn lunged for the man furthest to his right, and to his left Tathiel tackled two of the men to the ground, somehow grappling with both of them simultaneously. He heard Nunor bellow in anger, but the dwarf was out of his line of sight with a fifth man.

Tiryn brought his man down with a knee to the gut and a hurried toss, and straightened to face the last man, only to realize that he was already less than an arm's length away, sword coming down on him. Before Tiryn could dodge, a blast of blue-green energy struck the man in the chest, lifting him from the ground and sending him hammering into the far wall. He hit with a resounding thud, then slid to the floor and folded neatly at the waist, his sword clattering to the ground beside him.

Tiryn turned to find Eilonwy standing several feet behind him, one arm raised and palm out, wide eyed and shaking. Behind her, Brynne had shrunk back to hide in the small hollow between the two lower bunks, his book held up in front of him like a small shield.

More hurried footsteps could be heard from the deck stairs and the end of the hall, and Tiryn readied himself for additional intruders.

But it was Mathius that stepped through the door, mouth hanging open slightly at the sight. "Great Ones take it, what's going on in here?"

Behind him, Reed slid into the cabin, bare chested, with a small dagger in one hand. Just behind him were half a dozen of the *Kingfisher*'s crew, each of whom Tiryn recognized. One, the largest of them, Tiryn could even put a name to.

"Your men attacked us, Mathius!" Nunor growled, stomping his way around the fallen men, carving knife still in hand.

Mathius spluttered, raising a hand to Nunor, but Tiryn stopped the dwarf, holding an arm out between him and the captain.

"Easy, Nunor. These aren't Mathius's men." Tiryn

watched the way Mathius and Reed looked at the men slumped along the floor, noting the confusion in the captain's face, and the anger in Reed's. "They disguised themselves as sailors to gain access to the ship."

"I'm glad you can see that as well as I can, Tiryn," Mathius said with a sigh.

Behind him, Tiryn could hear Eilonwy fretting over her brother, and he turned to see her examining Tathiel's nose, which was red and swollen and trickling blood. Tiryn stepped over an unconscious man to inspect Tathiel himself. "You alright?"

Tathiel nodded, wiping fresh blood from his nose with the sleeve of his dark tunic. "I'll be fine. It's not broken. Bleeding will stop soon." He gave Tiryn a serious look. "Thank you for the signal, by the way. Two fingers on the left hand? Take two men from the left side?" Tathiel winced as Tiryn pinched his nose, feeling for a broken bone.

"I didn't intend for you to take them both at the same time. But I'm glad you caught it," Tiryn said softly. He gave the young elf a gentle pat on the shoulder. "You're right. Not broken. Bleeding will stop soon."

"What do we do with them?" Reed asked.

"Take them down to the lower level and put them in one of the cattle pens." Mathius looked at Tiryn apologetically. "It's all we can do, really. The *Kingfisher* doesn't have a proper cell. We can turn them out at a later port, but we should get out of here as soon as possible."

Tiryn nodded, and Reed motioned for the other crew members to start carrying the limp and unconscious men away.

One of them groaned as Reed grabbed him under the shoulders, and Nunor lurched forward at the sound. "Not that one. Not yet."

"Why?" Reed snarled.

"I want to talk to him first. Find out who sent him."

Reed hesitated, looking at Mathius, who, in turn, looked at Tiryn. Tiryn considered for a moment, then nodded, and Reed dropped the man back to the cabin floor with a disgusted huff.

"I'll start getting us ready to depart," Reed said, turning his back on them all and stomping from the cabin.

"I'll see if we can find Roland and the boys. We need to get out of here, in case more come." Mathius suddenly looked ill and kept glancing between Nunor and the man on the floor. Tiryn wondered if the idea of questioning a man didn't sit well with the captain, or if Mathius was worried about what the man might say.

"I-I think I'll stay right here, for the time being, Captain," a thin voice said from the back of the room. Brynne had found his feet again, and was leaning heavily against the wall, his book once more held tightly to his chest. "I suddenly feel much safer in present company."

"Master Brynne?" Mathius asked, his brows knitting together. "What are you doing here?"

"Brynne was here when they charged in. He saw the whole thing," Tiryn said.

Nunor rolled the groaning man at his feet over onto his stomach, pinning him in place with one boot pressing on his back. Mathius frowned, glancing once more at the man lying on the floor, then quickly nodded and left the room without another word.

Nunor grabbed the man's arm by the wrist and pulled it back slowly until the man's groans intensified and he struggled under Nunor's weight.

"Get off of me, you filthy creature!"

Nunor pulled his arm back further, slowly, and the man yelled, more from anger than pain. "I'd watch what you say, given the position you're in."

Tiryn knelt to the ground, one knee only a few inches from the man's face. "We just have a few questions for you.

Answer them, and you'll be taken to join the rest of your fellows."

The man's head turned slightly, eyes going up to Tiryn's, and the hate and anger in his eyes made Tiryn's heart ache. "And if I don't answer?"

Nunor growled, tugging on the man's arm, pulling it further back, and the man howled in pain. After a moment, Nunor loosened his tension and the man's screams abated. He instead cursed all of them with loud words, spit flying from his mouth.

Tiryn waited for the man to quiet further, then knelt closer to his head. "Elves and dwarfs don't work together very often. I might not want your arm to be ripped from your shoulder, but if my dwarf friend here does, I'll allow it. In the interests of peace." The man's breath was coming in heaves and sweat had begun to bead along his upper lip. "Now. Who sent you here?"

"Fuck off, long ears."

Nunor tugged again, and the man's howls drowned out the noise from the deck of the *Kingfisher* for several seconds. Nunor let the man's arm drop back into a slightly more comfortable position, and the man's shrieks eased into mewling whines.

"Who sent you? Please."

"We're King's Guard. The king sent us," the man gasped, eyes blinking away tears.

"And how did the king know that there were non-human passengers on the *Kingfisher*?"

"I don't know."

Nunor tugged again and the man screamed louder, one long yell that left his face red and the veins in his neck and forehead standing out grotesquely. Tathiel crossed the floor in a few hurried steps and shut the cabin door, giving Tiryn a pained look as he stood against it.

"There was a letter," the man choked when Nunor finally

released his arm. "The commander of the King's Guard received a letter, telling him you would be on the ship." He took a few quick breaths, the heat of them blowing over Tiryn's face. "You, and Ajax, former commander of the King's Guard and wanted criminal of the Etritian Empire."

Behind him, Brynne let out a startled squeak. "Ajax?"

"That letter was mistaken," Tiryn said quietly. "There is no Ajax on this ship." The man said nothing, only shut his eyes and dropped his head against the cabin floor. "Who sent the letter?"

"I don't know," the man said weakly.

Nunor pulled his arm back slowly, carefully.

"I don't know, I don't know!" the man yelled. "Great Ones damn you all, I don't know!"

"Nunor, please," Eilonwy called from behind Tiryn's shoulder. Her voice was thin.

Nunor growled, not looking up from the man, and continued to pull on the man's arm. There was a distinct popping sound, and the man's screams reached an ear-piercing climax. When Nunor dropped his arm, it lay limply on the floor at an odd angle to the rest of his body.

Tiryn sighed, motioning for Tathiel to help him bring the man to his feet. "That wasn't necessary, Nunor."

Nunor shrugged, lifting his weight from the man's back and retreating to his corner. "Probably not, but it felt good."

Tathiel held the man's weight up while Tiryn rotated the man's shoulder and tugged it back into place. The man glared at Tiryn the whole time, eyes bright with fury and pain. When it was done, Eilonwy opened the cabin door and ushered two of the *Kingfisher*'s crew in. The man went quietly with them, holding his damaged arm close to his body.

His eyes never left Tiryn's, and before he was led from the cabin, he stopped, looking from each one to the next. "If I meet any of you again," he said, his voice raw, "I will kill you."

When he was gone, Tiryn collapsed onto one of the lower bunks with a sigh. His hands were shaking slightly, and he laced his fingers together and let his arms hang between his knees to hide their trembling. Nunor was already back to his wood carving, but his movements were sharper and angrier than they had been before, and his lips were pressed together in a thin line. The twins sat together on the bunk next to his, Tathiel's arm wrapped around Eilonwy's waist, both of them staring at the spot on the floor where the man had been lying a moment before.

Mathius stepped into the cabin. His face was pale. "I would prefer it if nothing like that ever happened on this ship again, Tiryn."

"So would I."

Mathius swallowed hard, fidgeting. "We're ready to go, just waiting for the others to return. Best to put as much distance between ourselves and this town as possible, before more of them show up."

Tiryn only nodded, and after another moment, Mathius left.

Tiryn was still staring silently at that same spot on the cabin floor when Mathius's voice filtered down from the deck above.

They all jumped to their feet when Alastor rushed in, red faced and sweating. His breath was coming in hard gasps, and he could only wave anxiously over his shoulder, unable to catch his breath long enough to speak.

"Great Ones take it, what happened?" Tiryn half guided, half carried the boy to sit on one of the lower bunks while Eilonwy brought a skin of water. Tathiel, vigilant as ever, stood warily by the open door, eyes darting between the hall outside and those gathered around the boy.

"Attacked," Alastor gasped, motioning vaguely in the direction of the town. "Roland ..." He grabbed the water from Eilonwy's extended hand, gulping it down and spluttering.

"Slowly," Eilonwy said, sitting beside him. "You're safe now. Take your time."

Alastor swallowed another small sip of water, passing the skin back to Eilonwy and wiping the spilled liquid from his face. "We were followed off the *Kingfisher*." His words had a hurried, breathy quality to them, and his chest still rose and fell heavily. Tiryn could almost hear his heartbeat racing from whatever had happened to him. "Roland led them off while Jaimes and I hid in a tailor's house. But then we were attacked."

From his corner, Nunor growled suddenly, woodwork forgotten. "Damn cowards. Chasing after children."

Tiryn inspected Alastor for injuries, tilting his face up to find a large bruise just beginning to flower around his neck. "Are you and Jaimes alright?"

"We're fine." Alastor winced as Tiryn touched a graze along his cheekbone. He smiled, eyes brightening. "You should have seen Jaimes. Hit the man right over the head with a big roll of fabric. Poor bastard fell right over."

Tiryn ignored the profanity, motioning for Alastor to drink more water. "Where is Roland?"

Alastor's face fell, and he opened his mouth to answer, but someone else spoke up for him.

"I'm right here, Tiryn."

Tathiel stepped aside to let Roland through the doorway, Jaimes slumped tiredly under one of Roland's hands. Mathius and Reed both followed behind them, the former still sick looking and pale, the latter scowling deeper than ever. Alastor and Eilonwy both stood as they entered, Alastor rushing to Roland with a mixed expression of fear and shame across his face, and Eilonwy holding out the water skin and motioning for Jaimes to sit and rest.

"You're bleeding, Roland." Red stains dotted Roland's

shirt, along with a rather large spot on the leg of his trousers, which had a neat tear in the center. But he walked with no limp, and he showed no sign of pain as he looked Alastor's scrapes and bruises over.

"I'll be fine."

Tiryn was sure he would be, and the thought bothered him. "You threw yourself into the fray again, did you?" The irritation in his voice surprised even him.

There was a heavy silence, during which the *Kingfisher* rocked gently as she set off from the pier. Everyone was looking at him, and Tiryn felt his ears beginning to warm.

Roland nodded curtly, his jaw set. "I did. It was the only way to make sure the boys could get away."

Tiryn nodded, standing and going to their little cache of supplies. "Just be careful, Roland. We need you. We need each other." He selected a fat skin of water from their collection, hefting it lightly in one hand, eyeing Roland. "Wounds may heal," he said pointedly, and Roland's jaw tightened slightly at his words, "but there's no cure for death." He tossed the water skin to Roland, who caught it easily in one hand. Tiryn sighed, leaning against the wall of the cabin. "As it was, the boys almost ran back here into a trap. We had six members of the King's Guard pay us a visit only a little while ago."

Roland cursed under his breath, turning to give Mathius a hard look. His attention once more back on Tiryn, he said, "I had another five with me in town."

"Six," Jaimes piped. "Including the one that came after Alastor and me."

"Why would the King's Guard be interested in you, Roland?" Brynne asked in his high voice.

Tiryn had forgotten the small man was still in the room with them. He gave Roland a nervous look, but Roland was already answering the question.

"Because I travel with elves, probably. Anyone that travels with non-humans is considered a threat to Etritia." He turned to Mathius and Reed again, taking a small step towards them. "I'm more interested to know how the King's Guard knew we were on the *Kingfisher*. And how they knew we would be docking at that town."

"Roland," Mathius warned.

"I want answers, Mathius," Roland snarled. His gaze was fixed on Reed, who glared back at him with hard, flat eyes that somehow reminded Tiryn of a large animal's. Roland's hands flexed, balling into fists before slowly uncurling. "I want to know that we're safe on your ship."

Reed took a half step, bringing himself closer to Roland and placing himself between Roland and the captain. "I'm not the one that has betrayed you, Roland. I don't agree with what Mathius is doing, but—"

"I saw you passing a letter off at one of our last stops," Roland said. His fists were balled again, each uncurling motion slower than the last.

"Roland." Tiryn rose to his feet, but Roland waved him away.

Tiryn glanced around the room. Tathiel seemed nearly as angry as Roland, standing resolutely between Reed and the door to the cabin. Eilonwy was still sitting, surveying the room quietly, keeping herself between the boys and the men. Everyone else remained as they were, either oblivious to the changing tension in the room, or unconcerned with it.

"I saw you," Roland continued, "paying the barman in gold coins." Reed scoffed, but Roland ignored it. "Was the money to get the letter to Etritia faster? Or just to keep him quiet?"

"You misunderstand, Roland—"

But Roland had already moved in for the attack. His right fist came up under Reed's jaw almost fast enough for Tiryn to have missed it. Reed stumbled back, and Roland took him to the ground, beating him with more fists. Tiryn reached the two of them before Mathius had time to react, and he tugged the struggling Roland off Reed before more than a couple of hits could land.

"Roland, stop!" Tiryn wrapped his arms around Roland's torso and pinned his arms to his side.

Mathius knelt to help the bleary-eyed Reed sit up. "What in the name of the Great Ones is the matter with you?" He straightened, looking over at Roland. "He told you it wasn't him!"

"He's lying," Roland growled, twisting in Tiryn's grip. "Let me go, Tiryn. I've already lost too much of my family." Roland tugged at Tiryn's grip, trying to free himself. "I won't let this man get away with putting more of the people I care about into danger."

"Roland, you idiot!" Mathius cried. "The letter was going to his daughter."

"Mathius …" Reed said from the floor. He sounded confused, perhaps even concussed. "Don't …"

"Oh, shut up, Reed. He's ready to kill you," Mathius grumbled.

Roland stopped struggling. "What?"

Tiryn hesitated for a moment, then let Roland go. Roland didn't move.

"Reed has a daughter who lives a few days' ride from that shit stain of a town. Every time we go through, he sends her a letter and some money." Mathius rubbed anxiously at his face. "It's the only reason we still stop there."

Reed was getting to his feet, although slowly, and Roland held out a hand to him. "I'm sorry. I didn't know." His shoulders had relaxed, almost slumped, as the anger evaporated in a heartbeat; Tiryn was not at all surprised that Roland's voice had softened and taken on a hint of regret.

"It wasn't any of your damn business." Reed ignored Roland's offered hand, leaning some of his weight instead on Mathius's shoulder. "I told you I wasn't the one to betray you. That should have been enough." Reed's voice was firmer, his words taking on more of their usual roughness.

"It doesn't change the fact that someone on this ship has informed the King's Guard of our presence here," Tiryn said. He looked at each of the three men in turn, studying them for the briefest of moments. "They will try again, I'm sure. And they might send more next time."

Mathius and Roland straightened at his words, exchanging a quick glance between them.

"We should all be prepared." Tiryn gave Mathius and Reed a hard look. "All of us."

3 6

FERRAND

Ferrand took the stairs up his king's tower two at a time, cursing under his breath. The chill of arcane energy made his breath fog slightly, but he'd grown accustomed to the odd cold in Mothlenor's tower over the years. During one of the rare moments when Anna would actually speak to him, she'd said that Mothlenor intentionally put too much energy into his work, letting the excess spill over into the surroundings, leaving a stain. Anna was likely correct. The chill only grew worse over the years and seemed more concentrated closer to the door to Mothlenor's study. *That little witch is so clever, and she has that tight little ass ...* Ferrand felt himself growing hard, as he always did when thinking of Mothlenor's other adviser. *I should have taken her when I had the chance.*

The brief fantasy of bursting into her rooms in the middle of the night and fucking her until the sun came up delighted him. Imagined sounds of the little whore screaming for help that would never come distracted him for the few moments it took to reach the top of the tower. He might have paused to take care of himself right there on the stairs, the vision he pictured was so vivid and detailed, but

Mothlenor surely had ways of watching the winding steps to his study. He might lose his head for fondling himself so close to his king's most treasured work.

Besides, this is too urgent.

And he could find whores aplenty throughout town to ride until the roosters called—nearly everyone in the city was either destitute or nearly so. Everyone would do almost anything for a little bit of gold. Fathers sold their daughters. Mothers sold themselves *and* their daughters, often as a packaged deal. There was even a good demand for sons, though Ferrand himself wasn't interested in that. And Madam Moira had quite the collection of girls and women for the wealthiest Etritians to pick from. It seemed nearly everyone outside the castle walls was getting fucked in one way or another. And Ferrand wanted to keep himself off the receiving end for as long as possible.

He knocked on his king's study door, surprised it didn't swing open of its own accord when he reached it. Mothlenor must not have been watching the stairs after all.

There was a faint sound on the other side of the door, a grunt perhaps, followed by Mothlenor's voice. "I'm working. Come back later." The sound was faint, coming from a more distant part of the tower than the study just beyond the door.

"My lord," Ferrand began, wondering what his king might be up to, "I have news. It's about Ajax."

There was a sudden stillness in the air, followed by the sounds of movement and shuffling feet. "Enter, Ferrand."

The study door opened at Mothlenor's command, allowing Ferrand to step over the threshold and into the study. As ever, the desk directly in front of him was a disheveled mess of papers and small artifacts. The rest of the room was only a little better, and there was a small cauldron steaming lightly in one corner, despite a lack of fire to warm it. Mothlenor entered from the open doorway leading to the rest of his chambers, his grey hair mussed.

He was barefoot and tying an oversized silk robe around his waist. The robe made him look old and frail, but Ferrand knew his king could kill him in an instant if he wanted to. "What have you heard?" Mothlenor growled at him.

Ferrand instead started with an apology. "I didn't mean to wake you, my lord—"

"I wasn't sleeping, you imbecile. What have you heard?" Mothlenor repeated. From the doorway behind him, Anna appeared, hastily dressed in a loose gown, one hand smoothing the front of her clothing, the other taming her dark hair back to neatness.

Ferrand felt a hungry stab of anger at the sight of Anna emerging from Mothlenor's rooms, but tried to keep it from showing. "The attack on the *Kingfisher* did not go as planned, my lord. Half of my men attacked Ajax and the two boys while they were off ship. They were badly wounded. The other half have not reported in, and might have been taken captive. Or killed."

"Imbecile," Mothlenor snarled, collapsing into the large chair behind the cluttered worktable. "Your failure has tipped our hands. Ajax knows that we are following him and that we have a spy on the *Kingfisher*. It's only a matter of time before he figures out who it is."

"I thought you were going to leave the boys alone. They're innocent in all of this." Anna's voice was firm, and she scowled as she looked between him and Mothlenor.

Ferrand flexed the fingers of one hand, fighting the urge to leap forward and wrap his hands around her thin little throat. *The sounds she'd try to make would be so—*

"Unfortunately, our plans have changed, Anna," Mothlenor said, interrupting Ferrand's thoughts. "It seems we cannot rely on the commander's men to see this through."

"I sent my best men."

"Your best men were clearly not good enough if they can

be beaten away by one man and a couple of children." Mothlenor cast a quick disgusted look in Ferrand's direction.

"Those *children* are nearly men themselves," Ferrand said stiffly. He fumed in silence for a moment. Mothlenor's eyes were fixed on him. Anna leaned against the open doorway, staring at nothing. He met Mothlenor's gaze, staring at those angry hawk eyes and fighting down the unease they gave him. "I'll find another way, my lord."

Mothlenor finally looked away, huffing. "See that you do, Ferrand. I cannot tolerate too many mistakes."

"Can you somehow gain control of the ship?" Anna asked from her spot in the doorway. When she looked up, it was to Mothlenor, not him, and Ferrand grit his teeth against the retort that came to him.

Ferrand considered the idea for a moment, looking between Anna and his king. *What's that stupid bitch doing, sleeping with Mothlenor? Plotting against me?* He focused on Mothlenor's agitated face. "There might be a way. It could result in the capture of Ajax's whole party, if it works."

"Do it," Mothlenor said without hesitation. "Now go." He waved Ferrand off, then turned to Anna. "Both of you. Get out."

Ferrand felt a small amount of satisfaction at the shock on Anna's face at being tossed out of the tower as well, and he patiently held the door open for her as she glided across the room and through the doorway. He followed close enough behind that he could smell the oils she rubbed on her skin, and felt a carnal hunger stir in him at the scent.

He waited until the door had snapped shut behind them and they had descended a dozen or so steps. "Just what do you think you're doing, having sex with the king?" Ferrand hissed.

She didn't slow or even turn to look at him. "Sometimes he asks me to do things, and I do them. That's all."

"And would you do those same things for me?" He

reached out, wrapping an arm around her waist and pulling her against him. He could feel the curves of her body through the thin fabric of her dress, and he held her closer to him, pressing himself against her. She went stiff in his arms, giving him all the time he needed for one hand to squeeze at a small breast, and the other to grope at the warmth he craved. Her underclothes were missing, probably still lying on the floor of Mothlenor's bedchambers. "If I'd known I only had to ask …" he crooned in her ear. *Great Ones be damned, she's so—*

She spun on the steps, shoving him against the stone wall, one hand clutching his throat. Her nails dug into his flesh, obstructing his airway. She lifted him off the step he was on until his toes barely grazed the ground. *How is she so strong?* He struggled for air, clawing at her hand, but he couldn't pry her cold fingers away from his neck.

"I sleep with him because he asks me to, and he could kill me if I say no. He wants a Gifted child, one that he can groom and train to be his little pet."

She spat the last word at him, and Ferrand realized that the chill that had started where her nails met his flesh was extending down to his chest. Her eyes were burning with anger, but they were simultaneously filling with tears, and he couldn't help but stay hard at the sight of them.

She tightened her grip on him, and his vision narrowed until her angry eyes were the only thing he could see. He could still hear her voice, but it was muffled over the pounding of his heartbeat in his ears. "I only have a few years left until I am too old to give him what he wants. What do you think he'll do with me after that? Kill me? Lock me down in the dungeons until the smell of my rot reaches his tower, like he did with the others? Or will he keep me, because I have been faithful, and I've learned well under him? Will he keep me, because I can still be a good fuck, even if I can't give him a Gifted child?"

He could barely make out her staring at him, and the chill running through his body was slowly filling his lungs. What would happen when it reached his heart?

She released him suddenly, and he fell to the steps, somehow managing to keep himself from rolling down them in a crumpled mess. He massaged his throat with one hand, taking in large breaths of air. The chill in his body was dissipating quickly, and he briefly wondered if she had been using magic to hold him. It had to have been magic, she was too weak otherwise.

"Touch me again," she snarled at him, "and I'll kill you." He could see her bare feet as she turned and hurried down the steps again.

He took his time standing up again. His throat would be sore for a while, probably bruised as well. There was a wet spot on the front of his trousers, where he had apparently spent himself while she was choking the life out of him.

Interesting.

He took another deep breath, looking up to the high ceiling of the curved stairwell. It was surprisingly clear of cobwebs. *Perhaps spiders don't like the arcane energy here.*

He took the rest of the stairs slowly, and by the time he reached the bottom, he felt mostly normal. It was time to go hunting around town. He considered his options for a moment, deciding that it would probably take two women to do to him what Anna had just done.

Another call to Madam Moira was in order. And another visit from his twins.

3 7

MELONYA

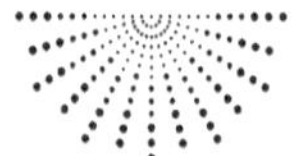

Melonya drifted languidly along, letting the warm waters of the current propel her through the ocean. She would have to surface soon; she could already feel the air she had breathed in a few hours before beginning to tickle her lungs. Just as she had to occasionally drop in altitude when flying to get a good breath of fresh air, she would have to breach the surface of the water to do the same soon enough. But not just yet.

She twitched her tail, using the motion to push herself deeper into the current, delighted by the tantalizing warmth. The ocean could be so cold at times, and the current was comforting in a way that she grew to appreciate more and more with each passing day. It also gave her a fairly accurate sense of time. Warm currents coming from further out in the ocean occurred twice a day, in the morning and mid-evening, and the time between each of those currents was broken up by a similar current that came from the shore, heading back out into the ocean. Melonya strongly suspected that they were what caused the tides along the coast.

Roland's book mentioned a tide, didn't it?

She was sure it had. She'd heard him that night on the beach, after he had confessed to Alastor his true identity.

He should have done that sooner.

The current was rolling away, and she couldn't be bothered to follow it any further. The dolphins around her did, however. They swam past her, chittering as they went. They were like big, blubbery birds in that way. Always flitting around, talking incessantly. At first they had been fascinated by her presence, and she by theirs. But each new pod she encountered amused her less and less, though they were still just as surprised and delighted by her.

At least they're somewhat intelligent.

Melonya had been surprised by the number of intelligent creatures she had come across in the ocean. She never swam down too far. It was both too cold and too far from her precious air supply. She wasn't sure how far down she could go before having to turn around. Besides, the idea wasn't all that intriguing. There had been enough to keep her entertained close to the surface.

She had told Roland about the normal sea creatures, most of whom had some degree of intelligence. She could pick out their minds from the darkness of the waters like spotting a light in the middle of the night. And aside from the humans on the ship above her, the dolphins shone the brightest. They were smart, but not smart enough to carry on a good conversation. Compared to her companions, they were sputtering candles next to a warm campfire.

Honestly, you'd be less annoying if you were stupid. I would just eat you, in that case.

She'd directed the comment at the chattering pod, not expecting much of a reply. To her surprise, one of them chittered angrily at her. Melonya couldn't be sure, but she suspected it might have been a comment on her size.

Melonya ignored the creature, continuing her lazy drifting through the water. She would need another nice scrubbing when she was finally able to surface for good. The salty brine of the sea was creating an unsettling slime on her scales. Jaimes and Eilonwy had done an admirable job on the Isle of Onia, but their efforts were already undone. She was surely an unappealing sight, and it bothered her to think that she might never get clean again.

There were other creatures deeper down, of course. She suspected that if she could swim deep enough, she might even find creatures that were just as intelligent as her companions. It was always possible. Not to mention more water nymphs, or even merfolk. She was shocked that she hadn't come across a family of mer yet. She knew there were bound to be a few around, even this close to the shore.

I hope I haven't frightened them off. I bet Eilonwy would enjoy seeing a mermaid.

She could even imagine her little companion's expression at the sight, and the thought made her chest rumble. Eilonwy called that purring, like a cat. Melonya was sure it wasn't quite the same, but it always seemed to happen when she thought of her twins.

She closed her eyes, letting the ocean carry her away, chest rumbling as she went. It was quiet and peaceful, with the fading chattering of the dolphins and her own low rumbling the only sounds she could hear.

Her purring grew louder. It even seemed to reverberate through the waters, startling a large school of fish away.

Melonya willed the purring to stop, not wanting to cause enough of a disturbance to upset the sailors above her. The rumbling in her chest stopped, but the sound surrounding her continued, growing deeper.

There was something else making that noise. Something very large.

Melonya thrashed her tail, spinning herself into a some-what upright position. Her wings were useless in the water, but she still had her claws. And if she grew desperate enough, her teeth.

From below her, far down in the ocean's depths, she felt the awakening of a mind like she had never known. The weight of it crashing against her own consciousness suddenly made Melonya feel very small and vulnerable. The intensity of this mind flaring to life was more brilliant than the light of a hundred fires, and Melonya was both awed and terrified.

The mental connection was made in an instant. Melonya couldn't have stopped it even if she had wanted to. It was strong, and felt both alien and oddly familiar. The mind she was connected to seemed to stir slowly, as if it had not been active for a very long time. After a moment, during which Melonya felt her heart pounding against her chest, the creature resting on the floor of the ocean spoke.

"Hello, Little One. You seem to be very far from home."

38

ELF

It had been nearly a year since her father's death, and yet she could still only find comfort from his loss in the shade of his burial tree. Her own Hometree had grown cold and inhospitable, despite her mother's continued efforts to care for it. Something had changed that afternoon, and there was no going back from that point on.

She leaned her head against the smooth bark of the burial tree and closed her eyes against the light filtering through the leaves overhead. "Papa …" she began. She clutched a golden stone to her chest, imagining it was her father that she held so closely. "I can't stay here anymore. I have to leave."

There was a rustling of wind through the branches, as if he might have heard her words. It was impossible, of course. Unless the old tales of death and rebirth were true, but she had never believed those stories.

"I'm trying to stay happy. For Mother. But losing you has been too much." She squeezed her eyes tightly together, trying to hold back the tears that always seemed to come when she visited her father. "And losing my brother, too."

She would have lost him at some point. *He had been*

human after all, and humans have such short lives. But she had expected another few decades with him, and losing him so soon and so unexpectedly had given her a wound that would not heal.

"Demons. In Vyris," she muttered, caressing the egg in her lap. "We had hoped it wouldn't happen again."

Another gust of wind rustled the leaves, and a distant rumble of thunder drew her attention back to her Homewood. She would have to leave soon if she wanted to outrun the approaching storm. She sniffed, settling against the smooth burial tree again.

"You told me it was the king of men that sent the demons before. To chase after my brother and the egg he had stolen." Of course, her brother never remembered that for himself. He hardly remembered his own name, after such a close brush with death. "It was surely him that sent them again. To kill you." She looked down at the egg in her lap, tracing a finger over the golden ridges that covered its surface. "And to try to take this back, of course." It was thanks to her brother that Mothlenor had not been entirely successful, though it had cost him his life. She closed her eyes once more, trying to block out the mental image the thought conjured up.

Her chosen brother, his dark hair plastered to his forehead with sweat, pulling her into one last embrace before making her flee on her own.

She'd taken the egg and run as quickly as her legs could carry her.

And when it was safe, she and a handful of neighbors had gone looking for her missing father and brother.

There had been little to recover, and little to bury.

She had survived, where her father and brother had died.

She stood, glancing back over her shoulder to give her Homewood one final look. Her mother wouldn't miss her until tonight, giving her plenty of time to get a head start on her new life.

"I'm leaving Vyris. I'm not sure where I'll be going. Southeast, perhaps? Across the desert? I know there are other elves out there in the world. I'm sure I can find somewhere to begin a new life." She leaned her forehead against the wood of her father's tree, sighing. "I'm sorry. I will always love you, even if you are gone. And I will never forget you."

She stepped around the tree, grabbing the reins of her father's old horse. A few feet away from her father's tree stood another burial tree, this one noticeably smaller and stunted. She brushed a hand against the wood of this tree as well, smiling sadly at the slight give it had at her touch. She hoped it would last, but it was unheard of for a human to get his own burial tree, and his soul might not have been strong enough to care for it properly.

"And I will always love you, brother. I know you had a family, even if you could never remember them. If I find them, I'll tell them how important you were to me, and how brave you were to protect this egg from Mothlenor's monsters." She leaned down, kissing one of the larger leaves that adorned its sparse branches. "Goodbye, brother."

With a final look back at her father's tree, she climbed into the saddle of her horse, tucking the golden egg into an empty bag strapped behind her leg. She pointed the horse away from her Hometree and led him from the only place she had ever known.

39
ROLAND

Roland had fallen asleep to the gentle rocking of the *Kingfisher*, leaning against the wall closest to Jaimes and Alastor. He had been more exhausted than he had any right to be, and it had been easy to just close his eyes and drift away into sleep.

When he awoke, it was to find himself in a steaming bathing room. The tub was large enough to fit a dozen people, the water clear and clean. And sitting against one edge, a glass of wine in one hand, water up to her collarbones, was Nevina.

Roland's shoulders relaxed at the sight of her, releasing tension he hadn't realized he'd been carrying. "Nevina."

She only smiled over her wineglass, offering him a spot beside her in the bath.

He obliged, not bothering to remove his clothes. This was a dream, after all. What did getting his clothing wet matter?

"This place again?" he asked, reaching for a nearby platter of fruit. He plucked a fat grape from the bunch nestled between a pair of juicy-looking apples and a group of small, brightly colored citruses. "I always forget about this place, until I find myself here again." He tossed the grape into his mouth, grimacing when he bit into the fruit and tasted nothing. "And I always forget that the food here is terrible."

Nevina's smile deepened. "I never ate anything in this place, so I have no memory of the taste."

Roland shoved the platter of bland fruit out of arm's reach. "I wouldn't recommend trying it now." He slid closer to her, and she turned her body towards him as he wrapped an arm around her bare waist. "I've missed you, Nevina."

"You seem happier," Nevina said, offering him her glass of wine.

"I am happier. I have family in my life again." He took a sip of her wine, surprised when the sharp tang of red wine passed his lips. "It's not like it used to be. Far from it. But things are better."

"And if you lost it?" Nevina's voice took on a serious tone, her smile dropping slightly. "What would you do then?"

Roland forced a short laugh. "What are you saying?"

Nevina didn't answer; her expression remained unchanged.

Roland pulled his arm away from her, leaning against the wall of the tub. "The spy, is that it? You want me to find whoever it is that sent word to Mothlenor that we're aboard the Kingfisher?"

Nevina grimaced slightly at the sound of Mothlenor's name, but still she said nothing, only staring at Roland as she took another slow sip of wine.

"Do you know who it is?"

"I only know what you know."

Roland sighed. "What do you want me to do?"

Nevina set her glass aside, leaning closer to him and pulling his arm until it settled against her waist again. "Find him. Find out who Ferrand's man is before he undoes all you've managed to do. Before he costs you your family."

"I'm only one man, Nevina." Her body was warm against

his; he could feel it even through his wet clothes and the hot water. "I'm not sure how I can do so much alone."

"But you're not alone." Nevina brought her hand up to his face, her fingers tracing his jawbone. "You have a family, don't you? Tiryn and Nunor will be there to help you. You don't have to do anything alone."

Roland leaned in for a kiss, and her face tilted up to meet his. She smelled faintly of rose oil and death, and her lips held the lingering taste of red wine.

When they parted, she leaned against him, her head nestled in the hollow of his shoulder. "I'm glad you're happier, Ajax." She inhaled deeply, settling herself against him more comfortably and closing her eyes. "I hope it lasts."

Roland said nothing for a moment. His real name was rarely ever spoken, and hearing Nevina say it brought back emotions and memories he had spent years trying to forget. So he remained silent for a moment, enjoying the way she moved against him as she breathed, staring at the steam still drifting off the surface of the water.

"Where are we, exactly? Somewhere in Etritia?" Roland looked down at her as she glanced up at him before shutting her eyes once more. "Have I asked you that before?"

"A few times," Nevina answered. "All I'll say this time is that this place was a cruel place for me in life. But in death …" She looked up at him again, a small smile playing her mouth. "In death, it is much more enjoyable."

Roland stared at her for a moment, burning the sight of her bright blue eyes into his memory. "You're so beautiful. I've missed you." She let him stare, patiently waiting until he leaned in for another kiss.

When their lips parted for the second time, Nevina once more nestled against him. The scent of death was stronger about her, and she seemed thinner and somehow less than she had been before. "Now that you have the book once more, will you tell me what Areanath's first clue is?"

"He never told you?"

Nevina's lips quirked, her eyes still shut. "He kept it from me intentionally, to keep his brother from getting it through me."

Roland nodded. "Alright." He held her closer, knowing their time was nearly gone. "To destroy the evil the king's death brings, seek out the beast with deep-sea wings."

"Hm," Nevina said weakly. "We already knew that part."

"There's more," Roland said, running his hands through her hair. "In the darkest depths of the deepest sea lies the treasure which you seek. Beast against beast, victory must be earned. All that is lost must be found again, before the tides have turned."

Roland's hands were empty, the weight that been leaning against him gone. But he could still faintly hear her soft laugh in the steam around him. "He always was a bad poet."

Roland smiled, leaning against the tub wall again. "I'll miss you, Nevina."

When he sat up, it was not in the warm waters of the bath, but in the chilly hold of the *Kingfisher*. His blanket, once draped carefully over his shoulders, had fallen into his lap, and gooseflesh had broken out across his exposed arms.

Roland sighed, reaching for the blanket and tucking it over himself. He cast a tired gaze around the room. Tiryn was gone, probably out on the deck, stretching his legs. Nunor snored from a far corner of the room, looking like an oversized child spread out on the floor. But on the top bunk closest to him Roland could see a shadowy figure sitting upright and watching him.

"Couldn't sleep either?" Roland whispered.

Alastor nodded his head in the dark, the motion hardly visible. "I wasn't sure you were awake. I heard you mumbling in your sleep."

Roland shrugged. "It was just a dream."

"A good one?"

Roland thought for a moment, trying to recall. He'd been with Nevina, and he had been somewhere he both did and did not recognize. "I don't remember. I think it was." Nevina had been trying to warn him of something. Roland shrugged his shoulders. "It's already fading." He pulled the blanket tighter around him, closing his eyes once more. "I didn't wake you, did I?"

"Not this time. But you have before. You never get too loud, but it gets to be so quiet some nights …"

Roland sat up again, opening his eyes to stare at Alastor. "Do I talk in my sleep often?"

"More often than not." Alastor's head tilted slightly. "Though I think it's been several days since the last time."

"Oh. I didn't know."

Alastor must have sensed something in Roland's voice. "We can't understand you or anything. It's just a bunch of muttering. Nothing to be embarrassed about."

"We?"

"Oh," Alastor mumbled. "Tiryn is usually awake, too. Sometimes Tathiel or Eilonwy." Alastor shifted slightly on his bunk. "Tiryn said to just let you be. That it's just old memories coming back, and that they'll pass."

Roland huffed, crossing his arms and casting a glare at the open doorway of the cabin. "He's probably not wrong."

Alastor drew in a long breath, holding it for a moment. "You can talk to me about them, if you want. Those old memories, I mean. It might help."

Roland smiled. "Perhaps I'll take you up on that someday. But not tonight." Roland closed his eyes again. "You should get some sleep. You never know what tomorrow might bring."

40

PYLE

Rawli was singing again, the damned fool. It didn't matter how many times he got a boot to the ass, he kept it up. It was a wonder he hadn't been beaten to death yet.

But then, they needed every man they had.

There had been twelve sent from Etritia to meet the *Kingfisher*, and it had been only bad luck that had put him in with the half dozen that went aboard and were captured.

Or good luck, perhaps.

The others might be dead, for all he knew.

"Will you quit that damned yodeling, you fucking fool," Orlen growled, punctuating the sentiment with a half-hearted kick in Rawli's direction.

Rawli screamed, though Orlen's boot had hardly touched him. The sound was piercing in the otherwise quiet hold.

"Elir damn you, Orlen," Roust muttered, pulling one of the rags the traitor captain had given them to serve as blankets tighter around him. "Just leave the daft bastard be."

"But his fucking singing is driving me mad!" Orlen protested, rounding on Roust. Orlen could complain as much as he wanted, but he would do as he was told eventually. Or risk having the stab wound to his ribs the filthy dwarf had given him punched mercilessly.

In such tight quarters, it was easy to learn how to hurt a man the fastest.

"I don't give a fuck what you think about his singing," Roust growled. "It's his screaming that I can't stand. Wakes me up every time, and here I was just dreaming about tossing around that busty bitch you keep moaning about."

Orlen made a face. "You take that back, you—"

"Shut up, both of you." Though he had kept his voice soft and level, they both instantly quieted, casting nervous glances in his direction. "It's not Rawli's fault that he got hit with that elf bitch's curse." He motioned to the snoring pair in the corner. "They seem to sleep fine, despite Rawli and his singing and screaming. So why don't you two shut your damned mouths and do the same." He smiled, and Orlen's eye widened slightly at the sight of it. "Or I'll find another use for your mouths that will keep you quiet for a while."

Roust pulled the blanket to his chin, turning away from the others with nothing more than a glare at Orlen. But Orlen shrank away, his eyes darting back and forth between his feet and Rawli. The stupid bastard had started singing again. "O-of course, Pyle. You won't hear another word from me."

"Good."

And it was silent for a time. Pyle himself was nearly nodding off, despite Rawli's racket. But then Orlen opened his damned mouth again.

"I think I hear someone coming."

Pyle wanted to threaten Orlen again for waking them all from their delicate slumber, but the light sound of footsteps on the stairs gave him reason to pause.

Someone was indeed coming.

"Probably just another sad excuse for a meal," Orlen grumbled. Then he pitched his voice louder, shouting from the far side of the cattle pen they had been imprisoned in. "Hey! *Hey!*" Roust and the others all jumped at the noise, and Rawli let out a pathetic wail. "Bring us something besides fish, you traitorous fucks!"

"*Shut up*, Orlen!" Pyle yelled. He tilted his head, listening. "It doesn't sound like dinner." Pyle got to his feet, wrapping his hands around the barred entrance to the cattle pen. The footsteps were off, wrong somehow.

"It's good to know that you're not all a bunch of fucking imbeciles."

The voice that carried through the dark of the hold was unfamiliar, and it wasn't until the stranger stepped into the dim light of a nearby hanging lamp that Pyle recognized the man that had come down to join them.

"You?" Pyle stepped back instinctively away from the tiny bars that separated the six of them from the visitor. "I recognize you from before. Inside the cabin, with those *creatures*." But the man looked different. More hostile. "What do you want?"

"To offer you your freedom." The man's voice was deep and slightly unnerving. And the way his eyes glittered in the darkness made Pyle think of an insect.

"Freedom? How?"

"I want your help with a task here on this ship."

Pyle hesitated.

"I can understand why you might not want to agree. But I assure you—you and I want the same thing."

Pyle scoffed, casting a glance behind him at the other men with him. Roust and Orlen were both listening with rapt attention. Arlyth and Domm were blinking themselves awake, looking around the cabin in confusion as if they had forgotten where they were. And Rawli … well he just kept singing.

Pyle turned back to the stranger. "What makes you think you know what I want?"

The stranger's teeth glinted as he flashed a smile, and Pyle had the momentary sensation of seeing himself through Orlen's eyes. This man was dangerous, and Pyle found himself fighting the urge to take another step back as the man drew nearer. "I want to make those monsters upstairs suffer. And I want to give you the chance to help make it happen. Is that not what you want?"

Behind him, Rawli let out a shriek, startling a curse from Orlen. Pyle remained unfazed, as did the stranger, whose eyes never strayed from his own.

Pyle stepped closer to the bars that separated him from a small hope of vengeance. The stranger's smile deepened slightly, sending a nervous shudder across the back of Pyle's shoulders.

"I'm listening."

"Good."

41
TIRYN

Tiryn sat slumped against one wall of their cabin, watching the twins and Nunor. Nunor was quietly whittling away at another piece of dried driftwood, making what appeared to be some sort of animal. There was a slowly growing pile of wood shavings on the floor at his feet, and an even slower growing collection of carved creatures on the bed next to his stool. Nunor was incredibly quiet when whittling; it seemed to keep him focused and calm in their little enclosure.

"What do you do with them all, Nunor?"

The dwarf looked up briefly at Tiryn's question then quickly resumed his work. "With what?"

"The animals you carve," Tiryn said, motioning towards the wood menagerie. "What do you do with them when they're done? Sell them?"

"I dunno." Nunor shrugged. "I've never done much whittling before. Might just toss them."

"Shame. They're rather good."

Nunor shrugged again.

The twins were equally quiet, each one reading from one of Jaimes's books. Eilonwy was lying on her back on the floor of the cabin again, both feet propped up onto the lower bed, a book leaning against her thighs. Her brother sat cross-legged on the bed next to her feet, another book balanced across his knees. Tathiel was also shelling a small pile of peanuts, occasionally tossing one into Eilonwy's waiting mouth. The sight was amusing.

Eilonwy caught a peanut with delicate ease, then tilted her head up from the floor of the cabin. "Can I keep the dragon? It looks like Melonya."

Nunor paused long enough to reach for the fist-sized figure Eilonwy had indicated. "Sure, I don't care." He tossed it down to her, and she caught it and tucked it close to her chest. "I can make you a better one, sometime. One that really looks like Melonya."

"I like this one." Eilonwy lifted it up for Tathiel to see, and he gave her a small smirk.

"You're still such a child." He tossed another peanut towards his sister. She caught it, then gave Tathiel a light kick to the knee, which only made his smile widen.

"Alastor and Jaimes might like to keep some for them-selves. You might ask them before tossing them away."

Nunor made a quiet, noncommittal grunt and continued working.

Tiryn was about to compliment Nunor's work again when Tathiel and Eilonwy both stiffened, and Tathiel's head jerked up from the book in his lap. "There's something out in the water."

Tiryn stood, ready to run up to the deck. Eilonwy sat up, and Tathiel and Nunor both rose from their seats, all of them facing the open door of the cabin.

"The mer are here!" Alastor's voice rang down the stairs from the deck. The sound was followed by hurried steps that halted halfway down before Alastor shouted again. "Tiryn, come look! There are merfolk!"

There was hardly a pause before all four of them were

rushing out of the cabin and up the stairs, Nunor bringing up the rear.

There were merfolk, alright. The whole ship was surrounded by the bubbling creatures, all of them darting around each other and splashing their finned extremities, trying to get a good look up at the deck of the ship. The mer were unsettling to look at, with slimy grey skin and large bulbous black eyes. Their flesh was mostly the thick blubber that other sea creatures possessed, with small scales covering their necks and torso in intricate whirls of blue and green shimmers. They spoke to one another in little clicks, sounding a little like one of the numerous pods of dolphins Tiryn and the others had seen.

Tiryn leaned over the *Kingfisher*'s railing, looking down at the sea creatures that had clustered beneath him. They looked up at him, then called out in a burbling chant, "Elf! Elf! Elf!" The word sounded almost like the bark of a seal, but it was still intelligible, and their excitement at seeing an elf made Tiryn smile.

"This is madness," a voice next to Tiryn grumbled.

Tiryn looked to see Reed standing beside him. "Do you normally see so many of the mer?"

Reed scowled, shaking his head. "They're only here because of you. They normally just leave us alone." He let out a low curse and left the port-side railing. "This whole voyage has become one long nightmare."

Tiryn ignored him, once more leaning to watch the merfolk in the water below. "Did you come to see the elves?" Tiryn called down. The mer were supposed to be intelligent creatures, and he hoped they would be able to understand his question.

The group chittered amongst themselves for a moment, then one of them called back up in a bubbling whine. "We come to see riders, elf!"

Tiryn frowned, thinking. *They came to see the riders?* Tiryn called over his shoulder for the twins, curious how the mer might have known about the young elves. *Surely it's Melonya's doing.*

Tathiel and Eilonwy were quick to come at his call, bringing Nunor with them, and the twins pressed themselves against the railing on one side of Tiryn while Nunor over-turned a small crate and clambered on top of it to see the spectacle below.

Tiryn gestured first to Nunor. "This is Nunor, a dwarf," he called down to the waiting merfolk. Their number had grown, and it seemed most of them were now clustered down below the four of them. At the sight of Nunor, they chittered between themselves once again, with half a dozen or so chanting cries of "Dwarf! Dwarf! Dwarf!"

Tiryn gestured next to the twins. "These are the riders, Tathiel and Eilonwy." On the far side of the twins, Jaimes and Alastor were leaning over the railing, watching the mer and smiling.

The introduction of Tathiel and Eilonwy brought on an uproar of chittering, followed by chants of "Riders, riders, riders!"

The twins smiled, Eilonwy going red in the ears.

"Thank you for coming to meet us. We've never seen mer before," Eilonwy said, tucking a loose strand of light hair behind her ear. "I've always wanted to meet your kind."

"We have wanted to meet riders, elf," the same merman replied. He seemed to be the one with the best grasp of language, and the merfolk clustered around him clicked and chittered their own sentiments at him. He waved them away with one webbed hand, the fingers thin and long. "Neria of the deep water sent us, and we come to see riders!"

"Neria?" Tiryn asked, turning to Tathiel. "Does he mean Melonya?"

Tathiel pursed his lips, thinking. The chattering of the mer was growing louder as more of the creatures surfaced and clustered on the port side of the ship. "I'm not sure. It's possible."

Tiryn frowned, leaning further over the railing and shouting to be heard. "Who is Neria?" On his right, he saw Roland and Mathius joining Nunor and watching the excitement of the mer family below them.

The merfolk looked from one to another, their chittering taking on a halting rhythm as they relayed the question amongst themselves. Finally, their translator looked up, craning his gilled neck to look at them.

"Neria is Neria, elf. Of the deep water."

Tiryn caught Roland's eye, but the man only shrugged.

"Mathius, this is ridiculous. We need to keep moving," Reed was shouting from the middle of the deck, arms crossed angrily over his chest. "Those creatures are delaying us, and we don't have much time to waste before we need to reach Carran."

Mathius sighed, giving Roland and Tiryn a sympathetic look. "Reed is right. We're already a day behind schedule. If we keep this pace up, we'll be late getting to Cusch to restock before turning around and sailing back to Hythe."

Roland nodded, shouting to be heard over the din of the mer. "You heard the captain, everyone. Time to say goodbye."

Eilonwy huffed in displeasure, but leaned over the railing to frantically wave a farewell. "I'm glad we could meet you. Please tell Neria thank you!" Tathiel put a protective arm around his sister's waist as she leaned dangerously over the water, using his free hand to wave as well. Eilonwy seemed to not notice his grasp as she called out more goodbyes.

The mer returned their waves, shouting varying chants of "Elf!" and "Riders!", then with a series of swift kicks, they disappeared into the water.

The sudden quiet was unsettling, until it was broken by Reed's shouts at the other crewmen to bring the ship back to course. Mathius sighed, leaving the railing and calling after Reed to let him do his job, dammit.

"I thought merfolk had tails, like dolphins?" Jaimes asked, turning to Tiryn.

"A common misconception, unfortunately," an enthusiastic voice answered behind them. Tiryn and the others turned to see Lord Brynne standing just behind them, craning his neck to peer over the railing at the vanishing merfolk. "They have legs and arms like humans, but their hands and feet are webbed to make it easier for them to swim."

"Why are they always drawn with tails, then?"

"Because those drawings were done by fools too lazy to do the proper research," Brynne answered with a sniff.

"Because a lot of people don't get the chance to meet them. Someone probably described them as sounding like dolphins, and the description was warped over time." Tiryn motioned for Jaimes and Alastor to leave the railing. "Come on, I think we've had enough fun for now. Back to work, you two."

Jaimes and Alastor groaned simultaneously but followed Roland's beckoning from the starboard side of the ship.

"Going so soon?" Brynne asked, his face falling.

Tiryn caught Reed's angry scowl as the man crossed in front of their group on his way to the helm. "I'm afraid we must, Lord Brynne. We'll just get in the way up here."

"Well," Brynne huffed, casting a dirty look at Reed's back. "I won't keep you, but you know where to find me, should the desire for invigorating conversation strike you."

Tiryn was sure the desire for Brynne's company would never strike him, but he nodded politely before ushering for the twins and Nunor to lead the way back down to their cabin. "Of course, Lord Brynne."

Eilonwy and Tathiel fell in on either side of Tiryn, each one a step ahead of him. Eilonwy leaned in close, checking around them for anyone who might overhear. "Who do you think Neria is, Tiryn?" she asked, tucking her hair behind her ear once more. Tathiel frowned at her, and she rolled her eyes, pulling her hair back from behind her ears and brushing it over the pointed tips.

"I can only assume they meant Melonya," Tiryn answered in a similarly hushed tone. They reached the bottom of the stairs and stepped into the cool darkness of the upper hold, Nunor waiting patiently for them. "And if not … perhaps there's something else out in the water with us."

4 2

MELONYA

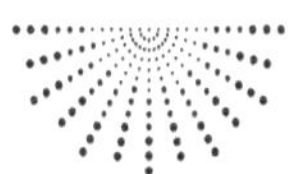

"Hello, Little One. You seem to be very far from home." Melonya heard the words before she could fully sense the creature that had awoken in the waters around her.

She was old, that much Melonya could tell. And with age came great power. Melonya felt that power stirring and collecting itself around her.

"*S-show yourself,*" she stammered. It was no use trying to hide her fear from the creature; she would feel Melonya's emotions just as easily as Melonya could sense her mounting curiosity.

"*It's been so long since I have met another like myself. But you are not quite like me, are you?*" The power that had been accumulating in the open ocean around her suddenly surged, and Melonya instinctively shuddered as a great *something* moved through the waters towards her. She sensed it looming closer, though she could not see it. Whatever the creature might be, she was large—several times larger than Melonya herself.

"*What are you, exactly?*" Melonya asked, steeling herself for the creature's approach. She sensed no malice, but that could

295

change in an instant. And she was clearly at a disadvantage, both in size and skill.

"I am Neria. That is what I have most recently been called, though I have had many other names." Neria's voice was smooth and deep, and she spoke with the careful lilt that Melonya had only ever heard from the elves in her Homewood. In the darkness around her, Melonya sensed the creature growing closer, and she could make out the indistinct shape of something large approaching from the depths of the ocean floor to meet her. A pair of warm red eyes glowed up from the deep below, and Melonya watched the eyes draw closer with each passing second. *"I was once known as Waterwing, and as Nausina, but lately I have only been Neria of the Deep. And I am a dragon, though I imagine you have already realized that."*

The red eyes and dark shape resolved themselves into an immense creature, lithe and long. Her scales were smaller than Melonya's own, and almost ghostly pale in their whiteness. Instead of wings, she possessed a large double set of fins about halfway along her length, and her tail ended in a streaming fin that waved through the water in a mesmerizing motion that Melonya could hardly tear her eyes from. She was much larger than Melonya, and she moved around the smaller dragon in lazy circles. She possessed legs in much the way Melonya did, though the claws that tipped them were massive in size. Each one could have torn Melonya in half in an instant, and Melonya tried to keep them well within sight as the larger dragon continued to circle her.

"As I suspected," Neria said, slowing her circling and coming to a stop in front of Melonya. *"You are not like me, are you? You are a land dragon, and a young one at that."* Neria's tail curled back on itself, the serpentine movement unnerving Melonya even as it fascinated her. *"What are you doing in the water, instead of the sky? Come to see how the other half lives, Little One?"*

Melonya felt the tickle in her lungs growing worse. She

would have to return to the surface soon. *"I didn't know there were sea dragons,"* she said, feeling stupid. She should have known. There were mentions of great sea creatures in some of the history books Tathiel had read to her as a hatchling. She had assumed that the accounts were of whales or families of mer, not of sea dragons.

"Alas, there is only the one left. My kind long ago gave themselves over to the eternal depths. But you have not answered my question." Neria laughed, the sound a crescendo of warmth over Melonya. *"Did Farnean send you? It would be in his nature to send a hatchling to awaken me, the old fool."*

Melonya hesitated, not sure what the great sea dragon was asking her. Who could she be talking about? Another dragon? There were no more dragons.

"I am the last of my kind as well, or so I believe. My name is Melonya. I've come to find the water amulet, to help my friends stop the rule of the human king."

Neria laughed again, though not unkindly. *"Your friends? Those in the ship above us, I presume? You consort with the small creatures of this world?"*

"Y-yes," Melonya answered, suddenly nervous. *"Two of them are my riders. I hatched for them. They belong to me, and I to them."* A momentary panic gripped her as she realized she was conversing with the only creature that would tell her the proper way for a dragon to behave. *"Is that not how it should be?"*

"That is not how it once was, but I cannot fault you." Neria let out something like a deep sigh, considering her next words. *"The world has changed much in my slumber. If you could feel their souls from inside your egg, and your own soul grew connected to theirs, then I cannot judge you for befriending them in the way you have."* Neria's tail unwound itself, and she made another half circle around Melonya. *"As for the water amulet, it is not far from my resting place. You are closer than you might think to finding it, Little One."*

Melonya felt her pulse quicken. To think they were finally reaching the amulet, and the first part of their quest was nearly over … *"Are you sure? The amulet is near?"*

A wave of amusement rolled from Neria, mixing with the aura of curiosity already emanating from her. *"Of course I am sure. I remember the day it was moved here. It is not far, but it might be a bit of a swim for you."*

"I need to resurface. I need more air." Melonya felt her lungs beginning to ache. She should have started the swim back to surface already. The nervousness that crept over her wasn't helping her composure, either.

"Go on. I can wait here for you, Little One. Tell your companions that you have found the amulet. I am sure they will be very happy to hear it. And perhaps you can tell me about them on the journey down." Neria's tail fanned through the water before her as she settled herself to wait. *"I can be patient, time is nothing to me."*

Melonya hesitated. *"You're really going to help me find the amulet?"*

"Of course." Another wave of amusement flooded Melonya's senses as Neria made an airy chuckle. *"I no longer want it down here with me. If you do not take it now, some other hatchling will just come along and wake me up to take it for themselves. Besides, a little company would be nice for some time. It's been so long since Farnean has come to see me, I suspect he might have chosen to move on to the eternal depths as well. Or whatever land dragons call it."*

Melonya was already clawing up to the surface far above her. *"We call it the great open sky."* She faltered, one claw pawing ineffectually at the water. How had she known that? She pushed the thought out of her mind, intent only on getting to the surface and close enough to pass the news of the amulet to Tathiel and Eilonwy. *"Please wait for me, Neria."*

"I will, Little One," Neria replied softly, and Melonya sensed her mind beginning to drift.

She would slumber, Melonya knew. I would take a few hours to reach the surface and return, and Neria had probably tired herself just with their short discussion.

Still ...

Melonya considered the little black book Alastor had inherited from his mother.

Areanath warned that the amulet would have to be earned. "Beast against terrible Beast", the book said. Is Neria supposed to be the other Beast? Would she try to fight me?

But she's another dragon. Surely not? And she said she wanted the amulet gone. Melonya continued to struggle her way up, convinced she was moving slower the faster she moved her legs. *And I sensed nothing malevolent from her. It would be a hard thing to hide.*

But perhaps it isn't so hard for someone as old as she is.

Melonya considered the idea of clashing with Neria to get the amulet as she made her way back to the surface.

I'll just have to take the chance, she decided. *It's the only way. If Neria wants to fight me, then so be it.*

The prospect of finally meeting another dragon, only to have to subdue her for possession of the amulet caused a shiver to run down Melonya's spine.

It's the only way.

JAIMES

"Try again, Jaimes. You too, Alastor."

Tiryn was staring at both of them intently, somehow holding both their gazes with the unblinking ferocity he only seemed to possess when instructing them.

Jaimes obediently replaced the triple stack of pebbles in his palm, closing his eyes and concentrating on the feel of the smooth stone against his skin. To his right, he heard Alastor huff through his nose. If Jaimes had heard it, Tiryn surely had as well.

Jaimes could understand his brother's frustration, and was himself equally annoyed. They had been practicing the same old spell for weeks now, yet Tiryn refused to teach them anything new until he felt they had sufficiently mastered this one small thing. At least they had moved from levitating a single stone to levitating a stack. The extra pebbles made it difficult to maintain control without them all toppling over, but Jaimes had figured it out soon enough. Alastor had taken a bit longer, but even he had mastered the task after only a few days.

Jaimes ignored Alastor's quiet complaint, instead feeling the weight of the stone in his hand. It was easy to find the connection between himself and the stone sitting directly on his skin, and from there, the connection between the first stone and the second, and so on. With a small effort and some mental acrobatics, Jaimes imagined the connection between himself and that first stone stretching out, while the connection between each stone remained rigid and taught. With the familiar sense of his stomach dropping as he released his will, the weight of the stone left his hand. He opened his eyes, searching Tiryn's face for a look of pride. Or acceptance. Or anything other than the blank look he always wore when instructing.

Nothing.

Tiryn was a tough teacher. *But a very good one*, Jaimes acquiesced.

Tiryn's eyes lifted from his own, focusing instead on something over Jaimes's shoulder. He gave a slight nod, and Jaimes was hit hard from behind. He fell to the ground with a grunt, Alastor doing the same beside him. He heard Eilonwy giggle as her weight fell on top of him. Tathiel snorted but managed to maintain his feet.

"Ugh, Tiryn, what in the names of the Great Ones was that for?" Alastor moaned.

Tiryn leaned over the boys, finally smiling. "Tomorrow we start mock combat training. You'll need to keep your focus while dodging hits from these two."

Jaimes frowned, letting Tathiel pull him and his sister to his feet. "You're joking, right?" He searched the floor around him. His stones were nowhere to be seen. He'd have to find new ones that stacked as nicely as those ones had.

Tiryn smiled again. "I'm very serious. We'll start out easy, maybe with the twins tossing things at you. Dodge them without letting your stones fall, and we can move on to swordplay. Roland has been kind enough to offer his assistance there, so that should be very instructive."

"Damn, Tiryn," Alastor muttered, pulling himself up with

a dirty glare at the hand Tathiel offered. "When do we get around to throwing fireballs and cursing our enemies?"

Tiryn shook his head, pulling a handful of pebbles from a pouch on his belt. "You can throw a fireball when you have learned to control fire. You can't learn to control fire until you have learned to control stones." With a small flick of his wrist, half a dozen small stones floated up from the palm of his hand, forming a circle and beginning a slow spin. They reminded Jaimes of the witch lights Tathiel conjured the night he and Alastor met Melonya.

With another small motion, the stones flew out from Tiryn's hand. Jaimes gasped, realizing the stones were headed for his chest. He flinched away, waiting for the peppering of tiny rocks against his thinning tunic. But it never came, and Jaimes opened his eyes hesitantly. In front of him, at roughly chest height, three little pebbles were arranged in a neat stack. The other three waited in front of Alastor, who was staring at Tiryn with a mixed look of shock and inspiration.

Jaimes plucked the stack of stones from the air, watching Tiryn's face take on his usual impassive teaching expression. "As for cursing your enemies, it's not something you should ever do."

"But—" Alastor started, but Tiryn silenced him with a raised hand.

"Once understood, curses are easy to implement, but impossible to remove. Why curse a man for the rest of his life in retaliation for a temporary pain he has caused you?"

"What about in battle?" Jaimes asked meekly.

Tiryn frowned. "There are no fast-acting curses. Curses are designed to cause prolonged pain and torment. If, in the heat of fighting, you need to kill a man, you kill him quickly and as painlessly as possible right then and there. Not in agony years from now.

"What about Mothlenor? Would you curse him?" This question came from Nunor, who sat whittling in the back corner of their cabin. He had been silent for so long, Jaimes had all but forgotten he was in the room with them.

"Nunor …" Tiryn sighed.

"No, I'm curious," Nunor insisted, letting his hands drop to his lap and watching Tiryn with his beady eyes. "He's killed so many of your kind. You told me he sent his men to burn down the town you grew up in. He practices dark arcane crafts. Some are saying he uses magic to make himself younger and healthier, so he can keep ruling. He's made his feelings about non-human species very clear. If you could, would you curse him? To pay him back for all of the pain he's caused?"

"Did he really burn down your entire town?" Jaimes asked.

"Yes," Tiryn answered. His voice was soft as he spoke, and the sound of it chilled Jaimes. "I grew up in Thessala, which was only a short trip east from the castle. It was easy enough for his men to reach. Ours was one of the first towns to fall, though we were lucky to lose only a couple of lives."

"So, would you curse him?" Alastor repeated Nunor's question.

Tiryn took a slow breath, relaxing his shoulders as he released it. "I think we're done for today. Try to see if you can figure out how to make your stones spin like I did. I'm interested to see if you can work it out." He turned to walk away, picking up one of Jaimes's books as he did.

"You just treat the center of the circle as the nexus," Jaimes blurted out. Remembering Tathiel encircled by his green-blue witch lights had helped him figure it out.

Tiryn turned, a genuine look of surprise on his face. "That's right." He smiled, and Jaimes warmed at the pride he felt. "I think you could grow to be very talented, Jaimes. I'm curious to see if you can demonstrate that technique tomorrow." Tiryn turned without another word and settled himself in his usual spot against the wall by the door.

"I never would have figured it out, Jaimes," Alastor said, one eyebrow raised as he looked Jaimes up and down. "You really are a lot better at this than I am."

"It was a lucky guess. And I'll always be here to help if you need it."

Alastor smirked, patting him on the shoulder. "Thanks, big brother."

Eilonwy smiled at the pair of them, tucking a strand of hair behind her ear. Jaimes glanced over at Tathiel as she did, knowing the unconscious motion always irked him. But Tathiel said nothing.

"I remember when we were learning how to control stones. Tathiel and I would play a game of catch with a nice rock. The first person to let it touch the ground lost. Do you remember, Tathiel?"

Her brother smiled, shrugging a shoulder. "I remember losing a good number of times. It was easy for me to throw the stone using magic, but always harder to stop the fall and catch it." He held his hands up, palms out, and wiggled his fingers. "You couldn't use your hands, you see. Only magic."

"Ah." Jaimes frowned. "Sounds complicated."

"It sounds fun," Alastor said, smiling. "Maybe we could try it next time we go to shore?"

"Sure." Tathiel nodded. "You just need to find a good rock. One that wouldn't hurt if it—" He stopped suddenly, stiffening. Eilonwy did the same, looking at her brother in concern.

"Tathiel? What's wrong?" Jaimes asked. Behind the twins, Jaimes saw both Tiryn and Nunor look up from their work.

"You don't think she's really going to go, do you?" Eilonwy asked her brother.

Tathiel shook his head, his gaze unfocused as he

answered. "I think she means to. Go, tell Roland. Get the course changed to follow her. I'll try to talk her out of it."

"Did Melonya find something?" Tiryn asked, closing the book that sat on his lap.

Neither Eilonwy nor Tathiel answered his question. Tathiel didn't seem to hear Tiryn's words, presumably too focused on trying to talk to Melonya to answer. Eilonwy was already rushing past Tiryn and out the door.

"Wait, Eilonwy!" Jaimes called after her. "You're not supposed to—" But Eilonwy was gone, the sound of her footsteps already on the stairs to the deck.

"Come on, let's go after her." Alastor ran out of the cabin door, Jaimes following behind. Jaimes paused in the doorway of the cabin, looking back at Tiryn.

Tiryn and Nunor had both gone to Tathiel, waiting for him to tell them what was happening. Tathiel still seemed to be communicating with Melonya, his brow furrowed and arms crossed tightly over his chest. Tiryn waved Jaimes away. "Go on, we'll stay here with him."

Jaimes turned and hurried after Alastor. They both made it to the deck, spotting Eilonwy almost immediately. She was arguing with a stoic Roland, the nearby crew eyeing her distrustfully.

"Please, we have to go after her. She could be in danger!" Eilonwy was pleading.

"I'm not sure what I can do, Eilonwy. We can't very well swim down there to help her, can we?"

"But maybe we can help her from up here. Tiryn can do something! Don't you remember what the book said?" Eilonwy's voice was growing louder and more pleading. "'Beast against terrible Beast', Roland. She's not the only one down there!"

"What's going on over here, Roland?" Mathius approached, drawn by Eilonwy's plaintive cries.

"Mathius, please! We have to turn the ship around. Someone could be in trouble!" Eilonwy clung to the captain's arm, and Mathius looked up at Roland in confusion.

"What's she talking about?"

But Eilonwy answered, looking between Roland and Mathius in frustration. "There's someone out in the ocean. Someone I care very much about. But she's about to do something stupid and reckless, and she could use our help."

"Someone out in the ocean?" Mathius's gaze flicked to Roland, who said nothing. "Not a human or elf, I presume?"

"No," Eilonwy answered softly.

"Is what she's saying true, Roland?"

Roland sighed, eyes fixed to Eilonwy's. "Yes."

"And is this … *someone* … truly in danger?"

"Quite possibly," Roland answered quietly. Jaimes frowned, looking over at Alastor. Alastor looked about as worried as Jaimes felt. *What was Melonya up to?*

"And can we do something to help from up here?"

Roland considered the question for a second, reaching a hand into the inside of his vest. Jaimes suspected he was reaching for the Dragon's Eye and considering their options. Eilonwy had been right. Tiryn probably could do something to help Melonya, and Roland's Dragon's Eye could be equally helpful.

Roland nodded slowly. "Quite possibly," he said again.

Mathius thought for a moment, looking first to Eilonwy's terrified face, then around the deck to the waiting crew. After a moment, he sighed. "Alright, girlie, which way do we need to go?"

Without hesitation, Eilonwy's arm shot out and pointed. "That way."

Jaimes and Alastor both looked up and across in the direction she indicated. It was on the port side, back towards the stern. The ship would have to turn nearly all the way around and leave the shoreline to reach the open stretch of sea Eilonwy pointed to.

Mathius looked back at Eilonwy, then at his crew. Most of them were glowering, and a few were shaking their heads. "You heard her, let's turn this ship around."

The crew broke out into an uproar. Reed stormed forward, glaring at Mathius. "You can't be serious! We'll be delayed! You can't just abandon your course to chase after some elf's friend."

Mathius growled at Reed. "I can, and I will, Reed. Someone needs our help, and we are going to give it, do you hear? Now get to work and turn this damn ship around!" Mathius stormed towards the stern, aiming for the helm. Roland followed, stomping up the stairs on Mathius's heels.

Reed seemed to hesitate for a moment, then turned and gestured towards the gathered crew. "You heard the captain. We're turning around."

"No."

The answer came from the largest of the crewmen, Evert. His brows were furrowed as he glared across the deck to Reed. "This has gone on long enough, Reed."

The surrounding men grumbled assents, and Reed raised a placating hand. "I don't like it either, Evert, but orders are orders. If we move quickly enough, we can still make it to Cusch before the weather starts to turn."

"Mathius broke the law when he let those *animals* on board. You should have done something then." Evert pushed his way through the men in front of him, stopping only a dozen paces away from Reed. "You need to decide which side you're on, Reed. Ours?" Evert motioned around him, indicating the rest of the crew. "Or theirs." He stabbed a meaty finger in Eilonwy's direction, and Jaimes instinctively stepped between her and the threat.

"What's going on up here, Mathius?"

All eyes turned at the sound of Brynne's raspy voice as he emerged from the hold.

"Dammit, Reed!" Mathius shouted, both hands on the helm. Roland stood close to him, fists balled and eyes on Evert. "Get Brynne and the children downstairs and keep them safe. Roland and I will stop this nonsense."

Evert took another lumbering step closer. "Choose, Reed. Which side?"

Reed sighed, stepping between Brynne and Evert and motioning for the Jaimes and the others to get behind him. "I will always choose Mathius's side, Evert."

Brynne's heavy book fell to the deck with an echoing thud. With the barest whisper of metal and a single wet gurgle, Reed tumbled down after it. Eilonwy let out a shriek, stumbling away from Brynne and the blood that flowed from Reed's neck.

"Shame," Brynne said. His voice was deeper, losing the shrillness Jaimes had come to associate with the man. "You would have made a good captain yourself, Reed." Brynne flicked his wrist, sending droplets of blood from the strangely curved blade that he held splattering across the wood in front of him.

"Reed!" Mathius cried, leaving the helm to rush down to his friend.

But Roland held him back, wrapping a hand around his upper arm. "Mathius …"

Jaimes saw what Roland was seeing. The two of them were quickly being surrounded by the other members of the *Kingfisher*'s crew as blades were drawn and the sailors advanced towards the two men.

Mathius and Roland were both unarmed.

Jaimes looked around frantically for a weapon to give them, but Eilonwy beat him to it. She found the two practice swords Alastor and Jaimes had been using for weeks, hefting one in each hand.

"Roland, catch!" She tossed both, and Jaimes watched them arc through the air before being caught neatly by Roland.

Eilonwy's hand found his, and she pulled him forward. "Run, Jaimes!"

Their prison was blissfully quiet and cool. Even Rawli was resting, his usual mutterings and singing absent in the dark hold. The others were still, cramped together in the pen that had held them for far too long now.

On any other day, Pyle would be grateful for the chance to get uninterrupted sleep. But this felt different.

There was a restless energy that set the muscles in his arms and legs twitching, and his fingers ached for the familiar touch of a weapon in his grip. The others felt it too, Pyle was sure. Orlen's eyes were constantly roving around the tiny room, and Roust's shoulders were tense beneath the blanket that stretched around them.

So when the quiet sound of footsteps drifted across the hold from the stairs, all eyes immediately shifted to the barred door.

Pyle stood, his hands balled into fists and jaw set. Behind him, he heard the whisper of cloth as the others stood with him.

"Eager, are we?" came the cool voice of their ally.

"Can you blame us?" Orlen asked. Pyle hissed over his shoulder, but Orlen continued. "We've been down here for days, weeks, I don't even know anymore. I want to kill every last one of those long-eared fucks for getting us trapped down here."

"Orlen!" Pyle snapped.

"Patience, Orlen," the man on the other side of the door said. "You will get your retribution, I promise you."

And with the sound of his voice, the door opened. Pyle hadn't even heard him working the lock.

Pyle hesitated, watching the man across from him. Brynne only smirked slightly at him, one eyebrow quirking up to give him an almost quizzical look.

Pyle stepped through the doorway, Orlen right on his heels. Pyle had to reach out and stop Orlen from storming right past him. "Weapons?"

"You won't need any."

"What?" Roust hissed behind him. "No weapons? What the fuck do you expect us to do against a ship full of—"

"You won't be going against a ship full of anything," Brynne said, cutting off Roust's petulant bitching. "You aren't the only ones I have working on this ship, but I need you for a very particular job."

"What's the job?" Pyle should have guessed that this man wouldn't rely on just the few of them do his work, but the idea of not getting their weapons returned was unsettling to him. His fingers twitched.

Brynne's mouth curled into an eerie smile, and one long figure crooked in a simple beckon. "Follow me."

Jaimes and Eilonwy made for the stairs down to the hold, Eilonwy using her free hand to send a spray of blue sparks over her shoulder. A sailor hot on their heels let out a scream, and Jaimes chanced a glance to see the man covering his face with his hands. Angry welts had broken out across his face and neck. Jaimes could hear Alastor's breathing on his opposite side as they ran into the half dark of the upper hold.

But the door to their cabin was shut, and Jaimes heard yelling and frantic pounding on the door. A heavy beam had been dropped across the door, though where it could have come from, Jaimes couldn't begin to guess.

Eilonwy dropped his hand, lifting both of her own and aiming for the closed door. Jaimes saw movement in the corner of his eye, but before he could shout a warning to Eilonwy, she crumpled as something flew through the air and stuck her in the head.

"Eilonwy!" Jaimes rushed towards her prone figure, but was tackled from behind before he could reach her.

Strong hands yanked his arms behind his back, and Jaimes fought fruitlessly to free himself. Behind him, he heard Alastor cursing and fighting with a second assailant.

"Stop fighting, or I'll leave you here to die." A pair of heavy boots stepped into Jaimes's field of vision, followed by a heavy metal cleat hanging from a spare bit of rigging. The cleat was flecked with blood.

"Roust, Arlyth!" The voice called to two figures Jaimes could not see. "Get Rawli and clear a path to the rafts."

Two sets of boots rushed around Jaimes, coming from the darkness deeper into the hold, half carrying and half dragging a third person between them. One of them seemed to be singing tunelessly.

"But what about killing the elves and dwarf?" the man pinning Jaimes to the floor asked. Jaimes struggled again as a thick rope was wrapped around his wrists, but it was in vain.

"We've done enough here to earn the freedom Brynne promised us. But we'll take the girl, for Rawli's sake."

One of the man's boots prodded lightly at Eilonwy's limp form, and Jaimes cursed, trying once more to fight free of the bonds that held his arms back. "Get away from her."

The tips of the boots turned his way, taking a half step closer. "Get them up."

Jaimes was tugged painfully to his feet, facing the man that had struck Eilonwy down. Jaimes didn't recognize him.

"Don't worry," the man said, one eyebrow raised slightly. "She isn't dead. Yet."

"You're one of the men that snuck onto the *Kingfisher* to kill my friends, aren't you?" Alastor said, and Jaimes tried to rush to Eilonwy's side, but the man that had tackled him still held him close. All Jaimes could see was a bright line of blood smearing the side of her face.

"They had a choice, young man. Turn themselves in for questioning, or face immediate execution." The man smiled eerily at Alastor, making Jaimes's skin crawl. "They chose poorly, and their choice still stands. They will die on this ship." The man gestured towards the stairs leading up to the deck, from where Jaimes could hear fighting. "You can either come with us, or you can stay here and die with them."

"We'll come with you," Jaimes said breathlessly.

"Jaimes!" Alastor's expression was one of shock.

Jaimes gave his brother a look that he could only hope Alastor would understand. "Trust me, it's our best hope."

Alastor hesitated, casting a glance at both Eilonwy, still unconscious, and at the shut and barred door to their cabin, from where muffled shouts and thuds could be heard. "Alright. We'll go with you."

"Excellent," the man said, looking over Jaimes's shoulder as heavy footfalls came down the steps. "Evert, I presume?"

Jaimes turned to see the large sailor descending the final steps and coming to stop between Jaimes and Alastor. He held a short sword in one hand, and Jaimes's stomach turned at the sight of blood on the blade.

Evert gave a curt nod. "Pyle?"

The man leading the King's Guards returned the nod.

"You ready to go then?" Evert asked.

"Grab the girl, if you don't mind. We have a score to settle with her." Pyle jerked his head towards Eilonwy's form, hefting the makeshift weapon he held as he stepped aside for Evert. The heavy metal cleat spun idly, Eilonwy's splattered blood making Jaimes's stomach tighten. "The boys have decided to join us as well. Are things moving along as Brynne hoped they would?"

Evert snorted. "Should be smooth enough in a short time. There were more loyal crewmen than Brynne had led us to believe. But not any longer." Evert sheathed the short sword into a loop high on his hips, letting his tunic fall to cover it.

No wonder they were able to attack so quickly, if Brynne had supplied them with weapons that could be hidden so easily. Jaimes wondered at Brynne's treachery as Evert bent to lift Eilonwy, tossing her casually over his shoulder. Jaimes winced as her head bounced against the huge man's shoulder blade.

Brynne had seemed friendly and kind, but he had been anything but.

He was a monster, a murderous spy, posing as an aloof scholar.

And Eilonwy and the others might die because of him.

Evert and Pyle led them to the deck and through the edges of the fighting. Jaimes looked away as they passed Reed's body, but there were many more that he could not avoid. Fights had broken out across the entire deck, most of them obviously one-sided, with large hulking crewmen with short swords hunting down the few that had tried to flee from the mutiny. But some men fought with only their fists, beating each other without a care for who they hit. The deck was painted with spilled blood, and Jaimes searched frantically for Roland and Mathius. They were no longer at the helm of the ship, which had been momentarily abandoned, but were at the fore end, surrounded by nearly a dozen men. Jaimes could only see flashes of red hair as Roland and Mathius fought off their attackers, and he made a quick plea to Elir to give them strength, and one to Imis for their safety.

Brynne was nowhere to be seen.

Jaimes waited until they were nearly at the rafts before acting. Pyle was leading them closer to Roland and Mathius with each step, though he was careful not to let them stray too close to the densest areas of fighting. Though Jaimes knew there was little hope of him escaping and running into the fray, he could still let their allies know what was happening to them.

He glanced at Alastor, who was watching him, waiting. Then Jaimes took a deep breath and bellowed with all his might.

"*Roland! Roland! They're taking us off the ship! Eilonwy is hurt! They're taking us—"* The King's Guard holding him clamped his hand over Jaimes's mouth.

Beside him, Alastor took up the cry. *"We're going to the rafts! Roland, you have to come—"* Alastor was silenced with a hand clamped over his mouth as well.

"Damn you both, you nasty cunts!" It took Jaimes a second to recognize Brynne, who now seemed taller than he had before. Even his face seemed different, though it might have been the menacing scowl scrawled across it. "Get them out of here, Pyle. I'll get the *Kingfisher* to shore and meet you where we discussed." Brynne disappeared back into the fray, slipping between two pairs of fist-fighting sailors.

Ahead of him, Evert stepped over the railing and settled into a waiting raft, depositing Eilonwy's body onto the floor like she was just another barrel of wine or roll of fresh leathers that needed loading. Jaimes went in after, the hand covering his mouth replaced with a quickly knotted rope. He carefully stepped around Eilonwy's crumpled body, wincing as Pyle stepped noisily on one of her hands as he followed Jaimes in. The man that had been holding Jaimes joined last, and Jaimes was finally able to get a good look at his face. There was an anger to his eyes that startled and unnerved Jaimes, but he found himself less wary of this other man than he already was of Pyle.

The next raft over already had a waiting occupant, a thin man who appeared almost entirely unaware of what was occurring around him. He simply sat in the middle of the raft, singing something Jaimes did not recognize. Alastor was shoved in to sit across from this man, who made no acknowledgment of Alastor's presence, then three more men filed in to fill the second raft.

They were swiftly lowered into the water by a group of sailors, and Jaimes could only watch as the deck of the *King-fisher* fell away from view, and the sounds of fighting began to dim. Jaimes cast a look across to Alastor, who was staring with nervous apprehension at the singing man in front of him.

"Do you see what the elf girl did to Rawli?" Pyle asked Jaimes, leaning in close to make himself heard. "Broken bones can be mended, but whatever she did to him will likely last forever." Pyle's gaze dropped down to Eilonwy, who lay pitifully in the bottom of the raft between them. "And something like that must be repaid in kind."

Jaimes tried to curse Pyle, tried to warn him not to lay so much as a finger on Eilonwy, but the words came out a garbled mess among the rope knotted around his head.

But Pyle seemed to guess the meaning behind Jaimes's muttering, and returned only an eerie smile.

The rafts hit the water with a hard thump and a splash, and Jaimes looked up to see the deck of the *Kingfisher* now an impossible distance away. And as he stared at the wooden rails as Pyle and Evert rowed them away, Brynne, easy to make out with his strange cloak, walked the length of the starboard rail and cut each of the remaining rafts free from the ship. The rafts fell one at a time, some smashing into the hull and breaking, others capsizing as they hit the water.

Jaimes was sure he could see a manic grin on the traitor's face as the safest way off of the *Kingfisher* was destroyed.

MELONYA

"I'm sorry, but this might be the only way."

Melonya waited until she had nearly reached Neria once more before telling Eilonwy and Tathiel what her plans were. She had expected resistance, especially after telling them about her encounter with the ancient dragon. Neria had already made her presence known by sending a large family of mer to the surface, and the twins were uneasy about the sea dragon's existence.

"You can't go alone, Melonya!" Tathiel pleaded. Of the two, he was usually the more cautious, and Melonya wasn't surprised that he was the one to make the attempt to dissuade her. *"You remember what Roland's book says. What if Neria means to trick you?"*

Eilonwy said nothing, and Melonya suspected that she was attempting to convince Tiryn or Roland to help her. But they would be too far away to lend any sort of assistance. She would be alone.

"I remember what the book says, but this is likely the best chance we have of getting to the amulet. If Neria means to trick me, then so be it, but I'm sure that's not the case." Indeed, she had contemplated the idea during her long struggle to the

surface. There seemed to be no point in Neria going back on her word. *"She's had the amulet for fifteen years. She could have taken it at any time. I think she really intends to be rid of it."* Her mental connection to her companions was growing weaker; she felt it thinning and fraying. It would break in a moment, and she would be out of touch with Eilonwy and Tathiel until she returned to the surface. If she returned at all.

The huge shape of the dragon Neria loomed out of the darkness. It had taken her less time to reach her than Melonya thought it might. Perhaps she was getting better at swimming in such dark and heavy waters, despite her lack of fins to aid her.

"Melonya, wait!" Tathiel's voice took on a panicked edge, but Melonya would not be swayed by him.

"It is the only way, Tathiel. I'm sorry. I'll be back soon. With the amulet. I promise." And with that, the connections broke. Melonya was alone, facing the unknown of the dark sea with only the word of a sea dragon to guide her.

"Hello, Little One. You've returned quickly." With the quiet power of an oncoming storm, Neria connected her mind to Melonya's. *"Shall we go? It is far, and we have much to discuss."* Neria seemed to come alive in the darkness around them, unfurling her great serpentine body and fanned tail. *"If you follow close behind me the trip should be easier and faster for you."*

Melonya did as she was told, and tucked as close to the great dragon's massive tail as she dared. As Neria began her descent, the current created by her movements pulled Melonya along behind her. The sensation was unpleasant and eerie and very unlike the soft tug of the tides she had grown accustomed to experiencing closer to the surface. It did little to comfort her unease at the possibility of fighting such a large creature.

"Why do you seek the amulet?" Neria asked. The same sense of amusement and curiosity she had sensed earlier rolled over Melonya. *"Do your companions intend to use it?"*

"No," Melonya answered. *"We hope to keep them from the king of men. He would use them to undo the world as it is known now."*

"And that would be regrettable?" Neria asked.

The question might have been rude, but Melonya felt the sincerity and confusion behind it.

"I think so. My companions think so. Mothlenor would destroy all sentient non-human life. Including mine, even though I am the last of my kind. Even yours, if he knew you existed."

Neria scoffed. *"The amulets could not undo me."*

"Are you certain?"

"Very certain." Neria sighed, her pace slowing slightly. *"I fear my time might be ending soon, regardless. I have slept for so long. There might come a day when another young hatchling comes to wake me, and I do not answer."*

Melonya drew closer to Neria's body, the morose feeling emanating from the dragon making her anxious. *"Do you have nothing left to live for? What about Farnean, do you not have a life together?"*

Neria scoffed again, and twitched her tail in agitation. *"Farnean is another land dragon, and it has been nearly a century since I last heard from him. I have searched the coasts time and time again for him, but if he still lives, he does so in such seclusion that I cannot feel his presence."* Neria paused, her massive head turning to look at Melonya. *"I do have eggs, but they will probably never hatch. Our time is ending, Little One. We do not have much left to offer this world."*

"You have eggs? Are you sure they would never hatch?" Melonya pondered the idea for a second, then blurted, *"What if I take a few back with me? Maybe there are riders above the surface that they will hatch for?"*

Melonya sensed Neria warm at the suggestion. *"I wish you could, but they need the cold of the deep waters if they are ever to hatch. And I fear it is just too unlikely for them to ever find a companion. You should count yourself lucky, Little One."*

Melonya let the matter rest, disturbed by the surety of Neria's words. They continued in silence for a few moments more, the darkness absolute even to Melonya's discerning eyes. *"Neria, do you intend to trick me? Do you want the amulet for yourself?"* Melonya's voice was blunt, and she hoped the small trickle of fear she felt went unnoticed by the larger dragon.

Neria slowed, her great body curling in the freezing waters around them. *"I will not trick you, Little One. That much I can promise."* She faltered, turning one great eye to look at Melonya. *"If I must be truthful, the amulet does call to me. It has a power that I find familiar to my own, and I can sometimes sense it in my dreams. But I cannot keep it. The amulets are not for us to use."*

"Why do you keep it close, if it haunts you?"

"To protect the others that live in these waters. If one of the merfolk were to become corrupted by it, I could not forgive myself."

"Corrupted?" Melonya asked. *"Are the amulets dangerous?"*

"Power can be dangerous, Melonya. And the amulets are powerful." Neria's body unwound itself as she continued diving deeper into the dark depths, pulling Melonya along with her. *"I hope, for your sake, that your friends are stronger than I am."* Neria's head turned once more to Melonya, one red eye glowing softly in the dark. *"We are very near. Can you continue alright? We are very deep for a creature used to the open skies."*

Melonya shifted uncomfortably. The pressure was pinching, and she wouldn't want to stay so deep for very long. But she could handle it for a short time before the discomfort became unbearable. *"I'll be fine for a while, yes."* She didn't want to admit to Neria that she found the darkness more unnerving and disquieting than the depths.

Neria laughed, the sound resonating throughout Melonya's mind. *"Very well. We can make this quick for you, Little One. The amulet is not much further."*

Melonya was once again pulled along beside Neria's great body as they continued their descent. *"Are you so sure that you want to be rid of the amulet? Would it not be wiser to keep it here, where it cannot be found?"*

A shiver ran down the length of Neria's long body, causing her fanning tail to twitch through the water just inside Melonya's vision. *"I do not want it so close. It is not for us to keep. It belongs to the people of the world above now. And I am not so sure I could ignore its call for much longer."*

Her answer intrigued Melonya. Perhaps Neria was old enough to know more about the amulets than she had her companions had been able to guess. *"Can you tell me about the amulets? Who made them? What are they really for?"*

Neria laughed again. *"Has their origin already been lost to the world?"* She sighed, turning her head once more to look at the smaller dragon. *"Very well, I suppose I can answer those questions easily enough. They were made by the Great Ones. You were correct in guessing their purpose earlier. They can be used to summon the Great Soul, the most powerful of the Great Ones. The Great Soul has the power to bring peace to the world. Or at least it was once possible. Who can be sure what might happen in this new age?"*

"The Great Soul is one of the old gods? One of the Great Ones?" Melonya wondered if that could be possible, if the Great Ones were no longer worshiped. Could the power of the Great Ones have died when they did? Would the amulets still function, if that were true?

Neria sensed the questions echoing from Melonya. *"Yes,"* she answered solemnly. *"And no. It is too soon to know for sure."*

"I don't understand."

Neria sighed, and a wave of annoyance and frustration rolled over Melonya's conscious mind. *"The Amulets of Power will still function, because the Great Soul still lives on. In a sense, anyway."* She turned to look at Melonya once more. *"It is too complicated to explain, Little One. I'm sorry."*

"I still don't understand, Neria."

"I know. There is nothing else I can do to help you. Perhaps Farnean would be better suited to this conversation, if he were still alive …" Neria stopped, pulling her long tail close. *"Look, Little One."*

Melonya left Neria's side long enough to examine their surroundings. The ocean floor was visible several meters below them. Melonya could see and sense small creatures scuttling and swimming along the silt bottom. Algae and other plants grew in colorful clusters, and many of them gave off a soft green glow that illuminated small patches of the sea around them.

"There is so much life here."

Neria let out a low sound, startling a few fish away. *"It's because of the amulet. They can sense its power."* Neria shifted, lifting her long snout to gesture at a rock outcrop that loomed out of the water. *"The amulet is in there."*

Melonya stared at the rock, squinting to see what Neria was trying to show her. As she stared, a soft ripple of arcane energy flowed through the waters. She instinctively tensed, baring her teeth as a blue light pulsed from a small opening in the rock that she had not seen before.

The light faded and the energy receded. Melonya relaxed, her eyes fixed on the spot where she could barely make out the opening to an underwater cavern. *"Is that the amulet?"*

"Yes." Neria seemed uneasy, her tail fanning through the water and sending silt eddying over Melonya's scales. *"You should go now."*

Melonya turned toward the large dragon. *"You won't be coming with me?"*

Neria retreated a few feet, coiling her tail around herself. *"I cannot. I haven't been able to fit inside that cavern in centuries."* Neria bared her teeth, the longest one the size of Melonya's legs. *"You should hurry."*

Melonya felt a shiver roll down her spine. *"What's waiting in there for me, Neria?"*

Neria shook her head, the tension in her coiled tail visibly easing. *"The amulet is there. But so are my eggs. And it is hard to see another dragon so close to my nest."*

Melonya stiffened. Neria's teeth were still bared, though she had made no move to attack her. *"I will hurry. And I promise that no harm will come to your eggs."*

"Just hurry," Neria snarled. *"I want the amulet gone from these waters."*

Melonya clawed her way to the dark hole that served as the cavern's entrance as another flash of blue beckoned her forward. *"I will return soon, Neria. Just wait for me."*

Roland sensed Mathius just behind him. The crew had them surrounded, and they took it in turns to swing at them. The sounds of their curses and jeers intermingled with the occasional crack of metal on wood. Roland thought he could hear Tiryn and the others shouting below deck, but he couldn't be sure.

"Roland!" Mathius shouted, shoving at his left shoulder.

Roland obediently ducked and turned, narrowly avoiding the crude overhead shot that had been meant for his neck. Roland instead pitted rough-hewn hardwood against an old broadsword, this one held by one of the greasier-looking men around them. They were all untrained and unskilled in combat. But there were plenty of them to go around, and he only held a glorified stick. *One well-placed hit is all it would take ...*

As if in answer, Roland heard the sound of splintering wood over his shoulder, and Mathius cursed. There was a sudden warmth as Mathius pressed his back against Roland's own. "Fucking shit, Roland." Roland felt the younger man panting hard. He blocked another strike before sidestepping a third, pulling Mathius along with him. "I don't think they mean to take us into custody." Roland grunted as Mathius's weight fell heavier against him. The captain was locked together with another fighter, the stump of the practice sword the only thing keeping the heavy blade from crashing down onto him. "They'll just wear us down, then beat us to death." With a grunt, Mathius's weight lifted off Roland. He briefly wondered if the captain had kicked his attacker in the gut as he had Roland during their brief spar.

"We have to go after the boys." Roland landed a heavy hit squarely on the jaw of a nearby sailor. "Eilonwy was hurt." He'd caught a brief glimpse of her slumped over Evert's back. There'd been blood, but Roland hadn't been sure how much, or where it had come from. "We have to follow before they get too far away."

"The others are trapped down below." Another man ran in for a tackle, and Mathius caught the charge and clubbed him on the back of the head with the broken chunk of wood still in his grip. The sailor crumpled to the deck instantly.

Roland could hear the steady thumping of something heavy against wood. Tiryn and the others must be trying to break their way out of the cabin. "They'll be fine."

"Off the port side, then?" Mathius panted, glancing over his shoulder to catch Roland's eye.

Roland nodded, already judging the distance to the port-side railing. There were only a couple of men blocking the path, apparently convinced that only an insane man would leap into the shallow waters this close to the shore. Or perhaps they worried about being pushed over themselves. "Now!"

Roland and Mathius both turned and bolted for the railing. Roland took the lead, batting his cracking weapon into the face of one man in their path. Something passed close by his ear, and the broken bit of sword Mathius had been holding split the face of another. Both men fell to their knees, clutching their wounds, blood spurting between their fingers.

Roland leapt, landing one foot squarely onto the hunched back of the man he'd hit, leaping from the broken bastard to land his opposite foot on the railing. Beside him, Mathius managed to avoid the second bleeding man and clambered up the railing in one quick vault. They jumped overboard together, landing feet first half a heartbeat apart into the cold waters of the ocean. The water was deep enough to receive them, but only just.

They surfaced, spluttering and gasping from the chill. The shouts continued above, and Roland hoped that Tiryn and the others had broken from the cabin and were continuing where he and Mathius had left off.

"C-Come on." Roland stuttered, swimming for the aft end of the ship. "Jaimes and Alastor said they were in rafts, headed for shore." He'd have to thank Jaimes for his quick thinking if they all made it out of this alive. But the *Kingfisher* was already close to shore; the rafts would have nearly made it already. Roland swam faster, willing the chill that crept into his extremities away.

"I think—" Mathius started, his teeth chattering. "I think there's a network of caves nearby. They must have taken the boys there." Mathius swam quickly with a practiced grace. "Roland, we have to hurry. The tide is coming in, and those caves will flood."

48
TIRYN

Tathiel was pounding frantically on the cabin door, shouting his sister's name. Nunor beat against the wall beside him, using his heavy axe to chip away at the sturdy wood. It had only taken an instant for the six King's Guards to rush the cabin door and bolt the three of them inside, but it was taking them far too long to break themselves out. They would never reach the deck of the *Kingfisher* in time to help Roland.

Tiryn carefully packed the last of Jaimes's books away into the boy's bag, dropping the wrapped package Jaimes seemed to have grown overly protective of on the top before slinging both the bag of books and Roland's old sword over one shoulder. Roland would need it, surely. *Wherever he's run off to,* he thought briefly.

"Tathiel, stop. The door is reinforced, you'll only break your hands." Tiryn placed a hand on the younger elf's shoulder, trying to pull him from the door.

"They hurt Eilonwy," Tathiel cried, pounding harder against the door. "I felt it, I felt her fall. What if they killed her?"

"She's not dead, Tathiel. Now stop." He couldn't be sure

what condition Eilonwy was in, but Tathiel was useless in his current state. He needed Tathiel's focus more than he needed his anger. "Tathiel. Stop," Tiryn's voice thundered, startling even himself. Above them, from the deck of the ship, he could make out sounds of fighting. The weight of Roland's sword was an uncomfortable reminder that they needed to hurry.

Tathiel finally stopped, one fist still set against the door, and turned to face Tiryn. His eyes were wide, the whites of them startling.

"Get the rest of the bags," Tiryn added softly.

Tathiel did as he was told, his face pale.

"Nunor." Tiryn stepped closer to the dwarf, one hand stretching out. "Give me your axe."

The dwarf paused, looking him over and panting. "The fuck I will."

"Nunor."

Nunor must have caught a glint of something in Tiryn's eyes, or heard the hardness in his voice. He passed the axe over in silence.

Tiryn hefted the weapon in one hand. He'd never used a dwarf-forged weapon before, but he recognized the weapon from his first meeting with Nunor. In Nunor's grip, the axe was a fierce and cruel-looking weapon. In Tiryn's, it looked little more than a toy. But the edges were sharp, and it would work well.

"Step back, both of you."

Nunor stepped away, eyes narrowed at Tiryn. Tathiel watched, frantically slinging bags and weapons over his shoulders.

With a hasty flick of the wrist, the axe spun from Tiryn's grip. Tiryn was strong, and the axe well-made and cared for. But it was the magic Tiryn had imbued into the throw that made the effort count. He had aimed for the section of wall that Nunor had already been hammering away at, and the force of the throw sent the axe through the splintered wall in an instant. The wall fell, whole timbers cracking and splitting into pieces. The axe came to rest in the stairs that led to the deck, the metal singing slightly as it stuck.

With a rumbling laugh, Nunor hopped through the hole and sprinted up the stairs, pulling his axe from where it had lodged itself as he ran. Tathiel made to follow, one hand holding the thin blade of the high elves, the other clutching a long dagger, but Tiryn pulled him back.

Tiryn sought Tathiel's pale green eyes, holding him in place. "Roland has already gone after the boys. He'll find your sister. She'll be fine." Tathiel nodded slightly, but his lips were pressed tightly together. Tiryn squeezed the shoulder he gripped. "Our job is to protect Roland's rear. To make sure he can get to them safely. We kill anyone that tries to follow him. Do you understand?"

"I-I understand," Tathiel muttered.

"Good." Tiryn shoved Tathiel forward through the hole in the cabin wall. He heard the faint sound of splashing. *Roland has jumped ship.* To Tathiel, he added. "We'll fight our way to the rafts and see if we can take one to the shore." Tathiel was running up the stairs, taking them three at a time. Already there was a sailor crumpled on them. *Nunor's doing, surely.* "When we get to the shore, you need to find Melonya and tell her what's happening. She needs to get back to the surface. The amulet can wait until another day, if need be."

Tathiel made a small sound of acknowledgment, dodging the thrust of a sailor that turned into the open doorway ahead of him. Tathiel opened the man's stomach with a quick jerk of the dagger and sent him rolling down the stairs. He continued, not looking back to see if Tiryn was following.

The man was still alive, hands clamped over his stomach and howling in agony. Tiryn's stomach turned, and he silenced the man's cries with a thrust of his own small blade into the man's heart. *Better for him to die quickly.*

Tiryn climbed the last of the stairs in a single bound, stepping onto the deck of the ship and into the sunshine. Already the deck was in chaos. Nunor was rampaging through the gathered sailors, axe swinging wildly. Tathiel followed behind, cleaning up Nunor's wreckage. The mutinous crew were putting up a fight, but they weren't trained to go up against an angry dwarf and a scared elf. Tiryn joined the fight, searching the crowd for Roland and Mathius. As he suspected, neither was to be seen.

The crew fell quickly. Several retreated across the deck, nursing injuries big and small. Most of the surviving crew fled, running below decks, dropping their weapons as they went. Nunor started after them, but Tathiel held him back. "My sister, Nunor. We have to find her."

Nunor grumbled, but he turned his back on the retreating men.

Tiryn walked the length of the starboard side of the ship, dismayed at the signs of sabotage he found. "They've cut the rafts free."

There was a hard, barking laugh behind them, and Tiryn turned to see Brynne standing at the helm. "It seems even that can't stop your friends."

"Brynne?" Tiryn stared at the man, trying to find the eager and frail scholar in the stranger that held the helm with calm ease. "What's going on?"

"What luck, what fortune was it, that you and your ilk would stumble upon the very ship I was already on?" Brynne sneered over the helm at them. "And what a pleasure it will be to kill your troublesome resistance while it is still only a fledgling."

Understanding hit Tiryn, and beside him Tathiel let out a low curse. "You are the spy," Tiryn said. "You were the one that told the King's Guard where Roland could be found."

"Yes, though I must admit I underestimated your capabilities." Brynne's sneer tightened into a grimace. "The same mistake will not be made again, and when Ajax is captured and returned to this ship, I will see to his death myself." Brynne motioned for a nearby sailor to take the helm. The sailor limped forward, his weapon lost and a cut to his cheek bleeding and beginning to swell, and Brynne stepped away from control of the *Kingfisher* without another word. "As for the rest of you, I'm not content to wait so long."

Nunor let out a barking laugh, shifting his axe back into both hands. "You're only one man, Brynne. There are three of us."

"It will only take one of us." Tathiel stepped forward, but Tiryn stopped him with a hand around his upper arm.

"No." Tathiel turned, ready to argue, but Tiryn cut him off before he could start. "Find a raft. Take Nunor with you. Get to Roland." Tiryn shrugged Roland's sword from his shoulders, dropping the bag of books he held with it. "And keep calling for Melonya."

Brynne was descending the stairs, slinking closer to where Tathiel and Tiryn stood. He drew a curved blade from a loop on his belt and plucked a discarded short sword from the deck. Tiryn drew his own blade, little more than a knife, and stepped between Brynne and Tathiel. "Go. I'll follow shortly."

Tathiel's angry sigh and the sound of cloth and metal snapping against wood told him Tathiel had picked up the discarded belongings and was retreating.

"I wondered if you might stay and fight, Tiryn. I've never had the chance to fight an elf fairly before." Brynne sidestepped to a relatively clear section of the deck, his eyes fixed on Tiryn.

Tiryn gave his small blade a pointed look. "You still haven't."

Brynne's sneer deepened, the expression grotesque. "We both know that's not your real weapon."

The palm of Tiryn's free hand was reaching an unpleasant

level of warmth, but he continued to carefully channel arcane energy there. "I'm curious if those are the only weapons you'll use, Brynne. It's not every day that I get fooled with something as simple as an illusion." Brynne continued his sidestepping, circling Tiryn like a slow hawk. "That is what it was, am I right? Perhaps tied to one of those books you always seem to carry around."

"Clever." Brynne's eyebrow raised briefly. "But I should expect as much from an arcane beast such as yourself, elf."

With a snarl, Brynne charged.

Tiryn almost hadn't caught the way Brynne's shoulders relaxed before he moved in, and the speed with which the man moved was startling. But Tiryn was still faster. He flexed his hand, and a small bolt of lightning exploded painfully from his palm, quickly followed by a second, then a third.

Brynne dodged the first, a feat Tiryn had half expected. The second Brynne glanced aside with the flat of his curved blade, even as the third clipped him in the opposite shoulder. The short sword fell from Brynne's hand as his arm writhed and he grimaced in agony, but still he rushed Tiryn.

The curved blade flashed, and Tiryn leapt back as it came slicing through the air in front of him. Brynne was terribly fast, and Tiryn sent out two more bolts of lightning before having to dodge another slicing attack from the curved blade. They both caught Brynne square in the stomach, and the man let out a howl of pain. But his advance continued unabated.

Tiryn met the next attack with his own blade, catching the fattest part of the curved steel against his knife. Brynne was stronger than he looked, but Tiryn had guessed that would be the case.

Brynne brought both hands down on the hilt of his sword, struggling to bring the blade down, but Tiryn held him in place.

"Impressive weapon, elf."

Tiryn flexed his free hand, the arcane energy still held in it making it numb. "It was my father's." With a snap of his wrist, Tiryn flung the curved blade from Brynne's grasp, then brought his opposite hand up to grab Brynne's face. One final burst of lightning burst its way from Tiryn's hand, and Brynne screamed as the arcane energy burned across his face. He staggered back, hands clasped to his face, his voice straining with the agony in his cries. Tiryn had fully expected him to collapse where he was, but he still stood.

"I'll kill you, you monster!" Brynne screamed, bulging eyes barely visible through his fingers. The skin around them was red and blistered. "I swear I'll kill you!"

Brynne staggered forward, and Tiryn raised his knife for a finishing strike.

A mass of blue-green arcane energy shot over Tiryn's shoulder, hitting Brynne in the chest. Brynne was knocked from his feet and sent flying into the mainmast, where he fell silent.

Tiryn turned to see Tathiel standing by the starboard rail, one arm still raised. "I found a raft." Nunor stood beside him, knuckles white against the axe handle he gripped.

Tiryn wanted to curse. "You were supposed to leave."

"Not without you, Tiryn." Tathiel pointed over the railing to the water below. "Now let's go."

Looking over the rail and into the water, Tiryn saw one remaining raft, intact and bobbing against the hull of the ship. Scattered around it was the wreckage of perhaps half a dozen other rafts, pieces drifting in towards the shore with the swelling tide. Closer to shore, Tiryn spotted the forms of Roland and Mathius crawling their way from the water and onto the sandy beach. And behind them, two more rafts were making their approach, heading for the two men.

Tiryn looked down at Nunor, stomach turning again at

the flecks of blood and gore on his face and beard. "There's a raft down below. Can you make the jump?"

Nunor scowled up at him. "You know I can't, elf."

Tathiel plucked Nunor's axe from his grip, then leapt from the railing without a word. Tiryn waited for the young elf to drop his bags and stash Nunor's weapon in the bottom of the waiting raft, then he turned back to scowling Nunor. "Don't worry, Tathiel will catch you."

Before Nunor could protest, Tiryn lifted him like a small child and tossed him over the railing.

True to Tiryn's word, Tathiel caught him, and was already dipping an oar into the water when Tiryn landed inside the raft as well.

"Do that again …" Nunor growled, "and I might take off your ears."

Tiryn took the second oar and began rowing as quickly as his arms would let him. "Tathiel, any word from Melonya yet?"

Tathiel shook his head. "Nothing. I keep calling for her, but there's no answer. She's too far away to hear me."

This time Tiryn did curse, letting it out in a low voice. "Roland and Mathius are already on the beach, but they're unarmed. We need to get to the shore before those men overtake them. They might know where Eilonwy and the boys were taken."

Tathiel nodded, his face grim. "The tides are turning, Tiryn. Remember Roland's book?"

Tiryn remembered. *Before the tides have turned.*

"Row faster, Tathiel. And keeping calling for Melonya."

The trip from the *Kingfisher* to the shore was only a few minutes long, but the seconds stretched out agonizingly. Alastor, mouth gagged and hands still bound, could only watch Jaimes for signs of Eilonwy's condition. It was lucky, perhaps, that he had ended up in the same raft she had been tossed into. Jaimes was always better at the medicinal crafts that his mother had tried to teach them. Jaimes seemed to be inspecting Eilonwy's head, using his knees to gently lift her limp body to lean against him. With his hands tied behind his back, there was only so much he could do, but he peered and peeked and did what he could, ignoring the sneers from the sailors around him. Jaimes looked up to Alastor, catching him watching. He only shrugged, but Alastor saw the frantic look in his eyes, and the way his chest moved as his breathing hitched. *Great Ones bless him*, Alastor thought. *He's nearing another panicked fit, but he's still trying to figure out how to help Eilonwy.*

As they reached the beach, a man jumped from each raft and pulled Alastor and Jaimes out and onto the sand, while Evert lifted Eilonwy and hefted her over his shoulder. Blood had darkened her light hair and was sticking to the right side of her face. Alastor's stomach turned at the sight. Surely Eilonwy would still be alright, even after losing so much blood. Pyle led the group across the sand, Evert following behind with Eilonwy. Jaimes obediently followed, unbidden. Alastor only hesitated a heartbeat before following his brother. Two men stood close to Alastor and Jaimes, keeping less than an arm's length between them, and the last three King's Guards brought up the rear. The one the King's Guards had called Rawli continued his intermittent singing and wailing as they trudged along.

They were led down a thin stretch of beach towards a rocky outcrop a few hundred meters ahead. A thick forest hugged the beach to their right, the sea lapping in against their left. As they walked, Alastor dug his feet into the sand, hoping Roland would find their tracks soon enough.

He'll find us, we'll be fine, Alastor repeated to himself as they walked, watching Jaimes as he continued to observe Eilonwy. She remained limp and unresponsive as they trekked across the beach.

As they neared the rocky outcrop, Alastor realized it housed a collection of cave entrances. Some were small and cramped, a few large enough to allow them all to enter side by side. The man leading their captors chose an entrance seemingly at random and stooped to enter. The pebbled floor was damp, sloping steeply down into the darkness. The walls were covered in dried brine, the salt crystallizing on the rough stone. Alastor searched for the rear wall, unable to see more than a few feet in front of him. The cave could have ended after only ten feet, or it could have continued for miles, digging into the earth to meet up with the great labyrinth of dwarfs' mines. It could also be home to wild animals. The thought made Alastor's spine tingle.

Eilonwy was dumped unceremoniously a few feet into the mouth of the cave, still limp and unmoving. She hit the ground with a wet thump, and rolled down into the dark.

Jaimes moved to follow her, but his upper arm was caught in a fierce grip by one of the King's Guards.

"Don't fight, boy," Pyle said, turning to see Jaimes struggling to break free of the man holding him. "We're doing this for your own good."

Alastor felt someone's hands on his shoulder, and before he could shrug the hand away, the rope in his mouth was cut away. The hand on his shoulder remained as whoever held him worked on the ties around his wrists.

Jaimes snarled as he was also cut free, and the man holding him began working at the knots on his restraints as well. Jaimes glared at the broad-shouldered man standing over Eilonwy. "She's hurt. I just want to make sure she'll be alright. Let me go to her."

Evert snorted, his lip lifting in a small smirk. "I'm sure she'll be fine. Animals have a way of surviving."

Jaime's ropes fell from his hands, and he tried to jerk his arm away from the man holding him. The sailor held fast, looking to Pyle for guidance.

"We'll stay here for a time. Brynne will send word when the *Kingfisher* has been taken, and he'll bring the ship down the coast to meet us. Until then, we—"

Alastor saw the flash of silver, and instantly knew Jaimes's intent. There was a howl of pain, and the man gripping Jaimes's arm fell back, clutching his stomach. He fell to the ground, fresh blood splashing against the dark stones. Alastor's stomach rolled again at the sight of it.

There were shouts of fury, and Pyle lunged at Jaimes. Jaimes was fast, faster than Alastor, but the King's Guard was quicker. He backhanded Jaimes, knocking him to the ground. He landed at an odd angle, and screamed as something snapped audibly. The dagger Roland had given him fell from his hand, red to the hilt.

Pyle knelt and picked the dagger up from the ground,

glaring down at Jaimes as he did. "Is Arlyth going to be alright?" he asked over his shoulder.

One of the other men walked over to inspect the fallen guard's wound. The injured man waved him away with a grimace. "I'll be fine, Pyle. It's just a scratch."

The other man shook his head, straightening to look over Alastor's head to Pyle. "It's deep. The boy got him right in the bowels. You can smell it."

Alastor could smell it, sure enough. The stench of rot and waste wafted to him. He watched Evert, who continued to glare down at Jaimes. The large sailor seemed unmoved by his ally's condition.

Pyle turned his back on Jaimes, motioning towards the cave entrance. "Take him back to the beach. See if you can get him back to the *Kingfisher*. Brynne can patch him up."

There was some shuffling, and a weak groan of pain from Arlyth. After a moment, the sounds were too faint to hear over the crash of the surf.

"We just wanted to help you, but I guess you've already been turned to the animals, like your man Roland was." Pyle hefted the blade, turning to Alastor. "Search this one, make sure he hasn't got a blade, too."

Alastor did have the dagger Roland had given him, and they found it tucked into his belt quick enough. Alastor wished he had been as quick thinking as Jaimes; perhaps there would be two men writhing and dying, instead of just the one. Pyle took the second dagger and looked between the two boys in his possession. Alastor was unbound and unhurt, but surrounded by two more King's Guards, and Evert stood at Pyle's elbow, glaring menacingly.

Alastor looked down at Jaimes, who lay on his back with both elbows propped up and his left leg twisted at an odd angle. "We're going to be fine, Jaimes. Don't worry."

Jaimes's eyes were wide and watery with pain, but he

nodded. His hands dug into the soft pebbled ground around him as he tried to keep himself sitting up.

Pyle's eyes narrowed, and he leaned to look Alastor in the eye. "I'm not too sure about that. Poor Arlyth probably won't make it back to the *Kingfisher*, and I don't take kindly to my men being attacked. And there's still repayment for Rawli's injury to be considered." Pyle's eyes lifted to the last King's Guard, and Alastor followed his gaze to find the man sitting just inside the cave entrance, his head tucked beneath his knees as he muttered incoherently. "But you're young. Perhaps some sense can still be beaten back into you."

Flipping Alastor's blade in his palm, Pyle struck Alastor in the stomach with the pommel. Alastor had expected something of the sort, but the blow knocked the breath out of him. His stomach roiled, and he forced down the bile that had risen to his throat.

Jaimes shouted, flinging a fistful of small stones and pebbles at Pyle's back. Alastor vaguely heard them splat wetly against Pyle's shoulder. The man took no notice. Pyle stepped back, giving Alastor a moment to regain his breath, then he motioned Evert forward with a jerk of the chin. "You can take care of the rest, I'm sure."

Evert struck, aiming for Alastor's ribs. Alastor struggled for air, leaning to shield his ribs from another hit. Evert struck his gut again. And again.

Alastor was sure he could hear Jaimes shouting, but he couldn't make sense of the words.

Evert stopped at last, turning to look at Jaimes lying prone on the ground. "Do you think we've beaten the animal out yet, boy?"

Alastor drew in several shaky breaths, his side pinching as he did. He tried to focus on Jaimes's figure, his eyesight blurry and narrowed. "Jaimes …" He blinked, his vision clearing as he did.

Half a dozen pebbles floated above Jaimes's palm, spinning in a lazy circle. His glare was locked on Evert, whose matching stare was aimed at the floating stones.

"Brynne knew that elf was teaching you magic," Evert hissed. "Mathius did nothing to stop it." Evert seized Alastor by the hair, pulling his head back. He felt cold metal against his skin, and he gasped at the pain the sudden jerk caused in his side. "Put the rocks down, boy, or I'll kill him. Put them down, and we'll leave. You can take your little elf girl and go your own way."

"No," Pyle hissed, stepping to wrap a hand around Evert's upper arm. "That wasn't the deal. You get Mathius and his ship, I get the elf girl."

"Do you not see what that monster is doing? He's got magic, Pyle!"

"Don't tell me you're afraid of a child, Evert."

Jaimes's gaze moved to Alastor, who was unnerved by the panic in his eyes. *He's not sure he can do it.*

"Alastor?" Jaimes asked, wide eyes blinking rapidly.

Alastor swallowed hard, the motion causing the knife at his throat to slip dangerously against his skin. "I trust you."

Jaimes's face hardened again, his eyes shifting back to Evert. The two men flanking Alastor each took a half step back.

"Pyle …" one muttered.

"Maybe we should listen to Evert. The boy has magic, Pyle."

"Shut up, Orlen!" Pyle gave one of the men a shove, then redoubled on Evert, blocking Jaimes from Alastor's view. "The girl stays here, dammit!" Pyle straightened, glaring at the heavy sailor. "Fuck off back to Brynne if you must, but the she-devil stays with me. She has a debt to pay, and I intend to—"

Pyle's words were cut off with a gurgled gasp, and his hand went to the side of his neck, his eyes wide. When his hand dropped from his neck, the fingertips were bright with blood. Pyle and Alastor both stared at the wet stains as Evert muttered a string of curses.

Evert shoved Alastor away from him, letting Alastor fall to the slippery cave floor with a grunt. Alastor's breath was coming in hard, wheezing gasps, and his vision was blurring slightly. But he could still see Pyle as the man stumbled back, his hand clawing at his neck as blood sprayed from his lips in hacking coughs.

Behind him, Alastor heard feet scrambling as the remaining King's Guards and Evert made a rush for the entrance to the cave. But they didn't make it far.

There were three sticky sounds of impact, and the men fell with grunts. Two of them collapsed immediately, their hurried retreat ending as they hit the pebbled ground. But Evert was still moving, clutching his chest as blood rolled between his fingers. The knife in his grip fell to the floor of the cave with a metallic clatter as he pushed himself upright once more.

Alastor looked to Jaimes, ignoring the distressing sounds of pain from Pyle and the skittering of pebbles from Evert's struggle to regain his feet. His brother's eyes were rimmed in red, his leg still lying askew, and his shirt and trousers soaked in sweat and sea spray. Two stones still floated above Jaimes's palm.

Jaimes narrowed his eyes, and Alastor shut his own as another stone whizzed past his ear and struck Evert with a sickening smack.

When Alastor opened his eyes again, Evert was still, blood oozing from a small hole in his forehead.

Jaimes's attention was on Pyle, who stared at the scattered remains of his men, his hands still clawing ineffectually at the stone lodged in his throat.

"Your men attacked us," Jaimes said, his voice hoarse. "*You* attacked *us*," he repeated, shifting to face Pyle better. "We defended ourselves, and your men were injured." He shook his head, his face twisting in pain and anger. "That could have been the end of it. Your knight is just in shock. He'll be fine, given enough time. There was no debt to pay."

Pyle made a noise of protest, garbled by the damage Jaimes's stone had caused.

"Shut up, Pyle," Alastor muttered, drawing a hitching breath.

Jaimes motioned over his shoulder with a nod. "Then you attacked Eilonwy. She might die." Jaimes grimaced, bringing his hand up once more. "If there is a debtor here, Pyle, it's you."

The last stone floating above Jaimes's palm was released, and Pyle's gurgling protests ceased.

In the sudden quiet of the cave, the sound of the surf rolling in was the only thing Alastor heard. He got to his feet with a groan, arm wrapped around his waist to clutch at his ribs. Jaimes rolled onto his back with a soft whimper, and Alastor struggled to close the few feet of distance between them. He fell to his knees, patting Jaimes on the shoulder weakly, wincing at the pain in his side. "It's alright, Jaimes. We're alright now."

"My leg is broken. I don't think I can walk." He propped himself back up onto his elbows, looking down into the darkness where Eilonwy's slim outline could be seen. "I need to make sure she's fine."

"I'll get you down there." Alastor stood, still holding his side. With some effort, he helped Jaimes stand, and led him over to Eilonwy. Jaimes's foot dragged awkwardly behind him, and he winced and moaned with every sliding step. Alastor helped him down slowly, until he was sitting next to Eilonwy. "Do you want me to try to set it?"

"No," Jaimes gasped. "Great Ones, no. We don't know what we're doing." He winced again, reaching over to pull Eilonwy closer to him. His hand went to her neck, and his shoulders relaxed as he found her pulse. "She's still alive. Can you find Roland? We're going to need help getting out of this cave."

Alastor nodded, turning to head out of the cave. His foot squelched loudly a few steps away from Jaimes, and water covered the top of his boot where he stepped. The front of the cave was worse, water already standing several inches deep in some places. He turned back to Jaimes, who had pulled Eilonwy into his lap to examine her head. "The cave is flooding, Jaimes."

Jaimes groaned. His head tilted back to rest against the side of the pebbled slope he leaned against. "I thought it might happen. Everything in here is wet, and the tide is coming in. Just as Areanath's poem said." Eilonwy stirred weakly in his arms, and Jaimes's attention was drawn to her fluttering eyes. "Just hurry, Alastor." He looked up. "I trust you, too."

Alastor nodded again and turned to wade through the encroaching water to leave the cave. He could find Roland. He had to find Roland.

The entrance to the cavern was smaller than Melonya had thought, and it had been difficult even for her to fit through. It was easy to see how Neria would no longer be able to slip into her nest, as large as she had grown over the years.

But once Melonya was through, the opening the cavern opened up, and she was able to move a little more freely. *"Neria,"* she called to the sea dragon. *"I'm inside the cavern."* Blue light strobed ahead of her, illuminating a long and jagged crevasse. Above her, smooth stone sealed her in. *"I can see the amulet's light."*

"Hurry, Little One. I don't know how long I can hold myself together."

Melonya scrambled along, using the rough edges of the cavern walls to pull herself through the water more quickly. *"Is it normal for sea dragons to be so protective of their nests?"*

"Yes," Neria growled. *"All dragons are possessive of their eggs."*

Melonya briefly wondered where her own egg had come from, if Eilonwy and Tathiel had found it abandoned in their Homewood. It was not a question she had ever considered, but Neria's reaction to another dragon entering her nest gave her reason to ponder her origins.

"What are you doing?" Neria asked, mild panic and anger strumming through the connection they shared.

"I'm still trying to make my way through the front of the cavern." It was hard going, and Melonya could feel her lungs beginning to pinch again. She would need fresh air soon.

"Do you see the amulet? Do you see my eggs?"

The stress in Neria's voice was beginning to grate Melonya's nerves. She dug her long talons into the hard rock to either side of her and propelled herself forward, tucking her legs close to her body to maintain her momentum. *"No. I can't see anything but rock and the amulet's light."* The tunnel she swam through began to widen, and the blue light emanating from the amulet grew more intense. *"I think I might be getting close. The cavern seems to be getting larger."*

"There is a room of sorts up ahead," Neria said. *"That is where my nest is. And that is where the amulet will surely be."*

The light flashed again, and Melonya saw where the tunnel opened up to form a large and irregularly shaped den. *"I see it."* She pulled herself free of the tunnel and let her body fall to the sandy floor of the nest. The amulet's light pulsed more rapidly, and she could hear a gentle hum emanating from the center of the den.

"Do you see the amulet?" Neria's voice had taken on a frenzied edge.

"I think so." Melonya eased herself closer to the light, which flashed so brightly it nearly blinded her. *"It's hard to see anything down here. The light is too bright."*

Neria let out a snarling growl that echoed through the water and the rock that separated them. *"Be careful!"*

Melonya obediently halted, scouring the seafloor for the eggs Neria had left so long ago. She saw nothing for a moment, until her gaze drew closer to the pulsating light. One single egg lay half buried in the sand not far from the amulet. From what she could see of it, the shell of the egg was little more than a transparent bubble. The whole thing was small enough to fit within one of Melonya's clawed feet with little trouble, though she did not dare approach it. The dark and misshapen mass within did not move or show any sign of life, and Melonya's heart ached. Neria was sure they would never hatch, and yet she was still fearful and anxious at the sight of another approaching their hiding place.

Melonya searched the rest of the den, the light from the amulet and the hum of energy making her head hurt and her eyes swim. There was a sandy platform in the center of the den, and it was there that the amulet seemed to be sitting. But there were no more eggs to be seen.

"I only found one egg, Neria. I don't know what happened to the others, but they aren't here."

"What?" Neria snarled again, this time louder than the first.

"Should I bring it out with me? So you can find a new place for it?"

"No! Leave it!" Neria let out a terrifying hiss, and the cavern shook.

"What are you doing?" Melonya stumbled, trying to keep her feet as the walls around her rattled.

"Stay away from it!" Neria screeched, and the den groaned as another shock brought a stone the size of Melonya's head down from the roof. *"Get the amulet and get out, before I bury you."*

Melonya jumped for the central platform, pumping her legs ineffectively through the cold water. *"Neria, stop! You'll destroy the egg."*

"Get away from it!" The cavern shook dangerously, and Melonya scrambled to swim to the top of the platform the amulet was sitting on. *"I told you to get out!"*

Melonya dug her talons into the soft clay and sand of the

platform as the cavern shook again. *"Please, I'm trying! I'll get the amulet and leave."*

Neria didn't answer, but the cavern continued to shake and groan as Neria hissed and growled just outside the rocky tunnel.

Melonya climbed the soft embankment, struggling to keep from falling without tearing the soft structure apart. The light from the amulet grew stronger, and she was forced to continue with her eyes narrowed into thin slits.

When she reached the top, the amulet flashed a brilliant blue one final time before going dark. The light seared itself into Melonya's vision, and no amount of blinking could erase the stubborn blue spots that clouded her vision.

The cavern shook violently, and several of the lightly glowing spots moved, jostling and bouncing against one another. Melonya blinked several more times, unsure if what she was seeing were true.

The platform she now stood on was not flat, as she had imagined it. It was instead bowl shaped. Within the deepest part of the bowl there were nestled together a dozen or more softly glowing eggs. They were nearly alike in appearance to the first she had seen on the seafloor, but these were full of life and energy. The dark masses within stirred and twitched with every shake of the cavern, and the clear shells pulsed in steady rhythm.

"Neria, I found your eggs!" Melonya called to the older dragon, hopeful that Neria might calm herself. *"They're fine! They're all alright!"*

"Get away from them!"

The cavern rattled again, this time the hardest of them all. The bowl tilted dangerously as one side of the platform crumbled. An egg rolled to the edge, the creature suspended within twitching madly. Melonya stretched her neck to create a barrier along the edge of the bowl, and the egg bounced gently against her scales and rolled back to join its siblings. The shell was soft and pleasantly warm, and Melonya felt a gentle tingling sensation where the egg had touched her.

She spread one wing over the bowl just in time to catch another rock as it tumbled from the roof of the cavern. The stone bounced innocently against the webbing of her wing and fell away into the darkness of the den's floor. *"Neria, stop this! You're going to kill your children if you continue!"*

The shaking stopped. *"Show me that they're alright."*

Melonya stilled her mind, giving more of her consciousness over to Neria. *"Look. They're fine."*

Neria's mind rushed over hers, and Melonya had the strange sensation of momentarily having little control over her own body. Neria's will overtook her own with little trouble, and the ease and speed in which it happened scared her.

But the sensation subsided quickly, and Neria retreated. *"There's one missing."*

"That ..." Melonya hesitated. *"That was the first one I found. It did not look like these."*

Neria's voice was still shaken and anxious, but the anger had all but disappeared from it. *"Please, just get the amulet and get out of my nest."*

Melonya searched the nest, her wing still stretched protectively over the nest. *"I'm looking for it now. It's up here somewhere."* Her gaze roved over the eggs nestled peacefully together. The gentle glow of their shells had settled to a duller shade, giving her enough light to search by without blinding her. *"There's so much blue. It's difficult to see where it might be."* A glimpse of dull stone caught her eye amid the soft and gelatinous eggs, and Melonya dipped her head to inspect it further.

Partially buried between two eggs was a stone object. Its shape was indistinguishable, but the gentle hum still filling the area seemed to be emanating from the object. *"I think I've found it."*

"Good," Neria snapped. *"Get it and get out of there."*

Melonya stared at the small sliver of stone visible among Neria's eggs, and the amulet let out one single pulse of bright blue light. Around her, the glow of the eggs brightened sympathetically before shifting to their more muted shade. For a quiet moment, Melonya could only sense the pulsating energy of the amulet. Even the chill of the water was lost to her. There was only the gentle hum of arcane power around her.

"Melonya!" Neria barked, and Melonya snapped out of her mesmerized stare.

"I'm coming." No wonder Neria wanted the amulet gone. Melonya had seen only a small glimpse, and it had caught her completely. She carefully extracted the amulet from the nest. Her clawed foot brushed against the eggs resting on top of the amulet, and she fought a shiver as another tingling sensation settled into her scales. The amulet was warm as she closed her talons around it, and the chill of the water was suddenly easier to bear.

The trip out of the nest went faster than the one in. Neria's continued growls and the increased pinching in Melonya's lungs hurried her progress, and she was facing the great sea dragon within minutes.

Neria's serpentine tail relaxed as Melonya wriggled her way through the opening to the cavern. *"I'm sorry, Melonya. I should not have tried to harm you. Perhaps one day you'll understand my behavior, but that does not excuse my actions."*

Melonya turned back to inspect the cavern. The rock had shifted, and there was a thin crack that ran down the length of the stone. *"Will they be alright in there?"*

Neria hesitated, shame bubbling up from her to meet Melonya's consciousness. *"The damage I have caused will not upset the nest. The structure will hold for as long as it needs to."*

"Are you sure?"

Neria's tail twitched, the fanned fins moving fluidly through the water. *"I am sure."*

Melonya opened the foot grasping the amulet. The stone in her hands was smaller than she had anticipated and the warmth it radiated was receding. The dark blue surface was covered in small iridescent lines that crisscrossed in uneven intervals. If Melonya could be sure it was entirely composed of gemstones, she might have guessed it was a large polished sapphire with diamond seams.

And it was split neatly in two.

"What happened to it?" Melonya asked. Would the amulet still work if it had been broken? She held the amulet out for Neria to inspect, but the older dragon shrank away from it. *"Could it have broken when I took it?"* She tried to recall the frantic moment when she plucked it from Neria's nest. *"Can it be fixed?"*

"It does not need fixing," Neria said calmly. *"It has been like that since it was magicked here, though I cannot tell you why."* She retreated further from the stone. *"It will still perform as it should. Just take it away from here."*

Melonya curled her long talons around it once more, concealing the majority of the blue glow from Neria. *"Will you help me return to the surface? I can't stay down here much longer."*

"Yes." Neria uncurled herself, pointing her snout toward the surface far above them. *"We must go quickly."* Neria's long tail suddenly whipped through the corner of Melonya's vision, and Melonya felt a wave of unease creep from the great dragon. *"Someone is calling for us."*

51

JAIMES

J aimes watched Alastor stumble his way out of the cave, his feet slipping and sliding with every step. Water sluiced down the curved cave floor, and when Jaimes pressed his palms against the shifting pebbles scattered around him to shift his weight, his hands came away wet and cold.

"Eilonwy, it'll be alright." Jaimes pulled her close to him, cradling her head in the hollow of his shoulder.

Her eyes rolled behind the lids, but remained closed.

Still unconscious, then. Jaimes brushed the hair from her face, his wet hand unsticking a few strands from the tacky mess of blood on the side of her head. He didn't want to see what Pyle had done to her, but he wanted to know that she would be alright.

He felt his way along her jawline up to her temple, searching for the injury. She made no response to his careful touch, but Jaimes wasn't sure that she couldn't feel any pain.

When he finally found the cut, he almost sighed in relief. It was shallow, but long and ugly, starting just above her left eyebrow and finishing a few inches above and behind her ear.

"You're going to be alright, Eilonwy," he whispered, bringing his lips close to her ear. "But I'm afraid you're going to have a nasty scar. Unless Tiryn can do something about that, too."

Eilonwy made no response.

"I wouldn't worry about a scar, though. I'm sure no one else will care about it."

Her skin was prickled with gooseflesh, and Jaimes felt cold water slush against his ankles. Panic swept over him as the water continued to fill the cave, audible now as it splashed against the cave entrance.

Jaimes took a deep breath, then pulled Eilonwy closer to him, until she was nearly in his lap. It was painful and awkward to hold her with his leg bent as it was, but it was better than both of them getting soaked.

"It's going to be alright," he said, more to himself than to Eilonwy. "Alastor is getting help." He swallowed against the knot that constricted his throat. "The water likely won't get too deep. We should be fine."

Pain washed over him as cold water brushed against his torn leg. He hadn't wanted to look at it, but he could tell that it was broken, and the sting of the saltwater told him the skin had torn along the outside of his calf.

"We're going to be fine." Jaimes gritted his teeth against the pain as a second wave of saltwater brushed against his leg. He wanted to scream, but his breathing was too heavy, too panicked.

He took another deep breath, holding it as he tried to block out the burning sensation in his leg. "You're going to be fine, Eilonwy. And you'll still look beautiful, even with a scar."

Another wave rolled over him, sending pebbles tumbling down onto his feet. He did scream this time, as the water soaked his legs up to the thigh and saltwater ran over his twisted and broken leg again.

"Great Ones … help us," Jaimes panted, each breath catching slightly in his chest.

He closed his eyes, leaning his head against Eilonwy's shoulder.

"Can anyone hear me?"

He waited.

"Can anyone help us?"

Still nothing. Jaimes choked back a sob as more water slid down to fill the little hole he and Eilonwy sat in.

"Please, can anyone hear me?"

"I can hear you, little one."

Jaimes looked up, searching the darkness around them for the source of the voice he had heard.

"We are coming."

"Thank you," Jaimes muttered into the empty cave.

Eilonwy shifted against him. "Jaimes?" She tried to slide off him, but her movements were slow and clumsy.

"D-don't move. Please." Jaimes gasped as one of her hands brushed dangerously close to his injury. "My leg is broken." Eilonwy stilled instantly, and he loosened his grip around her shoulders. "We're in a cave. It's starting to flood. You have a bad cut to your head."

Above them, from the mouth of the cave, he could hear voices.

"But we're going to be fine, Eilonwy."

5 2

LUKA

I t wasn't much like his father to make demands with no explanation, but Luka wasn't much for demanding answers from the family's leader either. Still, they had been following the *Kingfisher* for weeks now, and for what?

A few sightings of Roland and his young friends as they walked about various human towns?

Though the brawl had been interesting, and Luka would have gladly rushed into the fray to protect his father's friend if Myka himself had not been there to warn him off. His father had insisted that Roland could hold his own against five King's Guards, and Luka had been just as sure that he couldn't.

But when a slice to the leg did nothing more than slow Roland for a handful of seconds, Luka realized he'd been wrong to judge his father's friend as just another human. Myka was not one for making friends with just anyone, after all.

So they continued to follow the *Kingfisher*, and Luka kept a keen eye out for anything else that might illuminate his father's plans.

When the ship slowed in the water despite a gentle breeze

rolling down from further inland, he thought nothing of it. The *Kingfisher* had never truly sailed as the wind bid her.

It wasn't until he heard faint shouts from the deck and spotted a pair of rafts slide down into the water that Luka truly grew concerned. He watched the rafts come ashore, and he counted half a dozen men stepping onto the sandy beach with Roland's young friends in tow, bound and gagged with ropes. Luka truly wondered then if his father had perhaps known Roland would come to need them.

Luka hesitated, watching from the shadows of the nearby broadleaf trees as the men led the two young boys away. An elf girl was draped over the shoulders of the largest of them, unresponsive and smelling of blood.

Roland might be able to fight five King's Guards on his own, but Luka could not. Especially not without any weapon other than his hands and teeth. Those weapons were enough for the occasional wild animal that came across his path, but not for a sailor nearly thrice his size and his companion knights.

Do I follow, or retreat and warn Father?

Follow, or retreat?

Luka wavered for a moment, then stripped down to his skin, draping his tunic around the thick trunk of a nearby tree and knotting the arms together. The trousers he kicked into the underbrush, not caring if they were lost for good. Once his marker had been made, Luka shifted, falling onto all fours and darting further into the trees.

5 3

ROLAND

Roland pulled himself from the freezing waters of the sea, Mathius just beside him. His clothing clung to him, and he'd lost feeling in his fingers and toes several moments before. Behind him, he could already hear the shouts of the sailors that had followed them from the *Kingfisher* drawing nearer with each passing moment.

Mathius fell to his knees in the wet sand, the toes of his boots digging small holes into the smooth surface of the beach. "May Imis preserve Reed, for he was one of the best men I knew." Saltwater dripped from the captain's face as he knelt on the shore, and he wiped at his neck and cheeks with the soaked arm of his tunic. "And may Elir strike that bastard Brynne where he stands for killing him."

"I'm sorry, Mathius." Roland waited as Mathius slowly returned to his feet, his own muscles twitching and beginning to cramp. "I should have realized Brynne was the spy. It might have saved Reed."

"How could you have known, Roland?" Mathius asked, watching the approaching rowboats. "Brynne made himself out to be the perfect scholar, right down to the ink smear on

357

his nose and the damned books in his cabin. He even played nice with your elven friends. He was the perfect ally to you."

Roland wiped the drying seawater from his hands and face, brushing the salt already crusting along his skin away. "Nothing is ever that perfect."

"Fucking thieves," Mathius panted, hands on his knees. The shouts from the approaching sailors were louder now, and Roland could nearly count the men that had come to kill them. "They've already taken my damn ship … they could at least leave the rest of us with our lives."

Roland shook his head, flexing his fingers to stimulate the blood flow once more. "Forget about them, Mathius. We need to get to Alastor and Jaimes. They'll need our help, and Eilonwy is injured." A pair of rafts were cozied up on the shore nearby, and Roland made his way towards them on unsteady legs.

Mathius followed, wrapping his shivering arms around his chest. "They have swords, Roland. We're unarmed. They'll be on us soon enough."

Roland paused at the first raft, searching the scattering of footprints in the sand for signs that Eilonwy was up and walking. None of the footprints were small and light enough, and the tide rolling in was already erasing sets closest to the water. "Better get yourself warmed up, then. It'll be a rough fight. And Tiryn will follow us. Great Ones preserve us, he'll make it in time to help."

"I think I see them now," Mathius said, neck craning as he peered across the water. "I don't think he can row fast enough." He sighed, flexing his hands as Roland had. "Looks like it'll just be us."

"You forget he's an elf." Roland eyed the disintegrating trail of the men that had stolen Jaimes and Alastor. They seemed to be heading for a cluster of caves further along the shore, as Mathius had suggested. Roland turned back, hearing the splash of water and renewed shouting. Brynne's men had reached the shore and were disembarking, swords already drawn. "He'll make it momentarily, Mathius. No worries." Even as he said it, he wondered if it was true.

Mathius and Roland stepped forward on half-frozen legs to meet their pursuers. Mathius raised both fists in a hesitant stance, and Roland shook the few lingering nerves loose from his arms before lifting his arms in a similar manner.

The first fighter rushed them, running on the soft earth for Roland. Roland moved to intercept but was startled by a small reddish creature dashing from the nearby trees to lunge at the attacking fighter. The animal landed on the man's chest, knocking him to the ground, then clawed and bit the man's face. The man screamed, mostly from shock, and tried to fling the small creature from him. Three more of the animals streaked from the woods, and two of them lit upon the downed fighter. The remaining sailors came to a standstill, watching the attack with a mixture of disgust and horror on their faces.

The fourth animal slid to a stop at Roland's feet, hackles raised and teeth bared at the armed men.

"Myka?" Roland half choked. "Is that you?"

The fox at his feet turned his head to look up at Roland, his eyes strangely alert. It yipped once, nose dipping to point behind Roland.

Roland nodded, understanding the message. He glanced across the water, glad to see that Tiryn and the others had nearly reached the shore. "Tiryn will be here in a moment. He'll help you fight them off."

The fox made a sound somewhere between another yip and a growl, his bright eyes rolling. Roland smiled, imagining the quip Myka surely wanted to give. He grabbed Mathius's shoulder, turning him away from the confusion in the sand. "Come on, let's find the boys."

Mathius followed beside Roland, casting a final glance

behind them. "What in the name of the Great Ones was that?"

Roland's mouth quirked into a quick smile. "Some unexpected aid, it would seem." He once again eyed the vanishing trail left by Eilonwy's captors, trying to determine which cave they might have fled to. Up ahead, he could make out the vague shape of an approaching figure, though whether it was friend or foe, he couldn't guess. Water lapped at his feet as the tide continued to flow in from the sea, and the image brought up the last few lines of Areanath's first clue. *Before the tides have turned ...*

"We need to hurry."

They found Alastor staggering weakly just down the beach. One arm was wrapped around his waist, and his steps were slow and uneven. Roland ran to him and clutched both his shoulders. "Alastor, are you alright? Where's Jaimes?"

"Ah, I found you. Jaimes is in the cave," Alastor answered weakly. "I think my ribs are broken."

"Who did this to you?" Roland asked. He scanned the outcrop behind Alastor, searching for the others.

"Evert. Pyle broke Jaimes's leg, too. But don't worry, he's dead. They're all dead." Alastor turned, waving Roland to follow. "Come on, the cave is flooding. We need to get them out of there."

Mathius hissed a curse, stepping closer to the beach. "Is that one of those King's Guards? What the devil is he doing down here?"

Alastor and Roland both turned, spotting the body lying face down in the water some feet away. Alastor nodded. "Pyle called him Arlyth. Jaimes cut him pretty badly. Someone was supposed to be taking him back to the *King-*

fisher ..." Alastor looked up weakly, scanning the surrounding coastline.

Heavy panting behind them turned Roland's attention away from Arlyth's body in time to see another King's Guard rushing them from the trees, sword in hand. Roland stepped in front of Alastor, ready to intercept the attacker. Once again, the intercept was unnecessary; Luka ran in from the same direction the King's Guard had come from. He tackled the sailor, pinning him to the sand and beating the man's face with a flurry of hard punches. The young man was naked, save for what appeared to be a tunic wrapped and hastily tied around his waist. As he stood and turned towards the others, Roland was unnerved to see a smear of blood across his mouth and neck.

"That's the second time I've swooped in to save your hide, old man. My father was right to have us follow your ship." Luka smiled, eyes glinting. He picked up the fallen man's sword and held it out for Roland to take.

"I'm just glad your family is on our side, Luka. Did Myka send you to help us?" Roland took the sword and waved Alastor forward. Alastor, still clutching his side, led them towards the caves closest to the edge of the beach.

"That's right. Tiryn and the others reached the fight on the beach, and we cleaned those men up pretty well." He wiped a sweating forearm across his mouth, but it only smeared the blood more. Roland grimaced, but Luka continued, unaffected. "The younger elf was yelling about his sister. I'm sure he'll follow along in a minute."

Roland glanced back, and spotted Tathiel running to meet with them. "Alastor, which cave is it?"

Alastor pointed, indicating a small hole about six feet from what would normally have been the shore's edge. As it was now, water was rolling into the mouth of the cave and down into the depths. "They're in there. Jaimes can't walk, and I think Eilonwy is still out of sorts. She was only just coming around when I left to find you." Luka ran ahead, his bare feet splashing through the water, and Alastor started to follow at a more sedate pace.

"Alastor, just stay here with Mathius, we'll get to them." Roland put an arm on the boy's shoulder, stopping him from following the wyre into the cave. "Try not to move too much. Tiryn can take care of you."

Alastor started to protest, but with a glare from Roland and a gentle tug on his elbow from Mathius, he instead nodded lamely.

Luka was waiting just inside the mouth of the cave when Roland caught up with him. "They're a little way back. The girl is barely conscious." He stepped tentatively into the dimness of the cave. "I can smell blood, Roland."

Roland could smell it too, the tangy metallic smell mingling with the salty scent of the sea to make an unsettling combination.

"Most of it isn't ours." Jaimes's voice was weak and tinny, and Roland had a hard time pinpointing the direction it came from.

"Where is he, Luka?" Roland searched the darkness of the cave, but could see no more than a few feet from the entrance.

Luka took a few tentative steps further into the cave. "He's down here. Can you make it alright?"

Roland followed Luka's footsteps, keeping the young man well in sight. But he had taken no more than a handful of small steps before he misstepped, sending a shower of pebbles down into the dark and getting his foot stuck to the ankle in cold seawater. "Shit." Roland struggled for a moment before unsticking his foot, then shook his head at Luka. "No, I can't see my own damned feet."

Tathiel brushed past Roland's shoulder, startling him. Roland hadn't heard the elf approach, despite the slippery and unstable ground. "I'll go, Roland." Tathiel sent out a cluster of witch lights with a wave of his hand, and gave Roland a firm nod. His eyes were wide and frightened. "Don't worry, I'll make sure they're alright."

Roland hesitated then returned Tathiel's nod. "Alright. I'll be here, I guess."

The witch lights Tathiel cast gave the cave a soft blue-green glow, and though they didn't help Roland see very far into the depths of the cave, he could see the progress of the wyre and the elf as they made their careful descent. After a few minutes, Tathiel sent out another group of witch lights, and in the glow they cast, Roland was finally able to see the shallow hollow where Jaimes and Eilonwy lay.

Jaimes had pulled the young elf into his lap, cradling her against his chest like a mother might hold a child. She was awake, but seemed lethargic and weak. Jaimes sat with his back to the sloping sand and pebbles, one leg twisted horribly, water standing several inches high all around him. *The pain he must be in ...* Roland felt his jaw tighten as he watched Tathiel and Luka make their way down to him.

Scattered around him were several bodies. Most he didn't recognize, the lone exception being the large form of Evert. Blood had pooled in particularly large areas around Evert, and a second man was drenched down his front in sticky red ooze. Roland wasn't convinced they had suffered quite enough.

After another few minutes, Roland heard the low murmuring of conversation, and could only guess that Tathiel and Luka had made their way to Jaimes and Eilonwy.

"We're coming back," Tathiel called out, and Roland heard scuffling as they began the slow trip back.

The water was flowing in faster now as the tide seemed to be at its height. They had been in the cave for several minutes, and Roland briefly worried if Tathiel and Luka would be able to manage their way out with the unstable floor around them. He thought he could hear cursing and the occasional groan as someone stumbled. But they eventually made their way back into his view, and he helped them the last few feet. Tathiel held Eilonwy in his arms like a sleeping child, her head cradled against his chest, and Jaimes was slumped tiredly over one of Luka's shoulders, his broken leg sticking out at a grotesque angle.

The five of them emerged into the sunlight together. Mathius and Alastor were both where he had left them, and Tiryn was inspecting the bruises on Alastor's torso. Roland's anger flared at the signs of abuse on his nephew, but Tiryn patted Alastor on the back gently before letting him pull his tunic back over his head.

"Don't worry, Alastor. You'll be alright. No heavy lifting."

Myka and several of the men Roland had seen in the wyre encampment were also present. A few of them were shirtless and barefoot, and Roland suspected those were the ones that had changed into their animal form to fend off the attacking sailors. Together with Nunor they were gathering the collection of rafts and securing them to the higher shoreline, their bare backs beading with sweat and saltwater as they worked.

At the sight of them, Tiryn waved Tathiel over. "I want to look at Eilonwy first. Alastor told me about the blow to her head."

Eilonwy seemed to have become fairly alert, and Tiryn fussed over her for several moments, Tathiel hovering just over his shoulder. After inspecting her head and talking quietly to her, Tiryn declared that she would be fine in time, though she might have some memory issues over the next several days.

Jaimes waited patiently, face set in a grimace of pain as Tiryn saw to Eilonwy. Roland wanted to help, but broken bones were far from his specialty, and the break looked bad enough to need more delicate hands than his.

Luka joined him, watching Jaimes and Tiryn with his arms crossed over his chest. "There were four more bodies down there. They'd been hit in the chest and killed. Jaimes said he'd used magic."

Roland sighed, cursing himself. "I doubt he would have done it unless he felt it was needed."

Luka nodded. "He said the same man that hit the elf girl was planning worse for her. And another had a knife to Alastor's throat." Luka sighed, shaking his head. "I can't say that I wouldn't do the same in his position. But I think he feels guilty."

"He shouldn't," Roland growled.

"You ought to make sure he knows that."

Roland nodded. He turned away as Tiryn place both hands on Jaimes's leg, and the boy answered Tiryn's questioning look with a curt nod. The ensuing scream sent chills down his spine, and everyone stopped to turn empathic eyes on the boy.

"I've seen breaks like that, Roland. He'll be lucky to walk normally again."

"I know."

Roland caught Mathius's gaze as the captain looked down on the groaning and whimpering Jaimes. Mathius quickly turned away, focusing his attention instead on the departing *Kingfisher*. Roland left Luka without a word, going to stand next to Mathius. He remained quiet, giving the other man the chance to speak first. There was only silence for a moment, broken by Tiryn's hushed voice soothing the pained Jaimes.

"Alastor told me about what happened," Mathius said after a moment. "Brynne let the King's Guards that attacked Tiryn and the others free, and they're the ones that fled the ship with the boys and the elf girl."

Roland thought for a moment, staring back over his shoulder at the cluster of caves. "There's one missing," Roland said. "There were six King's Guards, plus Evert makes seven. There are four bodies in the cave, two more here on the beach …"

Mathius nodded. "Alastor said his name is Rawli. The one Eilonwy took out when they slipped onto the ship before." Mathius kicked at the sea foam that rolled in to cover his boots. "Alastor said the man wasn't right. Kept singing. It's why Pyle took Eilonwy."

"To make her fix him?"

"To make her pay for it."

Roland nodded, looking once more over at the young elf. Her brother knelt in the sand beside her, one arm wrapped protectively around her shoulders as she gazed numbly around the busy shore. Tathiel leaned close to her ear, speaking low. If she answered, Roland didn't notice.

"It's all my fault, Roland. I'm sorry." Mathius rubbed one hand against the back of his neck, his eyes dropping to his feet. "If I could have kept their faith, they wouldn't have felt the need to mutiny. I've failed as a captain." He glared down at his wet boots. "Twice now."

Roland sighed, shifting his gaze to Alastor, who was slowly lowering himself to sit in the sand next to his chosen brother. "No amount of faith could have kept them from this, Mathius. They were against you the moment you let Tiryn and the others come aboard."

Mathius shook his head, once again watching his ship sail away from him. "Do you really think it's as simple as that?"

"I do." Roland nodded. "Mothlenor has sown too much discord across the land. There aren't so many men left that might have made the decision you did. But if those men were truly *your* men, they would have followed you anywhere." He squeezed Mathius's shoulder gently.

Mathius sighed. "Perhaps I am not the same leader you once were, Roland."

Roland frowned. "Perhaps I'm no longer that same leader, either."

They stood in silence for another moment, the tide washing against their boots.

"What will you do now? Purchase another boat?"

Mathius snorted. "That was the second one I've lost in as many years. I don't think I was meant to be a captain. I'll find something different. The other merchants can handle my absence."

Roland began a reply, but a piercing cry cut him off.

"I'm coming, Eilonwy!"

Even Mathius seemed to sense the great dragon's distress. His eyes darted around them, searching for the source of the shout. "Who—"

A great spray of water erupted from the sea as the blue shape of Melonya sprang from its surface. Her powerful tail propelled her several feet into the sky, and a heavy mist descended as she spread her wings and lunged for the air.

Mathius stumbled back, hand reaching for a sword he wasn't wearing. Shouts rose from the gathered wyres, but none made a move to change their skins and attack.

Tathiel left Eilonwy's side, and together he and Roland waded through the surging waters to greet her.

"Eilonwy is fine, Melonya!" Roland shouted up to the dragon.

Beside him, Tathiel focused his words to her mentally, letting Roland hear his thoughts. *"Eilonwy will be alright, Melonya. Her captors are dead, and Tiryn says she will recover well."*

Above them, Melonya made one quick circle and descended, landing with a heavy splash and a spray of foam a few feet away from them. *"Neria said there was trouble, Tathiel. I came as quickly as I could."*

"The trouble is over, Melonya." Tathiel rushed for the dragon, and she wrapped a protective wing around his shoulders even as he tossed his arms around her great neck. "Where is Neria now? Did you fight her?"

Melonya blinked one large eye down at them. *"No, her word was true. She only wanted the amulet gone. She sensed the danger before I could, and helped me return to the surface. What happened?"*

"Roland," Mathius muttered, looking Melonya over. "That is a dragon."

"Yes, it is. Mathius, meet Melonya. Eilonwy's friend. For whom this latest mess started."

Mathius blinked several times, then gave a shocked nod. The wyres around them watched and waited, their tensed bodies relaxing as the immediate threat of danger subsided.

"Roland, what happened?"

Roland answered the question aloud for Mathius's benefit. "The ship's crew mutinied. Eilonwy was attacked and stolen off the ship, the boys with her. We fought our way to them with the help of our friends here. The ones that hurt Eilonwy and the boys have been killed, as well as the men sent to stop us from reaching them. The rest of the crew is still aboard the *Kingfisher*." Roland nodded in the direction of the departing ship. "It seems they'll get away."

Melonya's head lifted out of Tathiel's grasp as she twisted her long neck to look across the water to the *Kingfisher*. *"Neria? Will you help me once more?"*

A great roaring laugh rippled through Roland, and he sensed the strange energy of some ancient power surge from the depths before them.

"With pleasure, Little One."

All was silent for a second or two. Roland exchanged a look with Mathius, whose eyes had gone wide and his face pale.

The silent stillness that had descended onto the shore was broken when a huge white creature surged from the waters around the *Kingfisher*. A long tail wrapped twice around the hull of the ship, and a great maw of a mouth bit the helm of the ship clear away. Even with the distance that separated them, Roland heard the sounds of the ship being crushed and broken. With a sickening crunch of wood, the *Kingfisher* was torn apart in mere seconds, left as only so much driftwood. Beside him, Mathius groaned at the sight, but Roland only felt savage vengeance at the sight of the great dragon Neria wrapping her claws around one of the larger pieces of drifting hull and splintering it like a dried twig.

"The mer families in this area will hunt the humans down and kill them before they can reach the shoreline. No one will survive."

"Thank you, Neria. We are in your debt, old one."

Neria laughed again, though it was warmer than before. *"The debt is paid. I'm thankful Melonya was able to remove the amulet from my waters. This was the least I could do in return."* To Melonya, Neria added, *"Perhaps, Little One, we can meet again. Under better circumstances, I hope."*

"I would like that, Neria. Thank you."

With a quiet splash, Neria's long neck and head disappeared below the water's surface. One moment, great white scales glittered in the bright sunlight, wet and shining among the blue waters. Then there was nothing left of the ancient creature but the scattered debris of the *Kingfisher*.

Roland sighed, turning once more to look at Jaimes. Tiryn seemed to have finished what he could for the boy. Jaimes's leg was wrapped with the torn strips of several tunics, presumably donated by the wyres. There were several planks of wood strapped to the broken leg, forming a kind of caged brace around it. Alastor was helping Jaimes to his feet, Tiryn offering instructions even as Nunor hacked at a medium-sized tree branch to form a sort of crutch.

Eilonwy stood nearby, watching Jaimes as he tried a few experimental and hobbling steps, leaning against Alastor for support. Her face was a little vacant, but she smiled when Roland caught her eye.

Roland sighed again. "I think we're done here. Wouldn't you say, Mathius?"

Mathius only groaned, looking at the wreckage of the *Kingfisher*.

Roland shook his head, sighing lightly. He called to Alastor, and the boy looked up at the sound, eyebrows raised.

"Let's get you two home."

MOTHLENOR

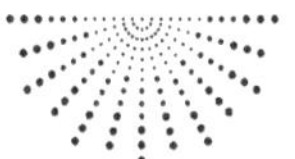

There were some days when it was difficult for him to find any comfort in his throne. His brother had sat in the damned thing for years and had never complained. *Perhaps Areanath was more suited to the simple comforts of his hall.*

Mothlenor took a moment to adjust his posture, searching for something slightly less uncomfortable, irritated with the infernal piece of furniture. *It doesn't matter, it's just a chair. It can be replaced.*

He had been saying the same thing for years, but had never brought himself to actually remove the throne his brother had used for so long.

He sat, back a little too straight and stiff, fingers drumming impatiently on the thin arm of the throne, as some pathetic fool mumbled at his feet. Ferrand stood next to the man; a mixture of unease and disgust colored his face a faint red. Anna waited at the back of the room, close to the door, ready to flee as soon as the dismissal was given.

Mothlenor could hardly blame her. The man before them was filthy, his stench rising to fill the room with the sour scent of wandering and ale. His hair was greasy and matted, his clothes threadbare, and the soles of his boots worn through to the toes. *This was one of Ferrand's men?* Mothlenor wanted to throw them both out of his hall, but he only grimaced as the stench around them grew deeper. It had been over a month since they had lost contact with the *Kingfisher*, and he wanted any update this disgusting excuse for a man could give him.

"Explain it to me again, fool."

The man kneeling before him tilted his head, as if he was not sure that Mothlenor had spoken. His quiet, incessant mumbling continued, almost too silent to be heard at all.

Ferrand growled, the burned half of his face twisting grotesquely. "Your king has asked something of you, you disgusting wretch. Now answer him!" Ferrand twisted a hand through the ragged tunic that hung from the man's frame, pulling him to his feet. The man let out a pathetic, half-hearted cry, but found his feet and stood before Mothlenor without Ferrand's aid.

Mothlenor waited, leaning forward slightly as the man's head tilted this way and that. His eyes were still focused on the ground, or on his hands, which he had curled around each other in a dirty long-fingered knot tucked close to his chest. Either way, he did not look up.

Ferrand made to strike the man, bringing his hand back to swing across the man's face, but Mothlenor stopped him with a single word.

"Wait."

They waited, and after a long moment, the man began to speak. "We stormed the ship. I went down, hit my head. Lost myself for a long time." The man's voice had an odd lilt to it, as if he were not accustomed to speaking. But his words were no longer a mumble, and Mothlenor sat back to listen.

"We were left in the dark, made prisoners, until a small miracle set us free."

"Who set you free?" Mothlenor asked.

"The scholar," the man answered. "The scholar, who was not."

"He means Brynne, my lord." Ferrand was staring at the knight, his one eye narrowed. "The spy I had on the *Kingfisher*."

"We left the ship. Returned to land. But now we had prisoners." The man seemed to think for a moment, remembering. His head dipped lower, and his hands beat gently against the sides of his head as he mumbled to himself. After a moment, his hands dropped and resumed their twisting. "T-two boys, and a long-ear girl. She was bleeding."

"Why take the boys?"

The man looked up, staring stupidly up at Mothlenor. He seemed to consider an answer for a moment, but only shook his head.

"Why not leave the boys on the ship?" Mothlenor asked, biting back the irritation he felt. Showing too much anger would only make the man scream and babble incoherently, and they had already suffered enough of that nonsense. "Why not leave them to die with the other traitors?"

The man shook his head again. "Not my choice." He beat his hands against the side of his head again, muttering under his breath. It was the same sentence, repeated over and over, though Mothlenor couldn't make out the words.

"Then what happened?" Mothlenor asked, hoping to pull the man back from the edge of madness again.

The knight's head tilted and his mumbling quieted. "We went to the wet place. To the dark place." The man's hands lowered, but hovered close to his face, as if ready to resume their frantic beating again. "There was shouting. So much shouting. So much blood. Everyone fell." The man's mouth hung agape, his eyes unfocused. "Everyone fell, and they left me. So I ran."

"You ran?" Mothlenor leaned forward, listening.

The man's fists rose to his head again, beating against this skull. "I ran, I ran, I ran." His breath was ragged, and spittle flew from his lips as he spoke. The fists beat harder against his head, and Ferrand took a startled step back as the man uttered an inhumane growl and fell to his knees. "I ran, and then I heard her. I ran, and then I heard her."

"Heard who?" Mothlenor stood and stepped quickly down the dais.

The man continued to beat at his own head, both fists knocking audibly against his temples. "I heard her, I heard her calling. I heard her, and she found me, and she was calling to me." With a painful cry, the knight smashed his forehead against the stone floor, then repeated it a second time before Ferrand or Mothlenor could rush to stop him. His muttering had returned, though it was louder and rushed.

"Who did you hear?" Mothlenor had to almost shout to be heard over the noise the knight was making.

Blood was smeared across the man's forehead, and a matching bloodstain was smudged across the cracked floor where his head had already hit it half a dozen times or more. And still the knight continued his unending chant, each iteration growing more desperate.

Mothlenor knelt to grip the man by both shoulders, pulling him upright and prying his hands from his head. Frightened eyes scanned up to him, then frantically flicked all around, wide and disturbed. Mothlenor grabbed the man's chin, pulling his face up to look at him more clearly. "Who did you hear?"

"I heard Imis," the man muttered, finally meeting Mothlenor's eyes. "I heard Imis, then watched as the Great One herself brought death."

"Imis?" Ferrand chortled. "He thinks he heard a dead god?" Ferrand kicked at the knight's back, though the effort was half-hearted at best. The man let out a piercing scream, his eyes clamping tightly shut. "The man's mad."

"Even the maddest among us can sometimes speak truth." Mothlenor knelt on the cold floor, wrapping his hands around the man's head and letting soothing energy flow down his fingertips. "Show me what you saw, and I can make it stop."

The knight fought at first, but as Mothlenor's magic trickled its way over his skin, he sighed, slumping slightly. "I saw Imis," the knight said softly. His eyes seemed to plead with Mothlenor, though he could not be sure what they asked for.

"I would like to see her. Will you show me?"

The man nodded slowly, and Mothlenor poured more energy through his fingertips and into the mad King's Guard in front of him.

Images flooded to him, unbidden.

The wooden deck of a ship, coolness on his skin as he went down into the hold. Vague shapes flitted in his vision, followed by a flash of blue-green light and a split second of intense pain. Then darkness and damp, and indistinct shouting. The metallic tang of blood filled his nose, and he rose to his feet to flee the sudden still-ness. Trees beat against his face, and rocks scraped against his hands and knees as he climbed.

"We are coming."

The words shook him, hitting him and sending him to his knees.

"We are coming."

He continued to climb, oblivious to the cuts to his palms and knuckles. He could almost see the ocean again, could hear the waves beating against the rocks.

"We are coming."

The ship was still out there, and if he squinted, he could see men standing on the deck, cheering.

"We are coming."

Not cheering.

Shouting.

We are coming.

A great white beast erupted from the waters around the ship, wrapping herself around the vessel and crushing it with ease.

Imis is coming.

Not Imis. A sea dragon.

A sea dragon destroyed the Kingfisher. *He saw men floundering in the water. He heard them screaming as they disappeared from the water's surface. The sea dragon came, and then she was gone.*

"We are coming."

"We are coming."

"We"

"Are"

"Coming. They are coming. They are coming."

Mothlenor fought to keep the man within his grasp, but Ferrand pulled him off Mothlenor. He hadn't even realized that the knight had pinned him to the ground and was screaming in his face. "They are coming. They are coming."

He kept the cry up until Ferrand was able to lock an arm under his chin and cut the scream off. But even with no air to breathe, his mouth and throat still worked to keep the chant going.

"I can't hold him for much longer, my lord," Ferrand grunted. "Get away from him, before he tries to kill you again."

Mothlenor returned both hands to the man's face, sending waves of energy down onto the man. "Let go, Commander."

Ferrand hesitated, but released the mad knight.

"Are coming. They are—*gaaahhhh!*" The knight's face twisted in agony, and the smell of burning hair rose to Mothlenor's nose.

The man fought to pry Mothlenor's hands from his face, but his strength was already fading, and Mothlenor held fast to him, dumping more burning arcane energy into his body, even as his flesh began to singe and his hair fell away in smoking clumps.

"They … are … coming." The man's voice was little more than a croaking whisper.

Mothlenor finally released him when his body was blackened beyond recognition. It fell to the floor with a dry cracking sound, soot rising from the clothing to settle against the stones. Two handprints glowed dully around the head, already fading.

Ferrand stood impassively, offering Mothlenor a hand as he rose to his feet. "Well?"

Mothlenor ignored the outstretched hand. "It was not Imis, but death *did* find the *Kingfisher*." Mothlenor looked to the doorway, but Anna was gone. "A sea dragon destroyed the ship. You can assume your spy is dead."

"A sea dragon?" Ferrand's malformed face twitched. "Did he know what happened to Ajax and the others?"

"No."

Ferrand scowled; the effect was disturbing. "We'll find him, my lord."

"See that you do, Commander." Mothlenor motioned down at the burnt husk between them. "The next time I do that, it might be you lying on the tiles in a smoking ruin."

His scowl deepened slightly, but Ferrand bowed. Straightening, he looked down at the dead knight, prodding one leg with the toe of his boot. "Who is coming, my lord?"

Mothlenor stared at the remains, the smell of smoke and boiling blood wafting in the air. "We shall find out soon enough, I expect."

Anna rubbed at her temples, trying to forget the scene she had just fled from. Thinking about it any longer would only make her sick again. *The sight of him burning like that had been one thing, but the smell ...* The memory of burning flesh and hair made her stomach roll, and she reached for the nearest thing to catch the bile that spilled from her mouth. She wiped her mouth clean, grimacing into her smallest cauldron at the puddle glistening at the bottom.

She set the defiled pot aside, content to wash it out later. Besides, she might need it again before the evening was over.

Anna stirred carefully at the larger cauldron in front of her, watching the liquid shimmer with the heat of the witch fire she had cast beneath it. *Nearly ready now, just a few more ingredients.*

Grabbing a small pot from the nearby window, Anna selected a few flowering bulbs and a handful of the oldest leaves and gently dropped them into the potion. One yellow bud drifted to the top, and she pushed it back down to the depths with her wooden spoon, giving the liquid a few more stirs. The potion flashed a bright yellow, then settled into a calmer shade of weedy green as the witch fire beneath it dimmed.

Anna hastily spooned some of the concoction into a small wooden cup, setting it aside to cool. The rest she divided into several glass vials, each no longer than her finger. They would only keep for a season, but they would surely all be used before they spoiled. *The women in the city are always in need ...* Great Ones knew they suffered far more than she had. And while this potion was harder to make than the ointments and poultices she normally spent her evenings on, the alternative was an unpleasant one to consider.

She worked in silence, and her thoughts drifted to one of the first potions she had ever brewed. Even now, she remembered the ingredients and the instructions clearly, though it had been years. Nevina, preparing to step into the role of Matriarch, had walked Anna through the process of making the potion that would render her body barren. Nevara waited patiently nearby, offering advice as she saw fit. For the first and only time in her life, Anna had been blessed to be instructed as the Gifted were, with both the current and future Matriarch watching her every move.

The potion had been a success, confirmed both by Nevina and Nevara. Yet when Anna had tried to duplicate the recipe only a year later, it hadn't worked.

She'd tried again and again, with the same failing results. And now she was forced to routinely make this simpler potion for herself.

She slipped the vials into a small leather pouch at her feet, then reached for the cup. It was still warm in her hands, and softly curling steam rose from the liquid as she stared at it.

Anna tipped her head back, bringing the cup to her lips.

But a strong hand reached over her shoulder and stopped her, pulling the cup from her mouth.

Anna cried out and turned to see Mothlenor standing just

behind her. His face was impassive, but she thought she could make out a hint of anger in his eyes.

"M-my lord. I didn't hear you come in." Her gaze flicked behind him to see the door to her chambers shut. How could he have gotten in without her hearing him?

"You ran out of the hall so suddenly," he breathed. "I was worried about you." Mothlenor gently pried the cup from her fingers and lifted it to his nose, inhaling the potion's scent.

His head tilted, and one eyebrow raised. "Sweet tansy. And creeping nettle." He looked her up and down, his eyes lingering briefly on her stomach. "You're with child."

"Y-yes." She wanted to look away from those piercing eyes, but she couldn't find the will to do so.

"Have you made this potion before?" The evenness to his voice never changed, but Anna feared what he might do to her.

"Yes."

"For yourself?"

"Y-yes, my lord."

The slightest frown crossed his lips and was gone. "And for the women in the city? I saw the extra vials. This potion does not survive long. And we aren't intimate so often that you would need so much, Anna."

Anna nodded, still unable to look away from his eyes. "Yes. When I heard what Ferrand—"

"Commander Ferrand." His voice remained so calm, and so deadly.

Anna corrected herself. "Commander Ferrand. When I heard what he and his men were doing to the women and girls in the city, I felt it was my duty to help them."

Mothlenor's lip twitched again. "As a member of the Coven?"

Anna relaxed slightly, knowing the answer he wanted to

hear. "The Coven is dead. It was only my duty as a witch that urged me to help them."

"You've been brewing this for that long? As part of your little clinic?"

Anna's heart sank. She should've known Mothlenor would find out about her clinics, though she had tried so hard to keep the knowledge from him. "Yes."

Mothlenor nodded slightly, then upended the contents of the cup into the bile-laced cauldron beside them and dropped both cauldron and cup into the washbasin. Anna winced as the remaining potion hissed when it touched the water. Mothlenor stepped around Anna, stooping to pick up the leather bag with the extra vials from the floor.

"I can have these delivered on your behalf, Anna. I assume the servant woman Ishta is expecting them?"

Anna swallowed down the fear that suddenly bit at her throat. "Yes, my lord," she murmured.

"I will find you a caretaker, and perhaps a servant or two to help you in whatever way you might need it." He plucked the pots of sweet tansy from the window, tucking both into the crook of one elbow. "Further potion-making will be done in my presence, and only in my presence."

Anna nodded, knowing it would be pointless to ask to keep the plants. If he knew Ishta had given them to her …

"And tomorrow, we will be married."

"My lord?" Surely she had misheard him. What need was there for him to marry her?

"It will be a small ceremony. And we will bed each other, as married couples do. And when the child comes—"

"What will you do with me then?" Anna interrupted. She was beginning to see where his mind was working.

Mothlenor frowned. "Nothing. You will continue to be my apprentice for the foreseeable future. You are more valuable to me alive than dead, Anna. Even after discovering this little trick of yours."

"And what about the child? My child?" Anna's eyes were filling. She had never wanted this life for herself, but to condemn her child to a similar fate ...

"That would depend on the child, Anna. You should understand that." Mothlenor looked her over, frowning slightly again. "A boy will become king after me, and must learn to take my place as only my true son can. An Ungifted daughter will be yours to raise, and we will try again, and hope for better luck."

"And if she is Gifted?" Anna sobbed. There was a chance. Her mother, whoever she might have been, was Gifted. It was the only reason she had been raised in the Coven.

Mothlenor smiled, the expression making him look almost hungry. "A Gifted child would be the most useful of them all, Anna. She would be well cared for, and trained in all the arcane arts I know. She would grow to be my greatest pupil, surpassing even you, I would hope. She would be my greatest treasure. She would someday be queen over all Azimar."

He turned on his heel, making for the door to her chamber. "Rest, Anna. The months will grow tiresome for you."

The door snapped shut behind him, the sound clearly audible in the sparse room. Anna fell to her knees, hands covering her face as she wept.

Ishta tucked a loose corner of heavy wool deeper into the basket she carried, better concealing the pile of soft and freshly laundered wrappings she had painstakingly scrubbed clean in the middle of the night. Dirk was certainly back in town, as Anna had suspected. The number of bloodied rags from mysterious "falls" had drastically increased in the last few weeks. It would die down after a few months, when Ferrand sent him off somewhere once again, but for now all they could do was try to stay on top of the damage he inflicted as more and more women stumbled into Anna's clinics with obvious knife wounds.

She made her way through the kitchens, giving her mother and older sister each a kiss on the cheek as she passed them. She couldn't help but notice the look her mother gave her as she leaned in. She knew where Ishta was headed, and she knew the reason for it.

But at least she does not know the full extent of it.

Her mother would likely cry herself into an early grave if she knew just how intimate Ishta and Anna had grown in the last few years. She always lamented the fact that her two oldest daughters had decided to remain in Etritia, while her youngest had managed to flee east with an attractive baker's son shortly after Areanath's death.

Ishta could have a life, a real life, outside Etritia's walls.

But it wasn't a life worth having if Anna was not with her.

Ishta opened the door from the kitchens to the garden just enough to slip through, turning to quietly shut it behind her. "Good morning, Lady Anna."

"Ishta."

The voice that greeted her was not Anna's soft and caring cadence. It was hard, cold, and grave.

Ishta turned in surprise, bowing low. "My lord, I'm sorry. I did not expect you here. Anna—" Ishta thought frantically, keeping her head low to hide her fear. "Anna often comes here in the mornings. I often pass her on my way out to the city. I thought—"

"You thought that she would be waiting here for you. To make another one of your little exchanges."

Ishta straightened, unsure how to answer.

Mothlenor stood before the garden bench that had so often been her secret meeting place with Anna. His hands were folded neatly in front of him, his face impassive and unreadable. When Ishta didn't answer, he tilted his head slightly, his brows raising, as if giving her permission to speak.

"I-I didn't realize you knew."

"I know quite a lot. Not much happens within the walls of Etritia that I don't eventually find out about." Mothlenor took a step closer, and Ishta took a matching step away from him, her back pressing against the handle of the door to the kitchens. "Did you think that the garden could hide you?" He waved a hand around them, and Ishta's eyes followed the movement. "It won't any longer."

The garden had been nearly destroyed. Almost all the thick overgrowth had been completely removed, the stumps of bushes pulled from the earth to leave gaping holes. What had not been removed had been cut back to such a diminutive size that a fat squirrel would have a hard time concealing itself among the branches.

"I let Anna run her little clinics without interference because I thought it would be good for her to have something to focus on besides our work. And the people of Etritia look to her as they might look to Imis herself." Mothlenor scowled at Ishta, his shoulders squaring. "They see her as a guardian, and as a savior."

"Then why step in now?" Ishta's throat burned as she fought back the anger that rose in her. "Why stop her from helping us?"

Great Ones, Anna had been right to always be so careful. Did I mess this up? Was I too careless?

"Things have changed. I need her by my side. We will be married tomorrow."

"Married?"

Why would Anna agree?

But of course, Anna never had the option to refuse.

"Though Anna herself will no longer be the one to run the clinics she has set up, I will not force their closure." Mothlenor reached into the inside of his robes, pulling out a leather purse that Ishta recognized before even reaching for it. "She made these last night. I took it upon myself to make sure they were delivered."

Ishta's hand closed around the end of the bag she had made for Anna, but Mothlenor did not release it. "I also know the two of you have grown ... *close.*"

Ishta's stomach sank.

"It ends now." Mothlenor's eyes narrowed at her. "I can make things very difficult for you, and for your family, if you do not obey." He released the bag, his eyes never leaving Ishta's. "Do you understand?"

"Yes, my lord."

Mothlenor only nodded, then motioned for Ishta to step

aside. She did so without hesitation, letting Mothlenor open the door to the kitchens.

For a moment, she had the wild image in her mind's eye of bashing him in the back of the head with the medical pouch. But the door shut behind him, and she let the thought fade.

Instead, Ishta stepped further into the garden, surveying the damage that had been done. Her mother would be devastated when she saw it.

On impulse, Ishta turned and lifted her eyes to the windows above.

There, in one of the windows of an upper floor, stood Anna. Ishta was sure it was her, though she could not see her face plainly. Something in the way she stood told her it was the woman she loved.

They stood for a moment, staring at each through the partitioned glass.

She wanted to rush through the castle, ignoring Mothlenor's threats. A life in Etritia was nothing if it was not with Anna. They could leave, as her sister had left, and start anew in some other place.

But she knew Anna would never leave the broken and the ill of the city behind. Not even for her.

Ishta was the first to turn away, leaving the garden behind.

57
ELF

She knocked on the rough wooden door, startled by her own hesitancy. This was definitely not her Homewood. Nor was it a Homewood at all, for that matter. Would she truly be able to find peace here in this strange place, in this strange world?

Soft footsteps sounded just beyond the door, and when it opened, the thin face of a woman roughly her own age was framed in the doorway. "Yes?" The woman's voice was firm, but not unkind, and it had the unfamiliar coarseness of the woodland elves that couldn't be found in Vyris.

"I was told to come here." She turned, noting with unease and mild annoyance that there were four elves loitering around behind her. "I am looking for the Elder."

The woman gave a gentle nod, then dipped her head back into the house. Only her thin fingers were visible, still curled around the door, as if she were unsure whether to open it wider or to slam it shut.

She might do either. She wouldn't be the first. And this world has seen more hardships than I had thought.

"Papa!" the woman called, and the word sent a flicker of pain through her heart. "There's someone here to see you."

She reappeared, opening the door a little wider as more foot-steps echoed within the house. "A highborn, by the looks of it."

"Nieve," a male voice from deeper within the house hissed. "It's impolite to say such things."

The door opened wider, and an older elf stepped onto the doorstep. His hair was only just beginning to be touched by grey, and it hung around his shoulders limply. He wore a thinning wool robe, belted at the waist with a length of cord, and she was surprised to see that he went barefoot.

She felt her eyebrows rise appreciatively. "I'm surprised that there are those in Azimar who still follow the old ways."

The man's eyes widened slightly, and he let out a deep chuckle. "There are a few of us." He crossed his arms over his chest carefully, the tips of his fingers resting against the opposite shoulders, and took a low bow. She returned the gesture, ignoring the rising whispers of conversation behind her. When she straightened, it was to see the Elder's eyes lit up and a smile on his face. "I must admit that it's been some time since I last met a Vyrisian. Do they still keep the old ways?"

"My parents did, yes."

"Did?"

She hesitated before answering. "My mother still does."

The Elder nodded slowly, the tips of his ears warming to a faint red. He bowed a second time, this one barely more than a dip of the head. "How can I help you, young lady?"

She swallowed, turning to see that the number of onlookers had grown slightly. "I've come seeking a new life. Here in Azimar. If a new life is possible. My name is Syrani." She fished under the hem of her tunic, pulling the faintly mewling creature that had wrapped itself around her waist out for the Elder to see. "And this is Halcia." Syrani swal-lowed again. "Will you permit us to stay here with you?"

The Elder's eyes widened, and he leaned in for a closer

look. Behind him, the woman gasped, forcing her way around her father to stand beside him. "Is that what I think it is?"

"Nieve," the Elder said, straightening and turning to his daughter. "Get some tea going, please. And prepare the guest room." The warm smile the Elder gave Syrani caused a small sigh to escape from her lips. "I think we have a lot to discuss, Rider."

JAIMES

Jaimes and Alastor were finally home, but their little inn
in Larten felt oddly cold and strange. It had been mostly
unmolested, though a few shutters had been damaged
and a family of rats had moved into the larder. They spent
the days outside, making themselves visible to the other citi-
zens of their sleepy town. It was the easiest way to let them
know that Harlan's boys had returned, though everyone kept
their distance.

Jaimes did what he could, though his broken leg gave him
more trouble than he could truly handle on his own. He
spent most mornings for the first week or so of their return
clearing the weeds and refuse from Silvana's garden. Mathius
helped, clearing the more stubborn weeds and helping Jaimes
maneuver himself around. In return, Jaimes told Mathius
about the plants in the garden, and their various purposes
and needs. Mathius listened intently, but Jaimes was sure
most of what he said just drifted right by the good captain's
head. Still, Jaimes was grateful for the company.

Alastor and Roland worked together to get the exterior of
the inn back into good repair, while the elves and Nunor saw
to the inside. Tathiel and Nunor had held a contest to see

who could kill more of the rats, and Nunor grumbled for days when he was beaten soundly. Eilonwy was quieter than usual, almost matching her brother's strong silence at times. Tiryn insisted that she should be fine in time. But Tiryn also insisted that Jaimes would someday be able to walk unassisted, and Jaimes wasn't sure either statement was true.

"Do you think you could care for these plants on your own, Mathius?" Jaimes asked, tugging at a well-rooted clump of grass. "If you needed to, I mean."

Mathius wiped the sweat from his forehead with one bare arm. "If I had to? Possibly." He grunted, tugging a weed free of the soil. "I'm not likely to go back to being a captain, that's for sure. Why not tend to a garden?"

"What about running an inn? Do you think you'd like to do that?"

Mathius looked over at him, squinting in the light. "What are you thinking over there, Jaimes?"

Without a word, Jaimes lifted the inn's heavy brass key from his chest and tossed it to Mathius. He caught it deftly, glancing down at it. "It's yours, if you want it." Jaimes and Alastor had discussed it the night before, and had passed the idea by Roland and Tiryn. They all seemed to be in agreement that the inn would be in good hands under Mathius's care.

"You don't plan on staying?"

"No longer than necessary." Jaimes ignored the implied question about his leg.

"Why me? Why not Roland?" Mathius's brow furrowed.

"Roland is a wanted man." Jaimes finally tore the grass free and tossed it over one shoulder. "And it might be selfish, but we'll need a place to come back to during all our wanderings. A home of sorts. For all of us." He worked at another clump of the intrusive grass, digging his fingers into the damp soil. "An inn would be a good cover for you, should anyone come looking for us."

Mathius bounced the key carefully on his palm, inspecting it. "I'm flattered."

"So you'll do it?"

"Yeah, I'll do it." Mathius looped the key around his own neck, glancing briefly at it again before letting it drop to his chest.

"I just have one request."

"Oh?"

Jaimes lifted the smaller key from around his neck, passing it to Mathius. "Will you keep Silvana's … my mother's room the way it is? And keep that key safe? It opens the chest with her books in it. They're important to me."

Mathius nodded slowly. "Sure, Jaimes." He looped the second key around his neck, then pointed at a large and savage-looking bush. "Now, what can you tell me about that ugly fucker over there?"

Jaimes smiled, and continued digging the grasses free as he told Mathius about the rest of the plants around them.

* * *

The days passed quickly, though not quickly enough for Jaimes. He knew the others were only waiting for his leg to heal more before they resumed the search for the remaining amulets. He suspected that the others discussed things without him, but he wondered if perhaps that was his own feeling of uselessness getting the better of him. In those moments, his only comfort came from sitting in the cool evening wind of the garden and conversing with Melonya. She kept herself hidden away during the day, but swept in with the evening darkness to stay closer to the inn overnight.

"Alone again, Jaimes?" Melonya's cool voice drifted over him. He had been waiting for her arrival, sitting with his back to the inn and looking out towards the ocean. It almost

seemed to call to him, despite all that had happened. *"You might heal faster in the company of friends."*

"It's too stuffy in there. I like the breeze." It was only half a lie, but Melonya wouldn't judge him for it.

"They worry about you."

"Do you worry about me?"

"Some." She seemed to huff, sensation rippling over him. *"But I know this will pass. You are stronger than you think, Jaimes."*

He said nothing, letting his mind sink deeper into the warmth emanating from her.

"We'll be leaving soon, I think."

Jaimes knew it would happen eventually. Roland had told them weeks ago that it would be safer for the twins and Melonya to return home, where the safety of their Homewood could better protect them from Mothlenor. But hearing the words still upset him. *"I understand."*

"We don't want to leave so soon. Especially not Eilonwy. She's very grateful to you for protecting her. She wants to see you healed and returned to your old self."

Jaimes started to reply, but the shuffling of feet behind him stopped him.

"Jaimes?"

It was Eilonwy's voice, and he turned to see her and Tathiel both silhouetted against the open door of the inn. They stepped closer, and in the half light of the setting sun, Jaimes saw that Eilonwy wore her hair down and over her ears, hiding the nasty scar above her left temple.

She was wringing her hands together, Tathiel's arm wrapped around her. "We'll be leaving tomorrow morning."

"Tomorrow?" Jaimes's voice came out in a soft whine, and he hated himself for the way it sounded.

Eilonwy nodded, biting her lip.

"We wanted to spend a little more time with you tonight.

We both owe you and Alastor so much, for taking care of Eilonwy when—"

"I didn't really do anything." Jaimes waved a hand to cut Tathiel off. "There's nothing to thank me for."

"We feel differently," Eilonwy murmured.

"Is there something you would like to do? Alastor tells me that you haven't had the chance to visit your father yet."

Jaimes frowned. It was true. Harlan and Silvana were both buried on a little hill just outside Larten's walls, but the climb was too much for him to manage on his own. "I can't. My leg …"

"I'll carry you," Tathiel said firmly.

Tathiel did carry him. Jaimes felt silly, cradled in the elf's arms like a child. Eilonwy led the way, a single witch light bobbing beside her.

Jaimes watched the inn shrink as they climbed the hill, still able to make out two figures standing watch in an upper window. *Roland and Tiryn,* he presumed. *Making plans for our next journey.* The sight reminded him of Harlan and Silvana watching out of the same window as he and Alastor played together as children. Jaimes choked down a sob at the sudden memory.

"Cold?" Tathiel asked.

"I'm fine," Jaimes managed.

When they found the markers for his parents, side by side, Tathiel sat him gently down on the soft grass at their feet, and Eilonwy set her light to hover between them.

"Do you miss them?" Eilonwy asked.

"Yeah." Jaimes wiped at his face, suddenly wishing he was alone.

The twins were silent for a time, letting him grieve in peace. After several moments, Eilonwy and Tathiel both sat in the grass beside him.

"Melonya found the amulet." Jaimes twirled a thin blade of new grass between his fingers, trying to ignore the growing pain in his leg from sitting so long. "I guess we did what we were supposed to do."

Tathiel nodded. "Yes."

"Can I see it? The amulet?" His question was soft. He wasn't even sure why he'd asked it. *Perhaps seeing will make this all a little less painful. Like it was really all worth everything that's happened.*

Tathiel caught his sister's eye, and she nodded. They seemed to understand his intentions better than Jaimes did.

Eilonwy was the first to pull her half of the amulet from under her shirt. A leather thong had been wrapped and tied around the irregularly shaped piece of stone, but the soft glow of power was still clearly visible.

Tathiel removed his, and the two elves leaned in close together, their foreheads nearly touching, and pieced the broken halves together as best as the leather ties would allow. The amulet's glow brightened in the spots where the two halves met, and Jaimes thought he could hear a gentle hum in the air. After a moment, the siblings separated, each tucking their piece of the amulet safely away.

"So it was worth it, then?"

"Yes," Tathiel murmured, touching the outline of the stone against his chest. "I can feel the energy and power within it. It would have been too dangerous if Mothlenor had found it."

Jaimes only nodded, shifting in discomfort. Even he could sense the energy emanating from it.

"Jaimes? Do you know what a Mark is?" Eilonwy asked timidly.

He nodded. "Roland explained it to me. Tiryn gave him one, right?"

Tathiel nodded. "And I gave Alastor his."

Jaimes frowned. "Alastor?"

"Tiryn taught us how to do it," Tathiel explained, his eyes boring holes into Jaimes.

"And I want to give you yours, Jaimes," Eilonwy said. "It's the least I can do."

"Eilonwy—"

"I don't remember very much from that day," she interrupted. One hand reached up to absently trace the scar from brow to tipped ear. "But I remember the sound of your voice in the dark. You comforted me when all I could feel was pain." She caught his eye briefly before looking away. "You might not think that you did much, but you did."

Jaimes was silent for a moment. "Alright."

Eilonwy looked up, eyes wide in the dim glow of her witch light. "You'll let me?"

"Yes. If you really want to."

Eilonwy smiled, and he realized he hadn't seen her smile since the deck of the *Kingfisher*, just before— "I really want to."

Timidly, he offered his arm out to her, and she took it gently in both hands. Her hands were cool against his skin, and as she focused her gaze on the inside of his arm, a tingling sensation crawled over him. Within seconds, the tingling focused on a spot on his arm a few inches above the wrist. After a few more seconds, the tingling turned into an uncomfortable burning sensation. He was about to ask her to stop, that it was too painful, when a bright rune flashed across his skin. It remained, glowing white against his skin for a brief moment before disappearing.

"What does the rune mean?"

Eilonwy frowned. "It means 'savior'. Alastor's said the same."

"Why did you choose that?"

"I didn't. The rune you receive is entirely dependent on your innermost self. It's supposed to be a true indicator of who you are."

"Oh," Jaimes muttered. "Roland's says 'friend', right? That's what he told me."

"No …" Tathiel said, hesitating. "His doesn't say 'friend'."

"Then what does it say?"

Eilonwy bit her lip, looking to her brother. Tathiel only shrugged. Her voice was quiet when she answered.

"It says 'king'."

WITCH

The witch sat alone in her little cottage, staring at the object in front of her. How such a thing had fallen into that old farmer's hands, she could never guess. But it was hers now. *And for the cost of a pain amulet, no less.*

It was smaller than she had expected, though the tales her mother had told her about such things never seemed to describe them well. Its surface was white, almost opalescent, with thin blue lines stitched across the surface. All in all, it was beautiful.

She traced one thin line with a finger. It was cold to the touch. *Probably dead, then. A shame, really.* Though what she would have done with a *live* one, she had no idea. Great Ones preserve her, the very thought chilled her.

A knock at the door startled her into a jump. It was raining heavily outside, the wind lashing water against her shutters. Winter would be coming soon, and it was cold and dark. Not the ideal time for a visit …

"Who is it?" she called, standing to face the door.

The voice on the other side was thin and afraid. "It's Lana. Please, open up!"

"Lana?" She rushed to open the door, ushering the young

woman in. "What are you doing here? Where's my son?" She'd never thought she would see this girl again, but here she was, alone.

Or not.

Lana clutched a small bundle to her chest, wrapped in dirty white linens. The bundle was crying, one hand reaching out to grasp at Lana.

"He's dead. The guards came for you, just as you thought they would." Lana was crying, the tears burning ugly tracks down her face.

Her heart wrenched. Her son. Dead.

Lana continued, groaning in anguish as the baby continued to cry. "The guards found him, and when he couldn't tell them where you had gone, they killed him."

The witch forced herself to breathe, taking the child from Lana and gently rocking it. The babe was cold, and she bustled to warm some milk for it. "How did you find me? My letter to him?"

"Yes. I paid a witch woman in Armyn two gold pieces to use it to find you." Lana seemed to be calming with the baby out of her hands. "My father threw me out when he realized I was already with child. He said I was useless for marriage, already broken like an old mare." Lana barked in a sudden laugh, and the witch looked up to see her vacant stare. "I thought if I could find you, give her to you, I might be able to start again somewhere …"

"You don't want the baby?" The witch found her arm already tightening protectively around the little girl in her arms.

"She looks too much like her father," Lana said softly. "And like you." Lana shook her head. "It hurts to look at her."

The witch pulled back the layers of cloth around the baby's face. Tufts of fine blonde hair framed a face with piercing blue eyes. "Does she have a name?"

"No."

The witch stared down at the baby, now quiet. "I had a sister once …"

"So name her after your sister," Lana barked. "I don't care."

The witch glared at the young woman and resumed rocking the small child. "What do you want for her?" She remembered the object in the other room, and only prayed that Lana would not notice it.

But Lana was quick to reply. "Only enough gold for me to reach the next town, and to get myself a room and some food until I can find my own way."

Without a word, the witch went to a nearby shelf and picked up a leather pouch, tossing it to Lana. "There. That should be enough. Is there anything else you want to say?"

Lana shook her head, stuffing the pouch into the top of her bodice.

"Then get out."

Lana did, slamming the door shut behind her.

The witch sighed, taking the pan of milk away from the fire. She stroked the baby's fine hair, smiling down at her. The baby hiccupped once, eyes and cheeks swollen from crying.

"There, there," she murmured. "Everything will be alright now, Arella."

THANK YOU FOR READING!

I hope you enjoyed *The Book of Water*.
Please feel free to leave a review on your preferred
storefront.

Reviews help other readers like you find my work, and your
support means I can continue doing what I love: Writing.

As always, you can stay up to date on publishing news and
special offers by joining my newsletter at
JacklynHennionAuthor.com.

Thank you!
Jacklyn Hennion

The Book of Fire
The Azimar Archives Book Three

ABOUT THE AUTHOR

Jacklyn Hennion is an avid lover of sweets and wine. She enjoys Netflix and video games, and often spends the evenings winding down with a bit of crochet work. She and her husband currently live in Oklahoma. *The Book of Death* is Jacklyn's first published novel.